8/14
LP
TRO

DISCARDED

Dog Gone, Back Soon

Center Point
Large Print

Also by Nick Trout and available from
Center Point Large Print:

The Patron Saint of Lost Dogs

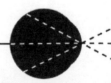

**This Large Print Book carries the
Seal of Approval of N.A.V.H.**

Dog Gone, Back Soon

NICK TROUT

CENTER POINT LARGE PRINT
THORNDIKE, MAINE

This Center Point Large Print edition
is published in the year 2014 by arrangement with
Hyperion, a division of Hachette Book Group, Inc.

The text of this Large Print edition is unabridged.
In other aspects, this book may vary
from the original edition.
Printed in the United States of America
on permanent paper.
Set in 16-point Times New Roman type.

ISBN: 978-1-62899-178-9

Library of Congress Cataloging-in-Publication Data

Trout, Nick.
    Dog gone, back soon / Nick Trout. — Center Point Large Print edition.
    pages ; cm
    Summary: "In one jam-packed week, veterinarian Cyrus must figure out
how to outsmart the evil veterinary conglomerate, win back Amy's
heart, solve several tricky veterinary cases, find a home for an orphaned
dog, and detangle himself from an absurd case of mistaken identity"
—Provided by publisher.
    ISBN 978-1-62899-178-9 (library binding : alk. paper)
    1. Veterinarians—Fiction. 2. Large type books. I. Title.
PS3620.R684D64 2014b
813′.6—dc23
                                                                    2014015608

For Whitney

Yet, taught by time,
my heart has learned to
glow for other's good,
and melt at other's woe.

Homer

← CONTENTS →

Dog Gone, Back Soon

Tuesday

Tuesday

PICK UP, PICK UP, PICK UP. NO, NO, NO!
Amy, it's me—me as in Cyrus—calling to
say . . . just wanted to say sorry, for this evening
I mean. Okay, I can come across as too . . .
inquisitive, but in my defense, a question is not an
accusation, you know?" I take a deep breath, let it
out in a long sigh, and realize too late that now I
seem impatient. "Look, I'm sorry. Maybe we can
try—"

The high-pitched beep in my ear tells me time's
up. Damn. I hang up, indicate right, and pull the
old Silverado into the parking lot of my new
home, The Bedside Manor for Sick Animals. I
slump forward over the steering wheel, driving
my head into the horn. Just like the missing sun
visor and broken reverse gear, the horn on Dad's
jalopy must be an optional extra because nothing
happens.

"What have I done?"

Yes, I say this out loud and to no one in
particular—a question leveled at two particular
facets of my new reality. It's January in northern
Vermont—ten below—and I've given up everything (and I mean everything) to rescue a decrepit,

if not derelict, building that aspires to be a veterinary practice. Rather than an inviting, brightly lit animal hospital, the place lies in shadows, looking haunted, a mugger's paradise or somewhere to score a drug that requires no prescription. Bad enough, but I've just spent the last ninety minutes blowing the best chance I've had in years of connecting with a woman I can't stop thinking about.

I get out and catch a snowman (correction—snowwoman) emerging from an idling car across the lot. It's her ruddy cheeks, flowing pink scarf, black Stetson, and puffy white ski jacket that create the illusion.

"That was quick," she shouts.

"I beg your pardon."

"I only called a few minutes ago. Margot. We spoke on the phone. Doc Lewis, right?"

"No," I say, "I'm Dr. Mills. Doc Lewis is the other vet at the practice. Can I help?"

If she's confusing me with my seventy-three-year-old partner-in-crime then she's clearly not from Eden Falls. Everybody knows everybody in this town.

I look past her as a second figure emerges from her car, the vehicle's interior light spilling over a tall, rangy character in a gray hooded sweatshirt.

"It's Tallulah," says Margot, and then, across the empty lot, she screams, "Gabe, the Unabomber impersonation has been done to death." And then,

14

in a normal voice, "My son, Gabe," before another drill-sergeant cry of "Don't just stand there! Help Tallulah out of the car."

Gabe does as he's told, pulling the hood back to reveal steel-rimmed glasses and a fuzzy 'fro of red hair. When he opens the car's back door, I glimpse what appears to be a large marine mammal. My double take has me rushing over to assist a half second too late to prevent the creature from sliding off the seat and flopping down hard on the rutted ice and snow.

Turns out, despite her pleading, seal-pup eyes and layers of blubber, Tallulah is actually an enormous English mastiff. She doesn't seem to have the use of her legs, making her a formidable dead weight.

"Let's get her up and inside. You got a towel or a blanket that we can use as a sling?"

Margot doesn't hesitate. Ignoring the biting cold, she unzips her coat (to reveal a particularly festive reindeer appliqué sweater) and slips it under Tallulah's belly like an enormous white cummerbund.

"How much does she weigh?" I ask, unlocking the front door and finding a light.

"One ninety-three," says Gabe, coming around to help lift.

The greatest weight ever recorded for a dog was an English mastiff—343 pounds.

"What was that?" asks Margot.

I don't bother explaining how I find solace in mumbling obscure facts and trivia during stressful situations but instead reply, "Would you mind calling Doc Lewis? Let him know I'm here and he can go back to bed."

If Margot nods or replies, I don't see or hear it, as Gabe and I grunt, strain, and stagger our way through the front door and on to the work space in the back. Tallulah is as nimble as a Zeppelin-sized float at the Macy's Thanksgiving Day Parade, her legs making drunken, halfhearted attempts at walking.

"It's my fault," says Gabe, breathless as his dog crumples to the floor in the center of the room. "Theobromine toxicity. She ate a whole tray of chocolate brownies I baked."

I consider the teenage kid pushing his glasses back onto the bridge of his nose. Theobromine is the ingredient in chocolate that is toxic to dogs. How many high school students would know this fact?

"When was this?"

Gabe consults his wristwatch. "Fifty-two minutes ago. We called our regular vets, Healthy Paws in Patton, and paged the doctor on call, but no one called us back. That's why we drove over here."

I decide not to mention that about an hour ago Amy had spotted the entire veterinary staff of Healthy Paws, loud and loose-tongued, on the far side of the noisy bar she had suggested for our ill-fated first date. I guess that explains why Gabe didn't get a call back.

"He's not picking up," says Margot, sans Stetson, letting me see where Gabe gets his hair color and texture. "My little girl's going to be okay, yeah?"

I grab my stethoscope and get down on the floor with her "little girl." Tallulah's out of it, neck out-stretched, head flat to the floor, eyes closed, jowls wet and droopy like a sad, sloppy frown.

I listen to her heart—thirty beats per minute—really slow, even for a dog of this magnitude.

"Has she vomited?" I ask.

"No," says Margot. She checks in with Gabe, who seems to deliberate before shaking his head in agreement.

I lift up a heavy eyelid. Tallulah's left eye is unfocused, eerily black because her pupils are almost fully dilated.

"Could you pass me that thermometer? On the counter."

Gabe obliges, but I catch the nervous tremor in his hand.

"This is your fault, Gabe," says Margot. "You and that girlfriend of yours."

"She's not my girlfriend," Gabe protests, but the blush in his cheeks begs to differ.

Margot folds her arms across her chest. "Okay, so what happened to this . . . friend . . . who happens to be a girl? Funny how she had to rush off."

"I told you, this has nothing to do with her."

"I even cooked a cobbler for supper. Why bother with brownies at this time of night?"

Still holding on to the thermometer, I realize where I've seen Gabe. Or rather, someone who looks like him. Remove the glasses and he's Art Garfunkel in *Catch-22*. (Hey, I happen to love classic movies, but if you prefer pop culture, leave the glasses on and go with *Napoleon Dynamite*).

Gabe ignores the question. "We need to make her throw up, right, Dr. Mills? I read online how that's one of the first things you do for chocolate poisoning."

I check Tallulah's temperature—97.2°F—way too low.

The most expensive dog ever sold was a red Tibetan mastiff named Big Splash, the price tag: $1.5 million.

I study Margot and Gabe. For all the similarities in their features, two distinct and separate facial expressions capture my attention: concern on hers, guilt on his.

Getting to my feet, I say, "This was a store-bought brownie mix?"

Gabe nods. "But I added chocolate chips," he says. "Lots of them."

"What's a lot?"

"Couldn't have been more than six ounces, half a bag," says Margot. "That's all we had in the pantry."

Six ounces of chocolate ingested by a 193-pound dog.

"And the chips were what, semisweet chocolate?"

"That's right," says Margot. "Hershey's."

The expression in Gabe's eyes has transitioned from shame through remorse to beseeching.

Tallulah's clumsiness, low body temperature, slow heart rate, and dilated pupils tell me Gabe may have been making brownies, but they were almost certainly laced with something more interesting to a teenage boy than chocolate chips.

I hear the chime of the old shopkeeper's bell that sits over the front door, and Dr. Fielding Lewis appears. It's after eleven at night, but he's still sporting one of his trademark silk bow ties—wisteria and blue plaid.

"Ah, I see the good Dr. Mills is already on the case. What's going on?"

"Sorry, Lewis. Ms. . . ."

"Stiles," says Margot. "Margot Stiles. And this is my son, Gabe."

Gabe manages a sheepish nod.

"Ms. Stiles did try to call you back and tell you not to come," I say, "but since you're here, maybe you could give me a hand. Where do we keep the activated charcoal? Tallulah has an acute case of semisweet chocolate poisoning."

Lewis considers the collapsed dog on the floor before eyeing me with overt skepticism. He reaches down, feels for Tallulah's femoral pulse, inspects her pupils, and claps in her ear. Tallulah doesn't even flinch.

"You quite sure of your diagnosis?" says Lewis, pulling a large plastic syringe from a drawer, filling it half-full of water, and ladling in enough black powder to make a gruesome-looking slurry. "Only, to me, it looks much more like . . ."

"Baking chocolate," I say, too loudly, snatching the syringe from him. "Yes, you would think . . . but Tallulah's clinical signs are practically pathognomonic."

"Patho-what?" says Margot, visibly suspicious of our contrived banter.

"Pathognomonic," says Gabe, deflecting her skepticism. "It means characteristic of a particular disease."

"Very good, young man," says Lewis. "You have a bright son, Ms. Stiles."

Margot appears to vacillate, caught between accepting the diagnosis and the compliment about her son. "Yes, well, if he'd stop playing on that computer of his and pay more attention to what's going on in the real world around him, perhaps my poor dog wouldn't be in this state. She is going to be okay, isn't she?"

"Definitely," I say, almost too quickly and in unison with Lewis saying, "Of course." The two of us share a moment of understanding of what we are keeping to ourselves. Time to clear the air.

"Lewis, would you mind taking some basic

information from Ms. Stiles so we can start a file for Tallulah? Gabe and I will set about getting her warmed up and starting some IV fluids."

Lewis looks like he actually does mind until I catch his eye and jerk my head in the direction of the waiting room, urging him to get Margot away from her son so we can have a word in private.

"Here," I say, handing Gabe a tower of clean towels and blankets. "Wrap her up in these while I grab an IV catheter and a bag of warm fluids."

Gabe does as he's told, creating an inviting nest, leaving Tallulah's forlorn face poking out like she's wearing a babushka. He kneels down on the floor next to her, closes his eyes, presses his pimply temple into the vast wrinkly dome of her forehead, and whispers, "I'm sorry."

Let me be clear, I don't do pep talks or shoulder squeezes with virtual strangers. For the past fourteen years I relished working as a veterinary pathologist. The only patients I examined were deceased. This line of work nicely avoided awkward, emotionally fraught confrontations with the pet-owning public, which was fine with me, until just over a week ago when I took over my late father's practice, Bedside Manor (yes, I appreciate the irony in this ridiculous name).

"If you must know," I say, squatting down and gesturing to the unresponsive brindle blob on the floor, "your dog is on the verge of a coma caused by the ingestion of tetrahydrocannabinol.

21

It seems pretty clear the canine ganja high is not a pleasurable experience."

Gabe can't meet my eyes. Interesting. It's definitely a little easier to do preachy over touchy-feely. So long as he doesn't think I'm offering fatherly advice.

"How did you know?" he whispers.

I smile. He's petrified. I could let him suffer a little longer but instead say, "Look, I'm not going to tell your mom, so relax." Gabe reaches out, pats Tallulah, and this rouses her enough to open her lids. Her eyes roll up, revealing waning crescent moons around the edges, the little-girl-lost effect noticeably compounding Gabe's sense of shame.

"For what it's worth, fatal marijuana ingestion is pretty much unheard of in dogs. And I knew because her signs were all wrong. Chocolate toxicity makes dogs hyper, nervous, with a racing pulse. Tallulah's clearly stoned. She's the one who got baked this evening. Here, let me show you how to raise a vein so I can place this catheter."

Gabe seems eager to be involved, to physically help out, and as we get her hooked up to fluids he talks about a recipe for pot brownies he found online. Clearly his use of the word *epic* differs from mine.

"Mom'll kill me if she finds out. I'll be without a computer for like . . . a *week*."

I flick some air bubbles in the line with my

finger just like in the movies. Gabe makes an Internet-free seven days sound like a sentence on death row.

"I swear I'd never harm her. She won't have any permanent damage, will she?"

I look over at Tallulah, resting comfortably, and think about Gabe's question.

Mastiffs rank number eight in the list of—how best to put this?—most intellectually challenged breeds of dog.

"No," I say, keeping the "not so as you'd notice" to myself.

"Thanks, Doc, for everything. You know . . . for keeping this . . . between us. I owe you."

"Sure, but don't worry about it."

Gabe presses his glasses into the bridge of his nose again. It's like a nervous tic.

"Where are you from, Doc? Your accent?"

I can't tell if he's making conversation or snooping.

"Here, originally, but I've spent the past twenty-five years in and around the Carolinas."

Gabe gets to his feet, visibly deliberates, and then asks, "You married? Dating? Got a significant other?"

Definitely snooping. Don't tell me he's trying to set me up with the snowwoman.

"Let's keep our focus on the patient," I say, nodding to the sleepy beached whale.

The kid regards me with a vapid expression

worthy of his frizzy-haired doppelganger when his mom walks back into the work area with Lewis in tow.

"How we doing?" she asks.

"Good," I say, as Lewis hands over the new file he's put together. "We've got Tallulah set up for the night. Pretty sure she'll be able to go home tomorrow."

Margot eases herself down, pinches both of Tallulah's doughy cheeks, and plants a drawn-out kiss on the dog's snout like the creepy aunt children try to avoid at family gatherings.

"Most expensive brownies of all time." Margot waves for a hand up. "Gabe, what do you say to the doctors?"

Gabe assists his mom before stepping over to Lewis, deferentially bowing from the neck. Then, pointing to the manila folder in my hand, he says to me, "You ever want to go paperless, let me know."

Margot lights up. "Maybe we can barter on the bill? My son's a genius with computers."

Lewis seems intrigued by the offer.

"Thanks, Ms. Stiles," I say, "but I'm pretty sure we won't be computerizing our record keeping anytime soon."

I hope that sounded like a polite refusal rather than a desperate need for actual cash.

Lewis reads her disappointment and swoops in. "We can sort out the bill tomorrow," he says, ushering them toward the front door. "Have a good night. Give us a call in the morning."

Neither of us speaks until the chime of the shopkeeper's bell confirms that they've gone.

"Baking chocolate?" Lewis says with a bemused smile.

It's nearly midnight, and this old man with his steely thatch of hair is not only wide awake, he's actually enjoying himself.

"I know. Lucky for me, marijuana poisoning was one of the few intoxicants I recall from my days as a vet student. In dogs, not people. I mean, I never—"

"Of course, Cyrus," says Lewis, stepping in. "Have to say, I'm impressed by your . . . your . . ."

"What?"

He searches for the word. "Benevolence," he utters, looking pleased with himself.

If this is a compliment, I ignore it. My motive was simple—figure out the problem and solve it. And also avoid an embarrassing scene.

"Smart kid, but obviously not smart enough," says Lewis. "Mom wouldn't stop going on about his addiction to computers. Let's hope that's the least of her worries. Now, to more pressing issues. You all set with your license to practice?"

"Yes, sir." If the "sir" sounds too formal, blame my time in the south. For the last three days, I was back in Charleston making sure I'm not going to get arrested for impersonating a veterinarian.

25

"Excellent. You get back in time?"

He's referring to my much awaited but postponed first date with Amy, one of the waitresses from the Miss Eden Falls diner in the center of town. Not much gets past Lewis. The phrase *an elephant never forgets* refers to the way these pachyderms pass on a genetic memory of directions and locality, including their loved ones' final resting place. Lewis may lack total recall, but he's clearly watching my every move.

"Yep," I say curtly, hoping he'll back off.

"How did it go?"

No such luck.

"Not well."

Lewis folds his arms across his chest, eases back in his stance, obviously awaiting details.

"Look, I'm out of practice at this dating game. Amy got this phone call that she simply *had* to take, so I'm twiddling my thumbs for a full twelve minutes and then she's all cagey about who it was and—"

"Well, knowing Amy it must have been important. She apologized for taking the call?"

"Yeah."

"But she wouldn't tell you who she was talking to?"

"She wouldn't answer any of my questions."

Lewis leans forward. "*Questions,* plural? Not a good idea."

"That's what I said. 'Maybe this wasn't such a

good idea.' And Amy said, 'Tonight or coming home to Eden Falls?' That was just before she stormed off."

"Let me guess, you replied, 'Both'?"

I hang my head in shame and then feel my left bicep squeezed by his trademark lobster claw grip and meet the slate gray eyes of this little old man.

"Take it from someone who's been married for fifty years," says Lewis, "women are not attracted to insecure, pushy men."

As if to emphasize his point, my right bicep gets the vise grip as well.

"Call her. Apologize." He waits a beat before adding, "Besides, isn't all this about second chances?"

How does Lewis do it, the way he manages to angle his head up, unblinking, to peek inside you?

"I saw what happened to you last week," he says. "Coming home, taking this place on. Something hibernating in your life woke up, right?"

I say nothing. Blame guilt or a craving for redemption, but I walked away from my old life as a respected pathologist (okay, there was the matter of a suspended license and huge legal bills) and committed to saving the late Bobby Cobb's floundering, debt-ridden practice. For fifteen years, after the death of my mother, I willfully never saw or spoke to my father again. Last week, Bedside Manor taught me what a fool I'd been. It's his legacy, all that's left of him, and I woke up because I caught a glimpse of something worth fighting for.

One last double-barreled squeeze and Lewis turns his attention to taking another rectal temperature on Tallulah. Our patient barely notices.

"Ninety-nine. Much better. Nice to upstage Healthy Paws," he says. "It's not often we get new clients from over in Patton."

Patton lies across the valley, and with a population five times the size of Eden Falls, it can sustain a mall, movie theater, and chain restaurants, making it a metropolis compared to our little town.

"Amy and I were out that way," I say. "The Yardarm. She saw them, the vets from Healthy Paws. Out celebrating I guess. The bar was packed and I couldn't make them out, except some guy with an annoying, distinctive laugh."

Lewis offers a sage nod. "Let me guess, braying donkey meets croupy pig?"

"That's the one."

"He's their office manager. And that laugh may be his most charming feature. According to Doris, he's declared war on Bedside Manor."

Doris is the Bedside Manor's only other employee—a chain-smoking, beehive-wearing, geriatric receptionist who makes it her business to know everything about everybody. I am not surprised to hear her gossip network extends out to Patton.

"Come on. War?"

"This is serious, Cyrus. Round these parts Doris provides better intelligence than a CIA drone. Healthy Paws was convinced you'd either default or sell the practice to them. Apparently our little trick with the free clinic last weekend has set them on edge."

Before I left for Charleston, we opened up the practice to the public, trying to attract new business with the promise of a free examination for their pets. To be honest, the accompanying free booze and munchies were probably the bigger attractions. Somehow we clawed back enough bad debt to temporarily stave off closure by the odious Mr. Critchley of Green State Bank.

"Look at this place. Sometimes I wonder if my father used the word *manor* instead of *clinic* or *hospital* to avoid false advertising. We're not in the same league."

Lewis steps into my personal space again, and I try not to flinch. "Sure, we lack their bells and whistles. But they're still worried about the competition."

"That's ridiculous."

"Not at all. Think about it, Healthy Paws is a national chain. Doris's source swears their doctors are jealous of the way we get to practice veterinary medicine. And I mean the scary type of jealous."

A scary type of jealous? Is that how I acted

when Amy insisted she had to take her phone call ten minutes into our date, going all wide-eyed and animated on me, feigning her apology as she giggled with the caller on the other end of the line?

I come back with a dubious nasal huff.

"I'm not kidding," says Lewis. "Healthy Paws eats up struggling practices for breakfast. Their unofficial catchphrase is 'If we can't have you, nobody else can.'"

What have I done? Gone for three days and now I've got a rival for Amy's affection as well as a rival for our business. As it is I'm hopelessly romantically challenged and Bedside Manor's already received last rites.

I take a deep breath, mustering renewed resolve. "Well, like you said, Lewis, this is about second chances. Yes, I'm out of my league, comfort zone, and probably, my mind, but if you're willing to fight then so am I. I mean how bad can this be? Surely a little competition will do us good?"

Lewis looks up at me with his piercing eyes, his tightening crow's feet adding to my unease. "Listen to me. This makes handling the bank look easy. Pay up and at least the bank leaves you alone. This is different. This is about professional reputation. This is about quality of service. Healthy Paws employees play dirty, and they'd love to expose our flaws and our antiquated ways. They'll try to highlight every weakness because for Healthy Paws this is personal. This is about humiliation. I wish it was just about competition, but I'm telling you, they don't want to compete. They want to wipe us out. They want to bring Bedside Manor to its knees."

Wednesday

L IVING IN THE APARTMENT OVER THE practice, my childhood home, feels like a blessing and a curse. Great commute in the morning but no possibility of truly escaping from work. Given this new development, maybe that's not a bad thing. If the rival practice thinks Bedside Manor is going to roll over and pee like a submissive dog, it's very much mistaken. And that's why I jog down the flight of stairs and step into the waiting room like the president stepping off Air Force One, a distinct pep to my stride.

It's my first morning of appointments since getting back to Eden Falls, and what's this? A Christmas miracle—the waiting room is full.

"Good morning, Doris. Don't suppose there are any urgent messages for me?"

From behind the reception desk, the mocking arch of her penciled-in eyebrows is all the answer I need. Damn. Still nothing from Amy.

"A word in your ear, Dr. Mills," says Doris, the summons enforced by a nicotine-stained index finger insisting I come closer.

"Looks like a full house," I say under my breath,

trying to contain my delight. "Guess the word must be out."

Doris eases back her chin and narrows her eyes as though she can't decide whether to pity me or stamp on me. For the record, Doris's loyalty still lies with my father, the late Doc Cobb, and she harbors a grudge for the son who was never there for him. I'm not sure I'll ever be forgiven (or if I deserve to be), but I sense there are moments, however brief, when she almost approves of what I'm trying to do to save this place. This might not be one of them.

"You seen this crew?" Doris asks. "Take a closer look."

Her eyebrows jump with a "well, go on then" ferocity, and I do as I'm told. It seems everyone on two legs, four legs, and no legs—a yellow python drapes over the shoulders of a teenage boy with what looks like brass knuckles tattooed into his neck—is staring at me, and to some extent, I see what she means. Dog collars and leashes have been replaced by lengths of frayed rope; cats are restrained not by carriers but by nylon shopping bags or ratty, partially unzipped ski jackets.

"Could have told you that free clinic last Saturday was a bad idea," says Doris. "All it did was bring back the low-rent pet owners we've already sent to collections. You won't get a dime out of this lot."

An imaginary itch at the back of my neck gets

the better of me. I hate public speaking, but I think this is the time to air an unpleasant truth.

I turn to address a blank but attentive crowd. "Ladies and gentlemen, um . . . thank you all for coming in this morning, but I need to draw your attention to this particular notice."

I point to my handwritten poster pinned to the wall.

PAYMENT IN FULL IS EXPECTED FOR SERVICES RENDERED.

"Hate to be so, um . . . so direct, but this is not a free animal clinic."

The room swells with moans and curses. I even catch a "told you" as pets perk up and people stand before shuffling out through the chiming front door as though they clearly came to the wrong place. In seconds, what was a packed waiting room has been pared down to just two people and two dogs. There's a straight-backed, stern-looking woman with an excitable, even squirrelly boxer by her side and a middle-aged man with a poodle. The man locks eyes with me, mulling me over. His face is beyond gaunt, his skin more translucent than ashen. The collar of his shirt gapes widely, accentuating the size of his head on a pipe-cleaner neck. And there's his black, almost woolly dog, aside from a few tan-colored whiskers around his snout. This scruffy specimen must be the biggest version of the poodle breed, the standard (as opposed to toy or miniature). He wears no leash, standing perfectly still, staring straight up at his master, oblivious to his surroundings as if bracing for a command.

"Here's the file for your first case," says Doris, handing over a wafer-thin folder.

I open it and notice there's no previous history—a new client with an address in the neighboring town of Patton. Interesting.

"Ms. Sauer and . . . Sox," I announce, noticing how all four paws of the tap-dancing fawn boxer are a brilliant white. "If you'll please follow me."

I lead the way to my examination room. The standard poodle never flinches, never blinks, so intent is his devotion to the sickly-looking man.

"I'm here 'cause I can't stand that other vet practice, Healthy Paws," says Ms. Sauer, "especially that . . . well, I won't say the word . . . but that . . . that Dr. Honey."

Ms. Sauer almost dry heaves as she says the name. She's a short woman with pinched features, twitching predatory eyes, and barely any lips on which to hang a pale pink halo of lipstick. Though her voice is shrill, her words are music to my ears. In my past life as a veterinary pathologist, I managed to avoid any and all banal banter with the pet-owning public. Now that I'm a *real* veterinarian, Lewis insists I be warm, straightforward, and engaging. What he's really saying is stop being so cold, unnecessarily scientific, and downright hostile. Well, when it comes to Ms.

Sauer, I'm all in, for here's a woman not only stroking my ego by asking for a second opinion, but bent on despising my professional rivals. I can hardly wait to hear more about this reprobate Dr. Honey.

"Here are his records." Ms. Sauer hands over a thick file of photocopied notes. "Sox is only a year old, and aside from vaccines and worming and what have you, these are pretty much all about his lump."

I look over at Sox. There's a lot of snuffling and throaty gargling going on as he snorts and sniffs his way around the room like he's rooting for truffles. That's when I notice his most conspicuous feature—his tail. He actually has one—not a nubbin, not a docked stump—a full-fledged wagging tail.

"Nice to see a boxer with a tail," I say, taking her notes.

"We got him from Nova Scotia. They don't allow docking."

I'm barely listening because I'm transfixed by the medical records, financial statements, and, of all things, a wad of coupons. The workup for what has been described as a red, raised, one- by one-centimeter hairless skin lump over Sox's right shoulder is both exhaustive and, from what I can tell, extremely costly. Ms. Sauer's MasterCard has been soaking up some serious dollars, and some of these tests appear to be, well, questionable, if not unnecessary. Why did Sox need his urine analyzed? What did a test for Lyme disease have to do with a skin problem? For now I'll try to give Dr. Honey the benefit of the doubt—and assume she was just being thorough, not gratuitous.

The glossy flyers find me less charitable. There's an offer for fifty dollars off all ultrasounds and X-rays, and one for free grooming or a soothing doggy massage if you get your dog spayed and vaccinated at Healthy Paws. Soothing doggy massage? When did choices in animal healthcare start to feel like shopping for deals on groceries? Apparently, a lot has changed since I graduated from veterinary school.

"So this mysterious lump, how long has it been around?"

"About a month," says Ms. Sauer. "She did all these tests, like the computer told her to, and we're still no further along."

"She being Dr. Honey?"

"Yes."

"And she . . . she . . . um, uses a computer to communicate?"

"No, course not," she snaps. "The place is paperless, computerized. Dr. Honey types into her laptop thingy and up pops a list of the tests and procedures needed to diagnose and cure the problem. Pretty fancy, only it didn't work so good with Sox."

I lean back and purse my lips, totally perplexed.

"Let me get this straight. Healthy Paws has a computer program that tells its doctors what to do?" I stop short of saying, "And how to think?"

"Exactly," affirms a wide-eyed Ms. Sauer, as Sox grumbles over what appears to be a toenail clipping under a counter, thankfully just out of reach of his ropey pink tongue. "Oh, they'll tell you it ensures 'optimal patient care.'" Out come the air quotation marks. "But I'm thinking it's just a fancy way of getting every penny out of you that they possibly can."

My eyes drift to the corkboard hanging on the green wall behind her. It's home to a collage of family photos, but it's the picture at its heart that has my focus. It's one of me as a boy sitting on my mother's lap, my father, Robert, smiling, his eyes half-closed, by our side. It's the only tangible memory I have of the three of us together as a family, and I wonder what the man who left me this ailing practice would have made of this brave new world of veterinary medicine. Bobby Cobb was your classic, old-school animal doctor, cut from the same cloth as Lewis. He lived to fix sick animals. Ask the right questions, get your hands on the animal, trust your five senses, use your brain, your experience, your gut instinct, and don't cut corners. Making money was never part of the formula. Connecting with the patient and the owner was all that mattered. No wonder Cobb was revered as a local deity while his business was going belly-up. How do I find a happy medium?

"Um, so how long ago did you notice the lump?" I ask, shaking out of my reverie, attempting to channel my late father.

Ms. Sauer stiffens. "You already asked that. Like I said, 'bout a month."

"Right. Got it. Getting bigger, smaller?"

Ms. Sauer shrugs. "Staying about the same."

Come on, Cyrus, keep going. Maybe the Healthy Paws computer program isn't such a bad idea, especially if it gives you ideas for what to say next.

"Does it bother him? Does he try to scratch it, rub it, lick it?"

"No, he couldn't care less."

What else? What else? And then, with haste, as though time is running out, "Oh yeah, and this lump, is it the only one he's got?"

My excitement at mustering a pertinent question only makes Ms. Sauer regard me with even more suspicion. Or is that regret?

"So far as I can tell," she says, becoming impatient. "Look, Doc Honey stuck a needle into it and had it sent off to be reviewed by some fancy pathologist. Even they couldn't tell me what it was."

I could let her know that every so often a sample will simply not yield an answer despite your best efforts, but instead I shake my head, purse my lips, and join her in a moment of eye-rolling astonishment and disgust.

"Now Doc Honey wants to put poor Sox under the knife and lop it off, even though she and her damned computer can't tell me what it is. She says it could be a bug bite, it could be cancer, but surgery is the only way to know for sure."

Hmm, boxers are the number one breed of dog for skin tumors, by far.

"What was that?"

"Oh, nothing, just thinking how skin cancer may be common in boxers but unusual in such a young dog." Though not impossible, I keep to myself. "Okay, let's take a look."

Sox leans into me, happy to deposit a dollop of stringy drool near the crotch of my chinos as I check out the strawberry-colored bald bump on the point of his shoulder. My fingers pinch and squeeze his mysterious lesion while my brain churns with the possibilities. Presumably the Healthy Paws computer wanted to test for Lyme disease in case the bump was caused by a tick bite. But what about a brown recluse spider bite? What about a cyst or an in-growing hair follicle? What if the program has a glitch or the computer goes rogue?

"I'd like to try sticking a needle into the lump, aspirate some cells, and take a look at it myself."

"What makes you so sure you'd do any better? And more importantly, how much will all this cost?"

Lewis warned me about the folks around these parts, suggesting they respond best to a no-nonsense honest approach that I, with my southern sensibilities, find perilously close to rudeness.

"Well, I'm pretty good with a microscope." She eases back in her stance, head canting to one side as her lower jaw slides forward to show me the entire lower arcade of her incisors. Did she learn this trick from Sox? I can't tell whether she finds me defiant or arrogant. Tactic number two—when all else fails, appeal to the pocketbook. "Tell you what, if I don't get a diagnosis, I won't charge for trying."

Even with that generous offer Ms. Sauer still deliberates, but she eventually consents. A few minutes later, armed with a glass slide smeared with cellular debris from Sox's lump, I head on back into the work area to find Lewis, coffee mug in hand, leaning into the counter with a copy of the day's *Eden Falls Gazette*.

"Morning, Cyrus. Good to see your mastiff looks better." Lewis raises his cup in the direction of Tallulah, who stands at the front of her run, tail wagging, eager for attention or perhaps a jumbo-sized bag of Cheetos. "What you got there?"

Lewis notices me dipping my slide into a series of small glass vats containing blue and crimson stains and waving it in the air like a Fourth of July sparkler. I need it to dry before I slip it under the microscope lens and unmask its secret.

"A second opinion," I say, taking a seat in front of the scope. "Disgruntled client from our mortal enemies at Healthy Paws. What d'you make of that clairvoyant computer program they've got over there?"

Lewis turns the page and takes a sip. "Ridiculous. You can't apply a set formula to fit every pet ailment." He meets my eye and winks. "Besides, takes all the fun out of it, right?"

"Maybe, but it probably makes good business sense," I say. "Maximal billing disguised as good medicine."

Lewis puts his mug down, closes the paper, and comes over to where I'm sitting. Again, he squeezes my shoulder with his best Vulcan death grip. I'm beginning to appreciate how the pain is proportional to the gravity of what he's about to impart. "The day I run a test or offer a pill simply to make money is the day I hang up my stethoscope. Let's you and I focus on good medicine, and the bills will get paid."

He's right. And then it hits me. "That's it. That's what we'll do. What you and my father have always done. We'll set ourselves apart by pro-moting our old-fashioned approach to veterinary medicine."

Lewis's fuzzy-gray-caterpillar eyebrows knit together as one. "Not sure we want to highlight the old-fashioned. Sounds antiquated, out of date, ready for the boneyard."

"No, no. I'm talking about our style: the way we practice and the services we offer. Think classic, vintage, and timeless. Think friendly, warm, and homey."

Lewis looks even more skeptical.

"Did you just say homey?"

"Okay, well at least you're friendly. But bottom line, it's personalized, not computerized."

Lewis concedes a nod. "Hey, maybe you should see if Tallulah's owner, Panama Red, can hack into their program and shut it down. Then we'll see whether the Healthy Paws vets can actually think for themselves."

I assume he's joking. At least I hope he is.

"Anyway, best get going. If you're free later this morning, I'd appreciate your opinion on one of my house calls."

"Of course," I say, slipping the prepared slide under the clips on the stage of the microscope, letting my fingers twitch and flutter with the focus adjustment knobs, cozying my cornea up to the eyepiece.

"Excellent," I hear over my shoulder. "Ask Doris for the directions." My reply is no more than a perfunctory grunt. I'm distracted by what Sox's sample is telling me, written in a familiar language of foamy cytoplasm and juicy round nuclei. My aspirate is good, plenty of decent cells—what I don't see is just as important as what I do.

"Sorry to keep you waiting, Ms. Sauer, but I have good news." I'm smiling as I return to the exam room, energized, relishing this opportunity to one-up Healthy Paws. "It turns out this little lump is indeed a true surgical emergency."

"Oh my God. What are you saying? Now Sox needs emergency surgery?"

Ms. Sauer drops to her knees, her permanent scowl resembling a downturned bass mouth, draping her arms around her boxer's neck as Sox sets to work, licking up her tears. My attempt at clinical levity has clearly backfired.

"No, no, no," I stammer. "Sox is going to be fine. The lump is what's called a cutaneous histiocytoma. It's totally benign. Most of them spontaneously regress." I can see I've lost her again. "Most of them disappear in a month or two on their own. See? It's an old veterinary joke."

Sniffling, wiping more drool off her eyes than tears, she says, "What is?"

"The need for emergency surgery. If Sox doesn't get surgery soon, it will be too late. You'll have missed the chance to make money because the lump will have disappeared."

I flash my brows, trying to convey "Get it?" but her thin lips compress into a pale and indignant grimace.

"That's not funny. You're telling me Healthy

Paws wanted to make my Sox have risky anesthesia and put him through a pointless surgery on a lump that'll go away on its own?"

"Well, I'm sure that wasn't their intent when—"

"I knew it. I knew that bitch doctor was trying to rip me off." I guess Ms. Sauer is angry enough to actually use the b-word.

"Please, Ms. Sauer," I say, hamming up the ecclesiastical open palms spread wide before me. "Let's just be glad I could make the diagnosis." But then, unable to resist, I add in my most syrupy voice, "At least you know Sox will be well taken care of at Bedside Manor."

I'm pretty sure she sees that my fake smile is more about gloating than sincerity.

Ms. Sauer sniffs deeply, gets to her feet, and deliberates before picking up Sox's leash.

"I'm grateful," she says, somewhat tersely. "And yes, I'll be transferring Sox's care to you. But that lot over at Healthy Paws haven't heard the last from me."

Though this threat of negative publicity for our rivals might prove useful, it doesn't sit well with me.

"Ms. Sauer, can I be frank? I'm not sure going to the State Veterinary Board or the *Eden Falls Gazette* is the best way to deal with this."

Sox shakes his head, saliva strands cartwheeling end over end, flecking the front of my shirt. Ms. Sauer looks appalled.

"Oh, don't worry. I wasn't thinking of either of those."

I reach forward to shake her hand. "That's great. I'm relieved."

She holds my grip, and I watch as the devil dances in her eyes.

"I'll simply be chatting to Doris on the way out."

Her smug grin coincides with the paralysis affecting my lower jaw as it becomes my turn to impersonate a heavily jowled and drooling boxer.

Everybody knows everyone in this town. And no one more so than Doris. The tale of what I imagine will soon be Sox's near brush with death is about to go viral.

← 3 →

WHEN I RETURN TO THE WAITING ROOM, the man jumping out of his seat and charging my way is not the man I expected. This man is stocky and mustachioed, hand out-stretched and ready for a shake, all business. I try to look past him to see what became of the sickly man and his devoted standard poodle. I wonder why they decided to leave.

"Cyrus. Pleasure to finally meet you. Guy

Dorkin. I was in the neighborhood and thought what the heck, take a chance on introducing myself even though I don't have an appointment." Dorkin makes a show of turning left and then right as though he's sizing up the empty room. "Looks like I didn't need one."

And that's when he lets loose with a feral, distinctive laugh that I instantly recognize. It's that skin-crawling mix of wheezy donkey bray on the inhalation and hyena cackle on the exhalation. It's the one I heard at the bar last night. The man refusing to let go of my grip is none other than the office manager of Healthy Paws.

I make three quick observations about his greeting. He's trying to crush me, he's trying to pull me toward him, and he's twisting his wrist so his hand lies on top. What's that all about? Managing to break free, I sense an unpleasant stickiness lingering in my palm. Hopefully it's only a remnant of the stiff gel he's using to enforce the *Tintin* cowlick at the prow of his hairline.

"Pretty ballsy play you made the other day." Dorkin's got to be my age—late thirties, early forties—his black cashmere coat over a pin-striped suit and matching silk tie a little too dapper, a little too sharp for these parts. And the mustache has to be an experiment that went wrong. Perhaps it started out as a full beard, morphed into a goatee, and got downsized to its present state. Not quite seventies porn star specifications, it still draws the onlooker to Dorkin's meaty lips and the sizeable gap between his two front teeth.

"Not sure I'm with you, Mr. Dorkin."

"Guy. Guy. Lighten up, fella." There's a mischievous slap to my upper arm. "The free clinic you ran last week. I totally get it. Speculate to accumulate. Either folks flock to you in droves or they take advantage and you never see hide nor hair of them again." He throws up his hands, the laugh replaced by a sympathetic consolatory headshake. "Guess you got your answer."

"We're doing okay . . . Guy," I say, accentuating his name while jutting my chin toward the front desk. "Busy enough. In fact, one of your new clients is just leaving," I say, nodding toward the reception desk.

Ms. Sauer, caught in a conspiratorial huddle with Doris, glances our way, the sibilant hiss of their whispers falling silent. I watch with satisfaction as Dorkin's expression begins with indifference, passes through a moment of confusion, explodes with a flash of recognition (not sure if it's the dog or the owner), and finishes with a mask of supreme concern. It takes him a few seconds to shake it off.

"Look," he says, still striving to be Mr. Congeniality, "I dropped by 'cause I got a phone call from Critchley at Green State Bank. He says you're definitely no longer interested in selling."

Dorkin's grimace insists Mr. Critchley must have made a mistake.

"That's correct. Bedside Manor is no longer on the market."

Dorkin shifts his weight and acts surprised. "Really?"

"Yes, really."

His theatrical moment of hesitation is broken by another signature burst of laughter, followed by a playful punch to my upper arm.

"Good for you, Cy. Good for you."

Cy. No one has ever referred to me as Cy. In a matter of minutes Dorkin's gone from total stranger to baptizing me with a new nickname. And what's with all this physical contact? Is the frat boy yearning for the good old days at Tau Kappa Epsilon?

"No, that's great. But—full disclosure—your timing could have been better. Okay, your timing sucks. I mean, I wish you the best, but it's a tough market, you know?"

In my head I can hear Lewis telling me, *They want to wipe us out. They want to bring Bedside Manor to its knees*. I can't help myself.

"So why was Healthy Paws interested in buying this place then?"

Dorkin makes a gun out of his cocked thumb and pointy index finger, aims it my way, and clicks his tongue. "Good question. But to answer it, you should know who you're dealing with."

I almost say, "A total douche bag?" but keep quiet.

"Last quarter, my practice kicked serious ass."

The "my" is not lost on me.

"Number one Healthy Paws in New England when you figure in per capita head of population."

I'm not much of an actor, but my attempt at awe may have come across as disbelief.

"Cause for celebration, I imagine."

"You betcha," says Dorkin. "Me and the vets went out the other night. Had a blast."

I nod, flashing back to the scene at the bar, wishing I could hit the rewind button and start over with Amy. Given the amount of background noise fueled by drunken revelry, I wonder which veterinarian forgot to put his pager on vibrate and missed the emergency call for Tallulah, the stoned mastiff.

"Anyhoo, my point is *I* crunched the numbers, so you know they're solid, and yeah, so long as I used one of our existing doctors from Patton, not a new hire, this place could serve as a satellite."

"Satellite?"

"Yep, deal with the minor stuff here, but essentially feed the decent cases back to the mother ship, where we can do things right."

Dorkin leans in close enough for me to fully appreciate his coffee breath. "You see, Cyrus"— his voice has dropped to a deferential whisper—

"I calculated this place to be unsustainable as a full-time facility. Why? Easy. Eden Falls doesn't have the population to draw on, and what you do have is never going to fork over the big bucks."

Dorkin flashes his brows as if he has provided proof positive, waits a beat, and then hits me with: "Hey, you and I should go out sometime, grab a beer."

If he punches me again, I might actually have to punch him back. Only I'll be aiming for his face.

"Yeah, you can be my wingman." Dorkin begins to sway at his hips, his hands open-palmed and stretched out before him as though he's beating out a rhythm on imaginary bongos. "You've got that brooding thing going on—good-looking and, best of all, that southern accent. Let me guess—Charleston?"

Clearly Dorkin's done his homework because Charleston is no guess. But good-looking? I've been told I have my father's kind blue eyes but I have nothing "going on" around the opposite sex. Just ask Amy.

And wingman? *I feel the need . . . the need for speed.* I swear I will never be Goose to his Maverick.

"Yes, Charleston. But you're telling me Patton, a town five times the size of Eden Falls, can support four full-time veterinarians, whereas Eden Falls can't support even one?"

Dorkin forces a sigh, as though he can't believe

I still don't get it. "See, we're coming out of a recession, people have to cut back, cut corners, and, for the first time, pets are paying the price. Look, I was invited to spearhead a national advisory committee on the future of veterinary practice for Healthy Paws, so this heads-up is current, accurate, and free of charge. Two words: buckle up. If the likes of corporate practices are bracing for a bumpy ride, mom-and-pop places like this are going to get tossed aside and left for roadkill."

There's the chime of the front doorbell. Ms. Sauer and Sox are finally heading out, Doris shouting after them, "I'll give you a call when it's time for his vaccines." Funny how Doris has cranked up her volume control to eleven, broadcasting Sox's imminent return to Bedside Manor for his future care.

By now I've had more than I can stomach of Mr. Guy Dorkin, and if I were sensible I'd excuse myself, politely thank him for stopping by, and avoid the risk of further confrontation. The trouble is he said precisely the wrong words—mom and pop. I bore witness to the sweat and tears my late mother and father invested in this place. Their presence fills every paint-peeling, water-stained corner of every room, and, for right now, I still need them by my side.

"You know, Guy, part of me suspects Healthy Paws is worried about the competition. Maybe you've got this the wrong way round. Maybe Bedside Manor is going to start drawing on some of that wealthy clientele in Patton."

I brace for a derisive laugh but it never comes. "Which bit of four—that's right, four—full-time veterinarians are you forgetting about, Cy?"

Though his expression remains wooden, the switch up from comical banter to sarcasm tells me I've struck a nerve.

"Four means we can provide care twenty-four/ seven. Four"—he flutters the fingers of his right hand—"means you can get an appointment on a Sunday. And, FYI, Healthy Paws is a publicly traded company, I'm talking, 'Hello, Mr. NASDAQ.' We operate state-of-the-art facilities in thirty-six states. We buy in bulk, direct from all the major drug companies and pet food distributors, so the prices we offer to our customers cannot be beat. Do you know what drives profits in veterinary healthcare? Food and drugs. Everything else is gravy, and let me tell you, pet owners lap up our gravy."

If he's waiting for me to counter with something unique to Bedside Manor, I'm not sure what I'm going to say. Our fax machine works? Just bought a new batch of hazardous chemicals for our archaic X-ray machine?

He concludes his monologue with, "You should drop by sometime. Love to show you around."

Though I'd rather take a cheese-grater to my

eyeballs, I force a smile and say, "Sure. And I appreciate your . . . insight, but I think I'll stick it out, give this place a shot."

Dorkin purses his lips and shakes his head, pained by my great mistake.

"I gave your father a chance to sell up, but he blew it, determined to stay the course, plying his outdated techniques even as they were going extinct. Remind me, how did that work out for him?"

He spreads his arms widely, as if to a congregation.

"What kind of a legacy did he leave for you to salvage?"

I look away, grind molar on molar, meet his eyes, and say, "The kind that matters. The kind that comes without a price tag."

I can't tell whether it's what I've said or his reading my sincerity, but I'm treated to the hyena-donkey hybrid laugh.

"I'm sorry, Cy. I respected your father, but times have changed. We live in a world of doggy day care, canine fashion accessories, Halloween costumes for pets, pet psychics, pet sitters, the list goes on and on. Veterinary medicine must evolve. The public demands it. If Fido's getting a pacemaker, then Fido's mom knows she can't just trade for a cup of tea and a slice of cake."

I wonder if Fido's pacemaker also comes with a soothing doggy massage.

"The days of James Herriot are over. He's dead and buried, and with him went his fossilized style of practice."

There's a hand squeezing my shoulder. I flinch, but he won't let go. "It's survival of the fittest, Cy, a dog-eat-dog world. Healthy Paws can offer you a path forward. Keep this place. Just operate with a different business model."

My eyes slide left and focus on his hand like it's a hairy tarantula.

"Don't say a word, just promise me you'll think about it. Here, take my card."

He reaches into his overcoat pocket and pulls out a business card. I stuff it in the front of my chinos without even looking.

"Cell number's on the card. And check out my Twitter account. Fifty-eight followers can't be wrong."

He's backing up toward the front door, unwrapping a stick of Juicy Fruit and jamming it in his mouth. Why do I wish he'd found something more carcinogenic, like chewing tobacco? Extending the thumb and pinky finger of his right hand, Dorkin mimes a telephone while mouthing, "Call me," before disappearing through the chiming front door.

← 4 →

WATCHING AS DORKIN'S BLACK AUDI spins out of the lot, I smell the nicotine before I feel Doris's presence by my side.

"Piece of work, isn't he?" Doris looks as though she can will his car to crash with her eyes. "Vulture. Bided his time. Waited until your father was ready for the hospital before swooping in. He called it a mercy offer, an act of charity for a practice about to die. You believe that?"

Now she's looking at me, and for the first time it's a different type of scrutiny. Her defiant streak has been directed elsewhere, at a common enemy, and I am being invited to join the rebel alliance. It feels like an olive branch, even if it comes with a painful reminder of my failings as a son.

"He still wants me to sell. Funny, last week his offer came with all kinds of stipulations—in particular, decent monthly production figures. Now he can't wait to get his hands on the place."

Doris reaches into the pocket of her ski jacket and pulls out her Zippo lighter and pack of Marlboros. "That's 'cause you've got him rattled." And then, after a beat of deliberation, "Some folks must be saying nice things about you."

This last remark comes out as more of a statement than a compliment, as though by stressing the "some" she wants me to know she's an undecided juror. Doris and I have a long way to go to achieve a decent thaw. Still, I'll take it. I watch the craving ignite in her eyes as she plucks a cigarette and tamps it down on the lid.

"Well, Dorkin's going to be disappointed. I'd rather burn the place to the ground than become a disciple of the Church of Healthy Paws."

Doris pulls tightly on the invisible drawstring of her sticky orange lips, forming an uneasy pout. "I've been here before, with your father. You ready for payback?"

I drift off, working on a slow, gravelly Russell Crowe impersonation from the movie *Gladiator*. "And I will have my vengeance, in this life or the next."

"What you goin' on about?" says Doris, showing me her unlit cigarette and heading for the front door.

I clear my throat without explaining. "Hey, what happened to that guy with the standard poodle?"

She shrugs. "No idea. Dog felt better or maybe his owner got cold feet about seeing you?" The bell chimes and she catches herself. "Eleven o'clock. Dr. Lewis wants you to meet him at Garvey's. Remember the way?"

"Of course."

"The farmhouse, not the main entrance."

"Got it."

And that's when she relinquishes a scary, lemon yellow smile. "And Dr. Lewis suggests you bring your wellies."

Whether Doris believes no explanation is needed or merited, I cannot tell, but I'm seriously worried. The prospect of what awaits me actually makes her giggle like a naughty schoolgirl.

EDEN FALLS is a "blink and you'll miss it" kind of place. No stop signs, no lights, no reason not to keep going. In fact, Main Street might be more accurately labeled Only Street. But Garvey's Nursery and Garden Center lies on the other side of a covered bridge on the far side of town, which is more than enough time to try calling Amy. Once again, it goes to voice mail. She must be screening my calls. I'm about to hang up, try back later, but even as I'm justifying my cowardice, I realize that's precisely what she would expect. Now might be the moment to be something I'm not—unpredictable.

"It's me." This time I overpower my insecure desire to clarify that "me" is Cyrus. "Thought I might drop by the diner at lunchtime. Not sure if you're working, but if you are, great. If not . . ." Keep going, easy-breezy. "Then . . . no problemo." *No problemo? What idiot says no problemo?* "Hey, I'd love to try to get together again sometime." Better, upbeat but still casual.

And then a thought hits me. "Think of it like me coming home to Eden Falls. It's all about second chances." I pause for a minute before pressing End.

What's gotten into me? I should be scheming for ways to beat back an imminent attack from Mr. Guy Dorkin. Instead I'm obsessing over a woman I barely know. Worst of all, I spent a restless night convincing myself that my decision to give up my former life in Charleston, to return home and breathe new life into Bedside Manor, was in no way influenced by something as cliché as an attraction to a potential mate.

In a moment of clarity, I tried to break Amy's spell by deconstructing the elements of her allure. Unfortunately her selflessness is hard to overlook. Here's a woman happy to put her education on hold (she was in a master's program over at UVM) and work a minimum wage job at our local diner in order to be there for her dying grand-father. There is, however, no denying her acerbic "take no prisoners" tongue, with words unleashed like bullets from an Uzi. Some say she speaks her mind. If I'm being honest, I think she speaks her heart. And yes, her facial features bear the perfect symmetry of an attractive woman, excluding her heterochromic (one's blue, one's brown) but no less hypnotic eyes, while she conveys an outward indifference to her looks. In another world this woman might not give me the time of day, yet here, in the northernmost reaches of rural Vermont, her beauty is not a tool to use or flaunt. If anything, she brandishes it like a test, daring you to look deeper.

Obviously, women are not my area of expertise. Taking this dare went against my better judgment. When I open up, I do so in carefully controlled increments; however, Amy makes . . . made me want to try. Okay, it's a ridiculous reaction to a woman I barely know from a diner and from being trapped with her in an X-ray darkroom, but I stopped redacting the bits of me I didn't want her to see—yes, even the intangible, emotional bits—because I could sense the possibilities. In short, I let down my guard.

I check the screen on my flip phone—plenty of battery and a decent signal. No excuses. Clearly this preoccupation with Amy is pointless. Best to go back to what works—clinical objectivity. Take in the bigger picture, weigh the options, spot the distractor, discard, simplify, and move on.

The vehicle in the cracked rearview mirror caught my attention long before the covered bridge. It's a gray minivan; and though the funhouse reflection makes it tricky, I'm pretty sure I can make out two figures inside—one white and one black. They've been on my tail since I left Bedside Manor, keeping a safe distance but now I'm certain I'm being followed. Two thugs looking to collect on one of my many debts, or a pair of contract killers hired by Dorkin? I indicate right at the sign for Garvey's. The minivan slows down then drives on, past the entrance. Maybe I'm confusing paranoia with astute observation.

In *Back to the Future*, Michael J. Fox used a DeLorean sports car as a time machine. My version is Dad's old Chevy Silverado truck, but it delivers me to a Garvey's far different from my childhood memories. For starters, the numerous post-and-beam buildings and glinting green-houses are new, creating the sense that Garvey's is a little village rather than a local store. This was the place Mom and I would visit for apple picking, hayrides, Halloween pumpkins, and our Christmas tree. Now it looks more like a theme park—a Disney version of Vermont.

The once run-down miniature golf course has been artificially enhanced by water fountains and an Eiffel Tower. Remnants of the seasonal maze that used to stand in a field of fitful cow corn has gone, replaced by a wall of twiggy but manicured privet more suited to an English stately home. There's a building devoted to skiing and snowboarding equipment and one for fishing and hunting supplies. The rusty swing-set and slides have given way to a state-of-the-art playground, the need for a dab of Mom's spittle or a tetanus shot traded for hand sanitizers at the entranceway.

As I curb crawl past the petting zoo, a young

mother carrying a toddler in her arms delivers the kind of death glare she might reserve for a suspected pedophile. She's obviously misread my look of surprise. Run-down stalls, a pigsty, and barbed wire have been superseded by imposing barns and white picket fencing. In the background I can still make out the remnants of the original farm—stanchions for livestock, silos, a milking parlor—but everything is conspicuously shiny, not a rusting piece of farm equipment or an abandoned tractor tire in sight.

When the asphalt of the neatly plowed and salty parking lot ends, the wheels of the Silverado lock into the icy ruts of a trail leading directly to the farmhouse. Lewis's empty vehicle is parked out front, and I pull up alongside. As usual, I make sure there's plenty of room to turn around without the need to back up. That's because Dad's old truck might be the only part of his legacy that always looked forward—its reverse gear doesn't work.

It's one of those bleak, pencil lead–gray mornings; the threat of more snow hangs in the bitter January air like a raised dagger poised to descend. Direct sunlight has been banished, and that's why the man in the sunglasses, who comes crashing out of the house and charging my way as I pull on a pair of my father's green Wellington boots, instantly strikes me as strange.

"No. No," he screams, hands waving over his

head as though I'm about to step on a land mine. "No solicitation. Not here."

Feet rooted to the spot, I raise a "I come in peace" wave that he chooses to ignore, almost barreling into me.

"Which part of private property don't you understand?"

The man has receding dark hair, center-parted and gathered in a ponytail, as though he's determined to keep every filament left on his head. The Kirk Douglas dimple chiseled into his chin is striking, but it's his mirror aviator sunglasses that have my attention. I haven't seen a pair like these in years. In my mind I flash to the prison guard in the Paul Newman movie *Cool Hand Luke*.

"I'm Dr. Mills, from Bedside Manor. I work with Dr. Lewis." I gesture to Lewis's truck as though this inanimate object will substantiate my claim. "Lewis asked me to meet him here to see a case."

For what seems like an eternity we stand there, inhaling each other's breathy clouds, the man apparently derailed by my explanation. He's about my height, six feet (like most men of five feet, eleven inches, I prefer to round up). I have no clue what's going on behind those mirrors, but without warning he winces and pounds a clenched fist into the center of his forehead.

"You got anything for a migraine in that bag of yours?"

He's noticed I'm carrying my late father's "doctorin' " bag.

"Might have some Advil."

I swing the bag up on my thigh and open it up.

"Don't bother," the man snaps. "Took eight hundred milligrams this morning. Didn't touch it. Got something stronger?"

"Afraid not," I say, beginning to notice an aroma hanging in the condensation between us. It's striking, the sweet smell of nail polish remover that is characteristic of a specific clinical disorder called "ketosis."

The man curses and stamps one foot into the snow like a warning from an angry goat. He's only wearing slippers.

"Test your glucose level this morning?" I ask.

The man eases his head back ever so slightly, but it's impossible to tell if he's impressed by my deduction. Blowing off ketones in the breath suggests poor glucose regulation, probably because he needs artificial insulin. Given the man's skinny build and the presence of visible scar tissue on the tips of his fingers, I'd go with juvenile diabetes, the scars the result of decades of monitoring his blood glucose with daily, tiny, painful pricks.

"Course I did," he snaps. "This"—he drills a forefinger into his temple—"has nothing to do with it." Then he growls, scoops up a snowball, and pounds it into his temple, holding it in place, savoring the temporary relief as a trail of icy water runs down his wrist and forearm.

"If it's that bad, Mr. . . . Mr. . . ."

He makes no attempt to bail me out.

"I'd suggest a visit to the hospital."

Off in the distance two men are headed our way. One of them is Lewis.

"Ah, there he is, I won't bother you any . . ."

But Mr. Ponytail is no longer listening. His back to me, he lopes off to the sanctuary of his house. The hostility and the social miscues make me wonder if he has some mental health issues and fears getting caught talking to a stranger.

Lewis saunters over, dressed like a farmer from central casting—ruddy faced from the cold, wearing a flat cap and green Barbour jacket.

"Cyrus, this is Mike Garvey Junior."

"Nice to meet you," says a heavyset man in a Blue Jays baseball cap. He also has that Kirk Douglas dimple in his chin.

We shake hands.

"Was that your son I was speaking with?" I ask, gesturing to the house, catching sight of a shadowy figure at the screen to the front door.

Mike Garvey Jr. waves, but the shadow disappears.

"Yeah. My son. Michael Garvey the Third. We call him Trey. Afraid he's not been himself lately. Acting a little weird."

"Doris mentioned the incident in his truck," says Lewis. "When does he get his license back?"

"Never lost it," says Mike, and then to me, "He failed a sobriety test, but his blood alcohol level was zero. Chief Devito had to let him go."

Interesting.

"Maybe your son's odd behavior reflects a problem regulating his diabetes," I say. "How old was he when you got the diagnosis?"

Garvey considers me, his expression caught somewhere between worried and impressed. "Two. But he never said he was a diabetic, did he?"

Lewis sees where this is going and begins to grin. "Told you he was smart, Mike."

Mike looks unconvinced.

"Maybe," he says. "But you can talk to Trey. Get right next to him. Not so easy with Ermintrude."

Ermintrude.

Lewis's grin refuses to wane.

"I'm sure Cyrus would be happy to take a look," he says, and they both turn to me.

"Sure," I say, sounding anything but.

Mike leads the way around the back of the house and down a trail plowed through the deep snow toward the main farm buildings that lie beyond the public's reach.

"Lewis tells me it's been a while since you lived in Eden Falls."

"Twenty-five years," I say.

"Ah, back when my old man was running the place."

"He was a smart man, your father," says Lewis. "Saw what was going to happen to dairy farms in this part of the world and did something about it."

Garvey cringes at the compliment, and for a few beats the only sound is the satisfying squeak of compacted snow under our every footfall.

"Guess so," he says, "at least he started out that way. Dad pushed the all-natural angle, the antibiotic-free milk, cheese, and yogurt long before it was popular. And no one was trying to sustain rare breeds of cattle, sheep, or goats. Throw in organic fruit and vegetables, expand into plants and trees, and he reckoned he could keep doing what he loved, keep farming, keep working." Garvey forces a laugh and shakes his head.

"Garvey's is part of Eden Falls culture," says Lewis as we walk three abreast.

"Oh yeah," says Garvey. "If you like mini-golf and a petting zoo. Dad got out because of falling milk prices. Cost him more in fuel and fertilizer than he could make in milk. Started selling off the herd, looking at other ways to work the land. Hey, now it's mine, I'm no better. See over there?"

He points to a clearing in the hillside.

"If we're still in business this time next year, I'll have a tow rope and floodlights, and with luck, kids will be tubing down there all night long. Not exactly my idea of farming."

"Maybe not," says Lewis, "but it's definitely mine."

Lewis catches my skeptical glance.

"It's true. I never liked farmwork. Hated the economics of whether a cure could be justified versus cutting your losses at a slaughterhouse. Garvey's is different. What's not to love when farm animals turn into pets?"

Pets? Now he's got me worried.

"This place has certainly undergone a major facelift since the last time I was here," I say.

"Had to," says Garvey. "Department of Public Health and Safety insisted on some of the upgrades. Insurance helped out when we took a hit from Hurricane Irene, but most of this is thanks to an equity loan from Green State Bank."

Ah, Green State Bank and the charming Mr. Critchley.

"I'm afraid the public likes its slice of farm life sweet smelling and pretty on the eyes. Here we are."

We've passed a row of stables (I'm relieved Ermintrude is apparently not one of the giant Clydesdale horses housed there), and Garvey leads the way into a large, airy barn. It's like walking into an animal husbandry class—steamy livestock busy chewing cud mixed with that authentic aroma of mud, manure, and damp straw bedding. The place is bright and warm, the V of the ceiling a good twenty feet overhead. Our presence incites a chorus of bleats and moos reminiscent of kids singing the Old MacDonald farmyard nursery rhyme.

"She's way down at the end," says Garvey, but I'm distracted, checking out the animals segregated behind metal rails on either side of the central aisle.

There's a spotted black and white sheep bearing four horns. *It's a Jacob, a breed thought to have originated in the Middle East around three thousand years ago.* Nearby stands a small black cow with a band of white fur wrapped around her belly. *She's a belted Galloway. Her coat packs four thousand hairs into every square inch, making it highly resistant to severe cold.* Aside from these useless factoids and an ability to identify obscure breeds, I haven't thought about the diseases of farm animals since I was back in veterinary school.

"C'mon, Cyrus," says Lewis, the two of them ahead of me.

I trot to catch up. "Are those pigeons, Mike?" I ask, pointing to the crossbeams near the ceiling. Hundreds of raucous gray birds appear to be roosting (and actively defecating) at the far end of the barn where we are headed.

" 'Fraid so," says Garvey.

"Flying rats," says Lewis. "Best not to look up, if you know what I mean." He doffs the peak of his cap. "You should have worn one of these."

"But there's so many of them. Are they a homing variety?"

"No idea," says Mike. "But they're good for business. Folks love having their picture taken with them. Sprinkle seed along your arms; see how many pigeons will land on you. Trey still holds the record—thirty-two. They seem to flock to him. Here she is. Dr. Mills, meet Ermintrude."

In an isolated stall, walled off from the other cows by bales of straw and hay, stands a fawn-colored cow with black hooves and a dark switch of hair at the end of her tail. I'm guessing a Jersey, but what concerns me is the way she's pressing her head into the wall. Based on the twitch and swivel of her leafy ears she obviously senses our presence, but it looks as if she's consumed by the worst hangover of her life.

The three of us cozy up to the fence, resting our elbows on the top rail.

"I remember you telling me you like comparative pathology," says Lewis to me.

"Me?"

" 'Disease is disease,' you said, 'whether you're human or a duck-billed platypus.' Well, here's your chance with a Jersey cow. Ermintrude's twelve years old and as you can see, she's lost a lot of weight despite a good appetite. What disturbs me most of all is what's happening inside her head."

Lewis consults with Mike, something passes

between them, and Mike claps his hands together and yells out loud.

Ermintrude startles as if she's snapped out of a trance, ears twitching, all four legs scrambling and uncoordinated as she skitters across the slick mud, going down on her front legs, bug eyes rolling back inside her head, black to white and black again. She's petrified and desperate to reach the sanctuary of the farthest corner.

"Not pretty, is it?" says Mike.

"How long has she been like this?"

Lewis does that thing with his upper incisor chewing on his lower lip.

"She's only been this bad for a few days. Right, Mike?"

"Right. But she's been acting weird for a while."

"Weird?" I raise my eyebrows and give the farmer my best "you're going to have to do better than that" glare.

"It started in the fall. Trey takes care of her, always has, and he noticed how she was . . . I don't know . . . pushy, rough, even a bit aggressive, especially around feeding time. We thought she's getting old, getting crotchety—hey, don't we all?"

"Speak for yourself," says Lewis.

"So we cut her some slack—until the incident in the petting zoo. Ermintrude's been a permanent fixture for years, not least because she's bomb-proof around screaming, pinching kids. But on this particular day she went postal on a five-year-old boy. Nearly kicked him into kingdom come. Trey saw it, but thankfully his mother did not. Otherwise, I'd be on the wrong end of a lawsuit for sure."

"I know this is not your area of expertise, Cyrus," says Lewis, "but I've seen how your brain works. You love the weird details about obscure diseases. Her calcium, magnesium, and glucose levels are fine. She's never had a fever, her diet is good, her lymph nodes are normal, and her pupil reflexes are normal. Her most striking clinical sign is her sensitivity to sound and light—"

"And the way she's become scary to be around."

"What d'you mean?" I ask.

"Put it this way," says Garvey. "You shouldn't go in there unless you've been trained as a matador."

"That's right," says Lewis. "I just wanted you to look at her, see for yourself, and maybe something will cross your mind that hasn't crossed mine. I've tried changing her diet, I've tried antibiotics, multivitamins, dietary supplements, you name it. And I've ruled out pretty much every common cause of neurological disease I can think of."

"She's going downhill and fast. Look at her," says Garvey. "If you can't help her, Dr. Mills, and soon, she's going to have to be destroyed."

If I look anxious, I hope that Lewis and Garvey will think it's just the burden of this responsibility. Truth be told, that's the least of my concerns. Lewis is right, I've always been obsessed with the minutiae of bizarre diseases, and though I came here out of a sense of obligation to my colleague, secretly I'm totally intrigued by this case, even if it is a cow.

"I'll do my best," I say, and even to my ear, this reply sounds totally insincere. Perhaps that's because I'm following my gut reaction, the knee-jerk response to what I just witnessed, Ermintrude's hypersensitivity to any kind of stimulation and the way it's identical to my recollection of a grainy video of similarly afflicted cows from Great Britain in the late eighties. Could the poor cow's affliction have anything in common with her caretaker, Trey?

Afraid he's not been himself lately. Acting a little weird.

What if Trey and Ermintrude have variations of the same disease? If so, and if this is what I think it is, the ramifications for me, Eden Falls, and a multibillion-dollar industry are incalculable. For one scary news cycle I might inadvertently steal more media coverage than the Kardashians. Air my suspicions to the FDA, prove them correct, and every single animal on this property will be destroyed before Garvey's, this third-generation Eden Falls fixture, gets razed to the ground.

"What's going on in that head of yours?" asks Lewis with a smile. "You on to something?"

I shake my head. It's scary enough even to think about my number one suspicion, let alone to air it. I'd best be wrong, because if not, Ermintrude, Trey, and Garvey's farm will be a national sensation for all the wrong reasons.

← 5 →

TWELVE THIRTY AND THE MISS EDEN FALLS Diner is chock-full of a rowdy lunchtime rush intent on receiving sustenance. I reckon I'll be lucky to catch sight of Amy, let alone chat with her. I attempt to flatten the top of my crown where an unruly cowlick always lurks, berating myself for not looking my best, when a bear claw lunges in my direction and grabs me by the sleeve.

"Cyrus, quick, take a pew."

The order comes from Peter Greer, editor in chief of the *Eden Falls Gazette*, and a good friend and supporter of my late father and Bedside Manor.

I plop into the seat opposite him in a tight two-man booth. It doesn't help that Greer's a big guy, spilling over the red-checkered tablecloth between us to initiate an awkward hearty handshake.

"Marvelous to see you, old boy."

"Is it usually this crowded at lunchtime?"

"Always a little argy-bargy around the trough in these parts. Not to worry, you get used to it."

Did I mention Greer was English, complete with an accent posh enough to read the news for the BBC?

"How's business?" he asks. "Thriving after my stroke of genius?"

Greer's referring to last Saturday's free clinic. It was his idea of a way to introduce me to the community.

"If I ignore the fact that everyone thinks Bedside Manor offers complimentary pet care and we never ask for money, then business is booming."

Greer leans forward, sweeps his hand back and through his dapper mane of hair.

"Look on the bright side, you've got the opposition well and truly riled."

"The opposition? Healthy Paws?"

Greer chuckles. "Oh, it gets better, but did you order yet? You should, or it's going to take forever."

My waist-high view of the bar and other booths is blocked in all directions by a writhing sea of overinflated down jackets. Where's the main reason I came here for lunch?

"There she is."

Though seated, Greer's height gives him an advantage as he waves for attention like he's hailing a London cab.

"Here you go," says Amy, sliding a plate across

the table. "Bacon burger and onion rings on the side."

"Marvelous," says Greer, "and I wonder if my dear friend, Dr. Mills, might place an order too."

Amy turns to me as though she never noticed I was there. No smile, no recognition. I stare into the magic of her distinctive eyes, rewarded with a blasé shrug.

"Um . . . what's good?" I ask, unbalanced by her distance and impatience.

She leans closer. "What's good?" she repeats.

I nod, but now I'm worried.

"Hmm, implicit in that question is the fact that you not only trust, but you value my opinion. Wouldn't you agree, Mr. Greer?"

"Wholeheartedly," says Greer, squirting ketchup onto his plate, onion ring in hand.

"It seemed like a simple question," I stutter.

"But it's not. It's about personal taste, preference, and mutual understanding. Oh, I could tell you what I'm supposed to say, 'Yes, the fish sandwich is fantastic,' because the chef noticed the frozen cod has passed its sell-by date and wants to get rid of it, but I'm not that person. Now, if you want to know what I'll be having for lunch because I like how it tastes, I'll tell you the Greek salad."

I glance over at Greer, who's got the ring halfway to his mouth and looks afraid.

"Greek salad it is. And . . . thanks for the

clarification." I say this with an absolutely straight face and watch as Amy tries to work out if I'm being sincere. It takes a while but there's a spark, the flicker of a weak connection between her lips and her eyes.

The crunch of the batter encasing the onion ring brings me back.

"My, my, that was rather strange. I take it the first date didn't go well?"

I rock back in my seat. "How did you know I went on a date with Amy?"

Greer chomps into his burger, chews, swallows, and says one word. "Doris."

It seems my failed attempt at a love life has become public knowledge thanks to my receptionist.

"It could have gone better," I say, peeling off my gloves and jacket.

"Well, I wouldn't be too concerned," he says.

"How can you say that? You weren't there."

Greer speaks from behind his fingertips to spare me the sight of half-chewed food.

"Because Amy's wearing lipstick. When she took my order she wasn't. I suspect she's powdered her nose just for you."

This disclosure makes me smile, pleased enough to snag one of his onion rings.

"The evening was a disaster," I say, drawing air into my mouth to cool off the steaming batter burning my tongue. "But it wasn't all my fault."

Greer's got a red dribble of ketchup on his chin that's hard to ignore.

"Go on," he says, happy to bite and chew, waiting for my story. His air is attentive, one of an experienced Don Juan, eager to share his wisdom on how to properly woo a lady.

"Things were going well until Amy got a phone call and insisted she had to take it."

"Obviously important."

"Obviously. And exciting and flirtatious and highly amusing."

Greer grabs a napkin and wipes his lips but misses the stray ketchup. "You were eaves-dropping on a private conversation?"

"Of course not. The bar was noisy. She talked in a corridor outside the bathrooms, but I had a perfect view of her body language. Twirling her hair around her finger, playing with her necklace, getting all wide-eyed, even . . . giggling."

Greer recoils, a little too dramatically. "Not giggling."

"Hey, she's never giggled with me. I can only assume this pivotal phone call was from an old flame and she was thrilled to reconnect. Even though she was on a date with me."

"How do you know it was a man? How do you know it wasn't a long-lost cousin?"

"Because I asked. She said it was someone from her past. Someone very special. Fine, but you leave me hanging for twelve minutes and then refuse to elaborate, that's just plain rude. What?"

Greer looks appalled.

"Hence Amy's lecture on the virtue of trust. Makes perfect sense."

"Hey, I was nervous. I wanted the date to go well, to be special. But the place was a zoo, and to top it all, she was obviously far more interested in someone on the other end of a phone than she was in me. Believe me, I'm not a control freak. I don't need to know every detail of her romantic past."

"And what do you know about her past, romantic or otherwise?"

"Next to nothing."

The ketchup finally dribbles onto a receptor that Greer senses, the napkin finding its target.

"Let me assure you she's well liked in this community, not least because she's taking care of her ailing grandfather, Harry. There's no one else. Her mother ran off with some guy to Montreal, and her father died of carbon monoxide poisoning."

Reading my horror, he adds, "Snowstorm accident. Few years back. Trapped in his car. Snow blocked off the exhaust pipe. Just went to sleep."

"That's awful."

Greer nods and swallows his last bite.

"You two have more in common than you know. Parents are deceased or estranged and . . ."

"And?"

"You're both . . . difficult to read."

I think about this. He's right, and I've got no comeback. However, I pick up on his use of the word *both*.

I lean in and lower my voice. "I've never known a woman like her. I've worked behind a microscope for the last fourteen years, and the only women I got to know were . . . well . . . straightforward, polite, scientific . . . okay, nerdy, if not demure. And southern women are just different. Tell you exactly what's on their minds. Not that that made my love life any easier."

Greer laughs.

"Let's hope Amy likes mint juleps, otherwise you've got your hands full with a bird of another feather."

"Glad you find this funny. My point is, if she'd rather be with someone else, then let's not waste each other's time."

Suddenly Amy swoops in with my salad. "Who's wasting your time?"

Her presence instantly shuts me down, my silence not helped by a guilty blush of embarrassment.

"Is it me or is it hot in here?" is all I can think to say.

Amy meets my eyes, and this time I sense she's traded frustration for mischief. "It's you." She's still holding the plate. "One Greek salad."

I reach out to take it, the tips of our fingers

touching, the contact a second more than necessary before she lets go. I thank her in a boyish whisper.

"You all set, Peter?"

"Stuffed like the proverbial pig. My compliments to the chef."

Amy rolls her eyes. "Here's the check. When you're ready." She slides a slip of paper across the table and disappears.

Greer snatches it up and hunches forward, elbows on the table, his face inches from mine, a green leaf-laden fork hovering between us.

"Take it from a man who knows a thing or two about women, this woman"—he thumbs over his shoulder—"is still interested in you."

My lips work on a mouthful of vegetation as I mull this over.

"If I were you, I'd ask for a second date, somewhere quiet and relaxed. For God's sake, this time keep the conversation light. Seducing a woman is not a medical emergency. It's rare for one's services to be required stat or for the situation to necessitate a painstaking history of everything that led to this moment. Simply put, let her come to you. Believe me, women want to reveal themselves, but to get to the precious fruit inside, you must peel back the layers with skill and tact and patience. Remember, old boy, romance needs to be cultivated, nurtured, and never rushed."

I stab a piece of feta and shake my head. All this from a man whose red silk boxer shorts were consumed by his mistress's Labrador while her husband was out of town.

"What were you going to tell me about Healthy Paws?" I ask.

"Oh, that's right." Greer reaches for his wallet and deposits a ten-dollar bill on the table. "Got a phone call from a Mr. Guy Dorkin this morning, office manager over at—"

"I know who he is."

"Huh. Well, Dorkin wants to follow your lead, wants to offer a free clinic and tour of his fancy digs over in Patton. Thing is, he wants to advertise in the *Gazette*. He's trying to win over the pet owners of Eden Falls."

I put my fork down. "What a total—"

"My thought exactly."

"But you know Bedside Manor is hanging by a thread. We can't afford to lose what clients we have left."

"I know. But what am I to do? Dorkin wants a full-page ad to run this Friday."

"Tell him he's missed deadline. Tell him there's no available space."

"Too late. He dropped by in person. One of my lackeys already took his money."

The curse slips between my clenched teeth.

"Sorry about that."

"Not to worry," says Greer, reaching across the

table to pat me on the forearm. "I'm already working on a cunning plan. The Dork is going to rue the day he advertised in the *Gazette*."

And with that, Greer eases himself out of the booth and, seeing Amy headed my way, winks and wishes me luck.

"All set?" she asks, even as she grabs my plate.

"Yes, thank you."

"Just the check?"

"Please," I reply. As she turns away I blurt out, "How are Clint and Harry doing?"

Despite the name, Clint is the *female,* funny-looking Lab mix her grandfather Harry calls his best friend. Last week Clint had a bad run-in with a wayward pork chop.

"They're great," she says, considering me, and it's like I'm watching a security gate slide back, getting my first unimpeded look at the person on the other side. "Kind of you to ask."

"Not at all," I say. "Give them my best."

She waits a beat. "Fixing Clint, you were cool under pressure," she says. "Now I've seen what you're capable of."

I do this nervous porcine snort thing that is definitely not cool. "I'm not sure that's true."

"No? Well, you've proven you can handle at least one tricky bitch."

She smiles. I hope she's referring to Clint.

Once again she makes to leave.

"Wait. Did you get a chance to listen to your voice mail?"

Amy comes back to the table looking confused.

"Um . . . see . . . I left you a message. Look . . . I know the other day, well, it didn't go as planned."

Nonchalantly she fingers the top empty buttonhole of her shirt. "Oh, so you thought you'd get to sleep with me on the first date?"

"No," I shout, causing a few heads to turn before regaining my composure. "Never."

"Never as in it never crossed your mind because I'm not your type?"

"No, I mean, yes, it's crossed my . . . I mean, no, I'm not that kind of man."

The smile wriggling into the corners of her mouth takes its time, enough for me to achieve maximal blood flow to my cheeks.

"And what kind of man is that exactly?"

Her standing over me, forcing me to angle my head upward, only exaggerates my discomfort. To my surprise she reads it, deciding to squat down so we're face-to-face.

"Hey, I'm sorry if I came across as . . ."

"Rude," I offer.

Amy puckers her lips. "I'll give you abrupt, maybe even snippy. But believe me, my behavior was for your own good."

I manage a slow nod, forcing the next question out of my mouth to change from "What's that supposed to mean?" to "Can we have a do-over?"

In her dispassionate deliberation, the room falls silent, joining me in a moment of breathless anticipation. Though there may be some truth to the notion that attractive women can go overlooked because they appear unapproachable, even unattainable, I wager Amy's single status is based on a frank, brutal honesty that is as unsettling as it is beguiling.

"Sure, why not?"

Is it me or does the background noise return to its former volume?

"Just as long as the green-eyed monster doesn't rear its ugly head."

"Green-eyed monster?" I ask.

" 'O, beware, my lord . . . the green-eyed monster which doth mock the meat it feeds on.' "

Did I mention Amy was an English major?

"Shakespeare," she says. "*Othello*. Referring to jealousy."

"I wasn't . . ." I catch myself in the nick of time and push down the urge to act defensive. It was being the voyeur, having to witness her irresistible smile and laugh, the ease with which this mysterious man on the other end of a phone captivated her in a way I doubt I ever could.

"Of course," I say. "Fresh start. Clean slate. Don't suppose you're free this evening?"

She winces, inhales between clenched teeth. "Afraid not, got plans."

And I can tell she's watching me, like this is a test, her unavailability bait, to see if the monster lurking inside me will bite.

"No problem," I manage, though I'm not sure she's convinced. "Another time."

"That would be nice," she says, softening. "I'll have my people call your people. And soon, okay?"

I KNEW IT. I knew I wasn't being paranoid. Parked on the other side of the street from the diner is a dishwater gray minivan. It has to be the one that tailed me to Garvey's. There's a figure reclining in the driver's seat, lying low, gangsta-style, behind the steering wheel, but I can't see his partner. Peeved, I succumb to a rare moment of spontaneity, schlepping across the mushy brown snow to confront them, squinting through the condensation on the inside of the window, only to be greeted by white teeth and an explosion of booming barks.

"Easy, Stash," commands a voice, winding down his window, bringing one hand up to his windpipe in the manner of a fake karate chop. The barking instantly stops, and that's when I recognize the gaunt, sickly guy I saw earlier this morning in the waiting room. Riding shotgun, sitting square and to attention, is his black standard poodle.

"Hey, Doc," says the man, looking pleased to

see me. "I've been hoping to catch you. Wondering if I can have a word. In private."

"What's this about?" I ask.

The man hesitates, checks in with his partner, Stash (strange name), before coming back to me, giving new meaning to the phrase *deadpan expression*.

"I have a favor to ask. A big favor. Something only you could appreciate."

If the request is meant to sound ominous, it does.

"You'd better explain," I say.

A car barrels past, spraying a frosty slurry down the back of my pants as a couple of satisfied customers exit the diner and head our way.

"Sure. Somewhere quiet?"

I'd offer to come around and sit in the passenger seat, but the dog doesn't look like he's prepared to move.

"I'm headed back to the practice. I can meet you there."

Before the man can reply, my cell phone rings.

"Where are you?"

No introduction. No pleasantries. Straight to it.

"Good afternoon, Doris. I just finished up lunch at the diner."

I drift around to the front of the van to avoid another oncoming car.

"Any chance you could . . ."

The request gets lost in a burst of static.

"Hang on." I walk up the street as though I can somehow divine better reception. "Can you hear me now?"

More disjointed, garbled consonants. I jog over to the diner side of the street.

"Any better?"

"I said can you pick me up a packet of Marlboros from the gas station across the way? And then you're needed on a house call."

"Doris, I'm not comfortable enabling your drug habit."

"Suit yourself, but I'll have to leave the practice unattended to get them."

She always knows just what to say. "Okay, fine, what's the address?"

She rattles off a street name I don't recognize.

"It's off Route 62, closer to Patton than Eden Falls."

"Patton?"

"Maybe you're starting to get a reputation."

I'm speechless. Did Doris just give me a compliment?

"Or maybe they just don't know any better."

She hangs up before I can reply.

I look back across the street for the gray minivan.

It's gone.

THE HOME of one Marmalade Succabone (yes, I asked Doris to repeat the pet's name) is a conspicuously lonely colonial surrounded by empty lots, abandoned half-finished wood construction, and what appears to be a green plastic Porta Potty lying on its side. Though the turn into their street boasts the professional masonry of a new stone wall, and rows of arborvitae welcome the visitor to desirable Deerfield Meadows, clearly the developer went belly-up after completing one property, leaving no sign of getting the rest of the project finished any time soon.

In the driveway sits a brand-new pink Jeep, a life-sized version of something Barbie might drive. I walk past thinking someone's awfully confident of herself.

"Dr. Mills?"

A girl stands at the front door, sixteen, maybe seventeen years old, wearing a flimsy leopard-patterned shirt over skintight black pants the likes of which I haven't seen since Olivia Newton-John in the final scenes of *Grease*. The trouble is, that's where the similarity to Ms. Newton-John ends. I don't know how to put this, and please, I'm simply being objective, not judgmental, but she's about five-two and I'm guessing two hundred pounds.

"That's me."

"Thought so," she says. "Come in," offering her hand to shake, an act that strikes me as a little odd for her generation and, at the same time, completely wonderful. She has a pretty face and there's nothing but warmth in her smile.

"I'm Charlie, Charlie Brown."

I must look confused.

"Short for Charlize," she adds, for explanation.

"Ah."

We stand in a foyer, with a formal dining room to my left and what looks like a family room to my right. The place is neat but cavernous and way too empty, as though it needs a lot more furniture.

"Your parents not home?" I ask.

"No," says Charlie, "it's just me and my mom, and she's at work."

I make a show of checking the time on my wristwatch.

"School's out early today?"

She purses her lips as though contemplating which excuse to use. "Gym. Last class. I skipped."

"In the pink Jeep."

"You like?"

"It's very . . . eye-catching," I say.

"Thanks," she gushes as though I've paid the finest of compliments. "Hey, come on through, and I'll show you Marmalade. Can I get you a drink? Coffee, tea, something stronger?"

Something stronger? I catch the way she's watching for my response. The kid's trying to get a rise out of me.

"I'm fine," I say, following her into an open kitchen, noticing a couple of framed photographs on the walls. They're of a woman, a stunningly attractive woman. And please, before you start to think I wear rose-colored glasses around the opposite sex or that northern Vermont is an oasis of beautiful people, let me differentiate between Amy and this particular female. Amy's beauty is a package deal. This is airbrushed into a professional glamour shot.

"That's my mom. Trying to look hot after the divorce."

"Really? Why? Not that she doesn't look hot . . . sorry, I shouldn't have said—"

"It's cool. Her therapist says it's a normal part of her recovery. They're both better off. It just sucks that Mom's either working or embarrassing herself meeting total losers online and Dad went off to live in Wisconsin. Married a bimbo and started a new family. Twins. They're actually really cute. There she is."

What looks like a furry orange medicine ball lumbers past only to be swept up into Charlie's arms (with some difficulty, I might add).

"Dr. Mills, meet Marmalade Succabone."

I reach out to pet an overinflated blimp of a feline.

"Wow, she's . . ."

"What?"

I struggle to find the words to capture Marmalade's dimensions.

"Voluptuous."

Charlie beams. "I like that," she says. "Voluptuous." She runs a hand over the creature's girth and the cat approves with a Geiger counter purr.

"What seems to be the problem?" *Aside from her morbid obesity and the real possibility of challenging the Guinness World Record for fattest living feline, which happens to be 48.6 pounds.*

"You're kidding," says Charlie Brown, having to readjust the position of the mammoth in her tiring arms. "Look at her. She's totally overweight. And no one knows why."

I could have breezed by this last comment, but my mind jumps all over it.

"You've already sought veterinary advice?"

For the first time I catch Charlie's confidence begin to slip, just like her grip on the uber-cherubic cat spilling onto the floor with a seismic thud.

"Yeah, well, we went to the local vet, but they're, like, useless."

"You mean Healthy Paws?" I say, and I realize that I'm at risk of breaking into a smile.

"Yeah, they haven't been able to help at all. You know they have hidden cameras in every exam room."

I'm surprised by this unexpected tidbit. We don't even have an alarm on the door at Bedside Manor, and they have cameras in every room?

"I'm not kidding, my friend Gabe came with me one time. You've met him."

Gabe. Mr. Pot Brownie.

"Yeah, he told me he met this vet last night who didn't snitch on him to his mom. And that you were cool and maybe could fix Marmalade?"

So Gabe's the reason I got this house call. It makes sense. High school "freaks and geeks," the ostracized, pretty, but overweight girl is best friends with the nerdy computer whiz with an affinity for marijuana.

"Gabe's into spy stuff. He spotted the camera in the ceiling."

Sounds like Napoleon Dynamite has been watching one conspiracy movie too many.

"Not sure what to tell you, but let's have a look at Miss Marmalade."

I don't have far to go to find the cat that ate Vermont.

"Is this a pantry?"

"Yeah. That's where we keep her food."

Marmalade sits in front of the door, grooming a paw, though I sense she would rather be chowing down on a juicy T-bone or a baby wildebeest.

I kneel on the hardwood floor beside her, sweep my tie over my shoulder (Marmalade seems to think it's a toy), and pull out my stethoscope to listen to her chest. Everything seems in order. Though I might best describe palpating her abdomen as like kneading dough, again, no abnormalities jump out at me.

"Anything?"

"Not really. Can I assume she's had her blood tested?"

Charlie reaches across a counter and picks up a file. She shakes it in my direction.

"Yeah, blood, pee, you name it, she's had it tested. I like this cat, but Mom? Mom adores this cat. She worships her. This cat can do no wrong."

I take a look, see the familiar Healthy Paws logo on everything, and once again note the doctor on the case, the "useless" doctor on the case, to be none other than Dr. Honey. Still, the data is not pointing to an obvious cause for the cat's weight issue.

"What's she fed?"

"Regular cat food. It's even diet. Take a look for yourself if you don't believe me."

"Of course I believe you," I say, noting her defensive tone.

We face one another, the orange colossus in my peripheral vision happy to bide her time at the pantry door.

"Why haven't you asked the obvious question?"

"Which one?" I ask, totally confused.

"Her name. Marmalade Succabone. Don't you think it's strange?"

"A little. But I've learned not to second-guess the names people give to their pets."

"Really? Not curious?"

It's pretty obvious she wants me to indulge her.

"Sure. Why Marmalade Succabone?"

She lights up. "It's her porn star name."

"I beg your pardon?"

"Her porn star name. You know, you take the name of your first pet, then you add the name of the first address you lived at and you get your porn star name. She's my first pet, and when I was born we lived on Succabone Avenue. Let's do you."

"Uh . . . no, no, I really don't think that's—"

"What's the name of your first pet?"

The shake of my head is met with narrowed eyes.

"Tommy," I relent, with a sigh.

"Very good. And the first place you lived?"

I think back, my memory pressing the Play button on a conversation with my late mother, Ruth, back when I was ten, her pointing out the car as we passed a street, saying, "That's the apartment where we lived until you were nine months old." The street sign flashes before my eyes, and my mind makes the connections, the blood rushing into my cheeks as I see the excitement, the thrill, ignite in Charlie Brown's eyes.

"I should be going," I say, straightening out my tie, putting my stethoscope back in the bag.

"Oh, come on. Not before you tell me."

I inhale, long and deep. "We first lived at Apartment Four, Lovelace Terrace."

Her nose wrinkles as she pumps a fist. "Works every time."

I shake my head and begin walking back toward the front door.

"Any chance I can hold on to this file? Take a longer look, do a little research?"

"Yeah. Sure."

We make it to the front door.

"You got a girlfriend, Dr. Mills?"

"That's a very, uh, forward question to be asking someone you've only just met."

"Well, do you or don't you?"

I think about Amy. I think about how she would respond to someone catching her by the arm and asking, "Hey, aren't you Cyrus Mills's girlfriend?"

"If you must know, and clearly you absolutely must, the answer is . . . not really . . . not definitively."

Charlie Brown seems inordinately pleased. "I'll take that as a no."

It's time to steer this conversation back to business. "I'm afraid there is a fee for this visit. Should I call your mother?"

"No," she says, way too fast and way too loud, reaching into the front of her pants. There's a whole lot of squirming and writing to extract what I think will be wadded-up bills. It's not. It's a voucher from Garvey's for ice cream.

"Um, I can just bill you. It's not a problem."

She shakes her head and says, "Here, give me your cell phone."

Suspicious, I hand over the phone.

She takes it like I handed her a religious artifact.

"Wow, Gordon Gekko called, says he wants his phone back."

Though I should be insulted about the criticism of my outdated model, I'm impressed by the reference to the movie *Wall Street*.

"You an Oliver Stone fan?" I ask.

She frowns, rocks her hand side to side. "*Platoon* was okay, but as Vietnam movies go, I'm all about *Apocalypse Now*. Martin was better than Charlie any day."

Wow, a fellow movie buff. I'm impressed. But not surprised. Probably too many nights spent at home alone.

Her thumbs begin clicking on the phone's keypad like she's typing code.

"It's okay," she says. "I'm a professional."

I'm left in no doubt.

"Here's what I'm going to do. *I'll* call my mom and have her drop off the money. I've put my phone number in your contact list so that if there are any problems, you go through me, *capisce*?"

If she's trying to distract me from her sketchy

behavior with a famous phrase from Coppola's *The Godfather*, it's not working.

"And, um, this just in . . . you need to get some friends. In the meantime, treat yourself to a sundae."

Charlize hands over the ice cream voucher, along with my phone. There are nine perfect holes, three rows of three, punched into the card, and the announcement—tenth sundae is on the house.

I thank her and step out into the cold.

"No," she says, "thank you, Tommy Lovelace."

6

IT'S THE ONLY OTHER VEHICLE IN THE practice lot—the gray minivan. It's got windowless double doors at the back and what was probably a business ad or a logo brushed out by hand with mismatched house paint.

Looks like someone still needs that *big* favor.

I jump down from the Silverado as the driver's side door swings open.

"You free to see me now?" asks the gaunt man behind the wheel.

Even though the dog next to him doesn't move a muscle, I can almost sense the creature's anticipation.

"Sure. Come on in."

The man swings his legs out to the side and shuffles to the edge of his seat, preparing to rise. His jeans ride up above his socks, exposing bony ankles and blue bruises on alabaster white skin.

"Need a hand?"

"No," insists the man, "we've got this. Stash, stick."

The command is quiet and relaxed, a throw-away line, but Stash leaps between the front seats and into the back of the van before emerging with a wooden walking stick balanced between his jaws. Somehow the dog negotiates the ninety-degree turn, the seats, and the steering wheel like a skilled waiter carrying a platter through a crowded restaurant. What the dog lacks in appearance (he sports a wild dreadlock coat) he makes up for with remarkable dexterity, depositing the curved handle in his master's open palm.

No reward, simply on to the next instruction. "Stash, stand." On a dime, the poodle spins around and comes to rest in a standing position adjacent to the open door. I note the way Stash drops his head and neck ever so slightly, bracing, locking his elbows, before taking the brunt of the man's trembling weight as he eases into a full upright position, the walking stick more for balance than support.

Seconds pass as the man sucks down mouthfuls of icy air before saying, "Stash, come." I hold the front door open and the two of them amble into the waiting room, no leash necessary, the dog's nose never more than a few inches from the man's left thigh.

"Why don't you give Doris here your details. She'll make up a file and then we can head over to the exam room. Just got to dump my stuff."

I raise my doctor's bag and keep moving toward the door marked PRIVATE that leads to the central work area.

"Won't need a file," says the man. "Only want a quick word. In private."

It's not easy to guess the man's age, but I'm betting he's a whole lot younger than he looks. A black woolen cap accentuates his baby-bird features and jug-handle ears, and I can't tell the color of his eyes because they live in the eclipse of his sockets. His leather bomber jacket looks empty and stiff, as if it's full of helium, the white fur collar drawing the eye to a garish Adam's apple, slung under the angle of his wishbone jaw, the cartilage sharp and agitated.

The pathologist in me imagines all sorts of grim diseases. He reminds me of one of those tragic final photos of Rock Hudson or Patrick Swayze. *A quick word*. How big can this favor possibly be?

Doris stares at me. Stash stares at his master. Doris is hard to read—leery or irritated or both. I'm pretty sure she thinks he's not going to pay for my time.

"Okay," I say. "This way."

I ignore Doris as she shakes her head and clucks her tongue. If the man catches her disapproval, he doesn't let on.

I gesture for the man to take a seat on the wooden bench, but presumably for practical reasons, he waves the offer away.

"What can I do for you, Mr. . . ."

"Better you don't know my name, Dr. Mills. Better you don't know nothing about me, period."

Uh-oh. Maybe Doris was right.

"Okay. Why don't you tell me what's on your mind?"

The man leans into the exam table for support. He flexes the fingers of his left hand, a subtle beckoning gesture, and Stash instantly sits and backs into a position so his flanks are touching the leg of his master's jeans.

"See, I spoke to people round town. They told me about you, said you were a good man, said you helped out a pregnant girl, found a missing dog, ran a free clinic."

Boy, everyone loves free.

"Figured you for the kind of guy who'd be receptive to my proposal. Figured you for a doctor with a heart. A doctor with a conscience."

Where is this headed? I flash back to when I was maybe six or seven, my mother taking the stranger-danger lecture to the next level.

Beware of compliments from people you don't

know. They want something you won't want to give.

I glance at Stash. This cannot be good.

"It's an unusual request, but you and I have a whole lot more in common than you know."

Now we're cut from the same cloth?

"I grew up round here as well. Like you, I eventually came home, only you got this practice and I got this dog."

I got Bedside Manor and he got Stash? What's that supposed to mean?

"And I wouldn't ask unless I was totally desperate and had nowhere else to turn."

"Let me just stop you right there, whoever you are, because if you're going to ask me to put your dog to sleep and this dog doesn't have a painful or terminal illness, then you're wasting your time."

The man recoils. "Not him. Not Stash. I want you to help put *me* to sleep, in so many words."

Should I be looking for the hidden camera? Is this a joke? Then the man arches into the table and the overhead light chases away the shadows, just for a second, and I see what lies beneath—the black hopelessness of eyes that are already dead.

"You're a man who can end suffering." His tone is in control, not accusatory. "Well, I think I've suffered enough. Modern medicine has given me a life in which I can lose everything and spend my days fighting insurance companies. Only thing of value left is this poor dog, and what kind of a life does he have?"

Maybe I could extol the dog's talents, drop a few platitudes about the way companion animals help us look forward, give us purpose, but in this moment it feels wrong—trite and woefully inadequate.

"You want me to help you kill yourself?" I ask, unable to keep the shock out of my voice.

"I'm not a well man, Dr. Mills. And I'm never going to get better. We're talking days, not weeks. What remains for me is miserable and inevitable and, most of all, undignified. I don't need pain relief. I need the pain to stop forever. I know you know what I'm saying. It's what you do. Delivering a dose of mercy because nature can take its course and shove it."

I'm not sure where to begin. Last week I was a doctor disturbed by the way pet owners get so personal, trying to suck me into their overwrought lives. Now I'm being asked if I'll be Dr. Kevorkian.

"Oh no," he says, clearly reading my shocked expression, "I didn't mean for you to do it." He laughs, as though I should be relieved by this clarification. "I just need the euthanasia solution, the barbiturate. Point me in the direction of the drug box, leave the key out or tell me where I can find it, and I'll do the rest. It'll be a break-in. You've got insurance, right? Police won't care. They'll blame kids looking for Special K."

Ketamine. Special K. He's serious, in the worst possible way; a tragic, disturbed, unreachable serious. This total stranger wants me to help him commit suicide, and his tone is so casual, so relaxed, he's like a neighbor who drops by to ask if he can borrow your stepladder or whether you can help him move some heavy furniture. It's surreal. But then Stash glances my way for a split second, and the reality of this predicament becomes plain and simple.

"I can't help you. I'm sorry."

The man cants his head to one side and a trace of acquiescence crawls between his gray, cracked lips, careful not to let me see his teeth and gums. It's as if he knew this was a long shot but worth a try.

"Hell," he says. "If the plane's going to crash, might as well lay down and go to sleep."

This is a man resigned to his fate. The time for anger and fighting has passed.

"Thanks for hearing me out," he says, heading for the door, Stash right by his side.

"But what about your poodle?" I ask.

The man hesitates and turns my way, visibly disappointed.

"He's a doodle, not a poodle. Australian. Fourth generation."

Uh-oh. In the sheltered world of veterinary pathology I've noticed the popular trend of mixing poodles with all manner of different breeds, earning the moniker "designer dogs." I've never met one in the flesh. Or should I say the fur. That's why it's so ratty—he doesn't shed and, by the looks of things, doesn't get groomed.

"Stash has Labrador loyalty with standard poodle brains."

"Got it," I say, noting the pride in his voice. "What's going to happen to him?"

The man shrugs inside his jacket, but the shoulders barely move. He turns away and doesn't look back.

"That's up to you," he says as the front door chimes and the two of them slip away.

What a strange comment, I think. *Why or how would his dog have anything to do with me?*

Doris sidles over as I watch Stash help the man get back into his van.

"Before you start," I say, "that is an incredible dog. Faithful, attentive, and really smart."

"Smart enough to be billed for your time?" Doris lets the question simmer for a few seconds before adding, "By the way, there's a doctor been holding on line two. Wants to talk to you about a case. Says it's important."

"Doris, why didn't you say so?"

I practically sprint for the phone in the work area because, for the second time in one day, my expertise is being sought as a second opinion. Perhaps I have misjudged general practice, thinking it would never tax my brain, days blurring with the endless monotony of vaccines and health checks. Yes, I'm rusty with the hands-on stuff and the challenge of extracting a meaningful history from well-intentioned but long-winded owners, yet fellow professionals still want a slice of what counts—insight, knowledge, and the ability to uncover the truth.

I press the red line two button on the phone.

"Hello."

"Is this Dr. Mills?"

A reserved female voice.

"It is."

"Well, well, well, you've got a nerve. This is Dr. Honey over at Healthy Paws, and I don't know where you came from or what kind of voodoo medicine you like to practice, but around these parts we don't go poaching cases from one another."

My silence is borne of genuine shock, but she keeps going. "Oh please, I'm referring to Sox Sauer, the boxer, small lump on the shoulder. Are you really so desperate? Would it help if I handed out your business card at our local dog park? You're like the veterinary version of an ambulance-chasing lawyer. Do not, repeat, do not let this happen again. If you do, I will be forced to seek legal counsel."

The line goes dead before I can say another word.

N O BRIBE, NO NEGOTIATIONS, NO PRE-emptive white flag. Right now I'm angry enough to risk life and limb, charging straight into enemy territory, a human microburst, rifling through Doris's reception desk in search of the Sox Sauer file.

There's a savage rap on the glass and then a pointy finger insists I cease and desist followed by an aggressive shooing motion that makes me retreat to the other side of the waiting room. Doris is on the other side of the window looking in with a murderous glare, my crime so serious, I watch as a half-smoked cigarette (you heard me right) swan dives off the ends of her fingertips and lands in the snow.

The front door chimes.

"What on earth are you doing, Dr. Mills? There's a precise system to my record keeping."

"Sox Sauer. I need his file. Now."

Doris comes around the desk and, making a point of keeping her eyes on me, shuffles a sheet of paper here, a bill there, and suddenly there it is in her quick yellow talons.

"You mean this, Dr. Mills?" Her words are clipped, an angry hornet determined to sting.

I take it, my nod all the thanks she will get. It's not the case notes I want. It's the phone number for Ms. Sauer.

"If Healthy Paws thinks I'm out to steal a client, I'd best find out what this client has been saying to them."

"Marjorie Sauer might act confrontational," says Doris, "but she prefers to whisper. Not like me. I prefer to see the fear in their eyes."

Why am I not surprised?

Back in the work area I dial the number from the page marked "Client Information."

"Hello, Ms. Sauer, this is Dr. Mills from Bedside Manor. Tell me, have you been in contact with Dr. Honey following our consultation this morning?"

"No."

"Oh."

"But that office manager called me up. Dork, Dorkus, or something."

"Mr. Dorkin."

"Yeah, him. Asked what I was doing at Bedside Manor this morning, and I told him, and he started out acting sympathetic, apologizing, wanting to know how Healthy Paws could do right by me and Sox, and I told him he could start by not trying to rip off conscientious and vulnerable pet owners by recommending unnecessary surgeries. And that's when he went off on me, telling me we're not welcome at Healthy

Paws—fired is what he said, 'You're fired.' Like he was Donald Trump."

There's a sniffle, a series of jagged little breaths, as Marjorie Sauer begins to lose her composure.

"Then, get this, he says he'd be happy to recommend alternative veterinary practices. I said, 'Don't bother, we'll be going to Bedside Manor from now on,' and that's when he did this weird laughing thing and said, 'That place will be in foreclosure by this time next week. You just burned your bridges, lady.' And then he hung up."

I was right. Dorkin did recognize Sox as a Healthy Paws client. And the guy's got an ugly temper. But here's the upside: he'd only be this serious about our rivalry for one reason—he's worried.

My cell phone begins vibrating in my pocket.

"Have no fear, Ms. Sauer. Dorkin's full of hot air. We're not going anywhere."

I hang up on one call and pick up the next, not recognizing the number on the screen.

"Hey, Doc, you free to talk?"

"Um, who is this?"

"It's Charlie Brown, remember? Marmalade Succabone, feline porn star."

"Right, Charlize."

"I, like, spoke to my mom, and she's going to be passing through Eden Falls on her way home. She's going to give you a check for the house call.

112

Any chance you could meet her at the diner on Main Street?"

"I suppose so."

"Great. Seven?"

"Okay. But wouldn't it be easier—"

"I'm just repeating what she said. You still wearing that ugly tie?"

"I beg your pardon. I happen to like this tie."

I study the narrow strip of one hundred percent woven microfiber polyester dangling from my neck. It's white with bold red stripes.

"Please! It looks like a candy cane. But don't take it off. That's how she's going to recognize you. That and my description of how you're totally hot!"

I catch the laugh just before the line goes dead.

FIVE OF SEVEN and I have my choice of several empty booths, picking one close to the front door with a view of everyone who walks in. I wonder if the diner's always quieter on nights when Amy's "got plans." Keeping my winter coat on but unzipped to adequately expose my "ugly" tie, I've barely settled in when a waitress I don't recognize appears by my side.

"It's Doc Mills, isn't it?"

She's young with spiky tangerine hair, some sort of sparkly piercing embedded in the skin adjacent to her right nostril, and a plastic tag that tells me her name is Mary.

"It is."

"Coming to see you tomorrow. My dog, Gilligan. Amy said if anyone can sort him out, it's Doc Mills."

I smile, buoyed by the idea of Amy talking about me behind my back, giving me compliments.

"I'll certainly try my best." I glance at my watch, nearly seven. "So Amy's off tonight?"

"Yep, she asked if I could fill in for her, and I can always use the extra money."

Ordinarily, I wouldn't push, but the twinge inside won't go away. "Oh, is she doing something special?"

Her nose twitches, making her piercing catch the light, and I fear she's on to me.

"Don't know, but she was picking up a dress from the dry cleaner and getting her hair done, so it sounds like. But listen to me going on, what can I get you?"

"Actually, I'm meeting someone. Should be here any minute." With Amy not here I have no intention of sticking around. As soon as Mrs. Brown hands over my check I'll be on my way. "I'll hang on if you don't mind."

"Coffee while you wait?"

"Why not."

"Cream, no sugar, right?"

How did she know? Just how much did Amy share about me?

"Great."

I ease back in my seat, wishing I'd brought something to read. I hate twiddling my thumbs when I could have been researching catastrophic diseases of cattle or Jenny Craig for cats instead of imagining Amy out somewhere nice, somewhere that necessitates a dress. Women get their hair done for one of two reasons—either to outdo the female competition or to attract a mate. What are the odds that this momentous date has nothing to do with the mysterious caller who could make her giggle?

"There you go," says Mary, placing the steaming mug before me. "Let me know if you change your mind."

I thank her and look up as a bearded man in a lumberjack shirt breezes by on his way to the counter. Five more minutes, that's all I'll give her and then this annoying Mrs. Brown can damn well drive over to Bedside Manor and drop off the check at my convenience, not hers.

Fifteen minutes later and I'm looking over my shoulder for Mary, wanting to pay for my coffee, when I notice a domino effect of male heads turning toward the front door. I join in and discover a woman hovering at the entrance— golden hair swept back and expertly pinned in place, meticulously applied makeup (the sort that's supposed to look like you're not wearing any), short white double-breasted trench coat, jeans, and knee-length leather boots. If this new arrival is Mrs. Brown, she either works for *Vogue* magazine or she's totally overdressed to drop off some money.

Why is she headed my way?

"Mr. Lovelace? Thomas Lovelace?"

"I'm . . . I beg your pardon?"

"The tie. Too funny. And so much more original than a pink carnation."

Pink carnation?

"I'm Dr. Winn Honey," she says, extending her hand for me to shake.

Winn Honey. Dr. Honey. Dr. Honey, the vet from Healthy Paws who hates my guts. Why on earth is this woman greeting me like we're on a blind date?

Dazed, fish-mouthed, and speechless, I watch as my hand drifts up and completes the greeting.

"Mind if I take a seat?"

She's already unbuttoning her coat, hanging it on the brass hanger at the end of the booth, and sliding across the seat opposite, the tips of the fingers of her right hand performing a minor adjustment to her coif.

"So sorry I'm late. Work." I get the whites of her eyes again, a sharp intake of breath. "But let's not go there just yet. Should I begin or would you prefer to start?"

The only reason I'm not drooling like a total moron is the adrenaline coursing through my body and sapping my saliva. The logic is irrefutable.

Given she used the name Tommy Lovelace, the mother of Charlie Brown and Doc Honey must be one and the same person.

It's the question I'm about to ask when my phone begins buzzing in my pants and I recognize the number of the caller. Amazing. At this precise moment, I can think of no one else in the world I would want to speak to more.

"Would you excuse me for one minute? I have to take this call."

"Sure. Want a refill?" asks my adversary, pointing to my empty mug.

"Why not," I reply, hurrying through the front door and out into the night.

I flip open the phone.

"She there yet?"

"Yes, Charlize, she's here all right. You want me to tell her how you set her up on a blind date with a veterinarian and not a porn star?"

There's a silence, followed by a sigh, followed by, "It was Gabe's idea. Okay, Gabe's and my idea. He figured I could use Marmalade as a way for me to check you out. We wanted to hook you guys up 'cause we both really like you, and Gabe wants to pay you back for being cool about the pot. And I'm sick of the way Mom's meeting weird men online and bringing them home on a first date like a sex-starved nymphet. It's embarrassing."

"You what? No, no, that's ridiculous and totally

inappropriate. I'm sorry, Charlize, you leave me no choice but to—"

"It's too late. Gabe already set this up through a dating website: Loveatfirstsite.com. But don't worry, he didn't use your name or anything to create a profile."

Any sarcastic "that's a relief" rebuttal escapes me as the surprises keep coming.

"Mom thinks you're Mr. Tommy Lovelace. The site sent her an email saying the two of you were compatible and you were eager to see if there were any sparks, any love at first sight."

Her amorous intonation is not helping her cause as I pace back and forth in front of the entrance to the diner, the fog in my head as thick as the fog from my breath. "Let me get this straight—you guys secretly created a dating profile for me and lured me here to meet your mom and she has no idea?"

"Just listen," says Charlize. "You can walk away at any time. That's why we gave you a fake ID and put you together on neutral territory. Mom has no idea who you really are."

"Clearly," I say, flashing back to her angry phone call about Sox Sauer. "So your worries about Marmalade's weight, that was just to set this up?"

"No . . . not really," says Charlize, but I detect a shift in her tone, brazen and defiant turning more uncertain, even introspective. "My mom actually did all those tests and she still can't figure out why Marmalade's so fat. Maybe you're smart enough to find out where she went wrong."

I can't tell if that's a challenge or a request. Either way, if the second case I poach from Healthy Paws happens to be Dr. Honey's own cat, I'll need an ambulance and then a lawyer.

"Coming clean as a veterinarian from the nearby rival practice might prove a little tricky, don't you think?"

"Maybe. But based on the type of man she usually ends up with, if you two hit it off, she'll find a way to forgive you. Can you say low self-esteem?"

For all her scheming and the burden of the shameful and outrageous position she's put me in, I can't help but admire her chutzpah.

"Walk away and she'll be none the wiser. Wouldn't blame you, especially if she starts blabbing about work and more work."

And, unintentionally (at least I hope so), this is where Charlie Brown sets the hook.

"Go back a minute," I say, stopping in front of a bulletin board to the left of the diner's entrance. "What details did Gabe make up about this Mr. Tommy Lovelace?"

On a bulletin board outside the diner, next to a handwritten notice of someone searching for a runaway teenager, there's a poster that pulls me away from Charlie's reply.

Healthy Paws and the
Eden Falls Knights of Columbus
present
Pet First Aid
A lecture by local Healthy Paws veterinarian,
Dr. Winn Honey, VMD.
Refreshments will be served
Freebies for your four-legged friends
Dogs Allowed*

"He kept it vague. Except what you do for a living."

Dogs allowed. But there's an asterisk. My eyes dart to the bottom. Where's the asterisk, where's the exception?

"Doc, you still there?"

I can't find it. "Sorry, missed that last bit."

"Gabe put down your job as movie reviewer for an online magazine. He didn't know what else to write. If it helps, he did say you love animals."

Dr. Honey is going to lecture here, in Eden Falls? First they hit up the *Gazette* to advertise for a free clinic and now they want to do outreach to pet owners on my turf.

"Okay. I'm going to see what happens . . . but forget about a fairy-tale ending. Your mother may be an attractive woman, but I'm not interested. Right now, I'd love to walk away, but it would be rude and hurtful and unfair to someone who's been conned by her daughter into thinking a

120

computer program just discovered her soul mate. And don't think I won't spill the beans if this gets messy."

The line falls silent, and for the first time since stepping outside in only a shirt and tie I feel the cold setting in.

"Sorry," she says, and I don't need to hear her weeping to know she means it.

"Charlie."

"What?"

"I'm not going to get paid for that visit today, am I?"

"No," she says, "not unless the sundae counts."

Back inside the diner, Dr. Honey has her back to me, sipping a coffee. The fact that she hasn't stormed off or come looking for me can only mean one thing—Mary the waitress hasn't blown my cover as Cyrus Mills. How long can that last?

"Very sorry about that," I say, squeezing back into the booth. "Rude of me, and I apologize."

"Not at all," says Honey, eyeing me with unnerving scrutiny over the rim of her mug before placing it off to one side. "Do I detect an accent, Tom? Sorry, do you prefer Tom or Tommy or Thomas?"

"Tom's fine," I stutter, "and yes . . . um . . . I lived in . . . Mississippi, for a while, slip in a little twang and drawl every now and then."

Dr. Honey sits up a little straighter, plays with the handle of the mug. "It's nice. I like it."

I'm guessing she's a little older than me, midforties, and I'm rewarded for staring with a big smile of overly whitened teeth. I'm speechless. This is why I've never been on a blind date. The only two questions that have popped into my head are "Do you work out?" and "How tall are you?" Both make me sound like a creep who wonders if she'll fight back or fit inside the tomb under my basement. I'm so not suited for this.

I'm glad I couldn't get a word in edgewise when she was reaming me out on the phone over Sox Sauer. Clearly she hasn't recognized my voice.

"Need anything else?" asks Mary, breezing by, glass coffee carafe in hand.

"I think we're fine," says Dr. Honey, placing her hand over the top of her mug. I pretend to sip, shake my head, and though Mary keeps going, she's not fooling me. I know I'm being watched. Amy's co-worker is obviously curious about the meeting between Dr. Mills and a beautiful stranger of the opposite sex. Suddenly that unpleasant writhing sensation in my guts at the thought of Amy out with another man lessens at the prospect of what Mary imagines she sees and might report back to Amy.

"You were about to go first," I say as though I'm familiar with the standard blind-dating protocol.

"Ladies first," says Dr. Honey, folding her hands in front of her on the table. "I like that." I fear she has her thirty-second elevator pitch down cold.

"My name's Winifred, old-fashioned I know, but friends call me Winn. I'm a veterinarian, so naturally I love animals. I'm a hopeless romantic, but from time to time I like to let my hair down, if you know what I mean. I love good food, good wine, good books, and good movies."

"Good . . . good," I say, slow nodding and feeling anything but. She pretty much covered every base. If I said I was an abstinent illiterate vegan hermit I'm pretty sure I'd still be in with a chance. "You work here in Eden Falls?"

See how I did that? Fake left, go right.

"No, I work over at a Healthy Paws in Patton."

"You like being a vet?" After a lifetime of being on the other end of this question, I know how this inane line of inquiry goes. "What I mean is . . . it must be so rewarding, but also so very sad, putting animals to sleep all the time."

Winn Honey looks down at the table and back at me.

"I promised myself I wouldn't bore you with tales of woe from work."

"Don't be silly," I say. I can't believe I'm staring into the sparkling green eyes of the enemy. This is so wrong. At the very least I should get up and walk away. "I'm fascinated with what goes on at a modern animal hospital." I know, I know, but at least I'm telling the truth. "I always wanted to be a veterinarian when I grew up." See, so long as I don't actually lie, this façade doesn't feel too bad.

"Oh, I don't know," she says on a sigh. "My boss is a total dick, pardon my French."

"Your boss?"

"Sorry, office manager. Today he made me call the animal hospital down the road," she points over her shoulder, "stood right in front of me while I shouted at their vet for stealing one of our cases. He has some sort of vendetta against them."

"Wait, this guy stole your case?" As soon as the words leave my mouth I want them back. How would I know the vet is a he?

"It's complicated, but my boss thinks that if I lose a case I must be doing something wrong. It was enough to get a second written warning in as many days."

She missed it, so I pounce. "Second?"

"Tuesday night I was on call, but I forgot to turn my phone to vibrate. Ended up missing an emergency."

Ah, Tallulah, the pot brownie–chewing mastiff.

"One more strike against me and I'm out, fired, time to look for a new job, and, thanks to a noncompete clause, I'd have to move out of the area."

"Noncompete clause?"

"Forget it," she says, wafting a hand in front of her face. "All it means is I can't afford to screw up on Saturday. I've got this stupid lecture to give here in Eden Falls at the Knights of Columbus. It's meant to drum up business, an excuse to show off our place. You should come, if you're interested."

"I am," I say, and then, ignoring the fact that I'd be instantly unmasked as Cyrus Mills, I add, "I will."

She seems inordinately pleased, as though by making this promise we already have a future together.

"Your turn," she says, and then, reading the fear contorting my face as nervousness, she reaches across the table to touch my hand. "First blind date?"

I nod, and then it strikes me that it may be possible for me to go forward, to maintain this lie, so long as I stick to the truth.

"Take your time," she says soothingly. "No rush. Whatever comes into your head."

"Well . . . I'm from Eden Falls. Obviously I like watching movies." My awkward, nervous laugh is genuine.

"Obviously," she says, showing me her teeth again. It's like she's coercing a naughty boy to come clean about his crime.

"Um . . . well, I would say I have a certain . . . affinity . . . to animals."

"Affinity? Interesting."

Only ten percent of men and women get a second date if they say they don't like pets.

"Yes, that I'm intrigued by what's going on inside them."

"Really. Like a pet psychic?"

Oh dear. "A little bit," I say, trying to think of ways to return to the secrets of Healthy Paws.

"Tell me," she says, trying to bail me out. "What's your greatest strength?"

I make a show of bringing my thumb and fingers to my chin. Obviously trust goes out the window and so does honesty. Logical and intelligent seem a little self-aggrandizing.

"Good listener," I reply. Which is code for "I'd love to listen to you gripe some more about your place of work."

"Greatest weakness?"

It's painful to watch the sincerity, the hope in her eyes.

"That's easy. Stubborn. Judgmental. Occasionally impulsive."

"Impulsive?"

Dr. Honey seems to like the sound of that one a little too much.

"I tend to jump to conclusions," I add. "Not always the right ones."

Her head lilts ever so slightly to one side. "Has that gotten you in trouble in past relationships? With your ex-wife . . . ?"

Oh, okay, she's fishing here.

"Actually I've never been married. You?"

She hesitates. Maybe it's the recollection of what went wrong or the worry of what she must confess. "Guilty."

Strange word, like she's committed a crime.

"Married for nineteen years."

"Irreconcilable differences?" I ask.

"Irreconcilable hatred," she snaps back, and I can tell she means it.

"Children?"

For the first time she appears a little flustered.

"Just one—a teenage girl. But she lives with her father. Wanted to stay in the same school system. I see her every so often. Essentially, it's just me, not forgetting the love of my life, Marmalade."

Well, well, I'm not the only one telling fibs. Has Winn Honey discovered that having a child seriously limits your dating options? And why was Charlie not referred to by name? Is the daughter caught up in some sort of misplaced anger at her ex? I know what it's like to play the blame game, changing my last name to my mother's maiden name and refusing to acknowledge my father's existence for fifteen years. It took his death and his dying veterinary practice before I realized, too late, what a fool I'd been. I wonder how far this jilted woman will go to compete with the much-maligned Mr. Brown in Wisconsin.

"Marmalade. I'm guessing an orange cat."

"Very good. Maybe you are psychic after all." This next smile is coy, not unpleasant, and, I imagine, has proven to be highly effective in the past. "Look, after my day I could really use

127

something stronger than a coffee. You fancy a real drink? We could take this conversation to a bar or, if you prefer, I've got a nice Chardonnay chilling at home."

The recollection of Charlie Brown gagging over her mother's penchant for one-night stands comes to mind as one of my Bedside Manor clients stomps through the diner's front door. Ethel Silverman is a crotchety old biddy who makes Doris look positively discreet and compassionate. Her raptor eyes spy me. She bristles but heads straight for the counter. How long before I'm treated to a surly update regarding her husky Kai's ongoing skin issues?

"Yeah . . . um . . . that sounds perfectly . . . fine, but . . ." *Think, Cyrus, think.* "But . . . I'll be honest . . . I wasn't sure this . . . encounter, was going to . . ."

"Let me guess, you prefer brunettes?" she says with a smile that barely masks her vulnerability. I see it, around her eyes, written in the fine wrinkles and lines of her carefully applied foundation, the insecurity, the permanent scar of being abandoned by your husband for another woman.

"No, of course not."

It's true, in a general, unprejudiced way, but she appears to catch the fact that my remark is more objective, less emotional.

"So what's the problem?"

"There is none. I thought this was a way to see if there was anything between us."

"And is there?"

"More than you can imagine," I say, reaching into my pocket and laying a twenty-dollar bill on the table. I want to get away before Ethel and Mary rat me out, even though I need change and don't want to give Dr. Honey the impression I'm trying to impress her with a big tip.

"Are you sure you're not married?"

"Absolutely not."

"Hmm." Once again she dazzles me with her smile. "You are very different, Thomas Lovelace. Strange name, but you have my attention."

"And you mine," I say, getting up. "So . . . um . . . email me, and I hope to take you up on your offer real soon."

At least at her house there's no risk of being unmasked as Cyrus Mills.

"I'm not kidding," I say, standing to shake her hand. And then, as a melding of truth and flirtation comes to mind, I can't help but add, "There's so much more about you I want to discover."

Thursday

← 8 →

I DIDN'T EXPECT TO SEE MARY FROM THE diner quite so soon, but thanks to her tangerine hair, she's the first (and only) person I recognize in a rowdy waiting room. It's Lewis's morning to see appointments, and sometimes it feels like we are polar opposites when it comes to our appeal as veterinarians. Lewis consistently packs them in with his magnetic attraction whereas I keep them away with my magnetic repulsion. Still, five minutes ago, I was the recipient of an unusual greeting from the bottom of the stairway to my apartment.

"Hey, you awake up there? You've got one waiting."

Ah, Doris, my cup of morning cheer, what would I do without you?

I grab the file on her desk (it lies alone, crisp and thin, adjacent to an imposing tower of case files for Lewis) and march over to Mary, trying to get a read on her impassive features. What if, after I left, Doc Honey asked her about the mysterious Tommy Lovelace? Is my cover blown? If so, how much did Mary share with Amy?

"He's outside in the car," says Mary, as soon as

I say hello, "gets easily stressed." She sticks her head out the front door and yells, "Drew! Drew, come on."

A redheaded man steps out of a pickup carrying a border collie in his arms like an awkward piece of furniture, and I usher the three of them back into the work area, making my apologies, claiming our other exam room is undergoing renovation (or at least it will if the practice can stay in business until the end of the month).

"This is my husband, Drew. He's apprenticing as a mechanic at the gas station down the road," she says, making the introduction sound like an apology for the calloused, oil-stained hand that reaches out for the greeting. It's heavy on crush, light on shake, the dog perfectly still in his arms. By still I mean rigid, as though the creature's been stuffed or needs to be defrosted. When Mary said stressed I think she meant scared stiff.

"And this is Gilligan," says Mary as Drew finally places the timid creature on the floor. The collie comes to life, running on the spot, a cartoon dog scratching for traction on the linoleum, scampering behind Mary like a shy child hiding behind his mother's skirt, or, in this case, black jeans.

"Come on out, Gil, come on."

Best I can tell, Gilligan is a handsome tricolor of black, tan, and white, with pricked attentive ears. His bushy tail is so tightly curled underneath him it practically screams "don't even think about taking my temperature." He won't allow me to make eye contact, burying his head into the back of Mary's knees. Perhaps Gil thinks if he can't see me, I can't see him.

"Very smart breed," I say.

"I know," says Mary, clearly taking this as a compliment.

"Fastest time to open a car window by a dog."

She looks confused.

"A border collie called Striker," I say. "Just over eleven seconds."

Mary consults with her husband, her expression suggesting they should leave while they have the chance.

I press on. "What's going on?" I ask, picking up pen and paper to take some notes when, as if on cue, Gilligan decides to give his version of the story. In the style of a cuckoo clock striking the hour, a snout pops around Mary's leg to deliver a snappy, ear-piercing bark.

I reel, a little theatrically, but get no response from either Mary or Drew.

"I'll start at the beginning," says Mary, as Gil lets rip with another bark. "Drew and I have been married about six months." Bark. "Few weeks after the wedding, we moved into my late grandmother's house." Bark. "Before that, Gil was fine, right?"

There's a pause, and Drew nods as Gil, the

canine metronome, times another yappy keening to perfection. Seriously, he has to be cracking 120 decibels, easily. His bark's a health hazard, but worst of all, and what leaves me speechless (and presumably hearing impaired), his owners don't seem to notice. They don't even blink.

"Ever since we've moved he's been acting weird." Bark. "Both of us work, and it's like he has separation anxiety." Bark.

I narrow my eyes, wince, and press my index finger deep into my ear canal, to no avail.

"He stays in the exact same spot where I left him." Bark. "Standing at the dining room window, waiting for us to come home." Bark. And then, finally, my features having contorted past "unpleasant wince" and ending at "unbearable torture," she says, "Is there a problem?"

The welcome silence hangs in the air between us. Seconds pass without a bark, and I get to savor the after hiss ringing in my ears.

"Sorry, just, um, having a hard time concentrating," I say. Mary looks at Drew; they share a shrug and a frown and both come back to me looking confused. "Gil's barking." I feel like I'm explaining the punch line of a joke. "It's quite . . ." *Careful, Cyrus, don't offend.* "Extraordinary. Don't want to miss anything important you might say."

"Right," says Mary, stretching out the syllable as though totally on board, making eye contact with Gil while placing an index finger to her shushing lips.

"Really? That's going to silence your bad-mannered dog?" I want to say, but I bite my tongue and brace for the pending rupture of an eardrum.

"He's not eating much, and he's losing weight, don't you think?"

Drew nods but remains silent, and, to my amazement and relief, so does Gilligan.

"Then this time yesterday morning, he had like, I don't know, like a seizure. Scared the crap out of me. That's when I talked to Amy, and she said you're the man to see."

Was this the last time Mary spoke to Amy or was there a gossipy update regarding my "date" with a beautiful woman?

"When you say seizure, what do you mean?"

Mary deliberates, the recollection visibly upsetting. "He was lying on the kitchen floor, legs out straight and stiff, out of it, and he'd wet himself. I kept calling his name, and it was like no one was home. That look in his eyes, I'll never forget it, it was like . . ." A tear gets away from her right eye. "It was like he was dead."

I glance over to Drew, wondering why he's not putting a consoling arm around his young wife's shoulder. I read sympathy but reckon there's a blue-collar emotional toughness holding him back.

"So you never actually saw Gil shaking or trembling or flailing?"

"No."

"And how long did it take him to get up and back to himself?"

"Maybe half an hour. He was staggering at first, out of it, like he was really frightened."

All this time Gilligan has been watching me while his body remains neatly concealed behind Mary's legs.

"Okay, let's have a look at him."

I step forward and to one side, coming around Mary as Gil makes an equal and opposite maneuver so he can remain invisible. I catch myself, change direction, and we repeat our dance, Mary our maypole in the middle.

"Drew, perhaps you could lend me a hand." An oily, calloused hand.

Seconds later Gilligan has been corralled as Drew kneels on the floor beside me. Based on the man's pallor and freckles, I'm betting on an Irish heritage, cheeks guaranteed to light up red with too much sun or too many pints. His dog is compliant but clearly terrified. I don't need a stethoscope to determine his heart rate; I can see it thumping against his rib cage like it wants out. And forget about palpating the contents of his abdomen. Gil's tummy is rock solid, constantly bracing for a sucker punch to the gut. I do, however, make two meaningful discoveries. The nerves from Gil's brain that control blinking, seeing, swallowing, licking, smelling, and, sadly, barking all appear to be in full working order. But I have a problem with the color of his gums.

"Perhaps you can help me lift his tail so I can take his temperature," I say, remembering one of Lewis's favorite tricks. *If you don't know what to say or do, take a rectal temperature, it will give you a few extra minutes to think.*

For a while Drew and Gilligan engage in their own version of Greco-Roman wrestling until the mechanic pins him and the collie submits to my thermometer.

Here's my problem. As a veterinary pathologist, I've always had a direct, physical path to the diagnosis. I was like the detective who always got his man, the culprit tried, convicted, and behind bars and I never had to worry about the motive. Now, in my second week of pretending to be a real veterinarian, unsolved cases are beginning to stack up. Ermintrude the crazy cow, Marmalade the fat cat, and now Gilligan, the neurotic collie. Yes, I've got clues, but I don't have nearly enough evidence to convict. I'm all speculation, hot air, and theories, surrounded by anxious relatives desperate for results. Where are all the easy cases? Where are the fleas or the worms when you need them?

"One oh three point two. To be honest, he's so nervous I'm surprised the glass didn't melt."

"What do you think?" says Mary, petting Gil as if she's offering an apology for the violation.

I take a deep breath. "His gums are too pale. He's anemic."

"What? Why?"

"Three possible reasons. Losing blood, not making enough blood, destroying blood."

"So which one is it?"

I consider what I've got to go on. No appetite, weight loss, seizure, and anemia. Each problem has dozens of possible causes—put them together and the permutations are endless.

"Not sure," I say, but as she deflates, I rush to add, "but I intend to find out."

Rather than relieved, Mary seems cagey. "Sounds expensive," she says. "What's your best guess?"

That's when I wonder if my referral from Amy was grounded in a respect for my clinical prowess or recognition that, in certain circumstances, I can be a soft touch. Happy to get extra hours at the diner, husband's an apprentice, lucky enough to be given a house to live in—more than enough clues to know money's tight.

"Tell you what, let me get a blood sample and I'll look at it myself. Hopefully I'll find the answer and save you the cost of sending it off to a lab."

They check in with one another, there are nods of approval, and the deal is sealed by a complimentary yip from Gilligan.

Despite the collie's fear and unyielding full-body rigidity, I get the necessary blood and see them out, Drew, as talkative as ever, offers a grim nod and a grungy handshake; Mary smiles, thanking me and insisting, "Amy was right," as Gilligan yanks her through the front door.

Right about what? Right to suggest I see her dog? Right about me being a bit of a nerd? She's gone before I can ask. At least that's my excuse.

With the purple tube of the blood sample safely inside my breast pocket, I head back into the work area, only to find Lewis perched in front of our microscope. He looks up as I approach.

"What, you think you're the only one who knows how to use it?"

"No, of course—"

"Look it."

Lewis gestures to the eyepieces. I take a peek and remark, "Otodectes cynotis."

Lewis shakes his head in frustration. "Keep it simple, Cyrus. Plain speak. 'Ear mites' makes a lot more sense to most people."

I straighten up, close my eyes, and wipe both hands down my face. "Right now I'd love to make a straightforward diagnosis like ear mites. Seems like every case is a mystery wrapped inside an enigma. I'm used to working for private diagnostic and pharmaceutical companies with deep pockets. Our clients demand quick answers or cheap solutions, preferably both, with nothing more than a laying on of hands."

Lewis gets to his feet. He's not much taller than a racehorse jockey, so I know he's used to angling his head way back to make eye contact.

"Trust me, folks will find a way to pay. What you need to worry about is how to spend their money. You might prefer to run every test in the book, but the best clinicians learn how to play the odds, cut the fat, and get to the answer by the shortest possible route."

"That's what worries me," I say.

As always, Lewis stands way too close for my comfort. I brace for some sort of physical contact. Oh, for a return to the eighties fashion of over-sized shoulder pads to buffer these touchy-feely moments.

"You ever play Clue as a kid?" asks Lewis.

I flash to the classic children's board game, laid out with the cards and playing pieces on our dining room table, Mom sitting opposite. Did my father ever join us?

"Of course."

"Good. And I'm betting not once did you give up and open the black envelope because you couldn't wait to know whodunit?"

My silence gives him my answer, and there it is, the hand squeeze to the shoulder.

"Cyrus, you're blessed with an amazing clinical memory, remarkable, if bizarre, observational skills, and okay, your logic can be a little eccentric at times, but start playing this new game and, while you're at it, enjoy yourself."

I try to twist my lips into something approaching a smile.

"Hey, I meant to tell you, I had a visit from Mr. Guy Dorkin of Healthy Paws yesterday."

"Yes, Doris told me."

Silly me, of course she did.

"She also mentioned you had a phone call from an irate Dr. Honey. You know this woman is speaking in Eden Falls this coming Saturday?"

Hmm, now that's interesting. No doubt Ethel Silverman will have informed Doris that I was spotted in the diner last night with another woman. However, the fact that I am not being directly linked to Dr. Honey suggests Ethel did not know who she was.

"I do, and I did. I met Doc Honey for coffee last night. Turns out she was put up to the phone call by Dorkin, for losing a case to Bedside Manor. But I don't think she's a bad person."

"Ah, that's who you were with."

Of course he heard. This town is way too small.

"Yes, and if you don't mind, I'd like to keep that between us."

Lewis narrows his sage gray eyes.

"Would that have anything to do with a certain waitress at the diner?"

"It would have to do with a desire for a measure of basic privacy. If you must know, I was tricked into a rendezvous. Long story. But I thought meeting Dr. Honey might provide valuable insight into what makes Healthy Paws tick and how we can overcome their assault."

"Wait up, why would Doc Honey reveal their secrets to the enemy?"

"Valid question," I reply, "but it'll have to keep. Did you know they have hidden cameras in their exam rooms?"

"Yes. They claim it ensures optimal customer service. What it ensures is that every vet follows the script, maximizes every billable opportunity. Big Brother is watching your every move so if you try to give a client a break, cut a diagnostic corner, you're busted on candid camera."

"That's unbelievable. And what's with this noncompete clause?"

Lewis rocks his head side to side. "Sadly all too common these days, but less so in a rural community like ours. Did she mention the range and the time?"

"No," I reply, not sure what he's referring to.

"Usually two years and thirty miles. Regardless of whether she gets fired or leaves voluntarily, the clause intends to prevent her working as a vet for two years within a thirty-mile radius of Healthy Paws in Patton."

"Wait. What if you've got kids in a school

system? What if your spouse has a job nearby? What about the mortgage on your house?"

"Unless you've put an awful lot of money aside, time to sell what you can and ship out."

"Wow, that sounds harsh."

"That sound is the juggernaut of corporate veterinary medicine, more than happy to mow you down. What else did your Deep Throat share?"

I flash to *All the President's Men. Follow the money.*

"That's a work in progress."

Lewis furrows his bushy brows. "My advice is to be careful. Dr. Honey may be finding out more from you than you from her. Remember, she works for Dorkin, and Dorkin plays dirty. If Bedside Manor's going to survive, we might have to get down in the dirt as well."

"What are you saying?"

"That kid, the computer whiz from the other night? Perhaps he could hack into a certain computer system that tells people how to act like a veterinarian."

"That's got to be illegal."

"Cyrus, I'm seventy-three years old, and as far as I'm concerned something is only illegal if you get caught."

I straighten up and blow out a disapproving breath.

"Hey, I'm floating ideas here," says Lewis.

"Ignore me. You getting anywhere with Ermintrude the cow?"

There's a moment when I think about sharing my suspicions about the diagnosis from hell. But although it's based on some troubling evidence, it's still circumstantial. Until I build a better case, I'd just be fear mongering.

"Still working on it," I say. "You got other cases to see?"

"Unfortunately," Lewis replies. "Don't suppose you could pick up one or two of mine? The wife's seeing a doctor at noon, and I'd like to be there."

"Sure," I say, "happy to. How is Mrs. Lewis?"

Lewis smiles the smile of a man whose love for his wife hasn't wavered in over fifty years.

"She's good. Told her all about you. Perhaps you could visit sometime. Bring Amy."

And with that he disappears back into the exam room, the throwaway line a carefully lobbed grenade, his passive-aggressive way of saying, "Sort out whatever's going on between you and Amy and make it right." Even if I know how, I wonder if I'll get the chance. It's quite possible my date with Doc Honey has turned her into Miss Scarlet, intent on killing me with the lead pipe.

"HERE, DR. MILLS. Dr. Lewis told me you wanted to help him out, so I picked this case especially for you."

Doris smiles as she hands over the file, a smile

borne of genuine pleasure. It's unnerving. I must be walking into a trap.

"Henry," I call, keeping a wary eye on Doris.

"Over here," says a man with a full head of white hair so curly it reminds me of Shirley Temple in *Heidi*. The man's beard is just as white, but the length more Hemingway than Santa. Still, he's packing enough pounds to make some extra money during the holiday season.

"You must be the new one. Heard about you. I'm George Simms; Henry's in the carrier."

George pumps my hand, and once again I make my apologies for using the work area instead of our "other" exam room that still bears a striking resemblance to a storage closet.

"Haven't seen you at the Inn yet."

"The Inn?"

"The Inn at Falls View. I own the place," says George. "Stop by, have a welcome drink on the house. And Chef's great. Though I leave him to it. I'm more comfortable with the bar and the front desk. Make sure our guests are happy. Should I let him out?"

"Sure."

George places the carrier on the floor, undoes the latch, and a miniature black panther yawns, stretches, and leaps onto a counter next to him.

"See the problem?" asks George.

"Can I assume it's the pink lesion on the tip of his nose?"

"Lesion." George grins. "If by lesion you mean the hideous deformity masking Henry's handsome features, then yes."

Henry has his back to me, tail up, busy investigating this new landscape. Finally, a problem I can solve, a physical abnormality I can see, touch, define, and treat.

"How long has he had it?" I ask.

"Months."

"Really?"

"Saw your father about it several times, Doc Lewis as well. Still growing. Getting bigger and uglier every day."

"Let's back up a little. Henry's what, an indoor cat?"

"Indoor and outdoor. Twelve years old and still a great mouser. Not a rodent on our premises, though he does have an annoying habit of bringing back his kills and leaving them on the doormat."

I watch as Henry leaps over a sink and discovers the microscope with much cautious sniffing and the occasional lick.

"And what's he been treated with?"

"We've tried creams, pills, and injections. Antibiotics, antifungals, steroids. Nothing's touched it."

We're having this conversation, but we're not looking at one another. We're both tracking the black cat with our eyes like he's an inquisitive toddler, disaster imminent.

"Has it been biopsied? If it's a tumor, I wouldn't expect any of those treatments to make much of a difference."

George chuckles. Definitely a Santa, he's got the "ho ho ho" down pat. "I'll be honest, Doc. Henry has certain . . . issues, when it comes to veterinarians."

And suddenly all I can see is Doris's nicotine-stained smile.

"Henry's smart, and he can tell the difference between being petted and being examined."

Henry begins swatting at a box of lens tissues, and I notice his paws.

"I see he's polydactyl. His paws. Extra toes." It's a genetic mutation. *Normal cats have eighteen toes. Polydactyl cats can have as many as twenty-seven.*

"That's right," says George. "I believe Hemingway was a big fan."

"Yes, sir."

Maybe George does prefer to impersonate a certain author from Key West.

"Well, I appreciate the warning," I say, picking up a clean towel, "but I'm pretty sure I can handle a kitty cat, even one with extra toes. If I wrap him up, swaddle him nice and snug, I'll be able to take a closer look."

"You're the professional," says George, stepping back as I unfurl my makeshift cape, ready to bring it on. "Only don't look directly in his eyes."

I do a double take. "Why not?"

"Just don't, is all."

Could be tricky, I think, given the location of Henry's problem on the tip of his nose.

Henry remains perched next to the microscope, grooming his neck in long, languorous licks, the barbs of his pink tongue catching in his fur. He seems totally unfazed until I close the distance between us to less than ten feet. That's when the grooming stops. I look back at George.

"What are you doing?"

He's zooming in with his cell phone, filming my examination. "Never know, might make you famous on YouTube. Go on, get in the frame."

Rather than lunging at Henry head-on, I come in at a tangent from his right side.

Male cats are more often left pawed, just like more men are left-handed.

Five feet away and the cat's ears begin to flatten.

Thirty-two muscles control the feline outer ear, whereas only six control the human's.

Using an oblique glance, I can see the lesion— fleshy pink, moist, and bulbous. It's as though the cat's wearing a red clown nose to impersonate Rudolph.

"Should exfoliate nicely," I whisper, inching forward.

"Exfoliate?"

Will I ever learn to stick with layspeak?

"If I can touch a microscope slide to his nose, I

guarantee some of the cells from the lump will stick to the glass and I'll be able to make a diagnosis."

"Can't wait," says George, for all the wrong reasons.

This is it. This is the point at which I must commit to the capture and restraint of the mutant beast. In my left hand I brandish the towel like a net. My right hand is ready to lunge, to scruff the back of Henry's neck, evoke memories of kittenhood, the sense of submission, of being carried around by his mother.

What follows is brief and noisy, but I'm the one screaming, not Henry. Though I've always thought I possessed quick, if not catlike, reflexes, it takes a feline to prove my reactions are pathetically slow. Henry nails me with a swat I sense rather than see, the pain of claws piercing flesh delayed until I stagger backward, a towel pressed into the bloody scratches on my forearm.

"You were lucky," says George, switching off his phone, his tone disappointed. "Didn't get you with his teeth."

I huff. "More than one way to skin a cat," I say, washing my wounds in antiseptic solution. "Time for a little chemical restraint."

George comes at me, suddenly animated, waving his palms in my face. "Sorry, Doc. No can do. Henry's got a heart condition. Doc Cobb tried to knock him out one time and nearly lost him. Scared me to death."

"There's always a risk with anesthesia, Mr. Simms, but based on this display I'm not sure we have a choice."

George sighs, studies the floor, and smooths down his beard. "To be honest, I brought him in today to give you, or should I say Bedside Manor, one last chance. In case you knew what it was just by looking at it."

"I don't understand."

"See, I was thinking of going over to that big practice in Patton. I told them about Henry and how he might need sedation or anesthesia, and they promised me he'd be fine. Said they've got these fancy monitoring devices, use them to anesthetize cats older than Henry all the time. You don't have anything like that here, right?"

"No, but . . . they promised, eh?"

George fidgets, refuses to meet my eye. "Look, I've always been loyal to Bedside Manor, but I've got to do what's best for Henry. Could you give me a referral?"

I finish drying off my arms, but the scratches continue to weep tiny tears of blood. Will Healthy Paws stop at nothing to increase their caseload? As far as I'm concerned the doctor who says he never makes mistakes is either lying or an impostor. And the doctor who promises something more than to do his or her best is asking for trouble.

"Here's what I'll give you, George—my

152

promise that I'll diagnose Henry's problem without resorting to sedation or anesthesia."

"How are you going to do that?"

"No idea," I say, more angry than defiant. "But my promise is just as valid as theirs."

George waits a beat, tips his head back. "Tell you what, I'll give you to the end of the week. No diagnosis and I'm taking Henry to Healthy Paws, referral or not."

And with that, St. Nicholas scoops Henry into his arms, deposits the cat in front of the open door of his carrier, and, after a moment of consideration, Henry chooses to stroll inside and lie down.

"Deal," I say, shaking his hand and leading him back into the waiting room, just as there's a strange trilling sensation in my pants. It's my cell phone; not a call, but a text.

Hey, want to get together this afternoon? Take me on a date?

Panic might have set in if the text had been sent from Doc Honey. Instead I succumb to shock—it's from Amy.

← 9 →

"THOUGHT YOU MIGHT APPRECIATE SOME-where a little quieter," says Amy as I hold open the door to the so-called Scoop-Shack. "January in Vermont; won't get much quieter than an ice cream shop."

We step inside one of those new buildings on the Garvey estate—half a dozen plastic tables and chairs sit empty, hedged in by glass-fronted refrigerators displaying assorted quarts and pints of sorbet, gelato, frozen yogurt, and ice cream. There's the sweet tang of vanilla in the air and the cheery flamingo pink and azure blue paint job does its best to help me forget the season. Finally we're alone, without distractions, and all is right with the world.

Amy takes off her scarf and unzips her jacket. "If we're frozen on the outside, might as well try on the inside, yeah? Oh, and if anyone asks, I was never here."

Is she embarrassed to be with me?

"What, you think this just happens? My trainer would kill me."

Amy drags the back of the tips of her fingers down the contours of her hips and thighs, showing off her figure, the defiance in her heterochromic eyes tempered by the flash of a smile.

"Flavors on the left, fixings on the right," she says, pointing to a chalkboard behind the main counter. "Ignore the politically correct lingo—small batch, fresh, organic—who cares, this place makes the best ice cream sundae you will ever eat."

"I remember. Can't believe they're still open year-round. Maybe you could grab us a table and I'll see what I can rustle up."

"Cookie dough, hot fudge, nuts, but hold the whipped cream and the cherry."

"Yes, ma'am," I say, guided by a big white pointy finger and a sign that reads ORDER HERE. There's no one behind the counter, but there is a small brass bell next to the till, the words "ring me" taped to the handle, Alice in Wonderland style. I ring, and from somewhere out back an old woman wearing tortoiseshell glasses, a red felt beret, and black fingerless gloves appears. Ringlets of long gray hair spill around her ears; cavernous laugh lines frame a wide mouth. Her chin may be free of the Kirk Douglas dimple, but she's not fooling me. The genes in this family are as strong as they are distinctive. This has to be the matriarch of the family—the original Mrs. Mike Garvey.

"Yes, dear."

I place our order (I'm going with chocolate

chip, and yes to the whipped cream) and watch as Mrs. Garvey flexes her Popeye forearms.

"You sort out Ermintrude?" she asks, head down, scooping away at the fluffy innards of a stainless steel container. "Saw you out back with Mike and Doc Lewis the other day."

Silly me. Apparently no introduction needed.

"Not yet." But then, thinking about the tragic case of their Jersey cow, "Maybe you can help? Don't suppose you remember where Ermintrude came from?"

"Of course. She was born here. We imported her mother, Clover, from a farm in Canada."

Since Eden Falls is less than twenty miles from the Canadian border, "importing" livestock is just a technicality.

"Clover lived to be fourteen."

"Not a bad age," I say.

"No . . . but now that I think about it, she started acting strange as well. Nuts on both, right?"

"Right. How do you mean, strange?"

"Mike would know better than me, but . . . jumpy . . . ornery. Your father put her out of her misery."

Note to self: check with Doris and see if the late Doc Cobb kept records on Garvey's livestock.

"Do you happen to know if he performed a postmortem?"

"Yes, I do, and no, he didn't," she says, almost sounding offended. "My late husband butchered her himself. Trust me, nothing went to waste. Nothing. There you go."

Mrs. Garvey buries a plastic spoon in the heart of each sundae and slides the cups my way.

For a second I totally ignore her, lost to bullet points of this new information—Canada; off-spring; nothing went to waste. Sadly, the checks keep filling the boxes for my dire diagnosis.

"Did Clover have any other calves?" I ask.

"Sure," she says, telling me how much I owe her.

What if Clover is patient zero?

Distracted, I root around in my pockets for cash and pull out the voucher Charlie Brown gave me—buy nine sundaes get one free.

"This any good?" I ask, sliding it over, followed by a five-dollar bill.

"Certainly," says Mrs. Garvey. "You a friend of Charlie Brown?"

"How did you know that?"

She lets her chin rock back into the fatty wattle of her neck. "This time of year, not many folks fill up one of these cards. Charlie's in here pretty much every day after school. I've tried to push the low-fat yogurt, but she won't listen. Too bad. Lovely girl. Here's your change."

I take it, but drop the coins into the tip jar. Charlie Brown, a pretty but sad teenager finding solace in ice cream. Struggling to deal with her parents' divorce? Is she overweight because her mother wants to abandon her, or does Doc Honey want to abandon her because she's overweight?

"Thanks," I say, picking up the cups and heading for Amy. Then a scary thought crosses my mind and I turn back. "When you said nothing goes to waste, you didn't mean that you actually"—I want to say "ate" but instead go with—"consumed your cow Clover?"

"Sure did. Burgers, steaks, roasts, you name it. A little on the tough side, but nothing a slow cooker can't tenderize."

"Got it," I say, but I'm not thinking about farm life and tough times and making the most of what you have. I'm thinking about Trey, Mike Garvey III, and this improbable but irrefutable link to Ermintrude.

"You took your time. Has my sundae turned into a frappé?"

"Sorry, just chatting with Mrs. Garvey is all."

"Ah, the overpowering allure of another older woman?" she says, taking her first swallow, savoring the moment before eyeing me (blue eye only). *Another?* Why do I feel as though this might be a reference to Doc Honey?

"No, the Garveys asked me to help them out with a sick cow."

Amy's right, this sundae is unbelievable.

"Farm work? Wow, Bedside Manor *is* in trouble."

I swallow my mouthful too fast and wince with the brain freeze.

"Left alone, I think we've got a chance. But right now our problem is the competition."

"Healthy Paws? Their practice name is almost as bad as yours."

She scoops another spoonful of frozen heaven into her mouth. I catch myself staring.

"That guy you pointed out the other night," I say. "Their office manager, Dorkin, you know much about him?"

"The guy with the freaky laugh?"

"Yeah, like a cross between a hyena and a braying donkey."

"More like a braying ass. He dropped by the diner a couple of times a few weeks before your father died."

That must have been when Dorkin was badgering the old man to sell the practice.

"Totally self-absorbed."

"How so?"

"The clothes. The car. The tips. This one time, he claimed he had a lecture to give at some conference in Vegas, wondered if I wanted to join him for the weekend."

I try not to imagine Dorkin's paintbrush whiskers tickling Amy's rosebud lips, but she's already read my agitated features.

"Please, give me some credit. He's like a seventies porn star."

Just then the door swings open and in walks Trey, ignoring the floor mat, work boots stomping a slushy trail toward the counter. Amazing, he's still wearing his *Cool Hand Luke* sunglasses.

"Ma," he screams. "You back there? Ma?"

Grandma Garvey hurries over as best she can, and Trey, clearly aware he's not alone, frantically urges her to come close so he can whisper.

"Does Trey always wear those glasses?" I ask, keeping my voice down.

"No idea," says Amy, leaning in. She's close enough for me to smell the soap on her long, pale neck—lavender. "He's always been, well, different. The mirror sunglasses only add to his mystique. Probably wears them to make you focus on your own reflection and not him."

My spoon hovers in front of my parted lips. *Focus on your own reflection and not him.*

"What?"

I want to kiss her (even more). "You've given me a fantastic idea." I push back in my chair and make to rise. "Just need to find out where he got them."

"Sit. I can tell you. Fancies Convenience Store, this side of the diner. Got a rack full up front near the checkout. Five bucks a pop, but I'm guessing no need to rush. Pretty sure they've only sold one pair."

Amy angles her head back toward Trey.

"Good to know," I say, settling back down.

"That's it? No explanation?"

I smile and scrape my spoon around the inside of my cup, trying to capture every last dreg.

Amy holds her own spoon upside down on her tongue for a second, biding her time. "My friend Mary called. Tells me she brought Gilligan in to see you."

"Oh, yeah. I seem to attract challenging cases."

Amy deposits the spoon in her empty cup. "I believe Fancies also sells earplugs."

I get the reference to the collie's incessant barking. "Gilligan is a little . . . nervous."

"That's the best you can do, 'nervous'? Muzzled by doctor-patient confidentiality?"

This is the Amy I was first attracted to—her sharp wit.

"And I hear you were asking after me the other night," she says.

"Uh . . . yes, well, only because—"

"I'm glad. I'd be disappointed if you hadn't."

It takes all of my willpower not to grin and ask: "You would?"

She sighs. "About the other night, the phone call at the bar. I was in a state of shock. I was distracted, and yes, rude. I'm sorry."

Instead of simply accepting her apology, my socially awkward silence is met with, "Well, what was your excuse?"

Whoa! Amy never gives me any room to hide. Now I've got to articulate my feelings. I'm reminded of a quote from the late Robert Altman's movie *The Player*: *I like words and letters, but I'm not crazy about complete sentences.*

"I guess I'm not used to being around a"—careful, Cyrus—"strong woman."

No physical blow to my body, but her eyes still pack a punch.

"You're going to have to clarify strong, 'cause I'm pretty sure this has nothing to do with what I can bench press."

"I mean confident, assertive."

"And you find this threatening?"

"Different . . . but in a good way." Despite clasping a cup full of ice cream, I run a sweaty hand through my hair. "Professionally and, yes, socially, I've enjoyed a somewhat isolated existence."

"Monastic or hermitic?"

I try not to smile.

"Look," she says, elbows on the table, lips hovering over interlaced fingers. "Most men use their sensitivity as a way to impress, if not seduce. Thankfully you're not one of those men. Your actions speak much louder than your words."

There's an awkward silence. Was that a compliment?

"That phone call. It was someone I haven't heard from in years. Someone . . . special . . . in my life. Last night was a complete surprise, a big deal. I know it's hard, Cyrus, but please, I'm asking you to leave it at that for now."

Oh dear. How I hate an unsolved mystery.

"I can't help being curious."

"Don't be," she snaps, and then, softening, "Look, I'm happy to take your jealousy as a compliment and not a flaw."

Special. Big deal. These are not "leave it at that" words. She wants me to back off but still be enamored? I stew, my argument for asking further questions building on the back of my tongue.

In my unease she tenses, straightens up, and I catch a crinkle of disappointment ruffling her forehead, as if she might have read the signs all wrong, that I might not be as interested in her as she thought. She shakes it off, perhaps putting on a brave face, and like a fool moving in slow motion, I miss my chance to set her straight.

"Anyway," she says, "my sources tell me *you* were out on a date?"

It's a daring comeback, her timing perfect, less of a deflection and more of a broadside.

"Well . . . I . . . don't think I'd call it a date," I say, my chuckle embarrassingly fake.

"Mary said you were with a strikingly attractive woman who couldn't stop trying to undress you with her eyes."

"Oh no, really, she was . . . no . . . and attractive? Mary exaggerates."

"Drop-dead gorgeous was Mary's actual description. Also head turning and sizzling hot. Don't act so surprised, you're an eligible bachelor. At least you would be if you'd tame that stupid cowlick on the top of your head, relax around the opposite sex, and learn how to use a napkin."

She points to the corner of her own lip, inviting me to attend to a smudge of fudge sauce.

"Eligible bachelor?"

She rocks in her seat, ready with the caveat. "For these parts."

If Mary or some other patron from the diner had recognized Doc Honey, Amy would have used her name. It seems we were both out with people who shall remain anonymous. At least, that is, until Honey gives her lecture at the Knights of Columbus.

"Unlike you, my meeting was not *special* or a *big deal,* definitely more business than pleasure."

She squirms, ever so slightly. Jealousy is making me more snide than quick-witted.

"Huh, will you be seeing her again?"

This may prove disastrous, but I can't help myself. "For someone who doesn't like questions, you're asking an awful lot of them."

She raises a "well, well" eyebrow above her brown eye. "Let's say it's a woman's prerogative."

I crack a smile and, to my relief, so does she. Maybe I haven't totally blown this after all. Maybe now would be a good time to toss out a compliment.

"Last night," I say, "I really wanted to tell you . . . to tell you how much—"

My cell phone rings. I try to press on.

"Coming home to Eden Falls has been, well, eye-opening, but meeting you has been equally—"

"Don't you think you should take that?"

I know I'm staring, and maybe my fixed eyes come across as disturbingly wired, but I want to convey, "No, this is more important."

With a sigh, I pick up, answering in a series of cryptic grunts and yeses, and ending with a weary "on my way."

Amy regards me. "Business or pleasure?"

"Business. Sorry, I'm needed back at Bedside Manor."

"Is everything okay?"

"Yeah, some kind of emergency."

"Oh, with who?"

"Someone called Mrs. Peebles and her dog, Crispin. You know them?"

Amy does a double take, scrapes back in her chair, and gets to her feet.

"Guess I made a mistake," she says.

The tension drops like an invisible curtain between us.

"I'm not with you."

She grabs her coat from the back of her chair and puts it on.

"Like I said, I can pretend the jealousy is a compliment. But not lying. If you're meeting Miss Drop-Dead Gorgeous again, have the decency to tell me to my face. I know for a fact that Crispin died three months ago!"

← 10 →

I DON'T KNOW WHERE TO BEGIN. AMY WAS correct, but so was I. Crispin the dog *has* been dead for several months, yet he *is* my emergency patient. How can this be? Sitting in my examination room is a distraught eighty-three-year-old Mavis Peebles, being comforted by her daughter, "Patricia, call me Trish," and a well-behaved, wonderfully silent yellow Labrador that has been stuffed by a taxidermist. Though I'm troubled by the wobbly castor fitted to the dog's left hind paw, I suspect the cause for concern is the small, lifeless creature cradled within the old woman's knotty hands.

"Donny Kutz usually sorts out these little setbacks," says Trish, "only he's wintering in Florida and won't be back until late April."

"Donny Kutz?" I ask, trying not to stare at the way Mrs. Peebles rhythmically strokes what might be the furry exterior of a small pocket pet, like a ferret. It's hard to tell.

"The taxidermist. Lives down near Stowe. We figured you'd be the next best thing."

"But Mrs.—"

"Trish, please."

"Trish . . . with respect, I'm a doctor. I work on living animals." At least I do now.

"Of course," says Trish. "We just . . . well, Mom thought you could try, being as Crispin was a patient here. We understand."

I glance over at the open file on my exam table. Back in October, Crispin was put to sleep for inoperable cancer, the details of the dog's final months documented in my late father's chicken scratch. His writing is almost illegible. Almost. One particular phrase jumps out and snags me— *great dog, great owner*.

Trish bends over her mother, preparing to lift her onto her feet.

"Why don't you show me what's wrong?" I ask.

The younger woman catches herself. She's probably in her fifties despite the standard age-defying tricks—professionally dyed hair cut short, silk scarf to hide the neck, bright red nail polish to draw the eye away from the pronounced veins on the back of the hands. She has chunky diamond studs in her ears. Conversely, Mavis has more gray than dye, more visible scalp than hair. She probably weighs about ninety pounds in her overcoat, her hand-knitted woolen scarf less about providing warmth than reinforcing her frail neck and preventing whiplash. I notice the twisted and gnarled joints of her hands doing all the talking— boutonniere deformity of the thumbs, swan-neck deformity of the fingers—classic signs of end-stage rheumatoid arthritis. She wears skin-colored hearing aids.

"Show him, Mom."

Trish steps aside as Mavis takes the shaggy weasel in one hand and shakes it at me like a lank pom-pom.

"His tail broke off," says Mavis, her voice little and uncertain.

As three pairs of eyes stare at me (one pair particularly unnerving), waiting for a response, I realize that I may want to run screaming from the room, but no part of me wants to laugh. Mavis is trembling, and though the possibility of her suffering from early Parkinson's crosses my mind, she appears genuinely scared. It's obvious Trish feels awkward and embarrassed to be here, but a burden of responsibility to her mother prevails. Why is the daughter indulging a bizarre desire to keep a dead dog—how best to put this?—alive?

"Mind if I take a look?"

I reach forward; Mavis Peebles is reluctant to let go.

Limber tail syndrome, often seen in out-of-shape Labradors that swim in cold water. Acute inflammation in the muscles of the base of the tail causes the tail to droop. The condition is also known by a particularly apt synonym—"broken wag."

I study the exposed surface at the base. The tissue could be described as brittle, even "crisp," but that seems insensitive given the dog's name. I'm guessing the break is between the second and third coccygeal vertebrae.

"How did this happen?" The question is aimed at Mavis, but Trish steps forward to huddle.

"He got it caught in a screen door." She's lowered her voice to foil the hearing aids.

"Um . . . this might seem like a stupid question, but that suggests a stuffed dog has been going outside in the middle of winter."

Trish checks over her shoulder and flashes her Mom a fake smile that, as far as I can tell, broadcasts "yes, we're talking about you."

"She takes him out in the backyard three times a day, just like she did when he was alive. It's a ritual, it's comforting. Even if Crispin just stands there. I think his tail must have gotten caught in the door as she wheeled him in this morning."

Maybe senile dementia, not Parkinson's.

"I'll be honest, Dr. Mills." This must be serious because she's whispering now. "I've tolerated this foolish, irrational delusion for far too long. If this . . . injury . . . is the last straw, that would be fine by me and my husband, if you get my meaning."

I peer around Trish and catch a glimpse of poor Mavis. She's looking off in the distance, stroking Crispin's head.

"Crispin meant the world to her, and I know how much she loves canine companionship, always has, but her arthritis is getting to be a serious problem. Simple things—turning door handles, switching on lights, opening the refrigerator—are becoming more and more difficult. She really needs to be in an elderly care facility. But she can't go because the decent ones refuse to take a dog, even a stuffed one. We've got more than enough room at our house, but unfortunately Lionel, my husband, is highly allergic to dog dander. You see my dilemma? As cruel as it may seem, it would be kinder if Crispin turned out to be beyond repair, if you get my meaning."

Trish steps back, pressing her hands together as though the case for the prosecution rests. Mavis looks up at me with the eyes of a frightened child who wants to go home. I never cease to be amazed by how attached people can be to their pets. This yellow Lab has physically remained in her life, yet she's still a wreck at the thought of something *more* debilitating than death causing him harm. Proof positive that this kind of bond can be both dangerous and unhealthy. This woman needs full-time care more than she needs a dead dog. It's normal to outlive our pets. Your dog dies, and you're left with the memories. Unless—unless you can't remember.

Something chirps inside Trish's handbag, and she apologizes and fumbles to silence the noise. In that moment, Mavis, unnoticed by her daughter, jerks her head in my direction, eyes coming into focus to meet mine, making me register the subtlest shake of her head. It's over in seconds—Trish awaiting the verdict, the fragile old lady back to patting Crispin's head.

Mavis can only be saying, "No, don't do it," which suggests she knows her daughter's real motive behind this visit. Or am I jumping to conclusions again? What to do? One of Lewis's many mantras pops into my head—*play for time.*

"Why don't you leave Crispin with me," I say to both of them. "I'll see if there's anything I can do."

Funny, both women look pleased, as though I've hit upon a solution worthy of King Solomon. For Mavis, it looks like I'm going to fix the tail. For Trish, I'm giving her mother a chance to accept the separation, softening the final blow.

"I appreciate your understanding," says Trish, raising a conspiratorial eyebrow as she shakes my hand, glad to have me on board. Mavis, with her daughter's assistance, eases up and onto her feet, dips low to kiss Crispin on his forehead, and shuffles over to me. Only now do I appreciate her fuzzy white bunny slippers with pink ears.

The arthritic fingers of her right hand beckon for me to come close.

"Thanks, Bobby," she says, and, making sure she's out of her daughter's line of sight, she delivers a sly wink.

Arm in arm they head out to the front desk,

leaving me alone with a deceased yellow Labrador on castors. Bobby was my father's name. Physically, aside from our eyes, we look totally different. Is Mavis so senile she's confusing her visit with a time when her dog and her old veterinarian were alive? But what's with the wink? What if Mavis Peebles is trying to tell me she's really a whole lot smarter than she's letting on?

I trundle Crispin through the work area and park him in an empty run. He's definitely got some mobility issues. Only when I slide home the lock on the run's gate do I catch myself. What's wrong with me? He's not going anywhere. Forget about antibiotics, now I'm the doctor who dispenses WD-40.

I leave Crispin's broken appendage with him. My game of pin the tail on the doggy will have to wait. Time to start working on my backlog of unsolved cases.

First up, Gilligan, the neurotic border collie. Yes, I like the idea of Gillie's owner, Mary, singing my praises to Amy, but more importantly, I have a decent lead to go on—a sample of Gillie's blood.

For the record, I enjoy anatomical or gross pathology, and no, I don't mean disgusting or yucky (I suppose for some all pathology is gross). I mean the inspection of disease with the naked eye. But give me a microscope to find a diagnosis and I'm in heaven.

As I cozy up to the counter of my makeshift

lab, everything is at hand, the process of slide preparation so well rehearsed in my memory I can put it on autopilot. Take a drop of blood, place on glass and smear with a deft hand, allow to dry using a warm—not hot—hair dryer, add a drop of stain for just the right amount of time, and voilà— you have a secret cellular story waiting to be read.

I pop my first prepared slide under the microscope and set to work. Four more slides and the result becomes conclusive. Gilligan is anemic, as indicated by his low number of red blood cells. But far more troubling is the fact that the anemia appears to be what's called nonregenerative. Normally if you're losing blood, your body notices and tells your bone marrow to make some more. Either Gillie's bone marrow doesn't want to or it can't. Bad enough to be running on empty, but worse when the only gas station around is closed.

Gilligan's file provides me with Mary's cell number, and I give her a call to explain.

"There's only so much I can discover here at the practice. Ideally I'd like to send off his blood for more tests, and, if you can swing it, we should get an X-ray of Gilligan's abdomen."

Mary's sigh of disappointment hisses in my ear. "Ah, you're killin' me, Doc. Can't afford both. Wish I could. You choose which one will give us the answer."

My turn to sigh. Not only have I got to cut corners to save dollars, but this way, it'll be my fault if I spend her hard-earned money and still don't discover what's wrong.

"Tell you what," I say. "Drop Gilligan off tomorrow morning. No food after midnight in case we need to sedate him. Let's go with the X-ray."

Mary thanks me, but even as I hang up, I'm packaging the vial of Gilligan's blood to send off to the lab. No, of course I can't afford to foot the bill, but somehow I've got to increase my odds of making a diagnosis, for the sake of Gilligan, and hey, if this gets back to Amy as a philanthropic gesture, so much the better.

THE NOVELTY of a little sealed envelope icon in the bottom right-hand corner of my laptop screen proves irresistible. Nobody I know (or want to know) would try to reach me by email, which is why I abandon the world of kooky cows and fat cats and peck the digital letter with the arrow of my cursor and wait as two new emails appear in my inbox.

From: Stiles, Gabe
To: Mills, Cyrus
CC: Brown, Charlize
Subject: Sorry!

Hey Doc,
  Sorry if I messed up. I still owe you for not snitching. It was Charlie's idea to hook

you up with her mom (yeah, I'm a rat), not mine. If you still need it, here's the link to your profile. My first dog was Jack and we lived on Hoffman Crescent, so you got lucky!
www.lafs.com
Gabe
P.S. Hoping my "covert mission" ;) will make us even.

I click on the link—purely to research my cover—and I'm incredulous at the depth of the deceit Gabe has created online. Apparently I want to go to Hawaii for my next vacation, the last movie I saw was *Platoon* (a little dig from Charlize), I have no brothers or sisters, I majored in communications at college, and, it seems, the best part about being single is the hope that "my quest for the perfect soul mate will end with you." Do women really buy cheesy lines like that? Don't ask me how, but Gabe even uncovered a headshot on file with my previous place of employment and photoshopped it to somehow make me look a whole lot better than I really do.

I close out the link and review the email one more time. He certainly had no problem throwing Charlie under the bus. And what did he mean by the "covert mission"?

The other email has been forwarded via

Gabe (from tlovelace@lafs.com). Clearly he's in control of this account and it's no less disturbing.

From: Honey, Winn
To: Lovelace, Thomas
CC:
Subject: Another date?

Hi Tom, Tommy, Thomas,
  I don't know what happened last night. It wasn't like any online date I've ever been on. It's okay to be nervous. It's okay to be shy. But what I liked best was the way you just wanted to listen, to let our connectivity unfold. Men constantly read me the wrong way. They say (not me) my looks make me unapproachable, out of their league. Either that or they'd prefer to talk with their hands and not their hearts, if you know what I mean. You're different, Tom, Tommy, Thomas, and different is a good thing. Wonder if you're free tomorrow night? Love to continue where we left off. My place? Call me.
Love,
W
XOXO

The L word? Hugs and kisses? My place? What have I done? At best I was confused, jumpy, and totally lost for words. How can Honey interpret my improv performance as sensitive, honest, and even respectful? It's bad enough to deceive her professionally, but manipulating this vulnerable woman's emotions is unforgivable.

I ease back in my chair, clasp my hands behind my head, and stare out the living room window. It's late afternoon, and what little light permeated this grim winter sky has finally given up, submitting to total blackness. With the shadows comes the uncertainty of what I have gotten myself into. Connectivity? There are two things Winn Honey and I have in common: loneliness and, at least on my part, desperation. But here's the difference: hers is rooted in divorce and the need for validation (at least I think so) whereas mine is out of choice and, I could argue, a quest for redemption. Maybe I didn't know quite what I was getting into when I took on Bedside Manor, but it was my choice. I chose to live in a frozen tundra void of humidity. I chose to take on a veterinary conglomerate by fair means or foul. For the greater part of my life I've chosen to be alone. I've learned to embrace the silence, to believe there's a difference between insulation and isolation. Now I'm not so sure. Out here, in the "real world," it seems there isn't a vaccine or nearly enough Purell to stop you getting infected by a truly dangerous contagion—hope. It's the possibility of not being destroyed by Healthy

Paws. It's the belief that there's something, I don't know, something unusual, even thrilling, about being around Amy and the chance that she might feel the same way. But now, for all the wrong reasons, I am responsible for inflicting hope on a lonely woman who didn't get to choose.

I press Reply on Gabe's email, insist he owes me nothing more, and ask him to forward this response.

> To: Honey, Winn
> From: Lovelace, Thomas
> CC:
> Subject: Friday night
>
> Dear Dr. Honey,
>   Yes, Friday night at 8:00 p.m. will work for me. I'd like to explain the real reason for being so nervous.
> Sincerely,
> Tom

Succinct, formal, and aimed at dampening her anticipation as gently as possible. Dr. Winn Honey deserves to be told the truth, and, though I hate emotional confrontation, an electronic explanation feels wrong. At least at her house I'll be out of the public eye when she comes at me with a can of pepper spray.

I abandon the online research, bundle up, grab

my doctor's bag, and decide to head out on an expedition, starting with an important purchase. The plastic bag hanging from the handle of the front door has other ideas. Inside there's a card with my name on it and a Tupperware dish containing a large slice of lemon meringue pie.

I open the card.

> The diner was all out of humble pie, but I hope this will work. I guess Crispin Peebles lives on! Now you know you're not the only one who jumps to conclusions.
> Call me soon!
> A

Ignoring the absence of "love," I leave the pie on Doris's desk for later and, as I jump into the Silverado, savor the gut-tingling thrill that Amy wants to make up with me.

This evening's version of cold can best be described as fierce. No one uses pleasantries like "crisp" or "brisk" this far north in January. I leave the truck to idle in the Fancies Convenience Store lot—praying the heater will finally kick in—and find what I'm looking for precisely where Amy said it would be. Up front near the checkout, a rack of a dozen minus one *Cool Hand Luke* aviator sunglasses. Make that a dozen minus two. Just as I'm about to pay, another item catches my eye. Next to a six-foot-tall cut-out cardboard primate is a shelf full of Gorilla Glue. It claims to be the toughest glue on the planet. Well, let's see if it's tough enough for Crispin's broken tail.

Purchases paid for, heading back through the center of town en route to an unscheduled but essential house call, I can't help but notice the two figures standing outside the diner. As I slow down, the truck's headlights pick them out, holding them like the flash of a single frame as I trundle past. It's a man and a woman, standing next to an outrageous, brilliant white Humvee. I keep staring as I roll along, but neither of them looks my way. They're facing one another, in each other's arms, wide eyes locked in . . . what . . . joy, mutual adoration. They're oblivious to the nosy curb crawler because they're entranced, their smiles ready to explode. The man is a stranger, but his five seconds in my high beams tells me all I need to know—taller than me and devilishly handsome. Sadly the woman is not a stranger.

Then again, maybe Amy is after all.

THE PITCH OF THE KEENING HORN
Doppler shifts as the angry car swishes past,
and only then do I notice I've been driving the last
mile with my high beams blaring. White knuckles
fused to the steering wheel, I've been barreling
into the night, following the contours of feta
cheese snowbanks and chasing the dusty snow-
snakes side-winding across the blacktop. I can't
shake the man's image, so vivid. I could pick him
out of a lineup. But it's the expression on Amy's
face that haunts me. I can think of no better way
to describe it—besotted.

Maybe I'm being paranoid. What if Amy's
expression was more nurturing than amorous,
more maternal than carnal? All I know for sure is,
in this sea of love, Amy looked as if she had been
saved by the hunky lifeguard, while I looked on,
flapping around in water wings, trying not to
drown. I am so out of my depth with this woman.
I yearn for the gift of the gab, when all I exude is
the "gift of the geek." If only this romantic limbo
stemmed from a failure to communicate. What if
Amy simply needs to understand the intensity of
my . . . crush. No, that makes me sound like a

horny teenager. Infatuation? No, that makes me sound like a stalker. Devotion. Yes, my earnest desire to get better acquainted. Who am I kidding? How can she feel comfortable around me if I'm still struggling to be comfortable with myself?

Multitasking with a cell phone (actually multitasking in general) is not my strong point, but I dial the phone number from memory, knowing it will ring at least ten times before it's picked up.

Make that twelve.

"Hello, Harry, it's Cyrus, Dr. Cyrus Mills. I'm the guy who helped out with—"

"I may be old, but I'm not senile. I know who you are. How you been?"

Harry Carp is Amy's eightysomething grandfather, the one she's nursing. She lives with Harry and his bizarre mutt, Clint.

"Good," I lie. "How's your dog doing?"

"Never better, thanks to you. You looking for Amy? 'Cause she's out."

"Actually I . . . um . . . wanted to ask you a question about Amy."

Harry pauses. "A bit quick for a marriage proposal, don't you think?"

"No, no, definitely not that. I . . . well . . . there's this other man . . ."

"What about him?"

Harry interjects this so quickly I can't tell whether he's being protective or disinterested.

"Well . . . should I . . . should I—"

"Should I what?"

"Should I be worried?" I blurt out.

I hear Harry catch a few nasal breaths, making me stew.

"I met him the other day. Just for a minute. Seemed nice enough."

Asking if he was a friend or boyfriend seems too direct, so instead I go with something more subtle. "So you've met him before?" Figuring that will at least tell me how long he's been in the picture.

"No, but—"

"But what?" I ask, jumping on the possibility of a flaw—convicted felon, debilitating speech impediment, on the run from the INS.

"I'll say this. Clint didn't warm up to him."

Clint took a while to warm up to me. Or maybe it was the other way around.

Neither of us speak for a full five seconds and then Harry comes back with, "I've got this quote for you."

"From Mr. Eastwood?" I know Harry to be a huge Clint Eastwood fan (every dog he's had throughout his life has been named Clint).

"Of course, but unscripted, from the man himself, not one of his movies. It's about pessimism."

Is it that obvious or does Harry simply see me as a loser?

" 'If you think it's going to rain, it will.' "

I come back with a nasal huff. "I thought you

might go with, 'If you're waitin' for a woman to make up her mind, you may have a long wait.'"

"*Pale Rider*, right?"

"Impressive, Harry. You take care."

MOST PEOPLE don't use the term *expedition* when describing an unscheduled house call to a sick animal. However, in my defense, this particular creature does merit the adjective *wild,* and besides, after witnessing the scene with Amy and her mystery man outside the diner, I'm grateful for the diversion.

I park around the back of the imposing building and notice a sign that seems tailor-made for me—HOTEL BUSINESS OR DELIVERIES ONLY. In the context of this evening's visit, I certainly mean business and I intend to deliver a cure. Next to the sign, a gridiron of light from a lead-paned window in a door guides me to the top of a short flight of salty steps and a copper doorbell. I press the buzzer but get no buzz. Hopefully it's ringing somewhere deep inside because the cold has already ripped off my ears, chewed away my entire face, and begun to feast on my brain. I'm used to living in Charleston, South Carolina. I don't do freezing, let alone negative digits. Doctorin' bag hugged to my chest, I stamp my feet on a thick rubber doormat, a bad chicken dance that does little to improve the circulation in my toes. Then I notice the mouse, dead and eviscerated, lying where the mat abuts the wooden siding, no doubt the sacrificial offering of a feline version of Hannibal Lecter.

A census taker once tried to test me. I ate his liver with some fava beans and a nice Chianti.

The door swings open to reveal the man I came to see—Santa Hemingway.

"Dr. Mills, what a surprise," says George Simms. "You should have used the main entrance for that drink on the house. Come in, come in."

I shuffle inside, the warm air filling my nostrils, every inch of exposed skin prickling as it begins to defrost.

"Actually I came by because I thought I'd have another go at Henry, if he's around."

"He is. This way."

I'm led down a narrow corridor, winding our way between logjams of housekeeping and room service carts, past the drone of washing machines and the aroma of fresh laundry, converging on the hubbub and heat of a hopping restaurant kitchen. Even if I ignore the vintage green-and-white-striped wallpaper, the floor gives away the age of this place. The number over the main entrance, 1853, is not a street address. Based on the subtle inclines and declines of the settled hardwood underfoot, I'm walking on the original flooring of a historic building.

"In here," says George, "though I'm pretty sure

Henry's sixth sense about doctors works just as well at home."

George holds open a door marked SECURITY, and I enter a room lit by the flickering glow of closed-circuit TV monitors. Eight LCD flat screens capture crisp black-and-white images of a series of empty corridors, what looks like a bar, a reception desk, the front entrance, and the rear parking lot.

"Fancy setup," I say. "Where's the casino?"

George smiles, grabs an empty swivel chair, and crab walks up to a desk cluttered with computers and keyboards.

"Had it installed a couple of years ago. Expensive, but worth it. Here's why."

George presses a key, and a screen in the middle showing an empty corridor begins fast-forwarding, the digital clock in the bottom right-hand corner whizzing through minutes and hours, people scuttling in and out of the frame, walking at double time, like in a silent movie.

"Half an hour ago, one of our guests claimed a piece of jewelry was stolen from her suite. Naturally she blames housekeeping. Thinks the maid has shifty eyes, a funny accent, insists I call the police. Guarantee, in the next half hour this same guest is going to let the front desk know she found it on a counter in her bathroom or in a drawer under an item of clothing and it was all a big mistake or her husband's fault. But just in case, I have this surveillance video, and I'm going through to make sure no one entered the suite other than the designated housemaid. I'm gonna keep at it, if you don't mind."

"Of course. Where's Henry?"

George spins around an adjacent chair so I can see the seat is actually occupied by a large black comma that slowly uncurls into Henry the predatory, polydactyl cat.

Cats sleep for two-thirds of every day, so twelve-year-old Henry has only been awake for four years.

"If you were hoping to jump him in his sleep, I advise against it. Henry prefers to doze, always one eye open, ready to pounce."

Ready to kill, I think, remembering the desecrated rodent on the doormat.

"No. I have a different plan." I set my bag down on the desk between George and his cat, extracting a box of glass slides, a pair of old oven mitts from my kitchen, and my secret weapon— *Cool Hand Luke* mirror sunglasses.

Probably wears them to make you focus on your own reflection and not him.

When Amy said this about Trey, it seemed like the perfect way to tackle Henry. At least it did at the time. Now that I'm here and Henry's sitting up and watching my every move, I'm not so sure.

As a cat, Henry will not recognize my face. He's

more tuned into body shape, body language, and the pitch of my voice. Trying a slow, sneaky approach is doomed. At the very least he'll bolt. Speed and surprise are my only hope.

With my back to him, I apply the mirror sunglasses and the oven mitts and, with the manual dexterity of a lobster, pick up a glass slide in each padded pincer. You know that feeling, the one when you're about to leap out of the plane and trust the parachute on your back? Well, neither do I, but I imagine this is what it's like.

"Do you have any idea how ridiculous you look?"

Ignoring the dissent, I take one step backward, perform a one-hundred-and-eighty-degree spin that may not be worthy of the late Michael Jackson but puts me exactly where I want to be, in the strike zone. It could be the flickering reflective dazzle from the monitors; it could be the two curious black cats that suddenly appear from nowhere, but the sunglasses are the silent equivalent of a SWAT team flashbang, the perfect distractor, allowing me to swipe both slides across the fleshy tip of Henry's nose and step back before he can say, "Ah, Clarice."

"Don't tell me it worked," says George, hitting Pause, freezing the frame, pushing out of his chair, and coming over to see.

Mirrors and mitts off, I inspect the greasy smears on the glass. I'll have to wait until I get home, but they look like decent touch preps to me.

"We'll see," I say, packing everything away in my bag. "I'll have to stain them up first."

George picks up Henry, or should I say, Henry allows George to pick him up. To be fair, the cat appears stunned, limp, and lost for words, as if I tossed a glass of cold water in his face for no good reason.

"Your father said you were stubborn. Fine by me if you cure my cat's nose."

It seems my father saw a stubborn streak as one of my few virtues.

"I'll let you know what I find. Good luck with your missing jewelry," I say, nodding at the screen. "I'll find my own way out."

"Thanks, Cyrus. Hey, the bar's the other way, if you still want that drink."

I consider hearty St. Nick clutching his black cat with the Karl Malden nose. What an odd but strangely compatible couple. Maybe I should take him up on the offer, especially after gathering inadvertent intelligence on Amy.

"Um . . . no, I really shouldn't but . . ." I can't help myself. "Do you happen to have a guest staying here who drives a brand-new white Humvee?"

Here's my thinking . . . Harry Carp said he only met Amy's . . . friend . . . for a minute, therefore he's not staying at their house. If you drive an expensive SUV and you're visiting Eden Falls, chances are you'll stay at the best guesthouse around.

"Of course," says George. "Mr. Marco Tellucci."

I expected a yes or no, not a name.

"Oh . . . right . . . and is, is he alone?"

"No idea. But I do remember he insisted on a king-size bed. Very specific. Why d'you ask?"

Marco Tellucci. Got to be Italian. Damn! Swarthy, suave, and, no doubt, a sexy accent to boot. Could I hate him any more?

"No reason," I say, backing off down the corridor the way I came. "I'll be in touch."

THE WORD *chill* in *windchill* feels like a cruel joke. I think the local meteorologists meant "windkill" and it came out wrong. Though the drifting snow sparkles in the truck's high beams like fairy dust, there's nothing magical about it. Round these parts the word *chill* is about as useful as the word *warm* in the Sahara Desert.

As I drive, the left, logical side of my brain comes back to my conversation with Harry. Harry said he'd only just met this Marco character. This might suggest someone who's not been in Amy's life for very long, but the phone call at the bar, the one Amy insisted she take, seemed like a conversation with an old friend, and she alluded to the fact that he was someone important from her past. Assuming the caller to be one Marco Tellucci, why did the Italian merit only the briefest of meetings with Amy's favorite relative? Has she been as secretive with Harry as she has been with me? "Seemed nice enough," said Harry. Nice enough for what?

A bend in the road catches me by surprise, sharper than I imagined, and suddenly I'm dazzled by the flash of brilliant blue and red light filling the cab and spilling across the right side of the highway up ahead. Instinctively my foot comes off the gas and I hit the brakes, the back end of the Silverado fishtailing but not enough to lose control. There's time to recognize Chief Matt Devito's police truck parked behind a vehicle that's nose-in down a trail between the trees. *Probably drunk,* I think, looking for telltale skid marks. But I don't see any, and that's when I recognize the vehicle—the windowless double back doors of a dishwater gray minivan—the gaunt man with his faithful labradoodle.

I pull over farther up the road, wishing I had a reverse gear in this stupid truck because now I've got to jog back though the knee-deep snow.

"Doc!" Chief Matt sees me coming, blinding me with his Maglite, the flashlight held at the side of his head, Hollywood-cop style. He's opted for a Cossack hat with earflaps over his standard-issue patrol cap. Less heat loss through his fashionably bald chrome-dome. "I was about to give you a call. Need your skill set to access the victim."

Skill set? Victim?

"What happened? Are they hurt?"

I keep pumping my legs, desperate for traction, trying to get past him, trying to get to the van.

"Doc, stop," says Devito, reaching out to grab me by the arm. "It's too late. The dog's alive, but the guy's gone."

Breathlessness takes me, and for a few seconds I slump, hands on hips, letting the shock and the sadness settle.

"You okay?" asks the chief.

I nod that I am.

"Yeah, it's just . . . I know this guy. Well, I met him. He came in earlier . . . with his dog."

"So who is he?"

The flashlight beam is back in my face.

"I don't know. He wouldn't give a name. I know the dog is Stash."

What I know feels too complicated for right now. Being economical with the truth is still the truth, and if the chief doesn't believe me, he keeps it to himself.

"Follow me and please, watch where you tread. I'm trying to minimize contamination of a potential crime scene."

Crime? What crime?

The van's parked a good twenty yards off the highway, down a narrow trail more suited to ATVs and snowmobiles. It's a whole lot easier to walk in Devito's wake.

"This is one of my spots for a speed trap," he

says. "Hide down here with the radar to get myself a DUI from the inn. That's when I saw the van. Didn't look like an accident. Made me wonder if I might have a lewd and lascivious instead."

First thing I notice about the minivan, the driver's side and passenger side windows are rolled all the way down. No smoke from the muffler, in fact not even a tinkle of cooling metal. The van's engine has not been turned over for some time.

"They're up front," says Devito, waving his beam toward the driver's door, "but the dog means business. You got a blow dart in your truck?"

He backs off as I make the final few feet to the front of the van. Just like that time at the diner, the gaunt man is slumped behind the steering wheel, but this time Stash the labradoodle is lying across his lap. As soon as I go near the open window, Stash lunges, barking with junkyard ferocity. I'm frightened, but more so by the fact that the man doesn't even flinch.

"Shine your light on me," I shout over the barking. "Stash needs to see what I do."

The beam swings into my face, and, staring back at the dog, I call Stash's name while delivering a fake karate chop to my windpipe. It's like pressing the mute button—one gesture and the only sound is the wind in the trees overhead.

Devito pans back to the open window, catching the devil-dog red eyes from the doodle's dilated pupils.

"Stash, sit."

I remember how I was struck by the gaunt man's crisp, confident commands, and I try to mimic them. Again, Stash is on it, backing his haunches up and onto the passenger seat, sitting perfectly square and to attention.

"Stash, stay."

This last one gets a tilt of the head and nothing more. It might be a canine version of "that's redundant, you idiot, I'm not going anywhere."

"Is it safe?" asks Devito.

Sir Lawrence Olivier in *Marathon Man* pops into my head, and you don't know how much I want to say, "Yes, it's safe, it's very safe, so safe you wouldn't believe it." But I just nod, and Devito shoos me back from the vehicle with a gesture he must have learned during Crowd Control 101.

Still wary, the chief opens the driver's side door to reveal a man with no more life in him than a crash dummy. I take in the scene—empty prescription medicine bottle in the well behind the gearstick, half-empty bottle of water, no seat belt, the man's white T-shirt peppered with tiny clumps of black fur. Of course, I already know this is a man with a death wish. I guess when I couldn't help him he decided to find another way. Windows rolled down, T-shirt, January in Vermont. Someone wanted to get cold—real cold—cold enough and sick enough to fall asleep and never wake up.

Eyes fixed on the dog, Devito leans in and pokes under the man's chin to feel for a pulse.

"Oh my God," he shouts. "He's still alive. I could have sworn he was—"

"Step back," I say, pushing the cop aside, squatting down next to the gaunt man, laying my fingers in the jugular furrow below his chin.

In seconds I pick up a pulse, not strong, not weak, but surprisingly regular. I turn to face Devito, shocked, about to agree that he is in fact alive, when I stop and realize something's off. My fingers haven't moved.

"I'll fetch the defibrillator from the truck," says Devito, starting to wade back the way we came, suddenly all animated.

"No wait, hang on a second," I call to him.

Consulting my wristwatch, I count as the hand spins through fifteen seconds, I multiply by four. Precisely seventy-two beats per minute; and that's the important word—precisely. Assuming severe hypothermia and a core temperature less than 82 degrees Fahrenheit, the heart rate should not be more than forty beats per minute. His chest does not move. He's not breathing. I raise the gaunt man's left eyelid. The pupil of his eye is fixed and dilated. He's definitely dead, but his heart keeps beating. Only one possible solution.

"He's gone," I say, standing up. I let the wind slash across my cheeks and allow myself a moment to appreciate the despair in this poor man's demise. What a strange resting place. Even his best friend couldn't save him, though based on the black fluff covering his T-shirt, Stash did everything he could to keep his master warm. Devito won't need forensic testing to discover the dog's saliva all over the man's ice-cold face.

"You're right about the pulse," I say. "But it's too fast for a dead man."

"I'm not with you."

"I'm saying he must have a cardiac pacemaker. The artificial beat doesn't switch off just because you're no longer alive."

To be fair to Devito, he seems genuinely disappointed that we're too late, and for a while the two of us just stand there, uncertain what to do next.

Like you, I eventually came home, only you got this practice and I got this dog.

What did the dead man mean?

"Why here?" I wonder out loud.

The chief pans his beam into the darkness beyond the front of the van, but there's nothing to see.

"Another twenty yards out that way and there's an overlook with a view across the valley." And then, as if something makes sense, he adds, "Faces west. Nice sunsets."

"Okay," I say, and start to explain exactly why the man with no name came to see me, and how, sadly, he took his own life because he couldn't wait for nature to take it from him.

Devito waits for me to finish before rifling through the various pockets of the dead man's jeans. Stash does not look pleased. Gingerly, the chief reaches over to open the glove compartment—empty.

"Seems like your client made an effort not to be identified."

The beam flashes on the lower part of the windshield at the dashboard. The thin metal plate with the vehicle identification number is missing.

"Bet I won't find a license plate, either," says Devito, straightening up. "What did you say the dog's name was?"

"Stash."

"Stash? Makes you think our John Doe was a drug dealer. Wonder if he knew Trey Garvey."

And I thought I was the one who leaped to the wrong conclusions. Trey fails a sobriety test, and Devito thinks he's on the trail of a Mexican cartel. Given the apricot fur around the dog's muzzle, my money would be on a nickname, a short version of "Mustache." It may be too dark for Devito to notice, but I keep this to myself.

"The man was terminally ill. I imagine the dog was the only thing making the last few months of his life bearable."

"Then that's how we'll track him down," says Devito, pleased with himself, jabbing a finger in my direction. "The dog will have left a trail. He's obviously been specially trained. So who trained him? And if Bedside Manor wasn't his regular vet, then who was? Your chance to play detective, Dr. Mills."

"I'll see what I can do," I say. "In the meantime, you might want to call a coroner."

I begin trudging back the way I came, careful to follow the trail.

"Whoa, there. What about the dog? I can't take him."

I dip down to see Stash, eyes still focused on his sleeping master, his body fidgeting for the next command.

"Let me try something," I say, coming around the back of the van, "so long as you don't mind me destroying your *crime scene*." In lieu of air quotations I go with a sarcastic rising intonation. Even so, Devito vacillates before waving his permission to go ahead.

The passenger-side door proves difficult to open, buried on the windward side by drifting snow, but as I swing it as wide as I can without a shovel, Stash keeps his back to me, unable or unwilling to escape his responsibility.

"Stash," I call, with the same forceful tone I used before. "Stash, come."

The doodle glances my way, just for a second.

"Stash, come." Firm, not angry.

This time the dog turns his entire body toward

the crack in the passenger door, appears to think about it, but turns back.

"Stash, come," I say, unable to keep the regret, the resignation out of my voice, and then, as if against his will, Stash tears free, squeezes through the gap, and jumps down, swallowed by the soft powder as he comes to my side. In the glow of the flashlight, I watch as the dog's head tilts back, ready for his next command—from me.

Friday

← 12 →

I T SEEMS I HAVE A TALENT FOR HARBORING dogs of mysterious derivation. Last week it was a fugitive golden retriever named Frieda Fuzzypaws. Almost everyone in Eden Falls thought Frieda was missing, everyone except her owner, a guy who wanted this dog out of his life, until he realized she was an integral part of it. In the short time Frieda was with me, I discovered I quite liked canine companionship. Okay, "quite liked" may be an understatement. Oh, she was needy and worshipped my refrigerator, but at least I no longer had to talk to myself.

Stash is an altogether different lodger. I've traded golden tumbleweeds for fur that undergoes a bizarre chemical reaction when combined with powdered snow to form grape-sized, snarly, and intractable balls of ice that cling to Stash's legs and undercarriage. Where Frieda craved physical contact, Stash appears content to be hovering at my side, but he's always by my side, a canine shadow, following me from room to room, including visits to the bathroom—and I don't think this is because he's needy or afraid. If anything, he appears to be on duty. Last night I was getting undressed for bed and he sat in front of me with something stuck in his mouth. My cell phone must have slipped out of my pocket when we were sitting together on the couch. This wasn't about being impressed by a retrieval instinct. This was about being scared by bright brown eyes that might be saying, "Lost something?" Those same brown eyes greeted me the moment I woke up this morning, inches from my face, seemingly chiding me for languishing in bed. And when I offered him breakfast, he wouldn't eat until I was working on my own bowl of granola. It's as though he doesn't quite know how to relax and simply be a pet.

Right now I'm pretty sure Stash is critiquing my attempt to secure Crispin's broken tail back where it belongs. Either that or he thinks I'm a total freak for even trying. Under his watchful eyes, I sit on the floor at the back of Crispin's run, beside me an open pack of surgical instruments, a can of WD-40 (I was serious about fixing that castor), and the bottle of Gorilla Glue.

"Not funny," says Doris, standing over me, trussed up in her downy ski jacket. She's glancing at the card I attached to the gate of the run, a card identifying this patient as "Crispin Peebles, 14-year-old Labrador, Broken Tail, DNR." DNR—do not resuscitate.

"Sorry," I say. "A little gallows humor. Didn't want anyone to not find a pulse and go hunting for a defibrillator." Assuming we've got one.

Doris isn't interested in an explanation, her twiggy index finger flicking back and forth between the two dogs. "Hard to tell which one's stuffed and which one's real."

She's right; Stash possesses an uncanny stillness and unblinking stare as he waits for my next command.

"Where are my manners? Doris, this is Stash, the labradoodle who—"

"Belonged to that guy found dead in his car last night."

There's no point in asking how. Of course she knows. But she used the word *guy*. Should I infer Doris has discovered the details but not the identity of the man?

"So if he wasn't from Eden Falls, then where?" I ask.

Her only response is to shrug her shoulders, but there's a glint of something that might be pleasure in Doris's eyes, something that tells me she's already on it.

"Well, Stash will be staying with me. At least for now. There, what do you think?" I get to my feet, gesturing to Crispin's tail, ignoring the stainless steel towel clamps holding everything in place until the glue dries.

The snappy upward curl at the margins of her orange lips is faster than a blink.

"It was your father's idea." Doris jerks her hairy chin in Crispin's direction. "Getting him stuffed.

Thought it was the best way for Mavis to stay independent."

"I don't get it. Mavis Peebles looks like she's in desperate need of a helping hand."

"Looks can be deceptive," says Doris. "Her daughter, Trish, she means well, but it's her husband, Lionel, who wears the pants and holds the purse strings."

"Lionel—allergic to dogs, right?"

"So he says, though I'd bet the only thing he's allergic to is losing his mother-in-law's inheritance. Trish and Lionel live in a fancy McMansion out toward Patton, but Mavis might spoil the feng shui when friends come over for cocktails, if you get my meaning."

Feng shui. There's clearly far more to Doris than Marlboros and big hair.

"You're saying Trish wants to be rid of Crispin so her mom can either live with her or go into assisted living, whereas Lionel would rather keep Crispin around so that Mavis remains in limbo. Not staying with him because of his so-called allergy, and not eating up her savings in a nursing home."

Doris clucks her tongue like she's encouraging a stubborn horse to move forward and hits me with an unsettling "you got it" wink.

"What do *you* think Mavis wants?" I ask.

"No idea," snaps Doris, visibly insulted. "You do realize the woman's old enough to be my mother?"

"Of course, I never meant to suggest—"

"And given my current pay, I can't afford a nursing home anytime soon."

"That's great, I mean, that I, that we, still get the pleasure of your company, still get the benefit of your . . . expertise."

My detour from salary to corny compliment fails to dent Doris's scowl. I can tell she's jonesing for a cigarette, eyeing a roll of bandage material like it might be worth lighting up.

"Probably wants her dog back in one piece," she says. "And while you're at it, a cure for arthritis. How should I know?"

Doris spins on her heels, nimble and light on her feet, her elaborately teased yellow hair quivering wildly as she marches off.

"I'm practically a spring chicken compared to Mavis Peebles," she shouts without turning back.

And I have to agree. Doris's scrawny legs do share certain characteristics with the domesticated fowl.

With Cripin's tail in a holding pattern (literally), it's time to use Stash for a special assignment—unmasking the identity of the gaunt man. This way I get to bypass the sleuthing incompetence of Chief Matt Devito, and I already have an obvious lead in the investigation—missing testicles. Somewhere along the way Stash has been separated from this part of his manhood. And if he's been neutered, then he's probably been vaccinated, tested for heartworms, treated for ticks, and the list goes on and on. Next clue, though they might not have hailed from Eden Falls, when you're living out your last few days on earth, I'm betting you want to stay close to home. If they're not clients of Bedside Manor, then who better to check out than a certain rival practice across the valley? I pluck Guy Dorkin's crumpled business card from my pocket and dial the number for Healthy Paws.

The phone is answered by a recording that insists I pay particular attention because their menu has changed. I'm asked if I have an emergency, need a prescription filled, want to leave a message for a doctor, need to make an appointment. Eventually I meet the criteria of "for all other calls, press 0" and get placed on hold, forced to listen to a sycophantic female voice asking if I knew that fleas could jump up to eight inches high. Yes!

"Hey, hello, howayya, this is Healthy Paws and I'm Popcorn, how can I be of service?"

Whoa there, what kind of a greeting was that? I'm exhausted. Did she really say her name was Popcorn?

"Hello . . . Popcorn, this is Dr. Mills, I work at Bedside Manor, over in Eden Falls."

There's silence on the other end of the line, not an "Uh-huh, I know it, yes, Bedside Manor," just total silence. I press on. "I have a dog, a black labradoodle, that answers to the name of Stash, and I wondered if it belonged to a client of yours."

Another silence and then with her mouth she hits me with a burst of "yeah, sure, okay, please hold" and the fawning female recording comes back, telling me how vital it is for me to get my senior dog examined every six months. Where's the elevator music?

"Looking to poach another case, Doc?"

It's Dorkin, the question direct, not a trace of levity.

"Um, no, not at all . . . I picked up a dog—"

"Does it make you feel better, asking my permission? Help you sleep at night?"

"What are you talking—?"

"You as good as accuse us of malpractice with Sox Sauer, so what's next? Animal experimentation? Operating a Ponzi scheme?"

What's got into him? I guess the gloves are officially off.

"I'm, well, I'm simply trying to find out if a dog by the name of Stash is a patient of—"

"No. No, it's not. Have at it. You're desperate for business. It's not one of ours. Knock yourself out."

I don't do snappy ripostes, and normally the option to hang up would trump my typical bumbling weak comeback. But when I made this call, I had Doc Honey on my mind.

"So that lecture you've set up in Eden Falls is . . . what? You feeling civic minded?"

An insolent huff hisses down the line.

"If you're that worried, come along. In fact we'd love nothing more than to hear you defend your particular brand of veterinary medicine. I'm sure you could enlighten us about the discovery of X-rays or the benefits of a thing called"—he splits the syllables for maximal debasement— "pen-i-cill-in."

"Brag all you like about your flashy equipment, Dorkin, but believe me, people pay attention to what lies behind the curtain."

"Good. I'll save you a seat, and we'll let the pet owners of Eden Falls decide where they can get the best care and the best value. How's that sound?"

He hangs up before I can say another word. Suddenly all I can think about is my upcoming rendezvous with Doc Honey. Like it or not, I have to come clean, to confess my sins to an enemy combatant, an enemy with a ready-made public forum in which to air my double life as the nefarious Tommy Lovelace. I'm doomed. At best, I'm a deceitful creep. More likely, around here I'm that hillbilly trying to exploit a sad and lonely doctor for kinky sex and insider information. Either way, it's not good for me or Bedside Manor.

SITTING AT the microscope with Henry the cat's slides, I'm reminded of the old days, simpler times, as the scientist who kept his head down, kept the rest of the world at bay, and lived his life with pain-free objectivity. The old Cyrus would have run screaming from a confrontation with Doc Honey. The old Cyrus would have been turned to stone by Amy's heterogeneous eyes, let alone her confidence. But it's taken Bedside Manor and less than two weeks in frigid Vermont to make me want to change. Sure, being cold and isolated (welcome to Eden Falls) ensures self-preservation and protects against humiliation, but inside, I realize now, I was as dead as most of my patients. Sometimes I think it might be easier to shake off this state of dreamy weakness, to put up my guard and retrieve a sharper, harsher focus. But for all my financial and emotional troubles, I can't and won't go back. These days, the comforting armor of the introvert, the second skin that fit me so well, is nowhere near as snug. And, for now, it can hang in my closet with the mothballs.

More often than not, as a pathologist, I'm given a slide, a biopsy, or a chunk of tissue, together with a note from the clinician telling me what he or she suspects I'll find. It's like being a wedding DJ—even if you have a great sound system, it helps to know the kind of music you'd like me to play. The thing is, if I can't deliver a diagnosis, it's the clinician's problem, not mine. Blame your own crappy technique, your inability to get me a decent and representative sample, but don't blame the pathologist. Now, forced to wear both hats, faced with this particular pair of slides, failure to make a diagnosis means another round of mortal combat with Henry, or, worse still, losing a client to Dorkin and Healthy Paws.

Though the cause of Henry's nasal horror may lie within these greasy smudges, it needs to be cajoled, carefully deciphered, and with only two samples available, there's no margin for error.

Calm, Cyrus, be logical. Think about what you know. I know George Simms said he tried antibiotics, antifungals, and steroids, all to no avail. Conclusion—the nasal lesion is not caused by a bacterial infection, a fungal infection, or an inflammatory process. Why? Because there's still a big fat tumor on the end of poor Henry's snout. Let's prove it with a Diff Quik stain.

I hold on to the first glass slide by my fingertips and dip it in tiny vats of blue and red dyes. Quick rinse, dry, and it's under the lens, my fingers tweaking the knobs that control the coarse and fine focus on the microscope, the prepared slide zipping back and forth, and in less than a minute I have my diagnosis—or, that is, I have *no* diagnosis. It's not cancer. It's not a tumor. All I see is cellular schmutz. That's what you get when you're reduced to little more than a snot-wipe sampling technique. Damn.

One down, one to go. One slide stands between

me and cat-scratch fever, a rabies booster, stitches, and a course of intravenous antibiotics. The mirrored-sunglasses trick will never work a second time.

There are plenty of staining options used to enhance and identify certain microbes, but pick the wrong stain and it's over. Think. Henry had no response to antibiotics. Why? What if the bacteria were resistant?

There's a pile of files next to me on the counter, and I dig out Henry's, flicking my way through the pages of messy notes until I discover which antibiotics Doc Cobb used. The world is full of bacteria, but my father chose well, starting out with a sawed-off shotgun approach, hitting a broad target before working his way to a more specific antibiotic, the pharmacological equivalent of a sniper's rifle. Still, nothing appeared to work. Why not? Common bacteria would have been wiped out. There's only one possible reason—Henry is not afflicted by a common bacteria.

This time I go to the cupboard. Stash, now seated, keeps an eye on the action. Maybe he's hoping for an Old Mother Hubbard moment. Instead, I'm face-to-face with remnants of my late mother's life, in the form of her meticulously organized collection of lab equipment—rare stains, a mechanical stop-clock, and a classic piece of school chemistry memorabilia, the Bunsen burner.

It's like following a Martha Stewart cook-book recipe. Fire up the burner, flood the last remaining slide with a crimson liquid, place in flame and steam for five minutes, take care not to flambé with the acid-alcohol and presto—feast with your eyes. Fingers twitch, the slide zips, and in less than a minute I have my diagnosis, scooching my chair back from the microscope and over to Stash.

"High five," I say with uncharacteristic sporty machismo, and, as if we'd spent years together perfecting the trick, Stash instantly raises a black paw and we connect. Without thinking, I pull his whole body into me, up and onto my lap, like he's a kid ready for a picture book story, and I bury my face in the soft, sweet-smelling fur of his neck as I whisper, "Good dog." It's over in seconds, but I catch myself—no, *we* catch ourselves, like that moment in the movie *Grease*, where Danny Zuko and Kenickie share a spontaneous bromantic hug, realize it's not cool, and separate like it never happened. There's a split second of direct eye contact, the shift from mutual affection to mutual embarrassment, and Stash leaps gazelle style from my lap as I glide back to my microscope and the bright red chains of tiny bacteria floating in clouds of seafoam blue.

Henry is the victim of an uncommon bacterium, a bacterium belonging to the same family of organisms that provides us with such delights as tuberculosis and leprosy. It's known as a mycobacterium, and it won't respond to your typical antibiotics. You need a special Ziehl-Neelsen stain (thanks, Mom) to unmask it. Now that I know what I'm dealing with, I can even pin it down to a particular species—*Mycobacterium microti*—the vole bacillus. And when I say vole, I mean rodents, as in the prey of a cat regarded as an excellent mouser. Now it makes perfect sense. Where's an infected, cornered mouse going to bite a cat? Right on the end of his nose.

There's a Walgreens pharmacy in Patton. It turns out they carry the 2% isoniazid ointment Henry needs to treat his nose. I can pick it up, drive over to The Inn at Falls View, and deliver the Holy Grail—diagnosis and cure. I'm almost tempted to perform a self-congratulatory fist-pump while releasing a protracted "yessssss." Almost.

"Doris, I'm just going to run over to . . ."

But Doris is outside, wading through a cloud of cigarette smoke, and the only person standing at the front desk is none other than the computer geek himself, Gabe.

"Hey, Doc, you got a minute?"

The Napoleon Dynamite look-alike seems pleased to see me.

"Um . . . sure . . . shouldn't you be at school?"

"Free study time," he says, as though I should know. He's still wearing his gray Unabomber sweatshirt (hood down, thankfully), but strapped across his chest and shoulder, he carries a laptop bag.

"Tell me this isn't about that dating thing again?"

"No, no way, Doc. That was Charlie, not me. This you're going to love. But we should go somewhere private. You know that dog's loose, right?"

Stash looks up at me, checks out Gabe, and comes back with what I might best describe as a withering stare.

"Yep. He's with me. Come on through."

I close the exam room door behind us, and Gabe's already pulling out pages of computer printouts and organizing them in piles on the stainless steel table. Straight away one unifying, striking, and disturbing feature jumps out at me— at the top and center of each page sits the Healthy Paws logo.

"What have you done, Gabe?"

Somehow Gabe manages to look more confused than I do. Oh no, now I remember his email—*P.S. Hoping my "covert mission" ;) will make us even.*

"What you asked me to do."

"I didn't ask for anything."

"Doc Lewis said you did. He said nothing dangerous, just a little creative snooping around, that's all. Help give you a leg up with the competition." He lovingly double pats the nearest sheet of paper.

"Hold on." My eyes race across the pages. They're spreadsheets, production numbers, undoubtedly confidential. "Stop right there, Gabe. This is totally illegal."

"Maybe."

"No, it is."

"Maybe, but only if you got caught and only if you were stupid enough to leave an electronic footprint."

I don't know much about Gabe, but one thing seems clear: when it comes to computers, he is far from stupid. Dorkin's sarcastic tone rings in my ears—*Let the pet owners of Eden Falls decide where they can get the best pet care.*

"Explain to me how you did this?"

"Too technical, too boring," says Gabe, "except the password stuff, which is always cool."

"It is?"

"Of course. It's key. Cracking the password is the best. You like puzzles? Of course you like puzzles. See, most passwords are logical, personal, and rarely random."

"Password," I offer. "123456. Trustno1."

"I said logical or personal, not stupid. It's the only way we remember them without writing them down. I've been to Healthy Paws lots of times with Mom for Tallulah's checkups. I've seen what kind of software and hardware they use."

"But how do you know Dorkin, assuming he's the one who sets the password?"

Gabe grins, loving his advantage. "I pay attention. I've watched the way Dorkin handles owners when they pay their bills. He plays favorites. If you're wearing lipstick and a short skirt, he's all, 'Sure, we can work something out,' otherwise, he's hauling you off to collections. Guy's a dick."

Neither Stash nor I disagree.

"Normally I start with the pet name angle, but the unrestricted part of the system told me Dorkin doesn't have any pets registered with Healthy Paws. Weird for someone running an animal hospital, right?"

This comment makes me wonder whether I'd best adopt Stash as soon as possible.

"So I get more creative. Personal dates—birthdays, his own, his kids', wedding anniversary, that sort of thing. Dorkin's divorced, never had kids, and his date of birth didn't work."

Gabe reads my alarmed expression. "Don't ask. Anyways, next up, the man himself. What do I know? I know he loves himself. I know he wears nice clothes, nice watch. Vanity and wealth. Naturally I check with the DMV and bingo, Dorkin bought a vanity plate for his Audi. I type in six letters—T-O-P-D-O-G—and, open sesame, I'm in."

I don't know if I should be impressed or patting him down to see if he's wired as part of an FBI sting operation.

"For a while I snoop around, mainly boring numbers, but then I think, why not check out Tallulah's record, calculate their markup, see how badly we were being ripped off. That's when I noticed things didn't add up."

Gabe has set up his evidence such that anyone with a little business savvy should be able to compare the master spreadsheet that Dorkin generates for himself with the individual monthly totals each doctor gets to see. All I can say for sure is that Doc Honey is significantly under-performing compared to her colleagues.

"I'm still not with you. Looks like rows of boring numbers to me."

"That's what you're meant to see. But if, like me, you love numbers, it starts to unravel. Here," he picks up one of Dr. Honey's monthly Excel sheets, "the doctor gets a percentage of everything he or she does, stuff like vaccinations, dispensing medication, running blood tests. If they don't bill, they don't get a paycheck. Dorkin, on the other hand, is on salary, but if you notice, he takes a percentage of all the nonclinical stuff the hospital has to offer, like boarding, grooming, pet food, chew toys, dog beds, dog outfits, you name it. Nothing leaps out until you compare the monthly figure each doctor actually gets to see with the number on Dorkin's master spreadsheet."

Gabe's index finger bounces between the figures for different months and different doctors and the pattern floats to the surface. He's terribly excited, in a zone, and I notice because I know exactly how it feels. Math nerd meets science nerd.

"The doctor's production figure is always less than they actually generate. So Dorkin's skimming?"

"Essentially," says Gabe. "Where he can, he's weighting the bills in his favor. Nothing big, nothing greedy, just a steady couple of hundred here and there from every doctor, enough to make a difference, not enough for them to notice. Over a year, even after taxes, he's got a sizeable increase in his personal revenue."

I look back at the figures again, and this time the fraud is obvious. No one gets harder hit than Winn Honey. I can't help but wonder whether he's punishing her. Personal vendetta?

"How many people know about this?"

"Me, you, and Fido."

"You didn't say anything to Charlie, did you?"

"No."

"Gabe?"

"Okay, yeah. But you can trust her."

My thoughts become sidetracked by the smart, funny, but ultimately unhappy sundae-loving daughter of my online girlfriend. I deliberate, stew a little, but have to ask. "Does Charlie ever talk about her home life?"

"You mean why she's fat?"

I'm not good at acting appalled so I don't even try.

"Her dad moved out a couple of years ago. Went to live with a twenty-three-year-old he met online. Now they're married, have two boys, twins. Charlie and her mom dealt with it in their own ways. The Doc went on the nerve diet, got in shape, and started dating younger men, maybe to prove a point. That left Charlie to feel abandoned by both parents. Dad's got his new family, and Mom doesn't want a teenage daughter cramping her dating options. I think Charlie eats to annoy as much as to forget."

"That's too bad. They've had a tough time," I say. "But you really shouldn't have gotten me involved."

Gabe looks more impartial than contrite.

"And it was wrong to hack into Dorkin's computer."

"Ah, c'mon, Doc, this is epic."

I hate to admit it, but he's right (or even righteous). The best I can do is to keep quiet.

"Face it, Guy Dorkin's totally screwed. Forget a little illicit porn or online gambling, this info can send him to the Big House. So why look so worried?"

Standing there, slack jawed, and, to be honest, a little afraid, I have what I can only describe as an out-of-body experience. It's as though I'm watching myself in the third person as I do three unusual (for me) things. Firstly, I realize my hand has been resting on Stash's head, and, unlike his previous master, it's not because I need the support. Secondly, though I am equal parts grateful and furious with Lewis for commissioning this damning little project, I sweep Gabe's proof into a pile. Lastly, and most troubling of all, I turn to Gabe and say, "I wonder if you might do one more thing for me."

← 13 →

I T IS TIME TO ADMIT IT—I'M FORMING A dangerous attachment to this funky-looking doodle. My revelation occurs the moment we turn left out of the parking lot. Stash sits in the Silverado's passenger seat, one eye on me, one eye on the road, and into my head pops an awareness of . . . concern. I'm concerned that I can't provide this animal with a seat belt or some other dog-appropriate safety device in the unlikely event of an accident. Is feeling a burden of responsibility part of falling in love?

We're heading into town, my phone already against my ear, calling Lewis.

"Where are you?"

"Sitting with my wife, having a coffee. Busy

appointments? Need me to come in and give you a hand?"

Damn. How does Lewis do that? I want to be angry at him for mobilizing the computer geek behind my back, but he's the dutiful husband, spending time with his dying wife, happy to hop to if I need bailing out.

"No, no, it's slow."

I glance over at Stash. I'm getting less creeped out by the constant scrutiny, though his look might be more "hang up and drive already."

"Sorry to hear about the guy with his labradoodle. You taking on another lost dog, Mr. Patron Saint?"

Lewis is referring to the moniker, the lasting tribute, my father acquired—the Patron Saint of Lost Dogs. When someone came across a stray dog or if a dog needed to be adopted because its owner was relocating or lost a job or died, the late Bobby Cobb posted its picture on a wall in the waiting room and made sure it found a good home.

"We'll see," I say, wanting to get back on topic. "Gabe dropped by. The kid who's good with computers."

"Really? Find anything?"

Amazing. No apology, no backpedaling for sending a minor on a counterintelligence mission. I press on as best I can, explaining Dorkin's little scam.

"What were you thinking, asking a kid to go cyber-snooping? What if he got caught?"

"He said he owed you. Asked if we wanted help setting up a practice web page and he'd do the work for free."

"So you suggested the veterinary equivalent of Wikileaks?"

"He was the one who mentioned hacking. Took me a while to realize this had nothing to do with horses. I thought it might give us some ideas about how Bedside Manor might compete. Know your enemy. Never imagined he'd find anything useful. Believe me, Dorkin's playing dirtier than us. You catch this morning's *Gazette*?"

"No."

"Grab a copy. And be sure to thank Peter Greer next time you see him. Dorkin must be furious."

What has Greer done now?

"Let me think about what to do with Gabe's information," says Lewis. "I'll be in shortly."

We hang up, and since I'm passing the gas station, I pull over, eager to grab a copy of the newspaper to see what the fuss is about.

The one gas station in Eden Falls is the sort that only offers full-service pumping. A kid bundled up like Shackleton darts around, popping gas tanks, topping off, running back and forth with credit cards.

I find what remains of a parking space next to their Himalayan snow pile, get out, and order

Stash to stay. Beyond the pumps and the forecourt is a one-story building divided into two parts. To the right, a mini-mart where, in addition to jumbo bags of Doritos, two-liter bottles of soda, and all the ice-melt, antifreeze, and snow shovels I could ever need, I'm hoping to find a copy of this morning's *Gazette*. To the left, bays of jacked-up cars and trucks float above men in dark blue jumpsuits. Country music plays in the background, accompanied by the rev of an engine, the rattle and hum of a torque wrench, and the echo of expletives. The place exudes a heady mix of oil, exhaust fumes, and testosterone. That's when I recognize one of the mechanics coming my way.

"Doc, everything all right?"

It's Drew, Mary's husband. He's wringing some sort of pale cloth in his hands and it's hard to tell where the oil ends and his fingers begin. But hey, the guy can actually speak.

"Thought you were seeing Gillie this morning. Something about an X-ray?"

"Right," I reply. "Of course." Of course I totally forgot that Gilligan the neurotic collie was coming in for an abdominal X-ray. And of course Drew can tell I forgot. "Doc Lewis is expecting him," I lie. "Just picking up a *Gazette*."

Drew gives me the slow-nod treatment, and for a second we both study the fascinating scuff marks on his steel toe–capped boots.

"Sorry about the advertising," he says.

"That's why I'm getting the paper."

Drew looks confused and points toward the gas pumps. "Those ads."

At each of the four pumps, above the price of gas, are glossy posters of adorable and painfully cute dogs and cats imploring their supermodel owners to take them to the best vets around, to Healthy Paws, "For those on all fours." Their Patton phone number is prominently displayed.

"Tried telling my boss . . ."

Though Drew natters on about the merits of supporting local businesses, I'm not really listening because an enormous, brilliant white Humvee has rolled into the lot. The tinted driver's side window powers down, and a voice orders, "Fill her up with premium." I can see two men inside and there's a lot of hand gesturing going on, direct eye contact and flying spittle. The man in the passenger seat is a stranger. The man in the driver's seat is the same handsome devil who held a limp and smitten Amy in his powerful arms the previous night.

". . . anyway, I tried. So we'll hear from you later?"

The guy driving the Humvee certainly could be Italian, in a stereotypical perfect-stubble, man-whore, Lamborghini-driving, *"bellisimo bambini"* kind of way. Is Drew waiting for an answer?

"Right. Yes. Speak to you later."

The mechanic ambles away, shaking his head,

probably thinking he should have gone straight to Healthy Paws.

I'm frozen to the spot, unable to resist the allure of the ugly white whale of an SUV. Obviously the two men inside are fighting, and I'm reminded of something Doc Honey mentioned in her email: real men speak with their hearts, not their hands.

In order to eavesdrop and gather some useful intelligence I start to cross the court, closing in on the Humvee, only to be yanked through one hundred and eighty degrees by the long arm of the law.

"Thought it was you," says Chief Devito, steaming coffee cup in his free hand. "You get anywhere with that trick dog, Hash, or whatever it's called?"

About to correct him, I think better of it.

"No. Nothing. How about the owner?"

The chief puffs out a plume of condensation in disgust. "It's like the guy never existed."

I try not to smile, but Devito reads my pleasure. Then he looks past me, noticing the white Humvee.

"Hey, isn't that the guy I saw out with Amy from the diner?"

I turn around, attempting to look like I don't know what he's suggesting, as the monstrous SUV drives away.

"Funny, 'cause someone told me you two were dating."

The chief raises his cup to me, savoring the last word as he heads back to his truck.

Nothing left but to buy a copy of the *Gazette*, join Stash in the Silverado, and discover what the fuss is about together. I find it on page seven, flashing back to my conversation with a tetchy, combative Dorkin. This explains everything.

Healthy Paws invites you to our
Open House and Free Clinic.
Come see the fucture of veterinary medicine.
Whether you've got a pocket pet or a
Great Dame, your satisfaction is our guarantee.
Free lice and tick shampoo for all
our pet-loving pubic.

The Germans coined the word *schadenfreude*, which means pleasure derived from someone else's misfortune. No one ever said schadenfreude leads to good karma. That's why I shouldn't be smiling, but I am, all the way to The Inn at Falls View.

During my recent nocturnal visit, I never appreciated how classy the hotel looks in watery winter daylight. Elegant might be a better word, the front of the historic building defined by a façade of seven ornate two-story colonnades to create a classic New England porch and deck with views of what was once a spectacular series of waterfalls. Thanks to a rock slide eighty years ago, the "fall" is little more than a trickle of its former self, a forgettable sightseeing opportunity. The inn, however, has clearly put some work into landscaping. If global warming ever kicks in, I could imagine myself in a rocking chair on the deck, sipping on a sweet iced tea, surveying their beautiful gardens. For now, I'll have to make do with spying a row of bright red poinsettias in hanging baskets.

Having noticed a PETS WELCOME sign, Stash and I park the Silverado, and this time the two of us stroll through a dark, expansive foyer, ignoring the wood-beamed ceiling and the cozy allure of a crackling log fire. We cross a football field–sized oriental rug and walk up to the reception desk.

"Cyrus, here again so soon. Need a Bloody Mary?"

Santa Hemingway seems to think I've got a drinking problem.

"No, sir. Stash and I thought we'd bring you a present. And by present, I mean a cure for Henry's nose. By Stash and I, I mean the dog I'm . . . fostering . . . for now."

"Wait. Cure?"

I explain my findings from the slide, the theory about the mouse bites, the reason why the previous treatments failed, and why this one will work. George listens in rapt silence, like there's going to be a test afterward.

"Unbelievable. Un—"

Just as he's about to split the word with what I fear might be a celebratory expletive, a couple of guests walk by and Santa doffs an imaginary cap before wishing them a pleasant day of . . . what? Igloo building? Ice sculpting?

Depositing the package containing the ointment on the reception counter, my hand is snapped up before I can have it back and subjected to a vigorous pumping. Then, as if this level of gratitude simply won't do, George comes around, pinning me in a bear hug, ignoring my stiffness and refusal to offer more than a halfhearted back pat. Stash stares up at me. I wonder if he knows an attack word that might allow me to escape.

"Can't thank you enough," says George, holding on to me at arm's length, his eyes glistening with tears. "Seriously. Hey, that reminds me, you got a minute? There's something I want to show you."

George leads the way through a door behind the reception desk, down another corridor, and into the same room as before, the one with the bank of video monitors.

"The other night you asked me about a white Humvee."

George starts playing with a mouse, pulling up images, consulting a handwritten note on a piece of paper.

"Did your guest find her missing jewelry?" I ask.

"About five minutes after you left. Here it is."

I look at the screen, at a still image from a ceiling camera obviously placed at one end of a corridor.

"I wouldn't normally do this sort of thing, and I don't need to know what this is about, but you've gone out of your way for Henry, so here goes."

George clicks the mouse, and a couple in conversation emerges from a room. The door is checked to make sure it is locked, and then the man offers the woman his arm, the gesture theatrical, formal, like a father offering to walk a daughter down the aisle. The woman takes his arm, the man, looking straight ahead, says something, and the woman's head snaps backward before she doubles over. It's more than laughing—she's breathless: she's cracking up. She's Amy.

"This is the owner of the Humvee. This is Marco Tellucci."

George freezes the image, Tellucci caught in an Armani-handsome pose—almost dashing—wearing a closed-lip smile as though he's so subtle, so amusing, he doesn't need to laugh at his own jokes. In the still, I catch a glint of light from a tear next to Amy's right eye, her brown eye, from laughing so hard.

"They came from room 21, a suite, nice king-size bed. And that's Amy, from the diner in town."

I struggle to make my sharp intake of breath not sound like a gasp. "Looks like they know each

231

other pretty well," I say, striving for disinterest, knowing I come across as aggrieved.

We bid George farewell, and I manage to keep my mouth shut until we're back on the highway.

"I can be witty," I tell Stash. "I may not have his looks or money, but I'm pretty sure there are some women who think I'm amusing."

I glance over at the dog riding next to me. Stash keeps his eyes straight ahead and locked on the road, a gesture I, in my vulnerable state, interpret as him saying, "Dream on, buddy" or "Some women, but not the one you *really* want."

I shudder. What's gotten into me? I'm seeking advice on a floundering love life from a dog. Is it possible my relationship with Amy is over even before it got started? Or, once again, am I simply jumping to the wrong conclusion? Snap out of it. I've come too far to click my heels and mutate back to being a cloistered introvert. There has to be a logical explanation.

I flash to Leonardo DiCaprio in *The Beach*, falling in love with the French girl who already has a serious boyfriend. *When you develop an infatuation for someone, you always find a reason to believe that this is exactly the person for you.*

I mean, it makes perfect sense that Amy might have a suitor or two waiting in the wings, poised to snap her up. As far as I know I'm still a contender.

Maybe it's time to step out of my comfort zone.

If this is the kind of man Amy usually prefers, then she needs to know that there's more to me than meets the eye.

Hanging on to the steering wheel, I fumble for my cell and dial her number.

"Hey, it's Cyrus, where are you?" Careful, too probing. "I mean, *how* are you this fine day?"

"I'm . . . good. What's going on?"

"Nothing. Just driving back from a house call. Hideous nasal deformity in a cat. I . . . I . . . was thinking about you."

"Really. You see a hideous nasal deformity and think about me. You saying I should get a nose job?"

"What? No. Of course—"

"So when are we going to graduate from ice cream to something slightly more . . . romantic?"

What? Is she asking me on a date? And if so, what's with Tellucci?

"You mean no jimmies with rum and raisin?"

"Exactly, but maybe we could keep the rum."

Forward *and* flirtatious.

"Um, that sounds great. How about finally grabbing something to eat at The Inn at Falls View?"

This is where I had originally planned to take Amy on our first date, but the offer gets away from me before I realize this is Tellucci's home base.

She hesitates, eventually stretching out the word

sure and sounding anything but. It's enough to make me *not* ask, "When?"

I can't help but notice how Stash has his head down and neck outstretched. His abdominal muscles appear to ripple. Either he's getting motion sickness or my side of the conversation is making him nauseated.

"You know, I bumped into our resident detective this morning. He says he's seen you out and about with a male model."

Okay, so I made that bit up, but I need to gauge her response.

"Devito's an idiot. Like I said, this was all in the past. Time to stop being so inquisitive, Cyrus, and let it go. I'm serious. It meant nothing."

It meant nothing. Isn't that what adulterers say about casual sex?

"Besides, I hear I'm not the only one working on a new relationship."

It didn't take long for the gossips of Eden Falls to have me sleeping with Winn Honey.

"You still there?"

"Please, relationship is too strong a word," I counter, "and only applicable if prefaced with the word *business*."

I count five Mississippis.

"I meant the black dog, the one belonging to that John Doe. Who did *you* think I meant?"

The laugh on the other end of the line tells me two can play at this game.

"Did you know that in the Australian version of Monopoly, they've replaced the little metal Scottish terrier with a little metal labradoodle?"

"Wow, someone's fallen in love."

I hear a voice in the background.

"Sorry, Cyrus, got to go. Harry's calling. Promise I'll be free one of these nights. So make this dinner date happen, okay?"

She's gone before I can clarify whether "free" means available or liberated. Either way, I'm certain Amy wouldn't want me to ask.

THE DETOUR back to Bedside Manor adds fifteen minutes to our ride. Let's call it clinical research, for there's a particular piece of property I need to check out.

The house stands alone, set way back from the road, and appears to be a fine Frank Lloyd Wright reproduction. This is the home of Trish, daughter to Mavis Peebles, sister (so to speak) of Crispin, the stuffed Labrador.

For half a minute, Stash and I survey the property. Amy's right. I am inquisitive. I'll even accept stubborn and relentless. But there are times when this approach to life can come in handy. And maybe this is one of them.

Back inside the truck, I dig around for two vital pieces of equipment—a snow brush with ice scraper (widely unavailable in South Carolina) and an empty plastic grocery bag.

"Time to test a certain somebody's immune system."

The passenger seat of the Silverado is proof positive that my late father transported a large number of pets. The upholstery resembles a calico seat cover of assorted colors of canine and feline fur. Thick nylon bristles make quick work of gathering a sizeable *CSI* pile of hair and dander that I bag and stuff inside the pocket of my pants.

"And from you, I need a little saliva." I hold out my hand in front of Stash's mouth. "Stash, lick." Nothing. "Stash, lick." Not a flicker in his eyes. Either this is not in his repertoire or, more likely, I'm using the wrong language.

"Stash, pucker up."

No dice.

"Stash, kiss."

The world goes black as sixty pounds of dog leap onto my chest and begin coating every exposed surface of my skin with a shellac of saliva from a serpentine tongue.

"Stash, sit, Stash, sit."

It's as if the feeding frenzy never happened, Stash calm and distant, me dripping drool and panting.

"Good boy," I say, pulling myself together, scraping saliva from my cheek, and rubbing it into both my hands like Purell. "Okay, let's go see who's home."

With a truck lacking a reverse gear, you've got

to love a circular driveway. I park, order Stash to stay, stuff a sticky right hand into the bag-o'-fur in my pocket, and head for the front door. It's open before I can find the bell.

"Can I help you?"

This has to be Lionel—turtleneck sweater, thinning black hair swept back and slick, brown corduroy pants, and plaid slippers. Very cozy. Where's the smoking jacket and the pipe?

Squeezing some fur into my gluey palm, I extend my right hand and rush forward.

"Dr. Cyrus Mills," I say, giving him little choice but to shake, clasping my left hand on top, preventing the quick getaway. "I was in the neighborhood and hoped I might have a word with either yourself or Trisha. Lionel, right?"

"Right," says Lionel, his welcome smile more like a wince of revulsion as he tries to wipe off his hands without me noticing and him seeming impolite. "Is this about my mother-in-law's dead dog?"

"It is."

He seems quite happy for me to state my business while shivering on his stoop. "Perhaps I could come in?"

Lionel still seems unsure, as though he might want to see some sort of veterinary ID or guide me through some radioactive decontamination chamber. In the end he beckons me into a stark mudroom.

"Appreciate you removing your shoes. There's a selection of guest slippers on the shelf behind the coat rack. What are you, size eleven?"

"Ten and a half," I say, stumbling sideways, one boot dangling off my ankle, grabbing his left wrist as I pretend to fall, imparting another snail trail. I make my apologies for being klutzy and find a suitable blue suede pair. Snazzy.

"Do you need to wash your hands?"

I shake my head and offer a manic smile as I wipe my hands down the front of my overcoat. What's gotten into me? Lionel's discomfort is almost invigorating as I follow him into a living room that looks totally unlived in. Two enormous white leather couches face one another, separated by a bare glass coffee table sitting atop a plush black-and-white-striped rug. Three of the walls are an oppressive flat slate gray, void of pictures or photographs, but the entire fourth wall is not a wall. It's a window of sorts, no frame, no curtains, just a single massive pane of glass offering a spectacular wintry view of forests and mountains to the north. It's like staring at a humongous Vermont postcard.

"Nice room," I say, plopping down into the couch, rocking all the way back, wiping my hands back and forth to appreciate the quality of the leather and to spread my allergenic payload.

Lionel is visibly uncomfortable. He sits down on the couch opposite.

"Sorry, Patricia is out. I happen to work from home."

I think I'm meant to notice his wife's proper moniker.

"That's nice. What's your line of work?"

"Marketing. But I'm, well, between jobs for right now. There was something you wanted to discuss?"

I give him the knowing nod, the one that says, "Don't you mean laid off and currently unemployed?"

"Yes, that's right, Crispin. Sorry, but there's something on your face."

I make a motion toward my own right eye, to better direct him toward this imaginary fuzz. Let's see if those allergies to dogs are real.

Lionel's right index finger works the corner of his right eye, depositing a sample dangerously close to the sensitive mucous membranes of his conjunctiva. This is too easy. It's totally unprofessional and possibly murderous (though what would the police charge me with— assault with a deadly hair? I doubt it) but this thing with Amy is making me bold, if not reckless.

"It's gone, it's gone. Must have been a piece of fluff. Yes, I wanted to discuss Crispin, your mother-in-law's stuffed Labrador."

Lionel composes himself, passes a saluting hand through his cultivated but failing crop of hair, and once more tries to sit. I note no hives on his hands or wrists, and he's not scratching.

"What about it?"

"Well, by mending the broken tail I'm worried I'm only achieving a temporary fix."

"Temporary. You think it will break again?"

"I mean it feels like we're not addressing the bigger problem. I know I'm just the veterinarian, my involvement is peripheral at best, but it seems obvious that Mrs. Peebles requires assistance in her daily life. A stuffed dog may offer low-maintenance companionship, but what she really needs is physical, if not professional, help."

"Mavis won't be parted from that dog. We've tried. This house has a separate apartment out back, less contemporary but nice all the same. It's hers if she wants it, but sadly, that dog and I can't be in the same house together, let alone the same room."

Lionel pauses for dramatic effect, and I can tell this is a well-rehearsed vignette. "Deathly allergic to canine dander. I have to carry an EpiPen every time I go out." He sighs, resigned to his sad lot in life.

"Wow, a sensitivity capable of inducing anaphylactic shock. Scary." No puffiness, not a welt, swelling, or hint of a wheeze. I note the corner of his right eye—normal blink, no edema, and no excessive tearing.

"Then, between you and me, maybe it would be

best if I tell Mrs. Peebles I *can't* fix Crispin's tail. Tell her it's time to say goodbye, once and for all."

"No, no, I don't think that's such a good idea."

"But then she could live here. Without an allergy-inducing dog."

"Yes, but think of the emotional upheaval. My mother-in-law is a fragile and sensitive soul. She's very attached to Crispin, and that kind of shock might be dangerous to her health."

"I see. I just thought that . . . well . . . given her physical limitations, this might be as good a time as any to cut the cord. Perhaps she could discover the benefits of a nursing home?"

This time Lionel pretends to ponder the suggestion.

"I'm led to believe they can be pricey," he says, straining to sound cursory, as though he hasn't researched it down to the last penny.

"Extremely. Though my colleague, Doc Lewis, prefers to call it financially crippling. Sold his veterinary practice so his ailing wife could be cared for in a decent facility. All gone. Seventy-three years old and he's having to work for me."

I'll take the recoil of his head on his shoulders as a sign of genuine surprise or concern.

"But what do I know? Ms. Peebles's finances are none of my business."

"Right," says Lionel, though I seem to have lost a part of him, no doubt the "what's going to

become of my wife's inheritance" part. "Well"—
he gets to his feet—"thanks for keeping me in the
loop. I'll be sure to discuss this with Patricia, but
for now, anything you can do to keep old Crispin
limping along will be much appreciated."

He tops off his cloying smile by folding his arms
across his chest, fingers tight and immovable
under his pits, as though he's pretending to be cold
to avoid further contact.

We exchange our goodbyes, and I traipse back
to the Silverado. Though Lionel has stopped short
of tattooing DNR on his mother-in-law's forehead
and warning every eager paramedic "you save her
life, you take her home," his sentiment feels pretty
much the same. Mavis's bunny slippers are not
welcome in his sterile lair. I may not know how
much he needs her savings, but I do know this—
Lionel is definitely not allergic to dogs.

← 14 →

GILLIGAN'S ABDOMINAL X-RAYS ARE
hanging on a white light-viewing box in the
work area; Lewis is sizing them up as if he's
trying to appreciate a piece of modern art that
could have been painted by a kindergartener.

"You just missed them," he says. "I told Mary

242

you'd give her a call once you looked at the films. This your new sidekick?"

I introduce Stash, who sits politely by my side, accepting a pat but otherwise remaining passive. He's like one of the Queen's Guard at Buckingham Palace, stoic and unwavering when on duty.

"He's staying with me till Devito figures out who he belongs to."

Lewis considers Stash, steps over to a nearby cabinet, brushes aside a half-empty box of bandage material, and pulls out what appears to be an old Polaroid camera.

"What you doin'?" I ask.

"Just a minute," says Lewis, framing Stash while the dog keeps his eyes on me. There's a click, a flash of light, and the buzz of fresh film emerging shiny and wet from the camera's base. Lewis grabs the undeveloped image by its matte-white border and begins wafting it back and forth like a fan.

"Put him up on the Wall of Fame. See if anyone recognizes him. If not, someone might want to adopt him. Here you go."

He hands over the Polaroid. Somehow Stash manages to look uncomfortable, awkward, like it's a photo for a mug shot or a school yearbook.

I put it in the breast pocket of my shirt but feel the need to come clean.

"To be honest, I was thinking about keeping him

myself. I know he's a ragamuffin, what with the dreads and the weird clip job around his face. But there's something . . . pathetic . . . about him. The way he's always . . . I don't know . . . on. It's as if he can't relax."

"Huh," says Lewis. "Who does that sound like?"

"I'm serious. He's very smart and responsive to verbal commands. I've tried 'at ease' and 're-lax,' but nothing works."

"I heard you met with his owner."

I finally tell Lewis about the gaunt man's sad request for help. "When I asked what was going to happen to Stash, he said it was up to me. I've no idea what that meant, but this feels like the right thing to do."

Lewis seems to brighten whenever I start getting sentimental. I take it as a cue to clear my throat and get back on task.

"Thanks for taking these." I nod at the black-and-white images of Gilligan on the viewing box.

"No problem, but I'm not sure I've been much help."

The three of us gang up on the X-rays. We're looking at a side shot and a front-on view of a canine belly with all its shades of gray.

"Maybe some more contrast will help," I think out loud. "You want to turn off the overhead lights?"

"Do what?" says Lewis.

"The lights," I say, pointing to the switch, just out of Lewis's reach.

Whether it was the gesture, the phrase, the insistence in my voice, or Lewis's hesitation, Stash trots over to the wall, stands up on his back legs, and with a practiced downward jerk of his snout, we are plunged into darkness.

Though my eyes are adjusting, our silhouettes turn to one another, sharing a tacit moment of appreciation for a talented animal before we turn back to the films.

It's a bizarre pattern of white commas, curlicues, and cedillas littering the film from the collie's stomach all the way through to his colon.

"Dimming the lights doesn't make it any less weird," says Lewis. "I've certainly never seen anything like it before."

I catch Stash turning back and forth between us, following our words like they're a verbal tennis match and he's the ball boy, poised and eager to help out.

"Let's back up. This . . . stuff . . . whatever it is, has to be inside Gillie's guts. And if it's white on an X-ray, it has to be dense enough to impede radiation."

"It could be bone. Chewed up, cracked, and splintered bone."

"Could be, and that might explain why he's losing weight and off his food, but how do you tie in the trembling and the seizures?"

"That's why they came to you, my boy. And now you've got carte blanche to find out."

I'm confused.

"Amy dropped by to see you," says Lewis. "She saw me working on Gillie and insisted I bill her, not Mary."

"She can't afford to do that."

"That's what I thought, but I used a little more tact. She promises Mary will pay her back, but she knows money's tight right now and, more importantly, she knows how much the dog means to her. I'm telling you, that girl's a keeper."

I let my head rock all the way back, eyes reaching upward for heavenly inspiration.

"Do I want to know?" asks Lewis.

"Probably not. See there's this other guy in the picture and—"

"Stop right there." Lewis's hand parachutes down and settles on my shoulder. "You know the most important thing I've learned in fifty years of marriage: honesty—with each other, but also with yourself. So, answer the question—why do you like this girl so much?"

Lewis gives me "the stare." I've seen it before. It's like being injected with truth serum, the way its kind intent makes you want to find the right answer.

"Okay. I've spent the better part of my adult years avoiding emotional risk, making sure I wasn't vulnerable to—"

"Heartache?"

". . . the allure of a beguiling woman. Look, Amy's unpredictable, pigheaded, and dangerously outspoken. But no other woman has ever made me feel that way."

"Then make sure she knows exactly that. If she prefers someone else, she's not the girl for you."

When Lewis shifts into paternal mode, I'm always gripped by trepidation, but here's the thing, these conversations always leave me with a certain calm.

Lewis beams. Lesson delivered, he shouts, "Stash, lights."

I don't know who's the quicker study, the labradoodle or Lewis.

"That really is a neat trick. But to more serious matters. Where are you with Garvey's cow, Ermintrude?"

"I'm working on it."

"And?"

"It could be bad. Real bad. But I'm still not a hundred percent certain."

"Then make sure you are and, no disrespect, I hope you're wrong. What are we going to do about tomorrow's lecture at the Knights of Columbus? Best if we go together. Form a united front."

The thought of having to defend Bedside Manor's antiquated ways to a room full of strangers while I'm getting the third degree from

Dorkin fills me with dread. Give me a root canal or a colonoscopy any day. And let's not forget the guest speaker, Dr. Winn Honey, eager to broadcast how her professional rival hides behind a porn star pseudonym so he can exploit lonely women through online dating.

"You really think I need to be there? I mean, you're the one who packs the waiting room. Eden Falls will be there to see you, not me."

Lewis eases back in his stance, begins to worry his lower lip with that chipped upper incisor.

"Is there something you're not telling me?"

Plenty, I think, feeling myself being seduced by the coward's way out. I could bail on this evening's date with Dr. Honey, drop her an apologetic email and claim I tried but never really felt a vital connection. Which is true. Then, if Lewis flies solo at the K of C, Winn is none the wiser and I get to focus on sorting things out with Amy.

Lewis steps around Stash, the statuesque lion by my side, drifting into my personal space.

"If you're worried about this turning into some sort of confrontation, don't. We're starting to build something special here at Bedside Manor, something authentic. We're not going there to defend—we're going there to flaunt."

His hands reach out to squeeze my triceps while his eyes reach out to squeeze my conscience. What's with the sorcery of a wise old man?

"You're absolutely right. I'll be there." Though I may have a black eye, a red handprint embossed on my cheek, and an ice pack held to my loins by the time I arrive. "What d'you think we should do with the stuff Gabe filched?"

Lewis gives me his best Cheshire cat impression.

"You're not to worry. Think of it as our weapon of last resort."

"Now you sound like Truman."

"Trust me," says Lewis. "I have a cunning plan."

"I mean, the kid hacked into their computer system. That's a felony."

Lewis releases his grip, the letting go almost as dramatic as the latching on. "Which part of 'trust me' don't you understand?"

I smile and excuse myself to call Mary at home, mumbling my way through an unhelpful description of Gilligan's bizarre X-rays, suggesting I drop by to take another look at him in his home environment. I follow up with a call to one of the few people in my phone's contact list.

"Hey, Doc, what up? All excited for your hot date?"

It's Charlie Brown, and I thought, given this time of day, that she'd be in class and I'd leave a message.

"Don't tell me, another gym class."

"You got it. If you're calling for advice, ditch

the cologne—it makes her sneeze. And don't laugh when she says she loves Rod Stewart or that her favorite movie is *Pretty Woman*, and don't ask to see her photo albums."

"Actually I was hoping you could gauge her mood for me."

"Hmm . . . okay . . . different. Definitely different."

"That's not helpful."

"But she is. Sure she's nervous and excited and stressing over every last detail, but there's something . . . different."

"Like what?"

"Like, like she had me check out what she planned to wear, and she puts on this short skirt 'cause she's got, like, great legs, and I tell her it looks too slutty. Instead of reaming me out, she actually listens to me and goes with nice pants. It's like she wants to do this right. It's cute."

This revelation is bad enough, but then Charlie finishes me off with: "I'm really glad. Different for my mom is a good thing."

Perfect, another dilemma to further complicate my love life.

"Will I see you this evening?" I ask.

"God no, I've been told to make myself scarce. I'm hanging out at Gabe's. Pretty cool nailing Dorkin, yeah?"

Gabe, what a blabbermouth.

"Look, you keep quiet about Dorkin, and I'll tell

your mom the Loveatfirstsite.com scam was my doing."

"Why would you do that?"

"Because she needs to know who I really am."

"The big reveal? So soon. Come on, play along for a while, just see what happens. I know you'd be good for her."

But in this phrase I think I hear an unspoken "you'd be good for *us*."

"This is the first date in forever where she's actually planning on wearing underwear."

Whoa, way too much information. "Look, Charlie. I don't want to upset you, or her, but it's not fair to deceive your mother."

Charlie waits a beat. "I totally get it. If this is going to work, you want things to be right from the start."

As far as I can tell, the only thing Charlie "gets" is the misguided and heartbreaking concept of "if my mom is happy, she will be happy with me." Unbelievable. I'm supposed to be dealing with patients who can't (or won't) tell me where it hurts. Instead I spend just as much time helping those on two legs as I do those on four.

"What's happening with Marmalade?" I ask, making a point of changing the subject.

"Not much. Fat as ever but still just as loved by my doting mother."

And there it is, the bitterness in her words

stinging my ear. Fat cats retain unconditional love. But not fat daughters.

"Anything you want to tell me about this, Charlie?"

"Nope. Except in my next life, I'm coming back as a cat."

She hangs up, and I decide the best way to prevent a panic attack over my upcoming revelation to the smitten Dr. Honey is to bury myself in some heavy-duty research.

Whichever way I come at her case, Ermintrude is a disaster. My number one pick for the poor Jersey cow is a disease that still has no blood test and, more importantly, no cure. One quote jumps out at me—"diagnosis means certain death." I think about Trey Garvey's mood swings, clumsiness, light sensitivity, and craving for sunglasses. It all makes sense. If only the connection between Trey and Ermintrude were a leap, a stretch—instead it feels like a logical step, and a short one at that.

In need of a distraction, I switch over to a series of articles on the weird metallic objects dogs swallow (guitar strings, pincushions, razor blades, tinsel, none of which look quite the same as Gilligan's X-rays) and then, during a lull in my attention span, pay a visit to the so-called Wall of Fame.

It's no wonder the Polaroid camera fell out of favor. The wall is a crowded hodgepodge of regular photos and homemade missing posters (I notice the one from last week—Frieda Fuzzypaws, the fugitive golden retriever). But it's the faded Polaroids that draw the eye. Despite the lack of direct sunlight, every canine in question appears to suffer from a severe case of jaundice. With no dates anywhere I can't tell how long the wall has been around, but in the absence of a serial dog snatcher, and given Eden Falls's population of little more than two thousand people, it's been a while.

The photos are arranged in neat rows, right to left. I retrieve Stash's photo and think about clearing a space for him in the middle, at eye level, but it doesn't feel right, altering my father's legacy. Each dog has a number printed on the white space at the bottom of the Polaroid. I guess that makes sense when you don't know the dog's name. I look at the last photo—a miniature pinscher, Lost Dog #41. Even as a still image, Stash comes across as anxious and a little too tightly wound. The man said, "It's up to you," and therefore #42 is staying with me. No need for a Sharpie or a piece of tape to put it on the wall. The Polaroid feels very much at home, back in my pocket.

About to turn away, my eyes settle on an object that's both out of place and eerily familiar. Hand-cut, roughly shaped like a dog bone, it is made from cardboard, with two small holes at each end to accommodate a long piece of string. I flip it over, flip it back, sigh, and smile. It's a sign (possibly in more ways than one) and I knew exactly what it would say, a bold font declaring "OPEN" on one side, and on the reverse: "DOG GONE, BACK SOON" (a witty alternative to "closed," or so I thought). I made it for Dad when I was ten, Mom providing the materials and scissors, and then proudly hanging it in the front door of the clinic. I'm amazed that he kept it, let alone put it on display. Maybe he liked its sentiment, the optimism, the lack of finality. Maybe it was his hope for a lost son. Whatever the reason, I unpin the sign from the wall and put it back where it belongs on the front door.

When I return to my laptop, a gnawing sense of guilt and regret guides me toward my email. This concerns Gabe. Who knew the kid would be such an accomplished hacker? When I asked for his help I was simply gathering information, doing a background check, perfectly reasonable. Now it feels more like an invasion of privacy and, worse still, a betrayal of trust.

I begin typing.

Subject: Abort Mission

Hi, Gabe,
    Please cancel my request for further information as discussed. It will not be necessary. Appreciate your discretion.
C

I press Send and have time to wipe my palms down my face and breathe a sigh of relief before a reply arrives in my inbox.

Subject: Too late!

Hey Doc,
　Already done. See attachment. Otherwise hit delete. Good luck this evening. Don't forget your sildenafil citrate!!!!!
G

Sildenafil citrate—the active ingredient in Viagra (hey, I'm a scientist, I know these things). Not funny, Gabe, not least because of that pixilated paper clip and what lies within its 124KB file.

Click on Delete or double-click the attachment?

Open it up and I'm not just jealous, I'm despicable, insecure. Amy's invasion of privacy is reprehensible. Delete it and I'm naïve, myopic, and deserve to look like a fool. After all, information is power, and, for a scientist, irresistible.

The email sits open, the arrow of my mouse hovering in no-man's-land. In the end, the interpretation of objective data wins over moral willpower and I click on the paper clip.

It's from the Vermont State Archives and Records Administration. It's a digitized copy of a legal document. It bears a notarized stamp, it hails from nearby Burlington, and, based on the date, it was registered some thirteen years ago.

I've stopped breathing, the vacuum inside my lungs amplifying the pounding of my heart.

There are details of witnesses, names I don't recognize, someone claiming to be a justice of the peace, but all I see is the two names at the bottom of the page that are very familiar.

An enormous corkscrew twists around my guts.

Mr. Marco Tellucci in one column, Amy Carp in the other. Groom and Bride. Bride and Groom.

It's a marriage certificate, and even though my index finger keeps clicking the Delete button, the image in my mind refuses to go away.

← 15 →

LET'S SKIP THE DENIAL PHASE AND GET straight to the anger.

"Do I look gullible?"

I like to think I'm simply airing the question, not asking the black canine in the passenger seat for his opinion.

"God damn it," I yell, slamming the steering wheel with my palm for effect. This time Stash glances my way. Though his raised eyebrows are probably the result of being startled, it's easier to interpret their message—"Yes, you look gullible to me."

Calm, Cyrus, calm. Consider the facts. The devil's advocate to my immediate right stares back, my shock, disappointment, and blossoming insecurity eager to give Stash a voice.

"Amy doesn't wear a wedding band."

It's called cheating.

"Amy lives with her grandfather, a man who, by his own admission, barely knows her . . . husband."

Maybe Amy was ostracized, their marriage a rebellious act driven by an irrepressible love.

"Now you're just being combative."

Thank you, I try.

"But what kind of a man ignores a wife nursing a sick relative, a wife forced to work all hours while he stays in a fancy hotel, cruising around in a gas-guzzling tank? Why not help her out, at least financially?"

If she's as independent as you think, she might not want his money. Better yet, she might choose to be his love slave.

A shiver courses through my body.

"Wait a minute. The phone call in the bar, the call Amy *had* to take. I witnessed her reactions and noted her body language. She was genuinely surprised. Marco Tellucci may be her husband, but she hasn't heard from him for quite some time. Yes, and that's why it was important, that's why they've been catching up. The bigger question is where has he been?"

Easy. Serving time in a federal penitentiary for what he did to the last man who went after his wife.

My inner monologue may be on to something, but it's time to ditch all this unproductive speculation. Like my mother, Ruth, used to say when she first got me interested in looking down a microscope: *Keep your mind open; weigh all the possibilities. Let the facts speak for themselves.*

Back at Bedside Manor, I had clung to the most obvious explanation until a computer ping announced a follow-up message from Gabe:

Subject: One more thing!

Hey Doc.
   Before you ask, I already searched for documentation of a divorce. Nothing out there.
G

I'm not sure whether I was more disturbed by this news or the fact that Gabe, a kid I barely knew, correctly anticipated that I would find his attachment irresistible. Do I really come across as shallow, impetuous, and, worst of all, entirely predictable? What has this thing with Amy done to me?

This leaves me with two other possibilities: "separated" or "getting a divorce." Either way, based on the video footage from The Inn, the relationship between Tellucci and Amy appears entirely amicable. The question I keep circling back to is why would Amy warn me off? Why would she want to test my faith in her, to challenge my ability to trust? She must know how much I struggle with these abstract concepts. And I'm not buying reverse psychology, begging me to let it go while secretly wanting me to find out. This may sound painfully naïve, but my best guess is Amy is trying to protect me. But from what? Did she marry into the Mob? Was the guy Tellucci screamed at in his Humvee a hit man?

My hand drifts over to the passenger seat and I watch it go, like it belongs to someone else, an *Addams Family* "Thing" mussing up Stash's poufy haircut. Now I see why some people turn to these silent creatures for comfort and support in times of crisis. No head games, no lies, no pain. I pull back my hand. Is this dog turning me into "some people"?

I glance over at the clock and see it's almost two. I am going to be late for a house call, to check out Gilligan the neurotic border collie. If I keep busy, keep moving, my mind cannot be caught, and there can be no reckoning, no obsessing. This revelation about Amy makes me want to revert to my old ways. Who needs all this . . . mess? Maybe it's time to shut the world out, box up my feelings for Amy, and focus solely on Bedside Manor. Hey, a little flirtation with Dr. Honey tonight may be the perfect antidote. If only Tommy Lovelace knew how to flirt.

We pull up to the driveway of an isolated ranch house—set back among junk trees, plaques of black mold on rotten white siding, ice patches on a roof in need of insulation. Off to one side there's a rusty car on breeze-blocks and next to it, under a tailor-made tarp, what can only be a snowmobile.

"Stash, stay." About to turn the engine off, I change my mind. Can't have the doodle getting cold.

Halfway up the driveway, the collie emerges from somewhere out back, barking, zipping through the snow, darting forward and leaping around.

"Do I look like a lost sheep?"

Someone might benefit from a little attitude adjustment. I'm referring to myself, not the dog.

"Gillie, no, stop that. Sorry, Doc. He'll be fine in a minute. Come on in."

Unlike my visit to Lionel's house, no blue suede slippers for me. I stomp on the doormat and step inside. I never had grandparents growing up, but if I had, this is how I imagine their house would have smelled—a potent mix of boiled cabbage and BENGAY. It's more distinctive than unpleasant, and I remember how this house was once Grandma's house. Mary's traded the riding hood for a red sweatshirt.

"Come on through to the back. Didn't think you'd be by so soon."

Gilligan leads us down a central hallway, and I take note of a formal dining room to my left (six Shaker chairs around a table, Tiffany-style lamp dangling from the ceiling) and a bedroom to my right (queen-sized bed, pink duvet, yellowing floral wallpaper). I enter a galley kitchen with a den and breakfast nook.

I note the peeling linoleum, chipped Formica, avocado-colored appliances. Curious about this retro style, I wonder where they're hiding the orange shag carpet.

"We've got big plans for the place," says Mary, making me feel awful and judgmental.

"Hey, you should see my apartment." As soon as the words get away from me, I realize, in the shock written on Mary's face, I might as well have said, "Don't worry, I live in a dump as well."

"I mean, this place has . . . great bones."

Mary looks as unconvinced as I sound.

"I hope there won't be a charge for this," she says. "It's not like it's my fault you weren't at the clinic when you said."

Back to money. Perhaps I should have just driven around for a while, taken my mind off Amy that way. Besides, impressing her friend seems unlikely to make a difference at this point.

"Sure. Let me palpate Gilligan's belly one more time."

To be fair, Gilligan is much better behaved at home. Oh, he's still squirrelly, running figure eights in and out of Mary's legs before I can latch on, but at least this time I get to maintain the integrity of my eardrums.

"Any more seizures?" I ask as I run my hands front to back, top to bottom, trying to trace the path of the mysterious metallic material lurking in his guts. I should be poking something sharp, something that makes me pull back my hand to discover a bloody fingertip, but Gillie and the divining power of my palpation give me nothing.

"No," says Mary.

"He's been vaccinated for rabies, distemper, right?"

"Of course."

Of course, that would be too easy. Then I notice his teeth, the way the incisors are worn down.

"Is he a rock chewer?"

"Not so as I've noticed," she replies.

Stop staring at me, Mary. I'm trying my best here.

"Did he defecate this morning?"

She hesitates, and I'm not sure if she's searching her memory or confused by the language.

"Bowel movement? Did he go to the bathroom this morning?"

"Yes. Why?"

"Could you please show me where?"

Mary opens the screen door out back and points vaguely in the direction of the tree line.

I excuse myself (as if I'm the one who needs to use the bathroom) and wade out into the snow until I discover a collection of excrement (or maybe I should say an archipelago of frozen tootsie rolls). I'm no expert on dog poop, but it looks pretty normal to me. I bag a sample and slowly head back, running out of options.

"Anything?" Mary asks.

"No."

"Not a clue?"

"No, I have plenty of clues. My problem is interpreting these clues on a shoestring budget. In my world, disease doesn't offer a friendly wave while shouting, 'Hey, check out this clue. It's pathognomonic.'"

"Patho-what?"

"It's a tell, a sign, a revelation that says find me and you will have your answer. Mystery solved. It's great when you find it, but it's rare. Gilligan needs more blood work, urinalysis, abdominal ultrasound. His clinical picture fits nicely with hepatitis, inflammation of his liver, but what's the cause—viral, bacterial, toxic, copper, idiopathic?"

"Idio-what?"

"Idiopathic, it's a fancy way of saying I haven't got a clue."

"Yeah," she says, letting me see the frustration in her eyes. "That's what it sounds like."

I tilt my head to the ceiling, close my eyes, and suck down a lungful of air. She's right. This woman needs an answer that I don't have. She's looking on as her dog refuses to eat, as his ribs stick out, as his waist sucks in, as he thrashes around on his side, helpless and afraid as an electrical storm sweeps across his brain.

"I'm sorry, Mary. I'm not having a very good day, and that's no excuse, but maybe Gillie needs to see a doctor who's a hell of a lot smarter than me."

The sensation is like bile rising to the back of my throat, but I must fight back the nausea and swallow it down.

"I'd be happy to give you a referral. No doubt Healthy Paws in Patton will be able to sort him out."

"That's it," says Mary, hands on hips. "You're giving up?"

I squeeze my lips into a bloodless gray line and nod, avoiding eye contact.

The Clint Eastwood quote crosses my mind. *A man's got to know his limitations.*

"I'll be sure to fax over all Gillie's information, and I'll mail out his X-rays from today. Make sure they don't waste money by repeating what's already done."

I make to leave, glance back, and see Mary busy cradling her dog's head in her hands, whispering the same mantra as me in his ear.

"Sorry, I'm sorry."

Through an oily cloud of smog I make out Stash, face pressed into the Silverado's windshield as soon as he sees me marching down the driveway.

"Get back on your seat," I say, hopping up into the warm cab. I've probably used about a quarter of a tank idling, but it was worth it for a fast getaway. I let up on the clutch and begin to roll forward. Suddenly Stash begins barking his head off. I slam on the brakes, thinking I've run something over.

Don't tell me Gilligan got loose.

But when I turn to Stash to see what the fuss is about, I can see he's barking at the border collie standing in the window. Gilligan must be up on his back legs, front paws on the sill, his rooting snout sweeping heavy curtains off to one side. It's the room to the left of the front door, the dining room.

He stays in the exact same spot where I left him. Standing at the dining room window, waiting for us to come home.

The exact same spot.

I lean over, plant a kiss on the top of Stash's head, and I don't care who sees me.

"Stash, stay. Mary, Mary," I scream, charging up the driveway. "There's something I forgot."

Mary opens the front door, and I rush right past her, ignoring the mat, traipsing snow across the floor, entering the dining room uninvited while she's fumbling for curse words.

This time, in true *Wizard of Oz* fashion, I pull back the curtain. Concealed behind the heavy drape, I discover the answer to my prayers. The elusive pathognomonic clue—the windowsill has been thoroughly gnawed and gnarled by canine teeth.

"What is it?"

The worn teeth—not a rock chewer, Gilligan's a windowsill chewer.

I can't speak, the smile on my face interfering with my ability to form words. Instead I do something wholly out of character for me. Blame the emotional upheaval of the day or the thrill of *not* sending a case to the evil empire. Maybe, most of all, blame the realization, the certainty, that I can do this. There's something tangible about how good this moment can feel. Impulsively I reach my arms around Mary, hugging her so tightly her feet leave the ground as we spin like a whirling dervish.

"What the—"

"It's the paint, Mary. The paint."

"I can see that. The dog's ruined that sill. I told you he gets separation anxiety."

I check out the adjacent window—same thing.

"Old house, you said."

"Yeah, so?"

Suddenly I can see it, the case unraveling, so obvious now.

"Those white flecks on his abdominal X-ray. They're flecks of paint."

Mary tilts her head to one side. "Wait. You said Gillie swallowed something metallic."

"He did," I say. "It's lead paint. Common in an older house. It would have been picked up on a home inspection if you'd gone through a Realtor."

I watch as the wheels begin turning behind Mary's eyes.

"But Grandma left it to us. No inspection needed. I never even—"

"Why would you? It hit me when my dog started barking at Gillie standing in the window."

My dog. How easily that rolled off the tongue.

"Chronic lead poisoning will make you lose weight and lose interest in food. Changes in mentation are common."

Mary frowns. I really need to rein in my lexicon, I mean vocabulary.

"I'm saying it'll make him act weird. Even cause seizures. He waits at the window, gets anxious, chews on the sill like an infant sucks on a security blanket, and gets his daily fix of lead. Gilligan is obviously in the forty percent of lead poisoning cases that don't show basophilic stippling in their blood." I continue to explain. "Little blue dots on his red blood cells—classic for lead poisoning. When you see them on a slide, you've got your diagnosis. But I didn't see them. I ruled out lead when I should have kept an open mind. It was a stupid mistake. I'm sorry."

"Don't be silly. How do we treat it?"

Damn, and I was doing so well.

"I can't remember. Something to do with thiamine injections. I'll look it up. No point in making Gillie vomit. Keep him away from the paint for now, but you need to get rid of it. All of it."

Gilligan has backed up in a corner, watching the show. I can't tell if he's expecting praise for his oral woodworking skills or denying culpability.

"You're incredible," says Mary, smiling before lunging at me with her own version of a celebratory hug. "Amy promised you'd fix him."

This time around I bristle, but mercifully Mary makes it brief.

"I'm calling her," she says, jabbing a finger in my direction. "Amy needs to know she's on to something special."

"I wish, Mary," I say, faking a smile. "I wish."

← 16 →

M Y HEART IS SKIPPING BEATS, MY MOUTH refuses to generate saliva, and there are butterflies the size of bats flapping around inside my stomach. And please, before you label this as cute, nervous excitement regarding my rebound date with Dr. Honey, this is all about dread—tongue-tied, knee-knocking, "I think I'm going to be sick" dread—at the thought of unmasking Tommy Lovelace as her pesky rival from Bedside Manor.

There's a bottle of red wine in the passenger seat where a labradoodle should be. So weird, the relationship between appreciation and loss, the "only realize what you've got when it's gone" syndrome. In part I'm referring to Stash after leaving him home alone tonight. I'm sure he's seated behind the apartment door, head angled up, waiting for my return (okay, I confess, I went back to check and he hadn't moved). But I am also talking about two-timing Amy and the way we never had a chance to see if our sparks could catch fire.

This time there's no pink Jeep parked in Dr. Winn Honey's driveway. Charlie Brown took her marching orders and hopefully went over to Gabe's without the need for a hot fudge sundae detour.

I turn off the truck's engine, reach over to grab the wine, and catch myself in the rearview mirror. Can the man in the reflection go through with this? Maybe a little romance is a good thing: a much-needed escape from Amy and a way of softening the blow for being a vet and not a porn star. According to Charlie, her mother is usually more than willing and able when it comes to dating the opposite sex. I can practically guarantee the patrons of the Miss Eden Falls diner will know I spent the night long before I sip my mug of morning coffee. Dr. Honey is a beautiful woman (the word *hot* should be restricted to temperature). She's intelligent and spirited, but let's face it, I'm struggling for the superlatives that count because compared to Amy, she doesn't have it. She simply doesn't wow me, and I'm pretty sure she never will.

"Be gentle but be clear."

I watch as my reflection winces. "Be gentle?" Please. This woman will go postal the moment I tell her who I really am.

"Okay. Get her drunk, slip it into the conversation, and run."

"Is that you, Tom?" asks the slim silhouette standing at the open front door.

"Yes," I shout, dropping down from the cab and

making my way up the driveway. "Parked on the street because my truck has a problem with reverse. Didn't know if you preferred red or white?"

"Someone hasn't been doing his homework," says Dr. Honey with a pout and a little offended shimmy of her head before smiling, reaching for the wine, and planting a kiss on my right cheek. "It's on my profile. Good to see you again."

I'm slow to let go of the pinot noir for so many reasons. Clearly Dr. Honey's been listening to her daughter's fashion advice—Levi's that show off a waspish waist and long legs, a white cotton shirt, ironed into submission, open at the neck, drawing the eye to an ornate gold necklace and not her cleavage. The effect is conservative yet classy, and it's disarming. No vamp or tramp. Why did I bring wine? It only adds to my deceit. *Confess, Cyrus, here and now, on the stoop.* At the very least I should hold on to the bottle in case I need something to defend myself.

"You okay?" she asks, ultimately snagging the bottle from my hand. "Looks like someone needs a drink. We're in the kitchen."

I follow, wondering if I'm meant to notice the Marilyn Monroe wiggle to her hips, and we arrive at the island soapstone counter. There's a sweating bottle of Chablis, a breathing bottle of Bordeaux, and an assortment of cheeses, crackers, grapes, and cured meats on a Provençal platter.

"Lovely house," I say, remembering this is supposed to be my first visit.

"Thanks. The only good thing my ex had going for him was money. I got to keep it, but the mortgage is a killer on one salary."

Ninety percent of pet owners fight more passionately for pets than money in a divorce.

Dr. Honey shrugs, raises the uncorked bottle of white in my direction, and I nod my approval.

"Your email the other day," she says, beginning to pour, the bottle steeply angled, quickly filling the glass to the brim. I notice the pale lipstick smudge on the rim of her glass—clearly not her first. "You always so . . . formal?"

Stop wringing your hands and cut to the chase.

"Uh . . . I should . . . There's something I have to explain."

Dr. Honey passes me my drink.

"Yes, there is," she says, chinking her glass against mine, a little yellow liquid slipping over the side, before taking a sip (make that guzzle). "The reason I make you nervous."

I begin to mumble, proof positive of her effect on me.

"So . . . um . . ."

In her narrowing green eyes I sense concern tinged with vulnerability. It's too cruel too soon. Better to wait for her blood alcohol content to rise to a more soporific level.

"Do you . . . model?"

She throws back her head, dazzles me with teeth, the muscles in her face relaxing with relief. Maybe I should have hit myself over the head with the wine bottle.

"The photos on the way in? Very observant. No, but that's nice of you. They were part of a motivational plan after the divorce. Weight Watchers and six months with a personal trainer, proof of a before and after."

She leans back against the island, rocking her pelvis forward.

"Before?" I stammer.

Dr. Honey laughs through her nose. "Oh, those are locked away in a safe deposit box."

"And your daughter? No pictures?"

She takes another swig. The glass is half-empty.

"No recent pictures. Let's just say the divorce and adolescence have taken a toll. My daughter's a beautiful girl, but she's not looking her best and refuses to have her photo taken. Please, try the prosciutto. It's from this little Italian deli across the street from work. Really good."

Dr. Honey pops a slice into her mouth and hands me a napkin. I act as though I didn't notice her trying to change the subject.

"So there *is* an upside to working at Healthy Paws," I say, cutting a slice of gorgonzola and thinking, *Hey, if she wants to vent, relieved to unload what might be another useful tidbit of negative information, who am I to stop her before I make my announcement?*

"Hardly. Though, assuming I keep my job, I'm supposed to be in Miami next weekend on the company's dime."

"Wow. Guess they can't be that bad."

"Yeah they can. It's a conference for Healthy Paws veterinarians from all across the country. Held twice a year. Attendance is mandatory."

"What is it, CE?"

She rocks back in her stance, puzzled by my understanding. How would a guy who reviews movies for a living know about continuing education?

I freeze, pretending to wait expectantly for an answer.

"No, it's more like a cult. Total immersion and indoctrination, twelve hours a day for two days. Lectures on how to read the client, how to improve the client experience, how to project empathy, not just sympathy."

"Sounds like psychobabble."

Dr. Honey puts her glass down.

"Shake my hand," she says, "like you're meeting me for the first time."

I surreptitiously wipe my palm across the back of my jeans, and we shake. She seems pleased.

"What?"

"Palm sideways, in the neutral position, eye

contact, and a smile. Mutual respect and genuine friendship."

Clearly these classes are a waste of time. And why is she still holding my hand?

"Watch out if I roll my palm on top. It says I'm a control freak. That's why they call it the upper hand."

I flash back to my first encounter with Dorkin, but manage to catch myself before using him as an example.

Finally she trades my hand for the wineglass.

"The main focus is how to squeeze more dollars out of every office visit. It's brainwashing."

"Will your daughter go with you?"

Dr. Honey flashes me a tight smile.

"Right now, I'm not sure she'd feel comfortable poolside in a bathing suit."

Instead of a response, I tease a grape from its stem and think about Charlize and what really motivates her to overeat.

"Part of me envies those vets in Eden Falls."

I jerk to attention. "Really?"

"Sometimes," she says, crunching into a cracker and washing it down with the last of her wine. I wonder where her tolerance lies and whether she can be an angry drunk. "I'd kill not to have to milk my clients for every last dollar, to not have to see a new patient every seventeen minutes or else. What a concept, taking your time, really getting to know the animals and their owners.

Probably end up making just as much money by earning trust and confidence."

Amazing, she's starting to sound like Lewis.

As she's freshening her glass, I notice the reason behind my first visit to this house.

"What on earth is that?"

My performance may be wooden and hammy, but Dr. Honey follows my pointy finger in the direction of the recumbent feline next to the refrigerator. It's hard to tell where the cat's love handles end and the folds in her beany-bed begin.

"This is my soul mate, the one true love of my life." She clip-clops over and scoops up the panther-sized creature, careful to bend at the knees. "This is my Marmalade."

In her cradling arms, Marmalade's high lipid content seems to take on a liquid state, her dimensions spilling in all directions, impossible to contain.

"Wow. Would it be impolite to ask how much he weighs?"

"Careful, Tom," says Dr. Honey, nuzzling into Marmalade's face but keeping her eyes on me. "You're talking to a woman who used to be 'big boned.' All I'll say is *she's* closer to thirty pounds than forty."

"Slow metabolism? Glandular problem?" I keep the phrase *that's a relief* to myself.

"I wish I knew," says Honey, putting Marmalade back down (I noticed her arms were starting to tremble from the effort). "I've spent a fortune on tests and everything has come back completely normal." Her eyes begin to glisten, necessitating a reviving hand waft to settle her emotions. "What kind of a doctor can't sort out her own cat?"

In the world of real dating this would be deemed a perfect opportunity to put a comforting arm around her. Naturally, I freeze.

"Based on what you just said, the problem can only be too much food and too little exercise."

"Go on," she says, clearly pleased that I'm taking an interest. "But keep in mind I'm the only one who feeds her. I know exactly how much she gets, down to the ounce." Dr. Honey knocks twice on the closed pantry door. "No way she's eating too much food." She steps in close enough for me to smell the alcohol on her breath. "I'm fed up with talking shop. I want to hear something about you and those movies you get to watch for a living."

"Well, it's not really all that exciting."

"Ah, come on now." She loops a stray lock of hair behind her left ear, places her right hand flat on my chest. "Tell me about your last review."

I remember what Charlie said and think about describing the plot of *Pretty Woman*. How far can I get before she figures it out? What if she's amused, embarrassed but thrilled that I made the effort to find out her favorite movie? Once again, I'm still leading her on.

The clock's ticking, and the cougar seems ready to pounce. Without preamble or plan, total desperation has me launching into a perilous stream of consciousness.

"Okay. It was a low-budget, independent film. First-time director working with what was essentially an improvised script."

I drain my glass of wine in two big gulps, Dr. Honey encouraging me with "keep going" eyes.

"There's this . . . single mom, and she's a good person, you know, but she's lonely and she's been hurt. Her teenage daughter has some . . . issues. The kid binges on ice cream because it numbs the pain of abandonment."

"Ugh, this sounds really depressing."

"No, no. It's more like a morality tale. See, there's this unique allegorical character in the mix, a pet cat, and this cat is morbidly obese, yet her mother doesn't care, because no matter what, she will love this creature unconditionally."

She slams her empty glass down on the counter, and I'm amazed that it doesn't shatter.

"Thomas, what's going on here?"

Suddenly, I feel the shift from blurting out thoughts to genuine brainstorming, as the pieces of the puzzle fall into place.

"Please, just give me a minute. It all makes sense. This mother's been hurt, she's in denial, but she knows there's a Prince Charming somewhere out in the world, happy to make her pain go away, a knight in shining armor more accepting of a cute, fat cat than he ever would be of a weak-willed, fat kid."

Flat palm on the chest tightens into a firm grip of my shirt.

"What's this about?"

"I'm getting to it," I plead, trying to back up as I spew sentences. "The plot gets really contrived when this stranger . . . truly, a well-intentioned man . . . gets caught up in the relationship, but by the time the credits roll, it's all good . . . everything gets resolved."

I'm buzzing with the excitement of the discovery I've just made.

"I don't know what you're up to, but you're freaking me out and you should go. Now."

It was the way Marmalade sat patiently in front of the pantry door when Charlie was around, as though the cat knew it would be worth the wait. Not so with her doting mom.

Dr. Honey's furious and visibly creeped out by my performance (who could blame her?).

"Please, I'm leaving and I'm sorry, sorry in more ways than I can say. But the solution lies with why the cat was fat."

"Get out," she snaps.

My upper body makes to leave, but my feet haven't moved.

"Because it was the daughter's fault."

"What?"

"It was Charlie. I suspect she's been overfeeding Marmalade."

"But why?" she whispers.

I take a deep breath because this is way out of my comfort zone.

"I'm guessing she wanted to prove a point. No matter how much she overfed Marmalade, no matter how bloated and slovenly the cat got, you never stopped loving her. Could you say the same about your daughter?"

By the look on Dr. Honey's face, that was as uncomfortable for her as it was for me. She turns away and takes a moment before grabbing a napkin as a makeshift handkerchief. Head down, a subtle rhythmic shudder of her shoulders is the only outward sign of her crying.

"It was Charlie who got me into this," I say, ready to explain everything.

Dr. Honey spins around to face me, tears running down her cheeks, napkin balled up in a clenched fist.

"Charlie?" she says in disbelief.

"I know she meant you no harm. I think she thought I could help."

"I don't understand. Who are you?"

I try to stand up straight, firing-squad stiff, bracing for my punishment.

"I'm Cyrus Mills. Dr. Cyrus Mills. Actually we spoke on the phone the other—"

That's as far as I get. Whatever made me think

I'd be the victim of a well-deserved slap across my cheek? Had I known Winn Honey's personal trainer was big into martial arts and kick-boxing I would have delivered my explanation in an email. Instead I'm dropped, laid out flat by a roundhouse kick to the side of my temple.

Saturday

← 17 →

THE WEATHERMAN WARNED OF A "dusting" of snow in the afternoon, which around these parts means anything less than a foot. That's why I'm hitting the road early, eager to escape a personal forecast that promises lengthy spells of anxiety, bursts of loneliness, and a deluge of self-pity. Rather than brood over last night's thorny encounter with the veterinary equivalent of Bruce Lee and my pending comeuppance at the Knights of Columbus, it's time to make a house call I've been trying to avoid for far too long.

It's not easy steering and changing gears when you've got a bag of frozen peas pressed into your left temple. Still, the swelling from Dr. Honey's karate chop is beginning to subside. I wish the same could be said for the tension between us. Before midnight I received a text from Charlie.

Mom's really mad!

I waited for more, but that was all she wrote. Maybe Charlie's phone was confiscated or maybe she sided with her mom, making me their common enemy.

Stash comes along for the ride. Thanks to Chief Matt Devito, our mystery man with the pacemaker is still John Doe and Stash's provenance remains unknown. Fine by me, and not just because I'm more than happy to look after a homeless Australian labradoodle. It's also that, in light of my recent emotional . . . challenges . . . I am appreciating a straightforward, transparent relationship with a dog.

I pull into Garvey's Nursery and Garden Center and park in the same spot as before, up by the farmhouse, but this time Stash and I walk the trail that leads to the main barn alone. No need of my doctorin' bag. There's no remedy for the message I'm about to deliver.

Before heading out I sat down with Lewis to discuss what I was going to say. I reviewed the facts of the case and tied them to the scientific data I had unearthed, and by the end of my presentation, not only did Lewis buy my argument, he agreed that we had an obligation to go public. Though he offered to join me, I told him this one was mine.

"If there are going to be fireworks," I said, "might as well blame the guy who lit the fuse."

Stash and I pass the outlying greenhouses and the petting zoo, dormant until spring, the clearing where they hope to groom a tubing park, and the snowy silhouette of the mini-golf's windmill. I feel like the heartless demolition man, here to erase the soul of three generations and an Eden Falls institution. Worse still, there's a second unsuspecting victim in this case. That's why I set up a date with the psychotic bovine, Ermintrude, her owner, Mike, and her ailing caregiver, Trey.

As soon as we enter the barn, my nostrils are overcome by the earthy, methane-laden steam heat of tightly clustered animals, my ears are assaulted by a command that reverberates in the post-and-beam heavens overhead.

"Get that dog on a leash."

It's a while before I see the man in the olive green jumpsuit, black beanie on his head, and familiar mirror sunglasses climbing down from a ziggurat of small, square, neatly stacked hay bales, lugging a pair toward one of the stalls. It's a perfectly reasonable request, until you appreciate that I don't have a leash on me and Stash walks to heel like he's the best of show. The doodle hasn't flinched once at the scurrying sheep or the hawking llamas. It's obvious he's totally unconcerned—eyes front, steady gait. Either aloof or bored stiff; it's hard to tell.

"Stash, stay," I command, and, without missing a beat, without turning to check, I keep walking, eyes on Mike Garvey the Third, watching him stop in his tracks, impressed enough to drop his bales and stare in awe.

"Ignore the dog, Mr. Garvey, and the dog will ignore you and your livestock. He's a highly trained dog. He won't be a bother, I promise. Your father on his way?"

Stash stands in the middle of the barn's central aisle, staring at me with perfect tunnel vision. You've got to love this dog. Trey is clearly impressed, and, truth be told, I am too.

Garvey grunts (at least I think it was Garvey and not the Gloucester old spot pig behind him) and marches over to Ermintrude's stall, cutting the orange nylon cord that binds the hay with a penknife and teasing it into mouth-sized wads to scatter in the trough on the other side of the railing. The Jersey stands in the shadows, head in the corner, trembling and disinterested.

"Something came up. He's not coming, and I'm busy," says Trey, brushing past me, nostrils flaring with disdain, returning to the haystack, climbing up and picking off the next layer. Does he hate me, veterinarians, or all human life-forms?

"But Mr. Garvey, you and your father suggested this time, not me."

He hesitates, inhales deeply, releases a throaty growl, and carries on distributing a bale to the goats, another to the sheep, before stomping back to grab more. Trey appears as focused as Stash, but unlike the disciplined labradoodle, obsessive-compulsive demons are at play. It seems this task must be completed before he can chat, and, from the looks of things, the bales are picked off in a precise order to whittle down the stack. No doubt the fodder is delivered in exactly the same order to each of the different livestock every day of the week. Clearly, Trey is a creature of habit.

I wait at Ermintrude's stall, the one nearest the haystack, serenaded by the repetitive coo of squatter pigeons, and try to get a read on the patient.

Cows perform over forty thousand jaw movements every day, but not this cow. She spooks and shudders sideways when I clap my hands. It's heartbreaking to see her xylophone rib cage, her spine craggy and sharp, slack muscle slung across bone, her sunken eyes, feral and beseeching. Then something moves in the shadows next to her, a bird maybe. She flinches, backs up, and I notice a small amount of green discharge forming a crusty halo around her left nostril.

"You still here," says Trey, marching over, palm clasped to his forehead like he's either forgotten something or his headache is back with a vengeance. "Speak to Dad, not me."

"But this concerns you, Mr. Garvey, as much as it concerns Ermintrude."

Trey straightens up, works a grubby index finger into his chin dimple (how does he angle a razor into that cleft?), and then, dipping his head enough to study me over the top of his sunglasses, says, "I ain't no cow."

"Actually cows are eighty percent genetically similar to humans."

Trey gives me a look like that figure might be on the low side.

"Hey, got anything for a migraine?"

"No," I reply, ignoring the déjà vu. "How long has the cow had a nasal discharge?"

Trey says nothing.

I try again. "A snotty nose."

It's hard to tell whether his silence is based on ignorance or irritation.

"Look, I'm no expert on farm animals, but your father asked me to find out what's wrong with Ermintrude. I have a diagnosis, and it concerns you too."

"Why me? I just look after her."

"I realize that, but your diseases are inextricably linked. You have what she has, and vice versa."

"So she's contagious?"

"Not in the way you're thinking. I'm not talking about a bacteria or a virus, I'm talking about an infectious protein, something called a prion."

"Sounds like a type of foreign car."

I'm pretty sure Trey's not trying to be funny. Jaw twitching, hands constantly on the move, shuffling side to side like a boxer waiting for the fight to begin—he's a nervous wreck.

"Prions are tough, really tough, can't be killed by disinfectants, can't be destroyed by normal cooking techniques. You know what scientists call prions?"

I'm not planning on waiting for an answer, but Trey shakes his head all the same.

"Immortal."

He takes a step back, and I know I have his attention. Now, how best to explain?

"I did a lot of research and tried not to come up with this answer. I took my time, weighed the history, the signs, the available diagnostic evidence. But I kept returning to the clinical similarities between you and the cow."

I want to rip off his sunglasses so I can get some kind of visual feedback. Watching my own awkwardness in the mirrors is not helping.

"You both dislike sunlight. Ermintrude presses her head into corners because, like you, she suffers from migraines, and according to your father you've both been acting a little . . ." *Careful, Cyrus.* "A little different. Not yourself."

His stillness has me more worried than his silence.

"You deserve to be the first to know, and either I can talk to your family or you can, whatever you think best, but when I leave here, I will be calling the State Veterinary Board. In a matter of hours, your parking lot will be full of camera crews, reporters, and network helicopters circling the skies overhead."

"Am I about to be famous?"

He seems to have brightened.

"In a way, yes. See there's only been one other

case like this in the entire United States and that was over a decade ago. It cost the American Beef Industry billions in lost exports. And that case originated in Canada as well."

"Canada?"

"Ermintrude's mother. She was imported from Canada, right? Started acting strange, slaughtered on the farm, and, as your grandma told me, 'Nothing went to waste, nothing.' Ermintrude's mother was patient zero, the source of the prions, the infected proteins. Some of her tainted body parts must have gotten into the food chain, a chain thankfully confined to your family and your livestock. I don't know whether your juvenile diabetes put you at greater risk, and I'm not sure why you would be immunocompromised, but you and Ermintrude must have consumed contaminated beef. Nothing would have happened for years, the prions lying dormant in your brains, waiting for their moment, taking their time, starting off slowly, causing a little depression, mood swings, a little clumsiness, working their way up to relentless migraines that laugh in the face of Advil. But they're immortal, remember, they cannot be stopped, and in a little over a year from the time of diagnosis, they'll . . ."

"They'll what?"

I swallow. For all the tens of thousands of cancers I've diagnosed during my career I've never been the doctor who delivers the bad news, forced to witness the crippling power of a few well-chosen words. I'm led to believe there's an art to it, a need to cut to the chase.

"They'll kill you. You might live with the disease for a year or so, but it's always fatal."

He should be hearing this from his family physician, not the new vet in town.

"Enough already, what have I got?"

"Trey, I'm sorry, but I'm pretty sure, not one hundred percent, but high nineties—"

"What?" he screams.

"Mad cow disease," I blurt out, causing him to rock on his heels.

"Whoa, whoa, wait a minute." Trey appears lost in a recollection, his face hardening into a frown. "You're a hundred percent certain that the only way I could have gotten this disease was by eating Clover?"

"Correct," I reply. "I'm afraid so."

The guffaw he releases comes from deep within; uncoiling from a titter to a boom, hearty and genuine, causing him to double over, stagger backward, and pick himself up.

This is not the reaction I was expecting.

He removes his glasses, and for the first time I see his eyes—hazel, bloodshot, and wet. Catching his breath, Trey wipes away tears with the backs of his hands.

"I'm a vegetarian, Doc. Have been since my freshman year at college, a year before Clover died. Never ate beef since. I can't speak for Ermintrude, but if she and me have the same thing, it ain't mad cow."

As I stand there, feeling as dumb as I must look, watching his eyes transition from relief to indignation, an enormous bird poop, sloppy and flecked with green, splashes on the center of my forehead, a milky bindi dribbling down my face.

Trey loses it, gasping for air, at risk of peeing his jumpsuit.

Fortunately I'm carrying a handkerchief.

"Should have worn a hat, Doc. Still, supposed to be good luck." Then he winces, driving his fingertips deep into the bridge of his nose, as if stabbed by another round of sinus pain. The Trey that comes back is exasperated and ready to explode.

"You'd best go before I start to think about how my dad's spending good money on an animal doctor who wants to give his son a fatal brain-eating disease."

"Now, Mr. Garvey, I never meant to—"

Spittle hits my face before the shriek reaches my ears. "I said go."

I take a step backward, determined not to wipe off the spritzed saliva on my chin, and look over at Stash. He's not moved, but he has changed his focus. His head angles up, checking out the birds perched on the rafters above. I follow his gaze up to the hundreds of pigeons roosting in the beams.

The Gloucester old spot pig waddles over to the railing—*white with big black spots*. The black dog in the aisle—*not a single white splotch anywhere.*

Pigeons. Pooping pigeons. But where, exactly, are they pooping?

Without saying a word I march down to the other end of the barn and slowly work my way back, checking out the stalls and the flooring for traces of avian fecal matter. And then, though I'm a little slower than Stash, I see what's been going on.

"Please, Mr. Garvey, just answer this question and then I promise I'll leave. When you feed Ermintrude, do you follow the exact same routine as I witnessed today?"

Trey growls but his reluctant shrug makes me press on.

"You feed Ermintrude first, right? She always gets the top, outer layer of hay?"

"Yeah."

"And the other livestock gets the deeper layers, not outer bales, always deeper."

"What's your point? I like to keep things neat."

"My point is you're feeding Ermintrude hay that's covered in pigeon droppings. The bales from underneath are protected by the top layer that always gets fed to Ermintrude because she gets fed first."

"And what, there's a Prius in the bird poop?"

"No, not a prion, a fungus. Coccidioidomycosis.

You can inhale it into your lungs or your sinuses, and then, if you're unlucky, it can work its way into your brain. Damn! That's why she's got the snotty nose. That's why you've got the migraines, the sensitivity to light, and that's why you're a little clumsy."

Trey appears taken aback.

"That's why you failed a sobriety test even though you tested negative for alcohol."

"I told Devito I never smoke pot, but he wouldn't believe me."

In the moment it takes Trey to relive his encounter with the chief, I glance over at the cow, meeting her big brown eyes and wanting to apologize. This is not about my failings as a farm animal vet. This is about manipulating the signs to fit a concept floating inside my head. This is about humility, my misdiagnosis as stupid as my correct one was inspired.

"This cocci-whatever, it's not going to kill me, is it?"

"No, but you need to be on the right medications. Get over to the emergency room in Patton, tell them you want to be tested for . . . Forget it, I'll write it down. Here, if you're positive, we'll treat Ermintrude the same way. Oh, and you're going to need to get rid of your pigeon problem. No more photo ops with the bird feed, okay?"

If I'm expecting a smile or a grateful handshake,

it never comes. Hopefully those social miscues can be corrected. Then again, who am I to talk?

"How much?" asks Trey, suddenly dead serious, sunglasses back in place like he's ready to play poker.

"Forget it. I'm sorry I screwed up. After the mental anguish I put you through, there's no charge for the visit."

Garvey twists his lips off to one side. "No, no," he says, shoving a thumb over his shoulder in the direction of Stash. "I'm asking about the dog. How much do you want for her?"

Stash held his ground the whole time. Twenty yards away and we still have direct eye contact. He's like a diagnostic talisman—first a collie, now a cow.

"Sorry, Mr. Garvey, but you couldn't pay me enough. The dog is not for sale."

← 18 →

AS I ROLL INTO THE PACKED PARKING LOT of the Knights of Columbus Banquet and Reception Hall I'm greeted by an illuminated sign that claims this facility is PERFECT FOR PARTIES, WEDDING ANNIVERSARIES, AND FUNERAL LUNCHEONS. Given my present state of mind, all three options sound anything but "perfect." Obviously I'm not in a party mood (okay, I rarely am), and if Amy's celebrating thirteen years of marriage to her Italian lover (it's lace and yes, I looked it up) you can count me out. Also, two forty-five in the afternoon seems a little late for lunch. So what does that leave me with? That's right, a funeral, and though I'm sure Dr. Honey would love to bury me alive, the only practice headed for that big clinic in the sky is Healthy Paws.

I park next to a miniature version of the Andes plowed into the back of the lot (turns out the forecast was right—just a dusting) and watch as the new converts to the Church of Healthy Paws stream from their vehicles and march to the main entrance, eager to hear the gospel from the new testament of veterinary medicine. To be honest, I hope Winn Honey can deliver a decent sermon. Yes, I know this sounds strange for a man who still winces when he probes the swelling above his left eye, but the way she's handled her daughter since the divorce seems more misguided than heartless. Born of hurt, it's no better than me abandoning my late father. I can do penance, but I can never truly achieve forgiveness. Winn Honey has a chance, and I wish her well (which is not the same as wanting to get within range of her hands or feet). I did my bit solving Marmalade's weight issues. Everything else—parenting techniques, abandonment issues, a quest for redemption—is *way* beyond my job description (and comfort zone). If I started a conversation, Charlie and her mom can finish it on their own.

I didn't know what to wear for this event, but I went with one of my father's tweed jackets and matching wool ties. It feels a little forced, a little too gentleman farmer, but at least I look presentable.

Once outside the truck I'm assaulted by a whipping wind that cuts and slices like a scalpel, drawing tears as I head for the door. The last thing I need is to look like I've been crying. Fortunately I don't recognize anyone as I dab my lids with a handkerchief until the infamous Ethel Silverman rounds the corner with her husky, Kai, in tow. I flash to the poster for this event, the one outside the diner—"Dogs Allowed*." I never did find out what that asterisk meant—behaves well with others, vocally restrained, unlikely to defecate indoors? Perhaps I should have brought the labradoodle. It's obvious Stash hates being alone. His parting expression, indelible, caught in the split second before I shut the apartment door between us, was more than sadness, it was disbelief, unable to accept the fact that he's out of a job, that I, the master he serves, don't need him.

I slow down, giving Ethel and Kai a chance to make their entrance, and then, heart pounding, on a deep breath worthy of a free diver, I step inside.

The hall is just that, a grim, airplane hangar of a room with weak fluorescent lighting struggling to permeate the gloom of windowless, wood-paneled walls. It's deceptively crowded because everyone has gathered at this end, so as soon as the door closes behind me I'm forced to bump, squeeze, and apologize as I try to move forward and get my bearings. The steady drone of conversation never wavers in the tight circles of talking heads, and I notice the occasional dog on a leash or cradled in an arm. It seems the congregation has been corralled to make room for neat rows of metal chairs in front of a podium and projector screen at the far end of the hall. No one seems keen to take a seat.

Scanning left and right, striving for curious not furtive, I catch a glimpse of Doris's yellow beehive, bemoan the fact that this is my best (only) social option, and then, to my relief, spot Peter Greer, the editor of the *Eden Falls Gazette*. At six-five, Greer is a skyscraper of a man, head and shoulders above the masses. I can't see who he's with, but since he's a proven Bedside Manor ally, that's where I'm headed.

Then she comes at me as a neon pink blur, a girl in a gaudy scrub shirt sporting hair bleached to the point of whiteness and gelled into a stiff crown of daggers.

"Canine, feline, or exotic?" She smiles (sincere but manic), and shakes three gift bags in my face.

"I beg your pardon?"

"You got a dog, a cat, or somethin' fun like a sugar glider or a chinchilla?"

I take in the Healthy Paws logo on her breast pocket and the plastic name tag above it—Popcorn—ah, their perky receptionist. If I were going to name a girl Popcorn, and I never will, this is precisely how I would hope she'd turn out. Her eyes are poached-egg-white wild, lips twitching with anticipation, effervescent to the point of bursting. She must have Red Bull for blood. Right about now, Doris is looking pretty good.

"A dog," I say, and with that moment of acknowledgment comes a surprising awareness, best described as delight. This brief warm-and-fuzzy sensation is quickly extinguished as a gift bag bearing the picture of a frolicking Lab puppy gets shoved in my direction. I peek inside and glimpse a bottle of flea shampoo, a Healthy Paws refrigerator magnet and bandana, and biodegradable poop bags in a bone-shaped dispenser.

"Thanks," I say with a polite smile, "but I'll pick it up on the way out." I have no intention of doing so.

Popcorn offers me a "suit yourself" shrug and zips off, presumably for a double espresso refill.

As Greer sees me coming, the crowd parts,

and in the shadow of his eclipse I see he's in conversation with none other than Lewis.

"Ah, ready to do battle, Dr. Mills?"

Greer reaches out and crushes my hand (I'm sure this is not meant to be intimidating), while Lewis takes control of my free shoulder with his usual death grip.

"Bring it on," whispers Lewis. "We can give as good as we get, and besides, we have home-field advantage."

I try to smile back, to be buoyed by Lewis's confidence, but the muscles around my lips and eyes betray me, twisting into a silent plea for mercy.

"Ladies and gentlemen, time to take a seat and let the fun begin."

I recognize the voice, the authoritative yet chummy tone, like he's introducing a fairground attraction. Over on the far side of the room, I make out the man himself, Dorkin, and next to him, in a smart business suit, none other than the Jackie Chan of Patton, Dr. Winn Honey. Fortunately neither of them seems to have noticed my presence.

"Excuse me, gentlemen," says Greer. "Mr. Dorkin has asked me to join him down at the front. Seems he has a bone to pick with me over the ad we ran the other day. Don't know what to tell him. Either my copy editor is an imbecile or a japesome wag." He raises his eyebrows at me, but to Lewis he conspicuously double-pats the breast pocket of his overcoat before drifting away.

"Do I want to know what that was about?" I ask.

Lewis grins. Today's bow tie is blue with a repeating pattern of playing cards and sharks. The symbolism is obvious—a card shark—a person who uses skill and deception to win. What has he done now?

I get the full upper-arm-squeeze, pep-talk treatment. "Dorkin found me before you arrived. He's going to give you a chance to say a few words, but I can tell he'd rather put you on the spot. If he tries to push your buttons in front of this audience, be yourself, be the doctor who has a passion for animals."

"Yes, but strictly speaking my passion is for the diagnosis, the thrill of solving a medical mystery. I mean, the pets are okay but, well, the owners, they just tend to get in the way of—"

His fingers find the ulna nerve as it crosses my elbow, their squeeze triggering my "funny bone." "Easy, Cyrus. Best leave the passion for pets and people to me, but Dorkin's sure to pick on you because Bedside Manor is your business. Don't waffle. Keep it brief. No one remembers a drawn-out, complicated response. Only brevity can deliver a knockout punch."

Why do I feel more scolded than inspired?

"You really think Bedside Manor can go head-to-head with Healthy Paws? Handle this level of scrutiny?" I wonder, suddenly unsure.

"Absolutely," says Lewis, but I pick up on the subtle quaver hidden in his vowels.

I'm reminded of *The English Patient*, the sandstorm scene where Kristin Scott Thomas asks Ralph Fiennes if he thinks they will be all right.

Yes. Yes. Absolutely.

Yes is a comfort. Absolutely is not.

"I'll be up front, with Greer," says Lewis. "You and I sitting together, not right, looks weak."

I could argue that together we demonstrate solidarity, but he's gone before I get the chance. I'm guessing there must be a hundred and fifty people in attendance, a good showing for a Saturday afternoon, with most folks drawn to the front. I notice a guy in a camo jacket on the aisle seat of the last row, a German short-haired pointer on one side, and at least four goody bags stockpiled on the other. Something tells me he won't be staying for long. I come around, slink into an empty back row via the side, and settle into a seat, nice and low. With plenty of space up front I'm a little surprised when someone plops down next to me.

"Hell-o," says Amy, bumping my elbow, acting all—dare I say—chipper to see me.

Involuntarily, I develop an acute case of tetanus, the muscles of my body stiffening, my spine turning rigid. I grunt a reciprocal hello.

"What's wrong with you?"

My mind jams with our last conversation, Amy shutting me down for being, oh, I don't know, a little curious about a man who turned out to be her husband.

"Nervous for your girlfriend's speech? You think she'll get annoyed if I sit here?"

Though she makes the question sound serious enough, mischief sparkles in her blue and brown eyes.

"What happened to the side of your head?" She prods an index finger into my temple before I can speak, causing me to flinch and suck saliva between clenched teeth.

"I slipped in the shower."

She stifles a laugh. "That's the best you've got? 'Cause I'm leaning toward lover's spat."

"We are not lovers," I snap, loud, insistent, and, unfortunately, the only voice in a room that suddenly went quiet. Everyone turns in our direction, Amy managing to join the masses with an overplayed look of surprise. From the podium, Dorkin picks me out, and, keeping his eyes on me, says something to Honey, who's standing by his side.

"Someone's in trouble," Amy says, barely moving her lips.

"She's not my . . . girlfriend," I whisper, facing forward, my cheeks still radiating atomic heat.

"Hmm, you might be right. Her death glare is

clearly aimed at you, not me. I'm sensing animosity, not jealousy."

I turn and take in Amy's profile as she fakes anticipation, like a kid eager for the show to start. Such long eyelashes. Why is she here and acting all . . . frisky?

Time to shut her down.

"Shouldn't you be brushing up on your Italian?" I ask.

She jerks back to face me, aghast.

"What do you know, Cyrus?"

"Nothing much. A name. A country of origin."

"Best keep it that way," she says, adding, "*non essere un cretino*," in a perfect Italian accent.

Dorkin interrupts before I can get any more information out of Amy. "Wow, what a fantastic turnout. Obviously the pet lovers of Eden Falls know the value of veterinary care, and at Healthy Paws, our veterinary care is remarkable. State of the art, open twenty-four/seven—fantastic value."

"If he keeps this up I'm going to puke," says Amy behind a cupped hand.

"But I'll get my turn later. Right now, it's my great pleasure to introduce Dr. Winn Honey, one of *four* veterinarians working at our *conveniently* located Patton office. Dr. Honey graduated from the University of . . ."

Honey bows her head, hands clasped together in front as Dorkin proudly rattles off her credits and achievements.

". . . and, last but not least, compared to Doc Lewis and Doc Mills, she's a whole lot easier on the eyes, am I right, gentlemen?"

If the gentlemen of the room agree, they keep it to themselves, and though Honey smiles, like no doubt she's had to so many times before, the sexist shot garners an indignant murmur, not a receptive laugh. She must have spurned Dorkin's advances in the past. That's why he's got it out for her.

There's a round of applause as Honey takes the podium and Dorkin settles into his seat in the front row, Lewis on his left, Greer on his right. The overhead lights dim, and up pops the first slide of a PowerPoint presentation: *Practical First Aid for Your Pets.*

"Thanks, Guy, for that . . . generous . . . introduction. And for all the women in the room, be grateful you didn't have to work with him *before* he completed his sexual harassment training."

"Whoa, snap," says Amy, over pockets of applause. "I can see why you like this girl."

But I'm not clapping; I'm staring at Dorkin. Lewis and Greer might have to hold him down. Why would Honey go straight off script and defy her boss?

"So, what follows is meant to be practical and easy to remember. Don't worry, there's no quiz at the end. Here are some of the most common emergencies you might face."

The audience oohs and ahhs over the picture of a forlorn basset hound puppy with a fiberglass cast on his front leg adjacent to a bulleted list that includes: fractures, open wounds, choking, heatstroke (not much chance in these parts), insect bites and stings, household poisons, and seizures.

Three more slides in, and it's clear that Dr. Honey is a gifted and effective orator. Nice pace, informative but entertaining slides, lots of direct eye contact. She's everything I am not in a public speaker. The audience is receptive, and I can see Dorkin relax and settle back into his seat as though he might be able to forgive her earlier indiscretion.

Twenty minutes later, my eyes slide over to Amy and she reciprocates, smiles, and goes back to the talk. But I keep staring. She seems so at ease, the . . . wife . . . who capsized my world. What a fool I've been to think that this funny, edgy, beautiful woman would be interested in me. Her choice of a man—no, husband—with his vanities, should tell me all I need to know. If this is her taste, she was always going to spit me out.

"What?" asks Amy, eyes forward, locked on the next slide.

"I, um, wanted you to know I didn't mean to find out about Marco Tellucci," I mumble. "It was an accident. George from the inn was reviewing some security video and—"

Amy raises a hand to silence me, leans in, her lips brushing my ear. "Cyrus, you can be the smartest person in the world—and the dumbest. You of all people should know everyone has baggage."

She takes my hand, gives it a squeeze, and leans back in her seat.

I'm speechless. Do all women speak this cryptic language that men like me cannot understand no matter how much they wish to learn? I've been wallowing in self-pity about having been one-upped by the Italian. I've seen the marriage certificate. It's fair to say a marriage is a little bit more than "baggage." What am I missing here?

Ten minutes later, as Honey gets to her conclusions slide, she has her first moment of hesitation, fumbling through her notes as though she's lost her place. It takes me a moment before I realize what's happened. Charlie Brown tiptoes down the row to take the empty seat on the other side of me.

"Hey, Doc, thought I'd come for the fireworks. Offer some moral support."

I introduce Charlize to "my friend" Amy and make a point of clarifying that Charlie is Dr. Honey's daughter.

"That's quite a shiner," Charlie whispers.

"I'll live," I say. "How are things between you and your mom?"

Charlie frowns, rolls her hand from side to side.

309

"Better. She made me come home, and we talked till two in the morning."

"You should know the evidence for the cause of Marmalade's obesity was entirely circumstantial and . . . well . . . postulating why it happened was . . . just a guess and . . . very unprofessional. I'm sorry if I—"

"I'm glad. It was time she knew. I wanted her to solve the problem; I wanted her to see what was staring her in the face. It's too bad you and mom didn't hook up."

I can tell Amy's listening.

"I should never have gone along with your dating scam. I only did it to get the inside scoop on Healthy Paws. That's all." And then, to test my theory, I add, "Besides, your mom's too attractive for me. I prefer a woman who's more plain, even homely."

The pain in my left shin tells me I was right.

"But guess who's going to Miami next weekend?"

I turn full on to Charlie. She's genuinely excited, and more than I might expect for a girl hoping to get a tan or sneak an alcoholic drink poolside. I reckon she's thrilled to be getting a chance to bond. Good for her. I wish I'd been smart enough to take the same chance when my father was still alive.

Dr. Honey puts down her laser pointer and says, "So . . . yes, I think, yes, that's the final slide."

Dorkin steps forward, clapping his hands as he

310

heads to the podium, encouraging the audience to join him in a show of appreciation.

"If we could have the lights up, Dr. Honey will be happy to take questions, and I encourage our colleagues from Bedside Manor to join in the discussion." And then as a calculated after-thought, "Assuming they wish to do so."

Dorkin directs his most insincere gap-toothed smile at Lewis and then me.

Almost immediately, Ethel Silverman is up on her feet.

"Thank you, Doc, for all . . . that . . . but what I want to know is why you and your fancy hospital are trawling for business considering Eden Falls already has a perfectly good veterinary practice."

I don't know whether to hug Ethel or scream at her. Talk about cutting to the chase.

"Well," says Dorkin, lighting up, "perhaps Dr. Honey would be kind enough to start us off."

It's as though Dorkin just downed Popcorn's stash of speed, virtually salivating at this gift. It's the perfect opportunity for Honey to deliver a coup de grâce, to make her audience bask in the tender caress of Healthy Paws while spurning Bedside Manor as they would spurn a rabid dog.

Winn Honey takes her time, looking not at Dorkin or Ethel, but out, to the back, to Charlie and me.

"Great question, and one that could only come from a client who's incredibly loyal to Bedside

Manor. See, we can try to compete, bully it, or buy it, but that kind of loyalty is about connections, personalities, a gut feeling between people and between people and animals. Healthy Paws has the toys, the fancy bells and whistles, we can run every test and provide every treatment option, but at the end of the day, what matters is how your practice makes you feel. Do they listen? Do they care?"

She waits a beat, but then her eyes target Charlie.

"As a doctor and as a mom, for far too long I've been guilty of valuing appearance over substance. It's bad enough to look and not really see, but it's far worse not bothering to look at all."

I catch the glint of a fat tear rolling down Charlie's left cheek.

"So let me answer this way. The reason we're here is to let you know you have a choice, and choice is a good thing, but choose to look, to ask, to dig, and please, dig deep, because what counts, what really counts, you won't find floating near the surface."

Ethel looks perturbed, whereas Dorkin looks like his head is about to explode.

"Yes, but to your point about choice," says Dorkin. "By definition you are making a comparison. Shouldn't we talk about what's on offer? Dr. Mills, perhaps you'd like to say a few words. Dr. Mills?"

Everyone turns my way, and the moment I have been dreading has finally arrived. I get to my feet, say, "No, I think Dr. Honey summed it up perfectly," and sit right back down. From the front, Lewis nods his approval—not exactly a knockout, but definitely brief.

All eyes turn back to Dorkin.

"Well . . . okay . . . but I'm sure Dr. Honey would love to tell us about some of the—"

"Actually I'm good. So, if that's all the questions, Healthy Paws thanks you for coming, wishes you and your pets the very best of health, and please, grab all the freebies you can on the way out."

There's another round of applause, the audience stands, and it's hard for me to see what's going on up front.

"What have you been up to, Dr. Mills?"

The question comes from Amy, who, like me, waits in the back row, letting the room clear enough to watch the action unfold. It's not exactly a silent movie, given that the melo-dramatic piano soundtrack has been replaced by the babble of people and the occasional canine yip, but it's obvious who's the villain and who's the heroine.

"I'm not sure," I reply as Dorkin jabs an index finger in Honey's face before pointing toward the exit. That's when Lewis steps between them, his habit of close talking finally coming in handy, as

Dorkin is accosted by Greer and served with a mysterious document.

"Oh no he didn't—"

"Didn't what?" asks Amy.

I don't reply, imagining Lewis in his card shark bow tie, prepared to use skill and deception to win, handing over the confidential spreadsheets to Greer. I see Greer's double pat over his breast pocket, their unspoken exchange that said, "Only if things get ugly."

"Didn't what?" Amy insists.

I shush her even though I can't hear a thing as Dorkin shoves the papers away, turning to leave as they flutter to the floor. Greer ignores them, reaches out with a big hand, and yanks, Dorkin spinning around, visibly shocked by the assault. For a second I think we might be in for a skirmish, but Greer has him by the lapels of his suit, lifting up, forcing Dorkin onto his tiptoes. I watch as the manager's body goes limp, hands thrown wide open in surrender. Greer releases his grip, rounds up his evidence, and hands it over.

The English editor has his back to me (I hope he's saying something facetious like, "Someone's in a spot of bother"), but I have a great view of Dorkin, eyes flitting back and forth, the recognition of being caught in his deceptions causing him to buckle at the knees. The Dorkin who addresses Greer is quite different—grievously wounded, submissive, and possibly begging for his life.

"If you don't tell me what's going on I'll—"

"I'm not entirely sure," I maintain, distracted by the way Greer whispers in Dorkin's ear, producing vigorous acquiescent nods from the Healthy Paws office manager. Whatever passed between them, Dorkin appears inordinately grateful and in a hurry to leave, storming up the aisle and past us toward the exit. "But it looks like it's all good."

A fist pummels my left upper arm.

"You are the most annoying, cryptic man I've ever—"

"He is, isn't he?" says Greer to Amy, suddenly next to us and looking pleased with himself.

"What did you do?" I ask, sotto voce, pulling him aside.

"All fine and dandy, old boy. Lewis insisted I only use your . . . discovery . . . as an insurance policy, just in case. When Honey went off message, I couldn't stand by and watch her career go into free fall. I made Dorkin an offer—to make *this* go away, *you* go away. No one knows about the embezzling of funds, Healthy Paws backs off Eden Falls, and Doc Honey gets to run the Patton office the way she wants it run."

"And Dorkin agreed?"

"What choice did he have? The only person who lost out is me. First decent scoop in years."

Greer winks at me, nods a chivalrous "good afternoon" to Amy, and follows the stragglers out of the hall.

Amy has her arms folded across her chest. I jump in before she can say, "Well?"

"We blackmailed Dorkin to make sure Doc Honey kept her job."

She appears totally unfazed by this revelation.

"Huh, see, wasn't so hard. But then you've still got competition?"

"What?"

I'm not really listening, preoccupied by the action up front: Doc Honey, arms wide open, rushing over to embrace Charlie Brown. They bury their faces in each other's shoulder, their grips tight.

"You're smiling, Dr. Mills."

"Sorry?"

I turn to face Amy, and she's looking up at me with those hypnotic heterochromic eyes. The rest of the room—and all its intrigue—falls away.

"Perhaps I've misjudged your Dr. Honey," she says, a smile toying with her lips, "but sometimes it's easy to bark up the wrong tree, if you know what I mean."

I can't tell if she's talking about herself or me. Is this flirting or taunting? What married person acts this way? This whole thing doesn't sit right because there's obviously something between us. I can tell I still have a chance.

"So, this might be a little last minute for a woman with your hectic social life, but how's tomorrow night for . . ."

My sentence trails off as soon as I see the change in her eyes.

"Look, Cyrus . . . right now . . . I can't," she starts.

I don't even let her finish. I raise my hand in defeat; it's time for this roller coaster to stop because I need to get off.

I turn and head for the exit, trying to extinguish the hope that Amy will call my name.

No need to worry. She never does.

Sunday

← 19 →

THERE ARE TWENTY STATES IN THE union, including Vermont, where there are no regulations regarding dogs riding loose in the back of your truck. If the dog falls out on a fast corner, you might get a ticket for failure to secure a load, but for the most part, legislation hasn't caught up to children, let alone pets. That's why I'm not too worried about Crispin, snug under a fluttering nylon tarp secured by bungee cords to the flatbed. Not that he's going to bark or complain about the cold.

My cell phone rings.

"His name's Seth Pickrell," says Lewis, sounding mighty pleased with himself. "Your mystery man. Stash's owner."

"How?" I ask. "And more importantly, does Devito know?"

I can't hide the element of panic in my voice. Does this mean I'm going to have to return Stash?

"Don't think so," says Lewis. "And I'm pretty sure I've covered my tracks. I got to thinking about what your doodle can do and came across this nonprofit called NEADS that offers assistance dogs for combat veterans, the hearing impaired, children with autism, people with physical disabilities. I called them up, asked them if they ever trained a dog named Stash. Turns out they did, only Stash has been missing for the past three years. Dropped out of their system."

"I don't get it."

"Your doodle was partnered with a fellow named Al Pickrell. Al lived alone, a little nothing place in the woods outside of Patton. Poor guy had Lou Gehrig's disease, and Stash was by his side to the end."

"And Seth is Al's son?"

"Bingo. A son who left home at sixteen, a son who, decades later, only returned to pick up his late father's dog. Seth wasn't a sick man when he took Stash. He didn't need a service dog. He needed a link to his dad. I guess it's just a little extra bit of grace that Stash could also help Seth when he got sick. "

"Wait a minute. You couldn't have gotten all this from one phone call. Is Gabe helping out again?"

"Please." Lewis scoffs. "Even though the family's from across the valley, I have a far better grassroots source."

Ah, Doris.

"I told the folks at NEADS we got suspicious when a service dog named Stash showed up with a guy who refused to give us a name or address."

"So they want him back?"

The line goes quiet for a few seconds. "That's up to you. They asked me to describe him, and, well, I might have left out the bit about his orange mustache. I figured you could call them back and correct my mistake or . . . maybe invest in a little hair dye to keep him all black. Either way, I told Devito we'd had no luck tracking down John Doe's service dog."

I eventually came home, only you got this practice and I got this dog.

Was Seth like me, another lost son looking for redemption? Was Stash his only and best connection to a father he never knew, a living link to a past he wished he could do over?

"And one more thing," says Lewis. "NEADS told me the magic words."

"I'm not with you."

"The command that will finally give that poor dog a chance to relax and let his hair down."

Lewis repeats the phrase, and I swear Stash glances my way as though he's heard what was said.

What a human hears at twenty feet, a dog can hear at eighty feet.

I hang up, pull off Eden Falls's main strip, and locate my destination, a goldenrod yellow doll's house with a wraparound farmer's porch. Looks like Trish came from humble roots. If she married up, I'm betting Lionel needs the inheritance money because they're overextended.

323

Snow-encrusted cars line both sides of the narrow street, but Mavis Peebles's driveway is a short, steep slope, so I pull straight in, praying a neutral gear and gravity will let me roll my way back onto the road when I'm ready to leave.

"Stash, come," I say, inviting him to exit on my side. He's coming with me because the flicker of a small orange dot on the dashboard tells me I need more gas. If I leave him in the warm cab with the engine idling, the Silverado won't make it to the nearest station.

The "toughest glue on Planet Earth" appears to be living up to its name. Crispin's tail is restored to its horizontal former glory, and with a little comb-over, you can barely see the join. I grab the back feet and associated castors, ready to pull the faithful Labrador off the back of the bed when I think back to my one and only meeting with Mavis Peebles.

"Thanks, Bobby," she said, accompanied by a conspiratorial wink. A senior moment or a secret communiqué?

For now I leave Crispin to guard the truck. Time to find out what my late father was up to.

Following a snow-blown path I take two steps onto the wooden porch, where a sturdy wrought-iron door knocker allows me to announce my arrival. Stash stands by my side, attentive but patient, doing a fine impersonation of Crispin sans castors.

I hear a TV being muted, a rustling movement inside, and the creak of floorboards.

I knock again.

"Just a minute," says a soft female voice as though from the other side of a powder room, attending to last-minute details in order to appear presentable.

The door swings open, and Mavis Peebles lurches forward in sturdy sheepskin slippers and a hand-knit woolen cardigan over a minty blue nylon housecoat.

"That's not Crispin," she says, pointing with her knotty arthritic index finger.

"No, Mrs. Peebles. This is my dog." I hesitate, the "my" still feeling conspicuous but pleasantly invigorating. "This is Stash." I look down and do a double take. Stash's perfect impersonation of the dead dog himself has been spoiled by an aberrant behavior new to this particular labradoodle—he's wagging his tail.

"I didn't want to leave him alone, if that's okay with you."

Mrs. Peebles looks more flustered than confused.

"Where's Crispin?" she asks.

I glance back at the truck, feeling guilty, tempted to allay her fears, but this is about far more than fixing her dog's broken wag. "Maybe we could come in?"

Mavis swivels around, full body, not just neck,

like she's taking stock, making sure the coast is clear prior to opening the door wide.

Before I can say thank you and step inside, a certain canine has barged past me in order to nuzzle and methodically lick Mavis's right hand as though saliva might be the breakthrough cure for rheumatism.

"Friendly, isn't she?" says Mavis, hobbling over toward a couple of straight-backed wooden chairs gathered around the heat from an old cast-iron radiator. Her gait is a side-to-side rocking motion, like an Emperor penguin's. "Can she have a cookie?"

"Of course," I say, taking in a small sitting room that's clearly been converted into a bedroom. Aside from the high twin bed underneath the window, there's an armoire, a series of built-in bookshelves, and a small TV. The sound has been turned off, but based on the overacting and the plethora of beautiful people this has to be a soap opera. The handsome stubbly face of a swarthy Casanova pops up, and unfortunately I'm reminded of Mr. Marco Tellucci.

On a table next to her chair (at least I assume it's hers because it's the only one covered with thick cushions) Mavis decapitates a ceramic yellow Labrador cookie jar, reaches in (accompanied by the sound of an electronic yap), and removes a small Milk Bone. Stash meets her eyes, waits for a nod of approval, gently takes it on his tongue, trots off to the other side of the room, and eats it slowly and methodically, lying down.

"Tea? Coffee?"

"No thanks," I say, as Mavis waddles off through an open door that appears to lead into a kitchen.

"Can I help?"

"No," snaps Mavis. "Sit," she commands, and I wonder if Stash's presence has made the old woman flash back to her days of training Crispin.

Dutifully I take the matching chair without the cushions. Now I see why Mavis chose them—rigid, upright, easier to get in and out when your joints are trying to rust stiff.

The items on the table next to the Lab cookie jar tell me how Mavis must spend her days: two balls of wool tangled around knitting needles (remarkable given the deformity of her hands), the remote control, and, surprisingly, a Kindle reader.

Stash, having finished his treat, races past me to see what's going on in the kitchen. What's gotten into him? In his hurry, he broadsides one of the cushions on Mavis's seat, exposing the edge of a small book. I reach over to tuck it back in, but the cover title gives me pause—*Wicked Hard Sudoku*. It's not the Boston slang that strikes me as strange; it's the notion of a senile geriatric having the mental capacity for complex mathematical games.

Leaning back in my chair I glimpse part of a galley kitchen, red cabinets, white appliances, and, disturbingly, Stash with his front feet up on a counter as though he's begging for more to eat. I hear the whistle of an electric kettle coming to a boil and the chink of mugs (guess I'm having tea). There's still time. I adjust the cushions to hide the Sudoku and turn on the Kindle. I don't have an electronic reading device and sometimes I wonder if they're only good for curious men to read *Fifty Shades of Grey* in total anonymity, but up pops Tolstoy's *Anna Karenina*. Not exactly mindless pulp. And then there's the "last" button on the remote—a travel show on PBS. Quickly I flick back to . . . whatever they call this show— *Days of Our Guiding Hospital*—apparently television for the mentally infirm.

"Thanks," I say as Mavis returns, handing me a trembling mug.

She carefully places hers on a coaster on the side table prior to easing down into her chair. Stash stands off to her side but out of reach for petting. Strange, I think, him keeping his distance, until I notice the four circular depressions in the plush blue carpet, spaced at the corners of a dog-sized rectangle. It's as if he's showing deference to the senior dog, not wanting to stand in Crispin's spot.

"You fix the tail?" asks Mavis, her focus on my lips, avoiding eye contact, as though she needs to prove how mentally infirm she has become. I am convinced it's an act, or at the very least, an exaggeration. Lewis would be all over me, insisting I tread cautiously, but the clinician in me needs the backstory while the movie geek can't help but think about David Mamet's *House of Games*, Joe Mantegna saying, *It's called a confidence game. Why? Because you give me your confidence? No. Because I give you mine.*

"What if I said no, Mrs. Peebles?"

Slowly her eyes ascend my face.

"Do you have doctor-patient confidentiality?"

"But you're not my . . ." I hesitate. "Sure," I say, "nothing leaves this room."

Mavis sighs, eases back in her chair, hands flopping down on the rests. "This was your father's idea. He knew I'd rather be crippled here at home than trapped in some hospital bed or my daughter's . . . space station."

"Idea? You mean having Crispin stuffed?"

Mavis leans over and picks up her mug with both hands, relishing the warmth.

"I'm not crazy or senile, but how can I care for a new dog? Most of the time I'm too sore to walk to the kitchen, let alone out of the house. I'm eighty-three years old. Who'd look after my dog once I'm gone? It wouldn't be fair."

"Hold on, Mrs. Peebles. You're saying my father told you to act a little . . . kooky?"

"No. I just improvise every now and then. It's not hard. Stare off into space, say something senseless or based on a childhood memory. Just enough to keep them guessing. No, Doc Cobb suggested taxidermy—low maintenance, quiet company, and guaranteed to look scary mad. The ban on pets at local nursing homes was a bonus."

"But what about your daughter? I got the impression she wouldn't mind whether it's a nursing home or her own home, she just wants you to get the care you need."

"Have you seen her home?"

"Yes, I have."

"You met Lionel?"

I take a sip of my tea, trying not to wince. It's acrid from stewing too long.

"Exactly," she says. "He might swear up and down how he'll make a nice apartment out back, but Lionel's always quick to chime in about his allergy. He'd love it if I croaked."

I should argue with her, suggest her son-in-law might find it hard to show his true feelings, but I reckon she's right. That's why I have no problem throwing Lionel under the bus.

"The allergy thing is a lie. When I visited, I made sure he came into contact with fur and canine saliva, the most common dog-related allergens. He never sneezed, scratched, or sniffed once."

Mavis's lips peel back to reveal her beaming dentures.

"Your dad told me I'd like you. So apart from trying to kill him, why would you visit his house?"

I flash my eyebrows and let a breath of exhaled air fill my cheeks. "Well . . . I, I don't know . . . Look, I managed to fix Crispin's tail. You want me to fetch him from the—"

"Sit back down. Why'd you visit his house?"

I shrug and wonder how Amy might reply. "Some people say I'm nosy. I prefer curious. I've always liked solving any kind of puzzle."

"I like puzzles," says Mavis, digging under her cushion to show me her "incredibly challenging" Sudoku. "But there's more to it than that."

"Not really," I say, working on an awkward smile.

The concavity afflicting her spine cinches a little tighter, a finger henpecking in my direction. "Yes really." Her grin captures every wrinkle of her face like the barometric lines of a low-pressure system. "Just like your father. Easily hooked, all in, and duty bound to do what is right."

"Please, he was the saint, not me. I just wanted to make sure you considered all your options. This way you know you can keep Crispin *and* live with your daughter, assuming you want to."

Mavis narrows her eyes but lets me appreciate a glint of satisfaction.

"Some might say you're meddling in matters that don't concern you."

I nod. "Fair enough, but they obviously mattered to my father. Think of it as carrying on where he left off."

"It's more than that," she says, taking a sip. "You're trying to finish the job." Mavis studies me, lowers the mug, and adds, "You're an odd one, Dr. Mills. Take it from someone who's pretty good at pretending to be someone she's not, it feels good to open up every now and then, let the world see what's on the inside."

I feel myself relax. Doctor-patient confidentiality works both ways. "Not me, Mrs. Peebles."

"Just like your father. Well, not quite."

"What do you mean?"

"Bobby Cobb was a lot smoother round the edges. He talked a lot about you."

"He did?"

"All the time. Worried about you being alone."

I let the word "alone" settle and then shiver from its emotional chill. Amazing. My father can still reach out and touch me through his devoted clients.

"But the lengths to which you've gone for me, it says a lot. You should let it show."

"I am who I am, Mrs. Peebles."

She reaches over to Stash, who shimmies sideways and leans in for a scratch. Even when he's getting attention he's intent on making it as easy as possible.

"Tell me," Mavis says. "When you and this dog are alone, how do you act?"

I think about it. "I don't act. But it's different with a dog."

"Is it?" Her lobster-claw hand makes gentle pincer movements behind Stash's left ear that have him transfixed. "You keep things simple, let the dog know how you really feel. It's not complicated. It's honest. Alone with a dog you're allowed to shine. Be the person your dog expects you to be. I got to see that side. Bet most folks aren't so lucky."

Now I'm getting pep talks from a crazy lady with a stuffed dead dog.

"Let me grab Crispin," I say, getting to my feet, Stash making no move to follow me. I head out to the truck. *Be the person your dog expects you to be.* Where did she get that phrase?

Poor Crispin slides out the back of the flatbed, and, hugging him to my chest, I carry him back to the house. He's incredibly light, literally a husk of his former self, but his importance is a weight that will never change.

"Shall I put him in his usual spot?" I ask, carefully docking his castors with the reciprocal depressions in the carpet.

In her excitement and the struggle to put down her tea and get to her feet, Mavis loses her grip on the mug, the spill pooling toward her Kindle.

"I'll get that," I say, heading toward the kitchen, but the black blur is already back, clean white tea towel in his mouth, plopped down in the center of the milky brown puddle. Obviously

Stash wasn't just scouting the kitchen for food, he was getting the lay of the land, a helpful recon mission.

"Good dog," says Mavis, mopping up the spill, glancing my way, truly impressed.

I say nothing, not because I don't have something to say, but because I'm afraid of what needs to be said. It's so obvious. This is what Stash was trained to do, loves to do, needs to do. His raison d'être is to be of service. That's why he follows me everywhere, why he hates to be left alone. Everything that makes me incredulous, in awe of this creature, is nothing but a trick, but to someone like Mavis Peebles, someone who needs him, it's the difference between opening a door or staying shut in behind it, the difference between light and dark, between leaving something lying on the floor or picking it up. Independence or a kind of imprisonment. It's as obvious as it is painful.

But what of Mavis's fears about adopting a new dog? Easy. I'd love to take Stash for daily walks, and, if ever there came a time, I'd have him back in a heartbeat.

That leaves the daughter, "Patricia, call me Trish," and her faux-allergic husband. Though Stash is inherently hypoallergenic, I can confirm that in Lionel's case, my "laying on of hands" met with no adverse reaction. Whether Trish approves, wants her mother to move right in, or stay put, that's none of my business. Again, if Stash needs a home, I'll be first in line.

"Mrs. Peebles . . ."

Twenty minutes later, my phone call made, I drop to one knee and take Stash's head in my hands. For all his loyalty, devotion, and unwavering service, it's time for me to give him something in return. We lock eyes, and finally I get to deliver the magic words.

"Stash. *Free time.*"

Part of me imagined it would be like hitting a switch, turning him off, the doodle slumping to the floor relieved to be off duty. It shows how much I know about dogs. Instead Stash lights up, spins on his back legs, charges off into the kitchen, and sprints back with a tea towel in his mouth, goading me into playing a game of tug-o'-war.

"Call me if you need anything," I tell Mavis, reining in the crazy doodle with a "Stash, sit" while tying the towel to the handle of the front door. Some time ago Trish had made sure the round knobs were traded for long handles to ensure better leverage. Now, with "Stash, door" (it wasn't hard to figure out), life is even easier.

"You're sure about this?" asks Mavis.

I'm trying to keep in the moment, to make the logical, practical choice, but with a newfound spirit of honesty, I say, "No, I'm not. I'm going to miss him. But somehow I know Stash is sure, and that's what counts."

Mavis escorts me to the front door, and I can't help but feel stung by the way Stash has already chosen to be at her side, not mine. Without saying a word, she gestures with a hand, encouraging me to leave, as though she's well versed in the art of difficult goodbyes—best to make them quick, clean, and final. What is it about people who've done some serious living? Instinctively, Mavis knows not to reach out, not to touch me, not to say more.

Shuffling down the icy incline to the truck—the man who came with two dogs, leaving with none—I resolve not to look back. Maybe the arctic air helps the blanket of cold objectivity settle in around me. It's not meant to make me feel normal; it's meant to make me feel less. I need to think of it this way: Stash gets to utilize his many talents and Mavis gets a new beginning. I pat the Polaroid memento I've been carrying around in my breast pocket.

Cautious of the slope and the possibility of black ice, I slip-slide my way to the truck, hop inside, and turn on the engine. Foot on the brake, gear in neutral, I'm about to roll back when the rustle of a lace curtain in an upstairs window catches my eye and I see a figure staring down at me—it's Stash.

He's only there for a few seconds—scruffy, intense, and unfailingly determined to make things better—but it is more than enough to feel good about my decision. I witnessed how Stash's training gave him purpose, but the cynic in me got to feel his gift. If he can lift me up, then for someone like Mavis, this dog is a life preserver.

← 20 →

I'D LIKE TO THINK THE DECISION CAME down to my training as a pathologist, but I can't ignore the phrase *be the person your dog expects you to be.* My life coach swami, Mavis Peebles, had a point about deconstructing my feelings and venting my inner monologue. Around Stash I was unguarded. I was the real me, and like it or not, this real me continues to gravitate toward a baffling and demoralizing waitress. In my old job, when something was dead or dying, I had to know why. If Amy refuses to come clean about the man who, on paper, is her husband, and there's still something to salvage in our floundering (hopefully not dead or dying) relationship, then I must uncover the truth by another route, by asking Marco Tellucci himself.

Figuring out the where and when was easy. A guy called Liam, working the front desk, took my call.

"Hi, Liam, I'm supposed to be meeting my

friend for dinner tonight at the inn, and I can't remember whether Mr. Tellucci booked for seven thirty or eight."

"Just a moment." A pause. "That's eight o'clock, sir."

So, still around and with limited dining options in Eden Falls.

"Thanks. And it's just the two of us, right?"

"That's what it says, sir."

The "who" is a little more tricky because in this context it's about who Tellucci has invited to join him. Yesterday, at the K of C, Amy shot me down for trying to set up a date for tonight. If she's the one dining with her husband, I'd have to lure him away from their table to face him, *mano a mano*. Or, I could storm in there, play the part of the rejected lover, and demand an explanation in front of the other diners. Or, I think as I stand under the hot shower with just over an hour to go before eight, perhaps it would be easier (and safer) to simply call his room.

I imagine myself as the high school geek (not much of a leap), the one with the crush on the popular cheerleader, the one who let her copy his homework because she said hello to him in class, the one who plucked up the courage to ask her to the senior prom, watching her laugh, gag, and recoil because she already had a date with the handsome quarterback. If only this meeting were a twenty-year reunion, and Marco Tellucci turned out to be an alcoholic, abusive womanizer, recently terminated from his place of employment and the victim of a senseless random acid attack to the face.

I step out of the tub, towel off, and watch my reflection appear in the steamy bathroom vanity mirror above the sink. Since there's a good chance Amy will be there I want to look my best, which means shaving for the second time today. I'm hoping for contrast with Tellucci, who probably prefers to show off a five o'clock shadow that grows out by eleven most mornings. Rummaging through my father's medicine cabinet door, I discover a bottle of Old Spice aftershave and an ancient tub of Brylcreem for men. I splash a few drops into my palms and slap my bare cheeks. Hardly the pheromone I was hoping for, and dipping my fingers into the sticky white gel, I'm not convinced "just a little dab'll do ya!" In order to overpower that pesky cowlick, my hair congeals into a greasy, slick helmet. What an idiot. I turn on the shower and start over.

Ten minutes later and I've moved from personal grooming to fashion. If this turns into an altercation I might do well to wear something substantial like chain mail or a Kevlar vest. But what if there's a dress code or I have to hang out in the restaurant waiting to pounce? Still out of my comfort zone but having learned my lesson, I iron a plain white cotton shirt. Though my father's old blue blazer feels a little too nautical to me, complete with tiny anchors embossed on the gold-colored buttons on the cuffs, it fits well enough. That leaves me with one more decision—wear a tie or sport an open neck. Part of me wishes I had a silk ascot or a thick gold medallion and a bounty of bushy chest hair, hoping to see Amy's reaction. But this is Vermont, and I'm only there for a reckoning. I tuck the tie (my one and only) inside my breast pocket, just in case.

First order of business is gasoline for the Silverado, and as I roll up to the pumps, a figure in a black ski mask suddenly appears at my window. I'm halfway into the passenger seat thinking I'm about to get carjacked when I remember the gas station is full service.

"Forty dollars of regular," I shout, squeezing two twenties through a crack in the glass just in case, and the would-be assailant disappears, leaving me with an unwelcome reminder of Healthy Paws—an ad, a glossy conspicuous banner strung over the pump. Only this one has been defiled. Oh, there's the familiar logo, the smiling faces on the pet and human models, but the last seven digits of the telephone number have been covered over with a strip of duct tape and replaced by different numbers handwritten in black Sharpie.

I check out the other pumps on the lot, each vandalized in the same manner. I could blame another round of bad luck for Guy Dorkin, a printing error with the advertising company. But something tells me this correction comes courtesy of Gilligan the collie, Drew's silent way of saying thanks. I'm not sure how he explained it away to his boss, but dialing the phone number for "the best veterinary practice around" puts you straight through to Bedside Manor.

On the drive to The Inn at Falls View, I finalize my strategy. Catching Tellucci alone will be preferable—more civilized, less dramatic. There could be an opportunity to accost him on a bathroom visit. He might receive an anonymous tip that a man in a blue blazer appears to be keying his Humvee. Either way, a confrontation *away* from Amy will avoid—no, minimize—her outrage (or at least I won't have to witness it), and I won't be subjected to a humiliating bout of comparison-shopping with her husband. Let's face it, I can't compete with the Italian when it comes to looks and money, leaving me with what—character? According to the Internet (which never lies), the top three winning traits men should exude around women are confidence, wit, and sensitivity. This explains everything. Intelligence, arguably my greatest strength, appears to be optional. Though the Italian may be smart *and* successful, I'm hoping his opulence comes courtesy of a trust fund, lifelong mooching, or some illicit activity that I can report to our hotshot detective, Chief Devito.

Ironically I park next to the white Humvee (pleased to see that salt and slush have soiled its showroom dazzle), jog up the steps of the main entrance and through the lobby, and head for the bar and restaurant.

"Hey, Doc, finally," says George, dressed in what appears to be a uniform of black pants, black shirt, and narrow black tie. "Here for dinner?"

"Yes, I'm meeting some . . . people I know."

"Excellent. And look at this."

He pulls out his smartphone and begins swiping his index finger across the greasy surface.

"See: before . . . after."

He's flicking between two photographs showing close-ups of Henry the cat's nasal deformity. It's been two days since I dropped off the medication. I wouldn't expect visible signs of improvement for at least a week, which is why they look identical to me.

"That's great," I say, remembering a scientific article describing how nearly forty percent of pet owners thought their dog's lameness got better despite being given sugar pills. If George is happy, I'm happy. Placebo effect or not, like Lewis says, "The owner's always right."

"Can't thank you enough," says George. "You want to wait at the bar? Grab that drink?"

It's at this point I realize my plan is riddled with holes. What am I going to do, spy on them? And what am I going to say? "Excuse me, but you seem to be married to the woman of my dreams."

"Why not," I reply, and George gestures for me to follow.

It turns out the bar is perfect—empty, dark, and offering a view into a romantically lit dining room dominated by an elaborate plaster ceiling from which hangs a monster of a chandelier. There's a round table for eight directly below and it's empty. Given the context of why I'm here, it's hardly surprising that I'm reminded of the movie *The War of the Roses. If love is blind, marriage is like having a stroke.*

I position myself on a corner stool where I can hide behind a floor-to-ceiling wooden support beam. Overhead, the sound of a string quartet on the speaker system stifles the murmur of diners in discreet conversation. It's a slow Sunday night in winter, but even so, George has strategically placed his patrons to fool new guests into thinking the place is far from dead. I half envy a bearded man, picking at his food, head buried in a book, and I notice the couple I saw the other day in the hotel lobby. I wondered whether they were on their way to some sort of winter sporting activity. Thanks to sunglasses and inadequate sunblock, their raccoon impersonations suggest the answer was yes.

"What can I get you?" asks George, coming around the bar.

Keep a clear head or loosen up?

"Maker's Mark, up."

While George fixes my drink they walk in, the Telluccis, arm in arm, headed toward a table for four. *Strange,* I think, *four, not two.* But the gods are on my side. Amy takes the chair with her back to me. That's when I notice, tucked into the far left-hand corner of the room, another woman with her back to me, her hair carefully pinned up into a bun; the young man facing me leaning in, animated and vaguely familiar.

"There you go," says George, sliding over a glass containing at least a double measure.

I nod, take a sip, and relish the burn in my throat as I spy Amy's hand resting on his, giving it a squeeze before letting go.

"I'll be in the kitchen. Let me know when your friends arrive and you need a table."

"Actually, George," I say, knocking back the entire drink like a shot, "I wonder if you could do me a favor."

A minute later and Mr. Marco Tellucci is headed my way, the recipient of a mystery phone call at the bar. George has been kind enough to give us a moment alone.

The Italian brushes past me, picks up the hand piece, and says hello to a dead line as I get down from my stool.

"Mr. Tellucci, I wonder if I might have a word in private."

He hangs up in slow motion, looks confused—

no, it's more than that, maybe wary or even afraid.

"Who are you?"

"My name is Cyrus Mills and I don't want to disturb your evening, but I'd like to—"

"Cyrus," he exclaims, clutching his chest like he's relieved when I was hoping for a heart attack. Without hesitation he steps over, hugs me, and plants a kiss on both of my cheeks.

"Amy has told me a great many things about you," he says with only a trace of an accent but more than enough to catch your ear, especially, I imagine, if you're female.

I consider speaking too slowly, cranking up the volume, and overenunciating as I say, "Amy told me nothing about you."

All I've got is a whispered, "Really?"

"But this is wonderful. Come, come, you must join us. I insist."

At this point he begins strong-arming me toward his table, and I reckon I've got about twenty seconds in which to tear free of his grip and run. I didn't bank on him shouting across the room, "Amy, look who I found."

Suddenly a moment of uncomfortable camaraderie must look more like a citizen's arrest and I freeze, the busted bad boy.

Amy spins around, gets out of her chair, and before I can soften the blow with a hasty compliment about how gorgeous she looks in a long-sleeved silky black dress, her eyes have dropped to the floor and she's shaking her head.

"Just couldn't let it go, could you," she says.

Part of me wants to come back with "when something's worth fighting for." But remember, I'm standing next to her husband, so I say nothing and let my crimson cheeks do the talking.

"Sit," says Tellucci, pulling back a chair for me opposite Amy, "let me pour you a glass of Prosecco."

He reaches for a bottle in an ice bucket before I can refuse, filling my glass with a practiced, deliberate hand and topping up two more. Though this is a table for four, it's set for three. Who else are they expecting?

"Here's to Cyrus," says Marco, "a man after my own heart."

We chink glasses and sip in unison as Marco signals to a waiter for another bottle. What's he up to? *A man after my own heart?* I have nothing in common with this man.

"You made poor George lie about a phone call," says Amy, "just to get Marco alone?"

I nod, sheepish, guilty as charged.

Amy shakes her head again.

"Then be my guest. Pretend I'm not here. But don't forget, I was the one who tried to keep you out of this."

She makes this sound slightly threatening.

Maybe I should be concerned about the Cosa Nostra after all.

Marco stares at me, apparently riveted by my curiosity.

"Okay . . . well . . . to be clear, you, Marco, are Amy's . . ."

"Life partner" and "soul mate" flash through my mind, but Amy gets there first.

"Marco is my husband."

Despite having seen the certificate with my own eyes, from her lips the phrase pierces me like a steel blade, shockingly cold and deep. I fumble for my glass and knock back a healthy swig of the fizzy wine, hoping to numb the pain as Amy turns to the Italian to add, "*Tecnicamente parlando.*"

Tellucci frowns but arches an eyebrow in agreement. What's that about? I want to ask but he's leaning into the table, eager for his next question.

"And . . . you've been . . . away . . . for quite some time."

"Away?" Marco parrots, making me want to suggest, "Kabul? The International Space Station? Leavenworth prison?"

"Yes, I live in San Francisco. Pac Heights. You know it?"

"Just the movie; Melanie Griffith, Michael Keaton. But you're not *from* California?"

"No, no. *Monterosso al Mare.* It's a small town in the—"

"*Cinque Terre*," I interject. "Never been, but I've read about it. Supposed to be very picturesque."

"It is," says Marco, visibly impressed. "You never said he was clever *and* worldly."

Amy places her empty glass down on the table just as George appears with the next bottle, eager to provide us with refills. Mine is empty as well.

"Perhaps we could take some water, still," says the Italian, "a little calamari and antipasto misto for three. Cyrus, you like anchovies, yes?"

Even though there was a question, clearly Marco never expected an answer. George pulls back the menus he was about to hand out and disappears to place the order.

I can feel the beginnings of a not-unpleasant buzz take hold. A sensible, less tipsy, but suitably humiliated Cyrus would swallow his pride and bolt, but this looser, slightly shocking version plows on, asking, "How'd you two meet?"

"In Burlington, at UVM," says Marco. "But work took me out west. Advertising."

Without asking, he tops off my glass.

"Would you prefer a pinot grigio with the appetizers?"

I think about Paul Giamatti in *Sideways*, and I'm tempted to order a merlot.

"I'm good," I say, thinking I'd best maintain at least some of my inhibitions.

Either Marco must place the same order every

night or George is clairvoyant, because the man in black appears out of my peripheral vision with a steaming plate of crispy rubber bands and an assortment of cold meats, cheeses, olives, and sparkly silver fish. He's kind enough not to say "*buon appetito*" as he lays it on the table and backs off.

I unfurl my napkin and place it on my lap.

"Forgive me . . . but you live in different states and uh, neither of you wears a ring?"

This earns me the full force of her blue and brown lasers like I've said too much. I bow out by munching on a little salami and what I believe to be a sweet pickle. Naturally it turns out to be the hot variety and, in the absence of the water (still not delivered), I'm forced to consume a deep draught of bubbly mind-sapping fluid.

"You okay?" asks Marco, quick to refill my glass with more prosecco, just in case.

I nod and notice how my head moves, but my eyes and brain take a split second to catch up. I sense the languid blink, the smile threatening to contort my lips even though there's nothing funny inside my head. Not drunk, but definitely woozy. I'm going to need to call a cab.

Liberated by my lowered inhibitions, I finally feel myself beginning to man up. After all, I'm the one who's been duped. Amy's the one with the explaining to do. Time to ask the kind of questions I will later regret. They have begun to stack up in the back of my throat when Amy drops her napkin on the table, jumps up, and rushes to greet someone over my shoulder.

"Charles," she exclaims.

I turn in my seat to see a tall, lean man in a black leather jacket and white cashmere scarf. Like the guy in the corner with Ms. Bun-Head (who appears to be hiding behind a menu) I've seen this man before, but it's not coming to me. Damn those bubbles!

More cheek kissing (I wish she'd stop pretending to be so European) and Amy, taking Charles by the arm, guides him to our table.

Marco remains seated, a serious look on his face. Is he jealous?

I put down my napkin and get to my feet as Charles comes over. Amy makes the introduction.

"Nice to meet you," I say, gesturing to the seat next to me, "perhaps George can set another place at the table."

"Thank you," says Charles, "but we're not staying long."

I'm not sure whom he means by "we."

"Kevin says you're good to go." He's addressing Marco. "He says it's going to cost you, him working a Sunday, but everything is in order. We should be able to sign the paperwork at nine o'clock tomorrow morning. George has let me use his office. It's being faxed over right now."

Marco and Amy look at one another, scream in unison, and hug. I'm totally confused.

The Italian, suddenly all teary eyed, turns to Charles. "I can't believe it's finally happening."

"Well, it won't if we don't get your John Hancock on these documents."

Marco knocks back his glass and stands. "This may take a while," he says.

"We can wait," I say.

"No, please, order your dinner. We want to get this done. Right, Charles?"

"Absolutely. Don't make me stay in this Podunk town any longer than necessary."

And in his flash of anger I recognize Charles. The man fighting with Marco in the Humvee parked at the gas station.

I stand again (this evening is more like a game of musical chairs), shake Charles's hand, and watch as Amy squeezes her husband in a tight embrace. No kiss, but she places her lips by his ears and whispers something out of earshot. Whatever she says, it causes Marco to burst into laughter. Am I about to get stuck with the bill? How much does this Prosecco cost?

Amy and I watch them go, letting the sensation that we are alone settle in before returning to our seats, our plates strewn with the flotsam of nibbled appetizers.

"Very nice man," I say.

"He is. He's wonderful."

George magically appears, though without glasses of water.

"Can I take your plates?"

Amy nods.

"And how about a menu for dinner?"

Amy looks at me as though she wonders if I might run out on her. Finally I have her alone in a quiet, intimate setting.

"Please," I say, "and a wine list."

I'm definitely going to need a cab.

George hands out his large leather binders. It's standard Italian fare, with a generous smattering of the usual phrases—shaved, glazed, infused, seared. Seems as though Chef needs to unload an awful lot of truffle oil. Amy's quick to blurt out "chicken piccata" as though she already knew what she wanted. Her haste is infectious, baiting me to say, "I'll have the same," but in keeping with my alcohol-induced theme of "dare to be different," I order a bottle of Vermentino and opt for a shrimp fettuccini, the choice causing Amy to flash me a questioning glance. What could be wrong with Sunday seafood hundreds of miles from the nearest coastline?

"What did you think?" she asks as soon as we are alone. "About Marco?"

Where to begin?

"Um . . . well . . . you're a lucky woman."

She hesitates, the wrinkle in her nose signaling her annoyance.

"Come on. I can practically see the wheels turning inside that brain of yours. Don't stop now. You've got to be curious."

"Oh, I'm curious. But I'm also . . ."

"What?"

"Sad. Yes, sad. Sad that we met each other when we did. Sad that my timing was off."

Her wrinkle vanishes, replaced by an earnest cant of her head.

"So when were you going to tell me?" I ask.

"I could ask you the same question," she replies without missing a beat.

My turn with a "you've lost me" crinkled brow just as Ms. Bun-Head stands up, tosses a glass of ice water in the face of her fellow diner, leaves her table, and heads my way.

"Oh my God . . ."

This inner monologue gets away from me as none other than Mrs. Crystal Haggerty, wife of Ken Haggerty, headmaster of Eden Falls Academy, dressed to display her ample cleavage and thighs, totters past on ridiculously high heels. She appears to wipe a tear from her eye as she hurries out of the restaurant. I look back to the young man at her table, wiping a napkin down his face, watching her go and realize where I've seen him before—he was the owner of a Lab puppy from our free clinic last weekend.

"You'd think she'd have a little decorum," I whisper, once Crystal is out of earshot.

"Because she's married?" says Amy, and then, hand on chest, hamming up her best Scarlett O'Hara accent, "Unlike certain ladies, *I* have a reputation to uphold."

I don't want to laugh, but I can't help myself, as the Lab owner asks for the check, drops a wad of cash, and leaves with his tail between his legs.

"Looks like someone made an improper advance."

Amy rolls her eyes.

"You have a lot to learn about women. Crystal has been hiding since we walked in. She knew she was busted. I guarantee that was all show to save face. No doubt she's headed to meet him right now back at the room she's already paid for."

I ease back in my seat and sigh.

"You got all that just from, what, female intuition and body language?"

"You bet," she says. "Oh, and that shocked expression earlier, when I said 'husband'—it might have won over your high school drama teacher, but not me. When were you going to tell me about computer boy?"

"You spoke to Gabe?"

"Of course not. But Charlie Brown did. I stuck around after you left the K of C yesterday. Thanked Doc Honey for her informative lecture and took her daughter out for a sundae. Hey, you want facts, you've got to play to people's weaknesses. You'll be pleased to know she's switched to low-fat, apparently she wants to squeeze into a bikini."

Hands clasped together (to stop them twitching), elbows on the table, I say, "Okay, it was wrong, but if you were me, wouldn't you have tried to find out who he was?"

"Yes," says Amy without hesitation.

"And would you have told me?"

"Course not."

I take a deep breath and reach for another drink. Here's the fork in the road, the turning point, old life or new? These past few days I've given up the first canine love of my life (yes, I admit it—love), cured a certifiable collie, and saved an Eden Falls institution. Put this way, it sounds like the stuff of Clark Kent. In fact all I've done is my job, my new job, a job whose best reward is the chance to give people and animals second chances. If this is my second chance, my only hope is that she'll cut me off before things get too awkward.

"Well . . . maybe this is easier knowing that you're a happily married woman. Being unattainable makes me realize how foolish I've been." My laugh is pure innocence. "I mean, I really thought there was something . . . I don't know . . . like when I was around you, something clicked inside me. Oh, not warm or fuzzy, no, it was more physiological, the way you switched on my sympathetic nervous system—increased heart rate, dilated pupils, dry mouth—totally beyond my control. I'm embarrassed to say you created these changes in me like no other woman I have ever met, and, not knowing you were spoken for, I enjoyed the way they made me feel. If that's the mark of someone who . . ." I catch myself just in time to avoid the next word—*fell*. "If trying to discover your mystery man came across as jealousy, then I'm sorry. But the truth is, I was . . . am . . . well . . . jealous."

Without saying a word we take a moment, staring at one another, before Amy pours me another drink. I take it, thinking, why not crawl into a drunken stupor and blame an alcoholic haze? Strange the way our silence is comfortable, easy, like with Stash when we had no expectations of each other, simply happy to share space and time.

Amy puts her lips to the glass, takes a sip, and says, "Charlie Brown thought as much. I mean, her mom's a great catch, especially for you, but the daughter sensed you were smitten—"

"Smitten. That's exactly the right word."

Just then, George appears with our meals and our new bottle of wine. My request for water sparks another bout of humble apologies and a promise that it will be right over. Despite the foreboding, the food is good, and thankfully, George has sufficient confidence in his chef that he knows better than to circle back and discover if everything is to our satisfaction.

"So I guess this will be our first and last supper," I say, spearing a shrimp.

Amy dabs the corners of her lips with her napkin and puts down her knife and fork.

"Okay, my turn. This was not how I planned to tell you about Marco. He is my husband, but I haven't been entirely honest with you."

My fork fumbles with a spool of fettuccine.

"Yes, we met when I was an undergrad at UVM, but what Marco didn't say was that he was a foreign exchange student over for a year abroad. During that year we became good friends, and ultimately he fell in love."

"Yes, I already got that, and it was incredibly uncomfortable the first—"

"Shut up, Cyrus."

This time I take a decent swig.

"He didn't fall in love with me. He fell in love with someone else."

"O-kay." I split the syllables, having no idea where this is going.

"They wanted to be together, and, for that reason, he wanted to stay in the country."

"Hold on. Where do you come into this?"

"Because the person he wanted to be with was another man."

"Um . . . so . . . Marco isn't—"

"He's gay. Always has been. We were best friends at college. I wanted to help him out, and he needed a green card to stay in the country. It's what friends do. Or so I thought at the time. I wasn't tied to another man, and Marco needed my help."

"Wait, so married in name only?"

"It's not rocket science. The truth is I haven't seen Marco for years. It didn't work out with his boyfriend. He moved to California, we tried to keep in touch, but it wasn't long before he vanished off the face of the earth. When you and I went out for that date, it was the first I'd heard from him since forever. He called me because he met someone, Charles, and they want to get married because it's legal in Vermont, but first he needed a divorce from me."

The muscles contorting my lips into a smile are way ahead of the pleasure swirling in my brain. Where's that bottle of Vermentino?

"So the faxing back and forth tonight is all the paperwork and . . . and . . . why the hell—"

I'm shouting, and the raccoons are suddenly more like meerkats—alert, erect, and attentive to my outburst.

I lean in and lower my voice. "Why didn't you tell me this sooner?"

"Because it was going away in a couple of days. What I did was stupid, but more importantly, totally illegal. I'm talking five years in federal prison and a quarter of a million in fines. I couldn't implicate you or anyone else, including my grandfather, in an illegal transaction to keep a foreign national in the country. I knew you were in the middle of this fight with Dorkin, and Dorkin's exactly the kind of person who might sniff around, find out what I did, and use me as leverage against Bedside Manor. Marco swore it would be quick and you and I would be able to pick up where we left off. And I didn't want you to think less of me. It was embarrassing. I hadn't reckoned on Sherlock Holmes not being able to let this go, nosing around, even hiring a hacker to investigate my computer records."

The air gets sucked from my lungs as I rock back in my seat, reach for another drink, catch myself, get to my feet, and scream across the room, "Can someone please get me a glass of water?"

Finally George scampers over with two glasses of ice water. I wait until he leaves to ask, "How could you be so sure you wouldn't lose me?"

Amy interrupts her eating, smiles, and says, "I wasn't. But I wanted to protect you. I figured I'd rather lose you by keeping you out than lose you by letting you in. Besides," she says, devilry dancing across her features, "I had to pay you back for snooping in my life. It was disturbing, though apparently, given the intensity of your feelings toward me, quite understandable."

"Hold on, that information was obtained under duress."

"Please, it was given of your own free will."

I drain my water, and this time George is there with a refill. As he pours, he slides a padded leather envelope in my direction as though I'm about to get the bill. Maybe he wants to let me know how much I've already spent.

I open the binder to find two items. Instead of a receipt there's a handwritten note.

Dr. Mills,
    Just wanted to let you know this dinner has been entirely paid for by Mr. Tellucci. He's insisted I put this on his bill. Also, in appreciation of your expert care of my cat Henry, I would like to offer you my finest suite, should you not wish to drive home this evening.
    P.S. I recommend you take me up on this complimentary night's stay. Chief Devito loves to catch drunk drivers!
Warmest regards,
George

The other object is a key attached to a small plastic fob bearing the number nine.

"What was that about?"

"Um . . . just business," I mumble, as an extraordinary—no, outrageous—idea begins to form inside my unchecked brain. In a dreamlike trance, I let it fly.

"Amy, this has been an evening of revelations, and in keeping with this theme, I have a proposal. It's totally out of character. It may be totally inappropriate, but I'm going to put it out there."

I push the padded envelope across the table, my chin inviting Amy to take a look inside. She takes it and opens it up on her lap in the manner of a book.

I clear my throat and ask, "How do you feel about a little adultery?"

The question hangs in the air between us like an echo, and for the longest moment nothing happens, Amy unable or unwilling to take her stunned heterochromic eyes off of George's note.

Suddenly she explodes, snapping the envelope shut, throwing her napkin down on the table, and getting to her feet as she takes my full glass of ice water and tosses it into my face. She storms off before I can mumble an apology.

Unbelievable. I will never understand this woman—no, make that women in general. I pick up Amy's napkin and wipe it down my face. That's when I feel the buzz in my pants and pull out my cell phone.

It's a text.

I look over my shoulder. I read the text again, then I notice the envelope, open it up, and begin to laugh.

George's note is still there, but the key to room nine has disappeared.

I place my knife and fork on my plate, push it away from me, get to my feet, and read the text one more time.

What R U waiting 4!

← ACKNOWLEDGMENTS →

Trying to write about a general practice veterinarian certainly proves that *real* animal doctors know a whole lot more than a specialist like me. Any mistakes or erroneous remarks regarding disease, diagnosis, and treatment are mine alone, fallibility my relentless impetus to learn.

I must thank Jennifer Fisher for her insightful suggestions on the early drafts and the wonderful team at Hyperion including Martha Levin, Betsy Hulsebosch, Tareth Mitch, Cassie Mandel, and Jill Amack. After five books together, you'd think I might have run out of superlatives for my editor, Christine Pride. Not so. Sharp, savvy, and spot-on, Christine's edits always manage to make me look far better than I deserve.

Jeff Kleinman, my agent, is the coach who knows how to get the most out of his players, inspiring you to try to deliver your best. Cheers, Jeff, I'm blessed to have you in my corner.

Now that my daughters, Whitney and Emily, have flown the coop, my wife, Kathy, bears the brunt of my desire to write, putting up with a husband prone to vapid looks, lost in thought, searching for the right way to tell a story. Her tolerance, patience, and unwavering support make these books possible.

Finally a big thank-you to Cathy Zemaitis and the folks at National Education for Assistance Dog Services (NEADS). What these incredible animals can do for those they serve is nothing short of amazing and I am thrilled to have adopted one of their so-called "Furloughed Favorites." Our labradoodle, Thai, has stolen my heart, making me a besotted, doting father all over again.

← ABOUT THE AUTHOR →

Nick Trout graduated from veterinary school at the University of Cambridge in 1989. He is a staff surgeon at the prestigious Angell Animal Medical Center in Boston; the author of five books, including the *New York Times* bestseller *Tell Me Where It Hurts*, *Love Is the Best Medicine*, *Ever By My Side*, and *The Patron Saint of Lost Dogs*; and he is a contributing columnist for *The Bark* magazine. He lives in Massachusetts with his wife, Kathy, and their adopted labradoodle, Thai.

The
Brothers of
Glastonbury

Kate Sedley

ST. MARTIN'S MINOTAUR
NEW YORK

www.minotaurbooks.com

ISBN 0-312-27282-0

First published in Great Britain by HEADLINE BOOK PUBLISHING,
a division of Hodder Headline

First U.S. Edition: January 2001

10 9 8 7 6 5 4 3 2 1

The
Brothers of
Glastonbury

Chapter One

It had been a good summer, with protracted spells of fine weather interspersing the colder, cloudier days of wind and rain. I had peddled my wares along the south coast of England as far as the town of Chichester before finally turning my feet towards home, making my way first to Winchester and then across the great wilderness north of Old Sarum, where I'd found a warm welcome in the isolated hamlets and villages that fringe that great and barren waste. By the time I was within two days' travelling distance of Bristol I was able to look back with ever deepening pleasure on the sights and sounds of those recent months.

I recalled warm nights, sleeping in the open under the stars, or sheltering with fellow wayfarers in the muffled darkness of some barn, exchanging views on the varied subjects of creation while small, nocturnal animals rustled beside us in the sweet-smelling straw, busy and unafraid. I remembered the chirruping of birds at dawn and the white mist rising knee-high across the meadows, the first bright rays of sunlight piercing it with broken shards of gold. I thought of evening shadows splashed across cottage walls and the pearled-grey shimmer of waterfalls and streams.

I had seen and wondered at the massive, rampant giant of Cerne Abbas, carved into a Dorset hillside thousands of years ago by our Celtic forebears, and marvelled at the

1

primaeval stone circle raised on Salisbury plain. More recently I had helped, for the sheer fun of it, with harvesting in the fields, sharing the workers' midday meal of bread and cheese, onions and barley beer, while the Harvest Lord kept strict watch on us to make certain that we took no more than our allotted time to eat and doze in the noonday sun. I had crossed the downs above Edington where Alfred, the greatest of our Saxon kings, had routed Guthrum's army six hundred years before, making Wessex safe for ever from occupation by the Danes, and had descended what is still called the bloody mound, passing the night at the Augustinian priory nestling in its lee.

And now, at the close of yet another day spent dawdling from village to village, in that soft, glimmering hush that lies somewhere between twilight and full dusk, as I neared the castle of Farleigh Hungerford I saw it awash with light from torches flaring high on its grey stone walls.

I was surprised, for I had passed this way several times – the castle being only a few miles from Bath, on the southerly heights that hem in that ancient township – and on each previous occasion it had been occupied only by such servants as were necessary to maintain and run it during the absence of its lord. But today that lord was in residence, a fact attested to by the press of people around the eastern gate and thronging the outer courtyard, as well as the pennants and surcoats of the men-at-arms, all sporting the Black Bull *passant* of the Duke of Clarence.

I knew a little of the castle's history for I had grown up in Wells, less than twenty miles' distance as the crow flies (and where gossip from within a far greater radius reaches our ears with astonishing speed). It had originally belonged to the Hungerford family, but their support of the late King Henry and the Lancastrian cause had deprived them of their lands. Fourteen years earlier, Farleigh had been granted by King Edward to his youngest brother, the Duke of Gloucester, when Prince Richard – and I too, for that matter, for we share the same birthday – was nine years old. But the Duke, since attaining manhood and marrying his cousin, the Lady Anne Neville, had chosen to live in the north, at Middleham and Sheriff Hutton. He had therefore rented out Farleigh to his older brother, the Duke of Clarence, who had large holdings in Somerset. Clarence's daughter, Margaret, had been born there only a year or so previously – but as I say, I had never until this time found His Grace himself within.

As I approached I could see that the gates had not yet been shut against the encroaching dark, and was wondering who might be expected at such a late hour, when the porter emerged from his room to inspect me and judge if I might be admitted or no.

'All right,' he grunted. 'You can pass. Hoping for a bed in the kitchens, I suppose.'

'Anywhere, friend. A stable will do me just as well.'

The man snorted. 'You'll be lucky! In case you hadn't noticed, the Duke's in residence. So what with *his* horses and those of His Grace of Bath and Wells, who's expected here at any moment, an empty stall'll be rarer than gold in a poor man's pocket.'

'A late call for the Bishop, surely?' I queried. 'It must be almost nine o'clock.'

The porter hunched his shoulders and rubbed a pock-marked nose. 'The Duke only arrived himself four hours since, and he's off again tomorrow just after midday. The way our lords and masters tear around the countryside fair takes your breath away! Never still! Here, there and every-where, like a swarm of bees.' He cocked an ear. 'You'd best

3

get on inside. I can hear the sound of horses' hooves.'

I could hear it myself, and just at that moment the lookout on the castle walls shouted warning of the Bishop's imminent arrival. Immediately, activity in the outer ward increased as grooms appeared, ready to attend upon His Grace and his retinue. The gates to the inner courtyard were flung open and the steward, together with other senior officers of the ducal household, emerged from a passage between the twin towers and crossed the bridge spanning the barbican ditch. I edged my way around the outer walls, past the west gate, to what I thought was an inconspicuous corner, not realizing quite how well illuminated it was by a burning torch just above my head.

The courtyard seemed suddenly, overpoweringly full of horses and riders, the former plunging to a standstill and breathing gustily through distended nostrils, heaving flanks sweating as though the animals had been pushed to their limit. Everywhere the light ran and caught on rich harness and jewels, on the gold, silver and azure thread that made up the saltire of Saint Andrew, blazoned on the saddle-cloths and sleeves of the Bishop's retainers.

Robert Stillington himself was splendidly attired in crimson velvet, his chaplain in dark blue silk. (The Church might constantly plead poverty, I reflected cynically, but however depleted its revenues, its princes made certain that they never went without.) The Bishop of Bath and Wells, by my reckoning, must at that time have been in his late fifties or early sixties, and had until the previous year held high office as Chancellor. Maybe the deeply-grooved, dissatisfied lines around his mouth had something to do with his removal from that post in favour of Thomas Rotheram, a close friend and confidant of the Woodvilles. If that were indeed so, he and my lord of Clarence would be able to sympathize and condole with one another, and vent their mutual spleen against the Queen's family.

A further commotion – a trumpet voluntary and the shuffling of feet as the men-at-arms snapped to attention – made me glance to my left just in time to see the Duke step into the outer ward to greet his guest in person; surely, I thought, an unlooked-for mark of distinction, even for a bishop. It seemed as though George of Clarence could not contain his impatience to welcome and make much of his guest. He flung a familiar arm around Stillington's neck, having first kissed him on both lined cheeks.

The Duke looked much as I remembered him, with the same great height and florid, handsome features as his elder brother. At first sight they could almost have been mistaken for each other, but a closer inspection revealed a sulky, disillusioned pout to Clarence's full lips, and a sag to the heavy jaw which suggested a man more at odds with life than King Edward had ever been. As always, the Duke was dressed magnificently, this evening in amber-coloured silks and velvets with a huge emerald ring flashing on one finger to match the buttons of his tunic. Just above his left elbow he wore a plain black ribbon, its ties fluttering in the gentle evening breeze, a token of his continued mourning for his sister, Anne, Duchess of Exeter, who had died at the beginning of the year.

Swinging on his heel, the Duke urged the Bishop forward towards the greater privacy of the inner courtyard, where, no doubt, Duchess Isabel and her ladies would also be waiting to extend their greetings. As they neared the bridge across the barbican ditch, my pack, which I had eased from my shoulders and was holding by its straps, slipped from my hand and fell to the ground. As luck – or divine providence – would have it, there was not a single person to screen me from the Duke, and the sudden movement caught the corner of his eye, making him turn his head. For a moment his stare was one of haughty displeasure, but then it changed to a puzzled frown. In the glare from the overhead torch he recognized, but could not place, my face; and as he assessed my clothes and calling the frown grew more pronounced. How could he possibly be acquainted with such a common pedlar? Still patently bewildered, and with a last, fleeting, backward glance, he vanished from my sight.

The castle kitchens were situated on the other side of the inner ward, close to the bakehouse and the well, in the vicinity of the north-west tower. I had been allowed to pass unhindered once the ducal party had entered the great hall, and was in fact less in the way than I had expected to be in the circumstances, the cooling ovens and quiet spits indicating that although the Bishop might be treated to a substantial all-night beside his bed, he and his retinue were not being fed on any lavish scale. Trays of wine and sweetmeats were being prepared, pastry coffins stuffed with dates and honey, apple turnovers and marchpane doucettes, but nothing that a man could get his teeth into. My heart sank. I had been looking forward to a share of the episcopal feast, but it was not to be. I should have to be content with such cold pickings as I was offered.

'His Grace sent word that he and his party would eat before leaving Wells,' one of the kitchen-maids informed me as she settled down to rummage through the contents of my pack. 'You haven't much left,' she accused me.

'I've been on the road all summer,' I protested. 'I'm on my way home to Bristol now. Stocks are low – like the food in this kitchen.'

She giggled. 'I'll get you something,' she volunteered, and was as good as her word, returning after some ten minutes with a trencher of bread and a leg of cold fowl. In her other hand she carried a tankard of ale, all of which she placed carefully on the floor beside me.

'Is that all right?' she asked.

I nodded gratefully. 'You're very kind.' Realizing suddenly how hungry I was, not having eaten for several hours, I took a large bite out of the meat before enquiring thickly, 'What brings the Bishop here on such a flying visit?'

A pair of big, rounded, pale grey eyes were turned towards me. 'How should I know? The Duke doesn't confide in me!' And she burst out laughing.

'You might have been privy to a rumour or two. In my experience, most gossip reaches the kitchens before anywhere else in a house – or a castle.'

My companion shrugged. 'Not here. My lord keeps his private business very close.'

This didn't tally with anything I had ever heard reported of George of Clarence, but I refrained from arguing the point. In any case, the girl had lost interest in the subject, picking up a small bone needle-case and hopefully asking its price. I guessed she was unable to buy it however cheap it might be, for I had never yet met a kitchen-maid with money in her pocket. I hesitated for a second or two, but I had had an excellent summer and could afford to be generous, so I closed her fingers round it.

'It's yours,' I said, 'if really you want it. But not a word to your companions, as I can't do the like for them. I have a mother-in-law and baby daughter waiting for me at home.'

She breathed her thanks with shining eyes and reached up shyly to kiss my cheek.

'You're married, then?' she whispered.

'A widower. By the way, what's your name?'

But I was destined never to know it, because just at that moment one of the cooks bawled at her to stop idling her time away and go to the bakehouse with the order for the morning's bread. The girl scrambled to her feet, blew me another kiss and went running, the precious needle-case safely stowed in the bosom of her dress.

I settled myself in a corner of the great room, unrolling my cloak from my pack and draping it over my legs, for even the warmest of summer days are likely to grow chill as the shadows lengthen. All around me scullions continued to work, banking down the fire for the night (but leaving just sufficient embers to be blown easily into life the following morning), preparing the all-nights of bread and cheese and ale for the most important members of the household, making sure the water barrels and log baskets were filled ready for the next day, and cleaning the spits on which the Duke's dinner had been roasted. The cooks checked their supplies of fish and meat for breakfast, knowing how displeased their lord would be if his table failed to impress the Bishop. Once, a chamber-maid, her arms full of bed linen, looked in for a chat with a friend, but soon scurried off again when an irate housekeeper came searching for her. Later, near midnight, three or four of the Bishop's lesser servants, those for whom there was no room in the guest hall or stables, arrived to find themselves a corner in which to sleep, either in the kitchen itself or the adjacent scullery.

I had by that time dozed and woken again, my rest being only fitful, in sharp contrast to the untroubled nights of the past three months. Guiltily, I recognized the reason. It was because I was nearing home and the curtailment of my freedom. Autumn and then winter would soon be closing in, and I had sworn to my mother-in-law, Margaret Walker, not to leave her and my child again during the bitter weather. Indeed, I had similarly sworn to myself as well, after the experiences of last January; and I knew that there was enough money to be earned in and around Bristol for all our modest wants, and more than enough with Margaret's wages as a spinner. But I knew also that those long, seemingly endless weeks cooped up within four walls, even though I could escape by day, would try my patience and good temper to the utmost.

As a young man I had hated confinement, the reason why I had been unable to become a monk at Glastonbury, thus flouting the dearest wish of my mother's heart. I had not completed my novitiate but, with Abbot Selwood's blessing, had quit the religious life for that of a chapman, and for the best part of three years I had been footloose and carefree. And then, as readers of my previous chronicles will already be aware, in the February of 1474 I had married Lillis Walker, who had died giving birth to our daughter eight months later.

My mother-in-law was pressing me to marry again. She wanted someone to share the responsibility with her for little Elizabeth, then three months short of her second birthday and growing daily more active. I had promised Margaret to think seriously on the subject, with the result that every eligible single woman and widow in Redcliffe's weaving community had been paraded for my inspection and, whether willing or not, inveigled into my company, the two of us then being left alone together. With the arrival of spring, I had thankfully made my escape and taken to the road.

I both understood and felt the necessity for a wife, but this time I wanted to make sure that there was more than mere liking and a sense of obligation on my part. On the second of October I should be twenty-four years old, at that period in my life between the callowness of youth and the harder-headed realism of middle age, and I was looking for love. Because the monks of Glastonbury had taught me to read and write I was familiar with several of the great romantic epics concerning such characters as Robin Hood and Maid Marion, Lancelot and Guinevere, and also with the *Roman de la Rose*.

I was in a strange mood in that late August of 1476, a mood which the past blissful summer had only served to heighten. I was in no frame of mind just at that moment to return home to Bristol, to the dull round of domesticity and fatherhood, but wanted instead to be plunged into some fantastic adventure, to become a knight on a white charger riding to the rescue of a damsel in distress. (Which, as things turned out, proved to be just as well, although the reality was somewhat more prosaic than my imaginings, as life inevitably is. All the same, I was to come very close to achieving the unbelievable, to becoming a part of that mystic, mythical world of our wildest dreams.)

I stirred with first light to find, early as it was, the scullions and kitchen-maids already up and busy, great fires burning on both hearths, one on either side of the kitchen doorway, baskets of newly baked bread being carried in from the bakehouse, shaving water set to boil in cauldrons, razors being stropped by the body-servants of both Duke and Bishop. I extracted my own razor from my pack, begged a little hot water and began scraping away at the night's stubble. (Because I am Saxon fair, my beard does not show as much as some men's, but I am never happy until I have removed it.)

I glimpsed my little kitchen-maid fleetingly, but she was too occupied running to and fro on errands for the cooks to be able to do more than wave from a distance. I filched some oatcakes from a table where they had been left to cool, sweetening them with a little honey. Jugs of ale had been placed ready to be carried into the great hall by the servers, and I managed to take several swigs from one of them without being noticed. After which there was nothing left to stay for, so I replaced my cloak and razor in my pack, and took it with me to the well just outside the scullery. I drew up a bucket of water to wash my face and hands, cleaned my teeth with the bit of willow bark I always carried for the purpose, and was ready to resume my journey.

The morning light had a brilliant quality, carrying the promise of another fine day. The scent of roses wafted over a nearby wall from what I guessed to be the ladies' pleasure garden, while the smells issuing from the bakehouse were no less entrancing, although the latter also had the effect of making me hungry. I had breakfasted very lightly for one of my height and girth, and could see no hope of getting more sustenance; everyone in the kitchens was far too busy. If I walked steadily, I reckoned, I would be inside Bath's walls by dinnertime, and I knew of several stalls and shops there selling excellent pies and pasties. So I shouldered my pack and made my way across the bustling inner courtyard, through the passage between the twin towers, across the barbican ditch and so to the outer ward of the castle.

The chapel bell was ringing for Prime. The chapel itself, a plain, rectangular building with buttresses at each corner and dedicated to Saint Leonard, stood close to the east gate, and as I walked by I was astonished to see that the Bishop was just about to enter. Accompanying him was the Duke of Clarence, still unshaven and looking more than a little annoyed at having been forced to rise so early. On a sudden impulse, I joined the little throng of servants and retainers following their masters in to worship.

Immediately my suspicions were aroused, for those sudden and inexplicable actions of mine usually meant that God was once more hovering at my elbow, nudging me along the path He wished me to take. He had need of my skills again; of that strange ability He had given me to unravel the tangled threads of wrongdoing and evil. I began my usual counter-strategy – even though past experience had taught me that it rarely availed me anything; you can't outwit the Almighty, but I always felt duty bound to try – and stood at the back of the congregation, bending my knees slightly in order to reduce my height and fixing my eyes on a wall-painting of Saint George slaying the dragon in an effort not to meet anyone's gaze. And it seemed as if I might have been successful when, the Mass over, everyone filed out of the chapel, the Duke and Bishop arm-in-arm leading the way, without my having been accosted.

I again hoisted up my pack, which I had left outside the door, and walked the few yards to the east gate. A young girl was just ahead of me, half running, half stumbling in her anxiety to reach the porter, who had that minute emerged from his lodge. I heard her call out him, 'Has he come yet, Burl?' And when the man shook his head she stopped in her tracks, biting her lower lip and looking worried. Some little drama was being enacted here, but it was nothing to do with me. I gave the porter a friendly nod before crossing the drawbridge and turning in the direction of Bath.

God, after all, had had no need of my services, and I was free to go home. Perversely, I felt bitterly disappointed. My pace slowed and my pack began to weigh heavily on my shoulders. I crested the rise and started on the long, dragging descent to Bath, nestling some five or six miles off, deep in its valley.

It was growing hotter by the minute and I was beginning to sweat. Such people as I encountered appeared to be as surly and as out of sorts as I was myself. The roads were dry and rutted, and passing carts threw up clouds of dust which made me sneeze and irritated my eyes. By the time I neared the Charterhouse at Hinton, I was feeling extremely sorry for myself.

I heard the pounding of hooves behind me and turned to look over my shoulder. A man wearing the livery of the Duke of Clarence reined in his mount beside me and slid to the ground.

'Roger the Chapman?' he demanded, and when I nodded he continued: 'You're to come back with me to Farleigh. His Grace so orders!' Then he added, unable to keep the note of incredulity from his voice, 'My lord says he has need of you.'

Chapter Two

I rode pillion behind the messenger back to Farleigh and we arrived just after ten o'clock, in time for dinner. Not that I could think about food just then, being led at once towards an upper room to await the Duke.

In both the outer and inner wards of the castle, carts were were being loaded and horses saddled ready for the ducal couple's midday departure. As one who carried most of his worldly goods upon his back, I never ceased to marvel at the amount of clothes and possessions deemed necessary by our lords and masters for even the shortest stay. As my guide and I passed within view of the south-west tower, its conical roof gleaming in the morning sun, two young pages dragged out a large, iron-bound, leather chest which I presumed belonged to the Duchess, judging by the fine gauze sleeve that trailed from beneath its lid. Behind them a tiring-woman stumbled beneath the weight of a red, velvet-covered jewel box.

It seemed that the Bishop, together with his retinue, had long since gone; as soon as breakfast was over, according to my companion. What business he had had with the Duke had evidently been completed the previous night, and His Grace must by now have been several miles along the road to Wells. I reflected how fortuitous it was that Stillington should have been visiting his diocese just as my lord of

Clarence was spending twenty-four hours at Farleigh. There was a whiff of collusion in the air, and I wondered what mischief they had been hatching together. But whatever it was, it would not affect my life, although the Queen's kinfolk might do well to beware. In the meantime, if my instincts served me aright, God had His own plans for me.

The messenger led me across the inner courtyard and up a short flight of steps to the great hall, where trestle tables were being laid for dinner. A twisting staircase in one corner brought us to a pleasant solar where the casements stood wide, flooding the room with warmth and light. I was almost blinded by the sudden glare, and was still trying to clear my vision when my companion bade me be seated while he went in search of the Duke. I groped my way to a stool and sat with my back to the window until my sight returned to normal, by which time I could hear footsteps on the stairs outside. The next moment my lord of Clarence, booted and spurred for his forthcoming journey, entered the solar accompanied by his wife and followed by a man and a young girl, the very one that I had seen by the chapel of the east gate earlier that same morning. I rose hastily to my feet.

I had never seen the Duchess Isabel close to before, and I was startled by her likeness to her younger sister, the Duchess of Gloucester. There was the same delicate colouring of eyes and skin, the same air of fragility that made me think of harebells blowing in the wind. She wore a loose robe of leaf-green sarsenet which imperfectly concealed the fact that she was pregnant – about five months gone by my reckoning, the dark circles beneath her eyes and the way she sank thankfully into a chair indicating that she was finding her condition trying. She already had children, the daughter Margaret who had been born at Farleigh, and a son called Edward after the King, his uncle. I thought that George of Clarence, had he been concerned for his wife's health, should have been content with the two he already had, for the Duchess looked a sick woman to me.

The Duke nodded curtly in my direction. 'I couldn't place your face when I first saw you yesterday evening,' he said. 'But then, when I noticed you again this morning at Mass, I remembered who you are. Our paths crossed last year when you saved my brother Richard from assassination.'

'I had that privilege,' I answered, bowing. 'His Grace the Duke of Gloucester has employed me once or twice on his private affairs, but I am a chapman by trade.'

Clarence seated himself in a carved armchair and pursed his lips. 'Yes, he told me all about you, how he offered you a place in his household and you refused.' He laughed mirthlessly. 'You're a fool, man! But I suppose you know that.'

'Perhaps, but I prefer to be my own master.'

The Duke shrugged and his blue eyes surveyed me with indifference. 'That's up to you, of course. The important thing at this moment is that I know my brother trusts you, and that I can therefore call upon you with confidence to perform a small service for me.' He waved a hand dismissively. 'Oh, nothing of any significance; not at all the kind of thing you've done for Dickon. An errand really!' He turned and beckoned forward the man and the girl. 'This is William Armstrong, one of my sergeants-at-arms, and this is his daughter Cicely, chamber-maid to the Duchess.'

The man was tall and thickset with closely cropped, curling red hair and a surly expression. The girl was as different from him as she possibly could be, the top of her head not reaching much above his shoulder. She had small, neat hands and feet, and a huge pair of violet-blue eyes beneath well-shaped eyebrows. Her hair was concealed under a linen hood, but from the few stray tendrils that had escaped their confinement and lay damply across her forehead, I guessed it to be a pale golden brown. She was not beautiful – her lips were too thin and there was a slight heaviness of the lower jaw – but when she glanced up and gave me an impish smile I was ready to swear that she was one of the prettiest girls I had ever met.

The Duke continued, 'Mistress Cicely is leaving us. She is going home to Glastonbury to her aunt . . .' He paused, looking to William Armstrong for enlightenment.

'Mistress Gildersleeve, my sister,' the Sergeant supplied gruffly. 'Cicely's to marry my elder nephew, her cousin Peter,' he added with pride. 'He and his brother, Mark, have their own business close to the abbey. They're parchment makers.'

'Yes, yes!' the Duke interrupted testily. He turned again to me. 'The point is, Chapman, that the said Peter Gildersleeve should have arrived here last night, ready to escort his betrothed back to Glastonbury and his mother's house this morning. Our being at Farleigh for twenty-four hours seemed the ideal opportunity for conveying Cicely thence with the least possible inconvenience to any member of my household. But Master Gildersleeve has failed to appear.' His Grace looked annoyed at this setback to his plans. 'Which is very inconsiderate of him. We must leave here no later than noon. I have to be in London by the middle of the week, and I cannot spare William to go with his daughter. He, on the other hand, is worried for her safety between here and her aunt's house at Glastonbury. So, Chapman! If this Peter Gildersleeve is still absent at midday, I am putting the girl in your charge, and will rely upon you to accompany her to her destination.'

I had no choice but to express my willingness to comply with the royal wishes. I did, however, raise one objection. 'Your Grace, I go on foot. I have no horse.'

The Duke frowned and drummed his fingers on the arm of his chair. 'Can you ride?' he demanded after a second or two's deliberation.

I acknowledged that I could, if forced to, adding, 'But I have not done so for some while.'

'Once learned, never forgotten,' Duke George replied shortly, and rose to his feet. 'I'll give orders for a mount to be ready for you in the stables. You can take the girl up behind you.' He moved towards the door. 'And you may eat your dinner in the great hall with the rest of us in ten minutes' time.'

The audience was at an end. He left the solar accompanied by the Duchess, who lingered in the doorway just long enough to bid the girl come to see her before quitting Farleigh. Then she followed her husband down the stairs and I found myself alone with William Armstrong and his daughter.

The former regarded me with a certain amount of suspicion. 'His Grace does right to trust you, I suppose. He seems to know you. I wasn't in France myself last year, so I can't vouch for his story. It really was you who saved my lord of Gloucester's life?'

'It was. And you may trust me with your daughter's, if that's what's worrying you.'

Armstrong sighed. 'Well, you look a strong lad, and I daresay you're handy with your fists if the need arises.' His eyes narrowed and he moved closer to me, lowering his voice so that Cicely could not hear what he was saying. 'But you're a good-looking fellow too, and my daughter's not long turned sixteen. A susceptible age, when girls grow flighty and don't necessarily want to do what's best for them. Cissy's future is assured with her cousin. She'll have a decent home and my sister to keep an eye on her. My nephews are fine, upstanding men in possession of a thriving business. Peter, especially, has a healthy respect for making money. My girl will want for nothing. But, as I said just now, she's at an age when a handsome face can easily turn her head. Do you understand me?'

'Perfectly,' I answered coolly. 'And I can assure you, Sergeant Armstrong, that your daughter's virtue is as safe in my hands as it would be in your own. Moreover, if we set off as soon as possible, on horseback, even with both of us in the saddle we should reach Glastonbury before dark. At this time of year, daylight still stretches well into the evening. There will be no necessity for us to spend a night on the road.'

He appeared satisfied, nodding in a grudging sort of way, then turned fiercely on his daughter. 'You behave yourself, mind, Cis! Do as you're told, and when you get to your aunt's find out what the devil's happened to Peter.'

'He's probably forgotten all about me,' Cicely suggested with a toss of her head. 'I don't believe he's any more in favour of this marriage than I am.'

William Armstrong shot out a hand and clouted her around one ear. 'You watch your tongue, my girl, or you'll get a beating.' He breathed heavily. 'It's high time you had a husband to tame you. Go on! Go and get your dinner. I'll see you again before you leave.'

When the door had closed behind her, he sighed. 'She's been motherless for the past three years, and that's why I asked the Duchess to take her into her household, so I could keep her under my eye. But I couldn't give her a mother's guiding hand, which is what a girl needs at that age.'

'Is that why you've arranged this marriage for her?' I enquired, expecting to be told to mind my own business.

But having started to confide in me, the Sergeant seemed unable to stop. 'It was arranged between my wife and sister when Cis was a baby. Peter was then eight years old and his brother four years younger. Mark would have been a more suitable match for her, being nearer to her in age, but Katherine, my wife – well, she knew that it was Peter who would inherit the parchment-making business when my brother-in-law died – which he did a twelvemonth since – and it gave the two women something to plan for. I was away a great deal, being then in the pay of my lord's father, the Duke of York. When he was killed at Wakefield, the December after Cis was born, I joined the household of my lord of Warwick; and after his death, His Grace of Clarence took me into his service. So I wasn't at home to say whether I approved of the match or no. But now I'm all in favour of it. Cicely was too young when Katherine died to marry Peter, and it wouldn't have been fair on my sister to saddle her with a headstrong child of thirteen. However, three years in Her Grace of Clarence's household has worked wonders. It's taught Cis discipline and how to serve others. She's ready for marriage now.'

A sudden frown creased William Armstrong's brow. 'But whatever has happened to Peter? Why hasn't the damned fellow shown up? I arranged it all by letter with Joan, my sister: the date, the place, the time. The Duke's chief clerk wrote and dispatched it for me, and both my nephews can read and write.'

'Some last minute business deal, a lame horse, a sudden indisposition,' I suggested. 'Any one of these explanations might be the reason. I'm sure there's no cause for alarm. Indeed, your nephew could still appear at any moment.'

* * *

But when dinner was over and the Duchess already ensconced in her litter, the Duke impatient to depart, there was still no sign of either of the Gildersleeve brothers. If Peter had been forced to send Mark as his deputy, it seemed that he must have been delayed as well.

Just before noon, therefore, I accompanied William Armstrong and his daughter to the stables in the outer ward of the castle, where a solid, broad-backed brown rouncy was standing patiently, Cicely's modest possessions already stowed in its two capacious saddle-bags. A groom held the animal's head while I mounted and then lifted my charge up behind me. Finally my cudgel, without which I refuse to stir a step, was handed to me and laid awkwardly across my knees.

'What's his name?' I asked, referring to the horse.

'Barnabas.' The groom watched contemptuously my inexpert fumblings with the reins. 'And you're to bring him back here tomorrow. Duke's orders.'

I doubted very much if His Grace had bothered his head with any such instructions, but did not say so, merely nodding in compliance.

William Armstrong clutched at Cicely's sleeve. 'Get your aunt to send word after me to let me know that everything's all right. We shall be in London for a day or two, and if I've heard nothing by the time we move on I'll leave word of our next destination.'

Cicely bent and kissed his cheek. 'Yes, Father,' she answered meekly; but the way she wrapped her arms about my waist and cuddled into my back belied her timidity. I decided I should do well to be wary of Cicely Armstrong. Had Peter Gildersleeve somehow learned that his intended bride was wilder than he had been led to expect, and got cold feet? I thought it improbable, but at least it offered a reasonable explanation for his non-appearance. (I did not know then that reason was not destined to be the most notable feature of what was to follow.)

It took me a while to get used to handling even so docile a horse as the brown cob, but as nothing I did appeared to throw him out of his stride or upset his calm good nature, Barnabas and I soon became friends. He responded in the most gentlemanly fashion to the slightest touch upon the reins, and his thick-crested neck and strong, sloping shoulders imbued me with a confidence which soon had me at ease in the saddle.

We had gone only a few miles before I felt able to strike up a conversation with my passenger and attempt to satisfy her insatiable curiosity as to how I came to be known by the Duke and his brother, my lord of Gloucester. I answered some of her questions and stalled others, eventually telling her bluntly that I had no intention of saying more.

'Well, it all sounds very exciting to me,' she said. 'A lot more exciting than making parchment!' Her scorn was withering.

'Making parchment is a very interesting job,' I reproved her, 'and requires great skill.'

'It may require skill,' she retorted, 'but it certainly isn't interesting. I used to watch my uncle doing it when I was a child. Scraping sheep and calf skins for hours on end is very, very boring.'

'Your cousins make vellum too, do they?' I asked.

She did not bother to answer, but pressed her little chin between my shoulder blades and worked her lower jaw up and down.

'Stop that!' I commanded. 'It's extremely irritating.'

Cicely giggled. 'I'll tell you something else about Peter,'

she said. 'He reads a lot. He has a chest full of dull old books and manuscripts that he's bought at fairs or from pedlars, and one or two that have been given him by the monks at Glastonbury. By the Librarian.'

'There's nothing wrong with reading,' I said sternly. 'It improves the mind. You'd do well to get Master Gildersleeve or his brother to teach you.'

'Can you read?' she inquired.

'Yes, and write,' I answered foolishly.

'Mmm. I thought perhaps you might. You're the strangest chapman I've ever met.' She cuddled closer. 'There's mystery about you, and I like that. *You* can teach me to read. How would that suit you?'

'It wouldn't suit me at all,' I replied, not mincing matters. 'In any case, once I've delivered you to your aunt, we shan't be seeing one another again. I shall find a stable for the horse, share his stall for the night, ride him back to Farleigh tomorrow and continue with my journey home to Bristol.'

There was silence for a moment, then, 'God may dispose matters quite differently,' was the sententious response.

It made me uneasy. Peter Gildersleeve's mysterious failure to show up at Farleigh Hungerford, coupled with my opportune presence in the castle, suggested that God did indeed have other plans for me, plans which undoubtedly included some element of personal danger if past experiences were anything to go by. Well, I had felt cheated when I had suspected that God, after all, had no need of me, so it would be hypocritical of me now to complain. Nevertheless, as always, my excitement was tinged with apprehension and resentment at this divine intervention in my affairs.

We stopped mid-afternoon to rest and refresh ourselves, buying milk and honey cakes from a beekeeper's cottage, and turning Barnabas loose to crop the surrounding grass. The sun was long past its zenith, but it was still extremely warm. On a nearby pond, ducks were swimming. One of the females was chasing another, squawking and quacking, neck arched in fury, water flying from the spread and speckled wings in a spindrift of iridescent drops. The fronded reeds, the colour of ripe barley, rippled as they passed. Cicely laughed and clapped her hands, encouraging the aggressor.

The shadows were beginning to lengthen as, later that afternoon, we made our leisurely way across the lower slopes of the Mendips. Sheep dotted the hills.

'These animals belong to the Pennards,' Cicely informed me. 'Peter and Mark buy some of their skins from Anthony and his sons. That is, I expect they do because my uncle always used to do so. This part of the holding is called the Sticks. I don't know why. That's the Pennards' house in the distance, and that's their shepherd's hut, there, in that dip below us.'

As she spoke, both house and hut disappeared from view as we descended into another fold of ground, then re-appeared as we mounted the opposite slope. Once more we descended to where the grey stone shelter, with its roof of moss and twigs, stood in the lee of a mound topped by a small, wind-blasted copse, before continuing down the stony track and skirting my home town of Wells.

We had only some five miles to go now, and every step of the route was as familiar to me as my own name: the receding line of the hills, the raised causeway which carried travellers dryshod across the stretches of waterlogged moorland, and the horizon perpetually dominated by the great, brooding hump of of the Tor. There, throughout the ages, contending religions had struggled for predominance. Our

Celtic ancestors had thought it to be the home of Gwyn ap Nudd, King of the Underworld, Lord of the Wild Hunt. Even today some people still believed it to be hollow, the haunt of fairies and hobgoblins. But with the coming of Joseph of Arimathea and, later, Saint Augustine, the Church had claimed it for its own and built the chapel of Saint Michael the Archangel on its summit. Yet who was to say for certain that Christianity had triumphed?

Hastily suppressing these heretical thoughts, I urged Barnabas to one last effort. As we plodded down through Bove Town, past the chapel of Saint James, I asked Cicely the whereabouts of her aunt's house and shop.

'What?' She had been strangely silent for the last half-mile or so, her former high spirits quenched. 'Oh! It's in the High Street, between Saint John's Church and the pilgrims' hostelry. The shop and work rooms are on ground level, with the living quarters over. You can't miss it; it's opposite the north gatehouse of the abbey.'

Indeed, as soon as I saw it, I remembered the place from six years earlier, when I had been a novice at Glastonbury (although I had not known then that it was a parchment maker's nor anything of its inhabitants). I drew rein, thankful to be at my journey's end, and slid from the rouncy's back, reaching up to lift Cicely from the saddle. Hardly had I done so than the street door flew open and a small, birdlike woman emerged, hands fluttering in agitation and violet eyes, a paler version of her niece's, brimming with tears. I could see at once which member of her family Cicely favoured, and reflected yet again on the amazing diversity of features and stature between siblings.

'Oh my child! My dear child! You managed to get here!' Dame Gildersleeve flung her arms around her niece's neck and burst out crying. 'I didn't know what to do for the best.

I thought about sending Mark or one of the men to Farleigh, but they're all out looking, and Mark flatly refused to give up the search to fetch you.' All this was punctuated by sobs which made her utterances difficult to understand, but both Cicely and I somehow managed to catch the gist of it.

The girl patted the older woman's shoulder and made soothing noises. A little colour had crept back into her cheeks and the sparkle to her eyes.

'Aunt Joan,' she urged, 'tell me exactly what has happened!'

Mistress Gildersleeve took a deep breath and attempted to speak more calmly. 'It's Peter,' she sobbed. 'He's vanished.'

Chapter Three

I could not immediately satisfy my curiosity by following Cicely and her aunt into the house, because the rouncy's welfare had to come before mine. I knew enough of horsemanship to understand that this was one of the cardinal rules; and I also knew it to be the reason why, as long as I had youth and strength, I should always go about my business on two legs instead of four. Not only did I hear and see more travelling on foot, but neither was I forced to place an animal's well-being before my own.

I was advised by a passing pot-boy from the George hostelry that there was a good livery stable in Northload Street, just off the market place, where Barnabas would be well looked after for a reasonable daily charge. I made my way there, and after satisfying myself that the stalls were clean and capacious and the straw fresh, I handed him over with a sigh of relief and returned to the Gildersleeves' home as fast as I could.

Cicely must have been watching out for me. As I approached, she appeared at the street door to greet and guide me upstairs to the living quarters, where, in an airy chamber directly above the workshop at the back of the house, overlooking the kitchens and a small, walled garden, sat a tearful Dame Joan. A bottle of what I discovered to be primrose wine and four mazers had been placed on the table, together with a dish of cinnamon biscuits and another of medlars, squashy and brown and bursting from their skins. A glance through the open casement showed me the tree below, in the centre of some neatly laid out flower and herb beds, with a narrow bench surrounding its trunk. There was money enough for comfort here, I decided, stealing a furtive and hasty look around the room.

Cicely urged me to sit down at the table with them, and poured me some wine.

'Aunt, this is the Duke of Clarence's messenger I've been telling you about. His name is Roger.' I noticed that she carefully avoided any reference to my true occupation.

Mistress Gildersleeve nodded, dabbing at her eyes, apparently too overcome with emotion to question my lack of livery as one of His Grace's men.

'What has happened?' I asked, sipping my wine and looking across at my erstwhile charge.

But it was Mistress Gildersleeve who answered. A great shudder convulsed her thin frame. 'Witchcraft!' she uttered, barely above a whisper.

'Aunt, please! Don't say that! We know nothing for certain.' Cicely got up from her stool and, stooping, put her arms around the older woman's shoulders. 'When Mark returns, or Rob or John, we might have better news. One of them may have discovered Peter's whereabouts or what has happened to him. No one can just vanish into thin air.'

Dame Joan's violet eyes widened in horror. 'He can if the Devil takes him!'

It was Cicely's turn to shiver, but she protested gamely, 'And what would Old Scratch want with a good, upright citizen like Peter? A man who says his prayers and goes to Mass as regularly as anyone in the parish.'

Dame Joan pressed her hands to her flushed cheeks. 'All

those books that he keeps in that chest at the back of the workshop – how do we know what's in them? They might contain incantations, spells, black magic. I can't read and neither can you. We wouldn't be any the wiser even if we studied them.'

'But Mark can read,' Cicely said impatiently, releasing her aunt and returning to her place on the opposite side of the table. 'He would know if there was anything blasphemous or . . . or wrong in them.'

'Mark may be able to read, but he only does so for business purposes,' Dame Joan reproved 'He doesn't waste his time filling up his head with nonsense.'

'Mistress Gildersleeve,' I interrupted, 'I should be pleased to know exactly what has taken place, all the circumstances of your son's disappearance . . .'

But, 'One of the maids has left already,' was the only response I got. 'Maud has gone back to her father's cottage in Bove Town. By now the whole of Glastonbury must be buzzing with the news.'

I looked appealingly at Cicely, who leant across and touched Dame Joan on the arm.

'Aunt, will you permit me to tell Roger the facts?'

The afflicted lady gave a little moan. 'Do what you like,' she said tearfully.

'Very well. Thank you.' Cicely clasped her hands together on the table. 'Perhaps Roger might be able to suggest a solution, you never know.'

She smiled at me, that tantalising, impish smile of hers, and it occurred to me that she was very calm for one confronted with the news that her betrothed had vanished. She also seemed suddenly more grown up. I made no remark, however, but poured myself another cup of wine and settled down to listen to her explanation.

* * *

As the interruptions and emendations of Dame Joan (in addition to my own questioning) made Cicely's explanation longer and more confusing than necessary, I shall set down the facts in narrative form as they seemed to me after I had sorted and assembled them into some sort of order.

It was now Tuesday. On the previous Friday, Peter Gildersleeve had announced his intention of visiting the Pennards (already known to me through my earlier conversation with Cicely). There was nothing unusual in this as, like their father before them, the brothers bought some of their skins from Anthony Pennard and his two sons, Gilbert and Thomas. He had therefore set out not long after dinner, riding the five or so miles between Glastonbury and Wells on Dorabella, a chestnut mare which belonged to the family. (If a second horse or a carriage for Dame Joan were needed, they were hired from the Northload Street livery stables.)

In the event, however, Peter had made no attempt to see either Anthony or his sons. The three men were from home that afternoon, but Mistress Pennard and both her maids had been indoors all day, not wishing to venture forth in the stifling heat, and they all declared that no one had called at the house. But Peter Gildersleeve *had* been seen on Pennard land, a fact attested to by one of the shepherd-lads, Abel Fairchild. Not only had Abel set eyes on Peter Gildersleeve, but the terrified boy also swore that the visitor had magically vanished almost in his presence.

By an odd coincidence – or perhaps it was not a coincidence: was it not just as likely that God had taken over the reins and was directing my every move? – this event had occurred on the very same stretch of ground across which Cicely and I had travelled earlier that afternoon, within those two folds of the Mendip hills where she had pointed out the shepherd's hut and the distant prospect of the Pennards' house. Abel had been following his flock down to the lower slopes, and had noticed Peter Gildersleeve descending from the copse towards the hut. He had watched him pause and stare around once he had reached level ground. Peter had then glanced up, recognized Abel and raised his hand in greeting.

At this point, the undulation had hidden both him and the hut from Abel's sight; but the boy was young and active, and it had been only a matter of seconds before he had ascended the opposite slope. In those few seconds, however, Peter Gildersleeve had completely vanished.

To begin with, Abel had thought nothing of it. He assumed that for some reason or other Peter had gone into the hut; so, being a conscientious lad and mindful of his master's interests, he had opened the door and looked inside to discover what the intruder was up to. But there was no one there. Feeling a little uneasy, although not yet frightened, Abel had walked slowly around the outside of the building, first clockwise and then withershins, but there was still no sign of his quarry, and the rest of the lower hollow was just as empty. Unease had begun to give way to panic. He had called Peter's name and once more searched the interior of the hut, but to no avail. The man he had seen alive and well only minutes earlier had disappeared without trace.

Abel was, by now, thoroughly scared. He'd scrambled up towards the trees and run as fast as his legs would carry him to the farmhouse. At first, Mistress Pennard had refused to listen, being too busy scolding him for leaving his flock unattended, but when at last she paid attention to his story, she had been sufficiently impressed by his general demeanour to send one of the maids back with him as far as the copse. There they had discovered Dorabella tethered to a tree and quietly cropping the grass. Of Peter Gildersleeve, however, there was still no sign.

The day wore on. Towards suppertime the three Pennard men had returned from Priddy, high on the Mendips, where they had been visiting Anthony's younger brother, Henry, and had been told the sorry tale. Abel had been sent for and closely questioned, whereupon all three Pennards had visited the site of Peter's disappearance to conduct their own search, but without success. Consequently, after supper, it had been decided that one of the brothers must ride to Glastonbury, leading Dorabella, and tell the Gildersleeves what had happened. It was reckoned that Dame Joan and Mark would, in any case, be growing worried at Peter's delay in returning home. Foot-pads and thieves had been plaguing the whole area for some months past, and they would be feeling concerned for his safety, even though there were still a few hours until dusk.

Such had been the events of the last Friday, and the Gildersleeve household had been in turmoil ever since. Had it not been for his abandoning of Dorabella it might have been assumed, by Mark at least, that there was a reasonable explanation for Peter's absence and that he had gone off about some secret business of his own. Peter, however, would never have left the horse for more than an hour or so; she was far too valuable to him. In addition (and as I already knew) he had been due to ride to Farleigh on the Monday to collect his betrothed and bring her back with him. Mark and the two apprentice lads, Rob Undershaft and John Longbones, had been out hunting for him every hour of daylight since.

'But of course they won't find him!' Dame Joan now

exclaimed, pressing her hands together until the knuckles showed white. 'He's been taken by the Devil! We shall all be outcasts!'

'Aunt! Will you please stop saying that!'

There was a sudden, underlying note of hysteria in Cicely's voice, and I noticed that she was no longer smiling. In the retelling, the eerie little story had begun to affect her, and she was beginning to share her aunt's belief in witchcraft and magic. Perhaps it was not so surprising that these mysterious events should have happened there, in the Vale of Avalon, where myth and legend abound, and where the bodies of Arthur and Guinevere lie in their great black marble mausoleum before the high altar-of the abbey...

If, that is, they *are* the bodies of Arthur and Guinevere. (Am I the only person to have my doubts? Probably not, but it's a brave man or woman who will voice them openly with so much of the abbey's wealth depending on acceptance of the fact.) Everyone hereabouts knows the story, of course: how, almost three centuries ago, seven years after a disastrous fire which almost destroyed the abbey, Abbot Henry de Soilly ordered his monks to dig in a certain place, where they found two sets of bones and a hank of yellow hair buried in the trunk of a hollowed-out oak tree. Also in the coffin, by the happiest of chances, was a lead cross with an inscription to identify its burden. Pilgrims have flocked to Glastonbury ever since, including, ninety years on from that fortuitous discovery, King Edward the first and his beloved queen, Eleanor of Castile, who, in a magnificent ceremony still reverently talked about two hundred years later, transferred the bones, carrying them in their arms, from the first tomb in one of the abbey's side-chapels to their present resting place.

And where Arthur and Guinevere are buried, might not

the spirits of Merlin and the evil Morgan le Fay also haunt the surrounding countryside? Succeeding abbots have tried in vain to separate the real Arthur from his mythical persona – but who will prefer oatcake if he can have a doucette? It's almost as if people enjoy being frightened.

I did, however, make an attempt to allay Cicely's fears by suggesting that there must be a perfectly straightforward explanation for her betrothed's disappearance.

'Then what is it?' she demanded. 'Tell me! I'm more than willing to listen.'

But naturally, when confronted with this uncompromising request, I was unable to find an answer. 'Let's wait until your cousin Mark and his men return,' I suggested. 'Let's hear what they have to say first. After all, they may have news.'

But when, half an hour later, just as darkness fell, the three returned home, they had nothing more to impart. There had been no further sighting of Peter since Friday afternoon, when he had last been seen by Abel Fairchild.

Mark Gildersleeve joined us above stairs, having first stabled Dorabella and sent his two apprentices to the kitchens in search of their belated supper. He had refused all his mother's offers of food, being, he said, too tired to eat.

He was very like his uncle to look at, having the same curling red hair and sturdy, thickset body, although he was, I judged, a good half a head shorter than William Armstrong. His expression was also less truculent, but he could be just as surly when unsure of his ground.

'Who in the devil's name is this?' he demanded, suddenly becoming aware of my presence.

So Cicely repeated her story, once again omitting the fact that I was not really one of the Duke of Clarence's men. But Mark was more astute than Dame Joan.

'Why doesn't he wear livery then?' he grunted suspiciously.

Cicely would have made up some story – I could see the sparkle in her eyes as she warmed to the deception – but I judged the time ripe to admit the truth.

'I used to be a novice here at the abbey,' I said, 'but I renounced my vocation to become a chapman, a calling much more to my liking. I am however known to my lord of Clarence, having done several small services in the past for his brother, the Duke of Gloucester.'

'He saved Duke Richard's life,' Cicely cut in, and smiled admiringly at me across the table.

I saw Mark shoot her a sidelong glance. He plainly felt it his duty to keep an eye on his volatile cousin. 'If you're a chapman, where's your pack?' he asked, his tone belligerent.

'I left it at Farleigh Castle. I shall pick it up again when I return with the horse.'

'What horse?'

Patiently, I explained about the rouncy and where he was stabled.

Mark Gildersleeve continued to stare dubiously at me. 'You sound a very strange chapman to me. What were these services you rendered my lord of Gloucester?'

Reluctantly, and as briefly as possible, I sketched in my version of the events which had linked me, in the past, to Duke Richard, but my listener's frown only deepened.

'If what you tell me is true,' he said when I had finished, 'why are you not a rich man? Why are you still a pedlar? God's teeth! Do you think I'm a greenhorn?'

Cicely was on her feet, spots of colour burning in her cheeks. 'You may not be green, but you're very ill-mannered!' she exclaimed furiously. 'Roger is not a liar! Do you suppose that my father would have entrusted me to the care of a stranger if that man hadn't been recommended to him by the Duke himself? And do you also then accuse my lord of Clarence of being a liar?'

I could see that her hot-headed defence of me was making Mark even more suspicious than he had been before, and I hastened to intervene.

'Your cousin is justified,' I told her soothingly, 'in finding my story at odds with my present condition. The fact is, Master Gildersleeve –' and I smiled placatingly at him – 'that I prefer to be my own master. I have never taken kindly to being at the beck and call of other people. Nor do I like being confined for any length of time between four walls, which was one reason among others that I quit the monastic life. As a pedlar, I do my own bidding and no one else's. My existence may sometimes be hard, but in terms of freedom I am a wealthy man.'

Mark grunted, his hostility fading somewhat. He poured himself more wine. 'I can understand that,' he conceded grudgingly, but then he grew more expansive. 'I've always known what it is to be my own master – or, at least,' he amended, 'to work for nobody except my father – and now for Peter, which is the same thing. Or very nearly the same . . .' His voice tailed off as he remembered his brother and, with a great groan, he covered his face with his hands.

Dame Joan, affected by this sign of despair, began to cry quietly, the tears trickling unheeded down her cheeks. Only Cicely seemed unable to express her grief – if, that is, she felt any. Instead, she asked, 'Where do you mean to spend the night, Master Chapman?' And I felt her kick her aunt's leg under the table.

I said hurriedly, 'I shall find somewhere, never fear. I've

38

money in my pocket and can procure a place easily enough at one of the ale-houses in the town. If I recall rightly, there are a vast number of them, so I'm certain of getting a bed. They can't all be occupied by pilgrims.'

Dame Joan shook her head. 'You must stay here,' she said, wiping away her tears with trembling fingers. 'We have only one guest chamber, which must now belong to Cicely until . . . until . . .' She could not bring herself to add 'until she marries', but continued bravely, 'You may sleep in Peter's bed in his and Mark's room.'

I glanced quickly at Mark to see how he would respond to this invitation to share his bedchamber, but, to my surprise, he raised no objection. He seemed rather to be sunk in a reverie of his own, not even looking up when Cicely exclaimed, with a clap of her hands, 'Good! That's settled! You deserve our hospitality after squiring me all the way from Farleigh.'

I tried to quell her exuberance with as stern a glance as I could muster, but she ignored me, laying a hand on her cousin's arm and giving it a little shake. 'Mark! Why don't we persuade Roger to remain with us for a day or two? On his own admission, he has solved other mysteries. Why shouldn't he give us the benefit of his past experience and try to discover what has happened to Peter?'

'Eh?' Mark blinked at her, obviously not having listened to a word she'd said, and Cicely was obliged to repeat her question. When at last he understood, Mark looked at me doubtfully. 'Would you be willing to delay your journey?' he asked. 'As I understand it, you were on your way home when you reached Farleigh. And what about this cob that has been lent to you from the Duke of Clarence's stables?'

I hesitated. Here was my chance – the one chance God always gave me – to extricate myself from whatever it was that He had planned. But, as on all the previous occasions, I could not do it. God had bestowed on me the gift of solving puzzles as well as endowing me with an insatiable curiosity. 'Nosiness' my mother had called it, and she was probably right.

'I can spare a few days,' I said. 'The weather is still very warm and the evenings light; my mother-in-law and child can do without me a little while longer. As for the rouncy, I doubt it's one of the more valuable horses in His Grace of Clarence's stables. Its absence won't worry the Farleigh grooms as long as they hold my pack in exchange for it. Besides, the groom who was instructed to saddle it for me and Mistress Cicely will probably have moved on with the Duke, and those left behind may care nothing for the transaction, or even know of it.'

'You'll stop then?'

It was impossible to tell from Mark Gildersleeve's tone whether he was pleased by my decision or not. But there was no mistaking the pleasure on Cicely's smiling countenance, nor Dame Joan's tearful gratitude, although I did not delude myself that either had any special belief in my abilities to unravel the problem of Peter's disappearance. I could only hazard a guess at Cicely's reason for wishing me to stay, and I resolved to keep a wary eye on that young woman. Dame Joan simply looked upon me as just another person to join in the hunt.

'I'll stop,' I agreed, 'for a day or two at least.'

Mark nodded. 'Well, the lads and I will be up at first light tomorrow morning to continue the search. Rob and John will go the shorter distances on foot. I shall ride Dorabella to Wells and beyond, so you'd better join me on that rouncy.'

I shook my head. 'I prefer to go my own way. Pardon me

for saying so, Master Gildersleeve, but this aimless wandering about the countryside is achieving nothing. You have been looking for your brother for four days now, and have found no trace of him. It's time to try other methods, to start asking questions, which you can, if you wish, leave to me. You and your apprentices would surely do better to pay attention to the business rather than Master Peter's return. He won't thank you to find it neglected, particularly as he is soon to be married.'

My advice was received with varying degrees of approval. Dame Joan stopped crying and roundly declared that it was the most sensible thing she had heard all day; Mark looked offended, but said that he would sleep on my offer; while Cicely appeared suddenly glum, presumably at the prospect of having Peter restored to her unharmed. It was all I could do to repress a smile.

But my mood sobered when I reflected on the unlikelihood of such an event ever taking place. I felt in my bones that if I did manage to find Peter Gildersleeve, he would no longer be alive.

Chapter Four

Dame Joan earned my undying gratitude by insisting that we must eat before retiring to bed. My stomach had been reminding me for the past half-hour that, except for the cinnamon biscuits and medlars, it had had no sustenance since the honey cakes and milk which Cicely and I had bought at the beekeeper's cottage. To my great relief, Mark Gildersleeve also admitted to being hungry now that he had rested a while, and suggested that his mother and cousin repair to the kitchen to see what they could forage.

But the practical Dame Joan said that we should all go. 'If the chapman is to be our guest, it's better he learns his way around the house as soon as possible.'

So Mark and I followed the women down the twisting stairs to the long passage which led from the front door to the back, past the shop and workroom and out into the garden, now shrouded in darkness. The kitchen, a single-storey building, stood at a right angle to the rest of the house, joined to it at one corner but without, apparently, there being any internal door connecting them. Its shutters stood open to the warm night air, and the candlelight spilled out across the slatted wooden walkway which surrounded it. The soft, contented whinny of a horse told me that Dorabella was comfortably settled for the night in her stable which, I judged, was situated somewhere on the other side of the kitchen.

As we were about to enter, an owl swooped low above our heads, screeching like the spirits of the damned. Cicely gave an echoing cry and clutched my arm, clinging to it longer than was necessary. At least, Mark Gildersleeve seemed to think so, roughly detaching her hand from my sleeve and deploring her stupidity.

'In God's name, girl, you've seen an owl before! What's got into you?'

'Leave the child alone,' his mother chided him. 'This business has made us all jumpy and uncertain.'

Inside the kitchen, a sleepy maid was still entertaining the two apprentices, who were nodding over the remains of their meal, plainly more than ready for their beds. Mark dismissed them to their pallets in the workshop, but not before I had had time to acquaint myself with their faces and to distinguish one from the other.

Rob Undershaft was the taller of the two, a stringy boy of some fourteen summers who had outgrown his strength, with bad teeth marring a none-too-ready smile, and pale blue eyes almost hidden beneath a fall of lank, fair hair (the sort of hair my mother always used to describe as 'straight as a yard of pump water'). John Longbones, despite his name and being about the same age, was nearly a head shorter, but no fatter. His hair was red but, unlike Mark Gildersleeve's, it was that harsh, uncompromising shade which is almost orange. His hazel eyes blinked a little short-sightedly at the world, and he had the pale skin and easy capacity to blush that afflicts most people of his colouring.

When they had gone, Dame Joan began shooing the maid around the kitchen, chivvying her to set more water on the fire to boil, and to fetch the rest of the cold bacon from the larder. This diminutive creature, however, seemed to stand in no awe of her mistress, grumbling roundly about having to work single-handed since Maud's departure for her father's cottage in Bove Town.

'You let Lydia get away with too much, Mother,' Mark complained angrily. 'One of these days she'll go too far and you'll have to dismiss her.'

'Lyddie's a good girl,' Mistress Gildersleeve retorted. 'Let her alone. We understand one another. Besides, I don't want her leaving me as well.'

'Why has Maud gone?' Mark demanded, frowning.

'Black magic, that's why!' And Dame Joan hurriedly crossed herself. 'The circumstances of Peter's disappearance unsettled her. And she won't be the only one to give us the cold shoulder if we don't be quick and find out what's happened to him.'

Mark sank on to a stool and rubbed his forehead with fingers that were shaking slightly. Dame Joan, on the other hand, bustling around, cutting collops of cold, fat bacon, pouring out measures of ale and heating them over the fire, setting Lydia to slice bread and unwrap a fresh slab of butter from its cooling dock leaves, seemed temporarily restored to cheerfulness.

It was only later, when we had finished eating and drinking, that she again became distressed; but it was a distress caused more by what their neighbours might be thinking than by any conviction that her elder son was dead. In her heart, it seemed, she was still expecting him to walk through the door at any moment, with some perfectly simple explanation of where he had been for the past four days hovering on his lips.

I could see that Mark was less sure of his brother's fate, and his mother's words about black magic had worried him. Whatever his affection for Peter – and I was not yet certain how deep this went – he knew that the business would suffer if a member of his family were tainted by any association, however remote, with sorcery, either as practitioner or victim.

After thinking profoundly for several minutes, he looked across the kitchen table at me. 'Did you mean what you said, Chapman? Are you willing to stay a while and see what you can discover regarding my brother's disappearance? It might be better, I agree,' he went on, turning to address his mother, 'if Rob, John and I continue to lead as normal a life as possible. If people perceive us to be untroubled, they may think we know more than we do concerning Peter's whereabouts. Well, Master Chapman? What do you say?'

'I'm willing,' I agreed. 'But, as I told you, I've left my pack at Farleigh Castle, expecting to be parted from it for no more than a night. In addition to my wares, it contains my spare shirt and hose. I may therefore have to borrow these articles of clothing from you. Fortunately I have brought my razor and the willow bark I use for cleaning my teeth with me.' And I patted the pouch fixed to my belt. 'As for my cudgel, which I left at the livery stable with Barnabas, I shall retrieve that first thing in the morning.'

'I'm sure Mark will be only too happy to lend you anything you need,' Dame Joan said firmly before her son could quibble.

Mark hesitated, then grunted his assent and rose to his feet. 'It's time everyone was in bed. I've been up since dawn and I'm tired.'

'We're all tired,' Cicely told him. She had been silent for the past half-hour, idly toying with the food on her plate, but now she appeared to have recovered her former spirits. Like her aunt, she seemed unable to visualize Peter's death. At present it was just a game to her; a game which might postpone, for a short while at least, her unwanted marriage. 'Roger and I have ridden all the way from Farleigh today. You might think of someone besides yourself now and then, cousin.'

Lydia, who was washing the dirty dishes, clattered them loudly as if suggesting that she, too, could do with a little consideration from time to time, and Dame Joan rose from her stool and went to help her. Joan seemed a good-hearted woman and one, I guessed, who had not been born to the creature comforts she now enjoyed – and who, moreover, had not allowed her pride to increase with her rise in status. I warmed to her, and determined to do my utmost to discover what had happened to her son.

Mark, Cicely and I made our way back across the darkened garden to the house, where the lamps and candles were still burning.

'Leave them,' Mark instructed. 'Mother will douse them when she comes in.' He added angrily, 'She'll never get any respect from that girl while she treats her more like a friend than a servant.'

'She might get love and affection, though,' Cicely suggested pertly as she preceded us upstairs.

Mark made no answer except to say, 'You know where you're sleeping, cousin. Have you unpacked your things?'

'I shall do so now. I haven't had time before.'

At the door of her room, Cicely dropped a mocking curtsey and blew us both a kiss. At least, I hoped that it was for both of us, but I could not help suspecting that it was really aimed at me.

I ignored her and followed Mark Gildersleeve into the adjoining bedchamber. It was a pleasant apartment. Its window-shutters were still set wide to the warm, scented darkness, and while Mark lit the wicks of two horn-paned lanterns, I was able to make out that the window itself overlooked the back of the kitchen and Dorabella's stable. I was also able to determine the bulky, black shape of the neighbouring house.

Turning back into the room, I noticed a substantial clothes chest against one wall, and a good-sized oaken cupboard carved with a pattern of acanthus leaves standing in a corner. The bed, with its blue damask coverlet and rubbed velvet curtains of almost the same colour, dominated the chamber, but it was the bed-head which caught and held my gaze. It was built higher and deeper than most others I'd seen, and between the two bedposts, also decorated with acanthus leaves, were set a variety of small drawers and cupboards.

Mark, who was sitting on the chest pulling off his boots, saw me staring. 'It was my father's bed,' he said, 'and his father's and grandfather's before that.' He went on in a deliberately flattened tone: 'He left it to my brother in his will. "To my son Peter, my second-best bed." This is my half, nearest the wall. You'll have to take the other.'

I had not realized until that moment that when Dame Joan spoke of the brothers sharing a room, she also meant that they shared a bed. It was a common enough practice and should not have dismayed me as it did, but for some reason I could not fathom I did not relish sleeping with Mark Gildersleeve, and I was relieved to see that a large feather bolster divided the mattress in two.

'What will happen when Peter and Mistress Cicely are wed?' I enquired, and was favoured with a wintry smile.

'Rather, what *would* have happened, don't you mean?' Mark countered. 'The answer is that I should have been banished to the chamber which my cousin is occupying at present, while she took my place in here. But do you truly believe that they will ever be married now?'

I clambered into bed, having stripped down to my under-garments, and lay back against the pillows, linking my hands behind my head. 'You feel there's no hope then of Peter still being alive?'

Mark closed the window, extinguished both lanterns and climbed in beside me. 'Do you?' he asked bluntly.

The darkness was absolute, thick and clinging like a fog, the heat suffocating, and I found it difficult to breathe. My heart beat wildly, and it needed all my will-power not to leap out and reopen the shutters. But I forced myself to remain outwardly calm, and gradually the sense of panic faded.

'Well, do you?' he demanded, irritated by my silence.

'No,' I admitted. 'No, I don't think I do.'

Given the close, fetid atmosphere of the room, it was inevitable that, when I did at last fall asleep, I should dream. As a child I suffered from frequent nightmares, but as I had grown older these were replaced by normal, if unusually vivid, dreams. My mother, to annoy me, had always insisted that they were due to overeating, but I could never bring myself to admit that this was true, and certainly some of them had an almost prophetic quality. Tonight, I dreamt I was standing on that same ridge of ground upon which I had stood that afternoon, where Abel Fairchild had been last Friday, looking down on the roof of the shepherd's hut below me. Away to my right, on the very lowest slopes of that part of the Mendip Hills, I could make out the Pennards' house. Someone was descending from the copse into the lower hollow, but his face was averted from me. I knew, however, without being told, that it was Peter Gilders-leeve. Then, with the suddenness that one experiences only in dreams, I was standing outside the hut, staring in through the window. But I could see no one inside, although I felt certain that I was not alone. I started to walk round and round the building, searching frantically for this other person, the sweat pouring down my body. And at that moment, a hand reached out and grabbed my shoulder . . .

'Wake up, man! Wake up! You're tossing and turning and groaning fit to wake the whole house!' Mark was sitting up in bed trying furiously to rouse me, his fingers digging into the top of my arm.

I propped myself up on one elbow, knuckling my eyes with the opposite hand. I realized that I was indeed sweating profusely on account of the heat of the room, so, still somewhat dazed, I pushed back the bed-coverings, swung my feet to the floor and groped my way to the window to fling wide the shutters.

The night air poured in to bathe my hot face, gratefully upturned to the starlit sky and the pale, cold radiance of a three-quarter moon. I stayed thus for several seconds, before a flicker of movement caught my eye, making me turn my head sharply in the direction of Dorabella's stall.

'What is it? What have you seen?' Mark hissed from behind me, and I realized that he, too, had left the bed and followed me over to the window.

'I thought I saw someone move, over by the stable, but . . . no, I can't see anything now. It must have been my imagination.'

'Let me look!' He elbowed me aside, leaning as far as he safely could out of the open casement until, at last, he drew his head and shoulders back into the room. 'Everything seems quiet to me.'

'I'm probably still half asleep,' I apologized. 'The room's so hot and stuffy. I've been dreaming.'

'So I gathered.' His tone was dry. 'You were moaning loud enough to wake the dead.'

'I'm not used to sleeping so confined.' But my explanation fell on deaf ears. Mark was busy with thoughts of his own.

'Stay here,' he ordered abruptly, pulling on a woollen bedgown and pushing his feet into a pair of flat leather slippers. 'I'm just going to make sure that no one's out there.'

'Let me come as well,' I urged, 'in case there's any danger.'

'No.' His tone brooked no argument. 'Two of us creeping about the house in the small hours of the morning are more likely to rouse the women, and they're sufficiently disturbed by this business already.'

I was a guest in his home, and was therefore forced to accede to his wishes, so I had to content myself with resuming my watch at the open window and trying to oversee his safety as best I could from there. After a few moments, during which he must have let himself out through the street door, I saw him turn the right-hand corner of the house and walk towards Dorabella's stable, which stood alongside the pump and the privy. The mare gave a soft whinny of recognition as he approached, then was silent again. Mark merged with the shadow thrown by the rear wall of the kitchen and vanished behind her stall, his passage marked only by a faint ripple of blackness.

The time seemed endless before he reappeared, but in reality I suppose it was no more than two or three minutes. He glanced up and shook his head, a gesture he repeated, along with a shrug of his shoulders, when he joined me once more in the bedchamber.

'You were mistaken,' he said. 'There's no one there. You must have dreamt it.'

He insisted on closing the shutters again in spite of my protests, and we both climbed back into bed, the thick feather bolster between us. However, I could tell by his restless tossing as he tried to find a comfortable position that he was now as wide awake as I was.

I rolled on to my back and asked, 'What do you think your brother was doing on the Pennards' land?'

'We buy our sheepskins from them.' Mark heaved himself over on to his left side so that he was facing me. 'What's so strange about that?'

'But he didn't go to the house to find Anthony Pennard or either of the sons. Not if we can trust the testimony of Mistress Pennard and the maids, that is.'

There was silence for a moment before Mark said curtly, 'I see no reason why they should lie.'

'Maybe not, but people aren't always as honest as they seem.' I raised my arms above my head and kicked aside some of the coverings in an effort to keep myself cool. 'Peter was last seen by Abel Fairchild some distance from the house, so it would appear to be impossible that any of the Pennard household could have had a hand in the way he vanished.'

My companion shivered. 'What do you think has happened to him?' he asked, his voice catching in his throat.

'I don't know,' I said. 'What do you?'

There was no answer for several seconds. Finally Mark admitted, 'Like you, I've no idea.' He spoke so quietly that I had to strain to hear him. 'Perhaps . . . perhaps, after all, my mother's right, and the Devil has laid him by the heels.'

'For what reason?'

'How can I tell?' His tone sharpened. 'I have no truck with Old Nick. But my brother is able to read. The monks taught him. Oh, they taught me too, but I was never the scholar that he is. Like my father before me, I know my letters well enough to run the business, to write out a bill or understand an invoice, but Peter reads for pleasure. He buys books.' Mark's tone was incredulous.

'You make the stuff on which they're written,' I pointed out. 'Maybe that explains his interest. All the same, why should the fact that he can read mean that a man is in league with the Devil?'

Mark repeated, more or less, what Dame Joan had said to me the previous evening: 'Who knows what's in those books he keeps in the workshop? There's a chest of them there, full to the brim.'

'Then, if you'll permit,' I suggested, 'my first task tomorrow morning will be to go through the lot of them and see what they contain.'

'You can read?' His surprise was hardly flattering.

'I was taught by the monks, as you were. If you recall, I told you that at one time I was a novice here in the abbey.'

'So you did.' Mark began to settle himself for sleep. 'I was right. You're a very unusual chapman.'

'Perhaps. But do you give me your permission to look at your brother's books?'

He yawned, suddenly tired. 'Yes! As you please! You have my blessing and a free hand to do whatever you think necessary. I must open up the shop again tomorrow so that the people of this town can see that everything is normal. Goodnight.' And he yawned for a second time.

I tried to compose myself in order to snatch what few hours of the night were left to me, and had just succeeded in drifting across the borderline of sleep when Mark Gildersleeve once more shook me awake.

'What now?' I murmured irritably.

'I've been thinking,' he said, 'and it's occurred to me

that Peter's attitude towards his books has changed in the past few months.'

I was puzzled, and suddenly fully alert. 'How do you mean?' I asked.

'Well, he used not to mind who took them out and read them – not that any of us did; Mother can't read, and neither can Rob or John, and as I've said, I wasn't interested – but he used to encourage all of us to look at the pictures if we wanted to. He even made the attempt once to teach Rob Undershaft his letters. Anyone who came into the shop was welcome to inspect his latest acquisition.'

'But no longer?' I prompted when he paused for breath.

'No, not for some while. I remember that one day I saw him locking the chest, a thing I had never known him do before. When I questioned him as to the reason he flew into a rage and told me to mind my own business. And that was unlike him; Peter was usually a placid man. It took a lot to upset him.'

'Has he been short-tempered about any other things?' I asked.

'Not that I can recollect. No, I'm sure he hasn't. On the contrary, he's been . . . happy . . . excited, I suppose, is the only way I can describe it. I thought that it was because of his approaching wedding, but he and Cicely have never been that fond of one another. The marriage was arranged years ago by Mother and my aunt Katherine, and I half expected Peter to repudiate the match when he grew older. He didn't, however . . .'

Once again, I had to intrude on my companion's reverie. 'This excitement, then, that you thought you detected in your brother – it had nothing to do, in your opinion, with Mistress Cicely?'

'No, I don't think so. I came to realize after a while that

it wasn't *that* sort of anticipation. Peter was like . . . like a child hugging a secret,' Mark added with a flash of inspiration. 'Yes, that's what it was. How stupid I've been not to see it before. He had a secret.' And Mark sat bolt upright in bed, his fingers picking restlessly at the coverlet.

'And it had to do with his books?' I suggested.

He turned to peer at me through the darkness. 'It must've done, don't you think? Why else had he started to lock the chest in the workshop?'

'You could be right,' I agreed. 'Now, lie down again and get some sleep, or neither of us will be good for anything tomorrow. I'll look at those folios of his first thing in the morning, after breakfast.'

My companion grunted. 'The chest may still be locked,' he said, 'but I think I might know where Peter keeps the key.'

Chapter Five

Mark and I both rose at first light, neither of us able to sleep once the sun began to probe the shutters. We were glad to throw these latter wide to allow cool air into the stuffy bedchamber, before descending to the pump between the stable and the kitchen in order to wash away the soil and sweat of night.

While I waited for Mark to finish (for his ablutions naturally took precedence over mine) I seized the opportunity to examine the dusty earth, and noted that it had been scuffed over as if to erase all trace of footprints. I found this strange. Why should my companion have troubled to do this if his were the only ones to be seen?

Mark must have seen me looking at the ground, for he paused in the act of rubbing himself dry to ask edgily, 'Have you found something?' I pointed out my curious discovery and there was a moment's hesitation before he said with forced jocularity, 'Oh yes! I was just being over-cautious, I'm afraid. I thought the sight of footmarks might upset the women if one of them ventured outside this morning while I was still abed. As it turns out, of course –' he shrugged and spread his hands – 'we are up before them.'

It was an unconvincing explanation, but maybe just unconvincing enough to be true. For now, therefore, I accepted it, but determined nevertheless to keep a close eye on Mark. He had betrayed a hint of resentment when talking about his brother's inheritance of their father's second-best bed, which had aroused my ever-ready suspicions. Whether or not I was being unfair to him, only time would tell.

I washed and dried myself, cleaned my teeth with my willow bark and then went to the privy before rejoining Mark in his bedchamber. Fully dressed, I followed him downstairs again to the kitchen to eat breakfast and shave, using water heated by Lydia, the little maid. Seen in daylight, she appeared neither so pale nor so diminutive as she had done the previous evening, but even so, the top of her head barely reached to the middle of my upper arm. By contrast I seemed a giant, and her swift, delicate, birdlike movements made me feel awkward and gauche. The two apprentices, already seated at the table eating their oatmeal, were blear-eyed and only half-awake, tired after yesterday's long and futile search. Dame Joan and Mistress Cicely had not yet put in an appearance.

While Lydia plied me with bread and ale, oatmeal cakes and a piece of fresh fish, I, too, fought against the desire for slumber. I had had a disturbed night after the fatiguing ride from Farleigh Castle and could willingly have crawled back between the sheets to sleep until noon. But I had work to do, and the sooner I buckled down to it, the sooner I should be free to continue my journey to Bristol.

It was one of the perversities of my nature – and, I suspect, a common characteristic of most people – that, while I had been free to do as I pleased and go wherever the fancy took me I had had little desire to return home, but as soon as I had committed myself to the concerns of others I longed to see my daughter and mother-in-law again. However, I had promised my services to Dame Joan and

Mistress Cicely and could not now go back on my word. And I was unable to suppress entirely the thrill of anticipation which always gripped me when faced with an apparently unsolvable problem – and one, moreover, which might prove perilous. If, in this particular case, magic and witchcraft were involved in Peter Gildersleeve's disappearance, then I could do nothing except guard myself as best I could from the evil spirits responsible. But I did not really believe that God would lead me into that kind of danger; bodily danger, yes, but surely He would not imperil my immortal soul!

When we had both finished shaving, I suggested to Mark that I should inspect his brother's chest of books before doing anything else.

'I'll walk to the stables later and fetch my cudgel,' I said, 'but I'm curious to see these folios of his.'

My host laid aside his razor.

'They're not all folios. Many are quartos and some octavos.' There was a certain pride in his voice, mixed with annoyance at Peter's extravagance. He went on, 'You can come with me now. I'm off to the workshop.'

He turned to the apprentices, still lolling over their breakfast. 'Rob, I need you to help with the scraping. John, you get down to the vats and rescue those skins we set soaking last Friday, before all this trouble came upon us.' As the last named reached the kitchen door, Mark called after him, 'Mind you act normally! If people start asking about my brother, you're to say we're not worried. Tell them you think I know where he is. Have you marked that?'

John Longbones sighed, nodded and went on his way. After a few moments, we followed him across the garden before turning into the workroom at the back of the house. Here I saw various skins, all sheep except for one calf's hide, laced on to wooden frames and stretched taut, ready to be scraped to a smooth, even surface. Mark and Rob Undershaft donned leather aprons to begin the day's work, and the former indicated an iron-bound chest in one corner.

'That's where Peter keeps his books, Chapman.' His tone was indifferent, almost as though he no longer cared whether I inspected them or no.

'Did you find the key?' I enquired.

For answer, Mark delved into the pocket of his jerkin. 'It was in one of the drawers of the bed-head. It occurred to me last night that that was where it would be. It didn't take long to find. Here! Catch!' He threw me a small iron key. 'Now, Rob and I have a lot to do.'

He picked up one of the rounded sticks, which he referred to as a strickle, and started work on the nearest sheepskin, methodically removing all remnants of grease and fat. The apprentice was already busy on another, and between each scraping the skins were doused with a lye of hot water and soda, which simmered in a cauldron over a fire on the workshop hearth. The smell was unpleasant and made my eyes water, but both men assured me that I should grow used to it in time.

But I did not need the key for the chest was, after all, unlocked. Slowly, I raised the lid and peered inside. The musty scent of old books rose to greet me, and I lifted them out carefully, one by one. In order to keep the parchment from cockling, nearly all were bound with heavy boards, some covered in silk, others in velvet, and decorated with tassels or buttons or copper studs arranged in patterns; one lay on a bed of ivory satin in its own special cedarwood box. Several had gilt clasps, but these were easily loosened. There were histories, including Geoffrey of Monmouth's *Historia Regum Britanniae* and William of Malmesbury's

Gesta Regum Anglorum, devotional works, romances, a very fair copy of *Cursor Mundi*, and a hunting treatise, *The Master of Game*, by one of the past Dukes of York. But although I spent until dinnertime turning the pages and reading as much of the contents as I could, I discovered nothing of magic or witchcraft or or any other subject which might link Peter Gildersleeve to the black arts, nor explain the strange way in which he had vanished. Eventually, disappointed and dispirited, I replaced the books in the chest and sat, my back propped against the wall, watching Mark and Rob Undershaft at work.

They had by now finished scraping and dousing, and were scouring the skins with what I thought to be sand, but which, on inquiry, I learned to be finely powdered limestone.

'You *can* use sand, but this is the handiest thing for us to use in these parts,' Mark said, and I remembered that long ago one of the abbey brothers, who knew about such matters, had instructed me that the whole area, including the Mendip Hills, was formed of limestone . . .

'So this is where you are!' Cicely's voice accused me, and I turned to see her standing in the doorway. 'I've been searching for you for ages.'

'And now you've found me,' I answered coolly, conscious of Mark's suspicious glare. 'What do want with me, Mistress?'

She pouted at this formal mode of address, but merely said, 'You're all to come to dinner. Aunt Joan says we're to eat together in the kitchen until more help can be found for Lyddie. She won't have her overworked, carrying food upstairs to the solar.'

Mark muttered something under his breath, but made no further protest. He and Rob took off their aprons, running their fingers through their hair in a vain attempt to be rid of the dust, and I copied them, with as little result.

'What have you been doing?' Cicely asked as we walked across the garden. It was now well past ten o'clock and the sun was already mounting the heavens. Only a few faint clouds stencilled the relentless blue vault of the sky, and the heat was merciless.

'With Mark's permission, I've been looking through your cousin Peter's books.'

'And what did you discover?' She spoke a little breathlessly, abandoning her provocative manner.

'Nothing that need disturb anyone. It's a perfectly innocent collection, more respectable I should guess than the libraries of many an abbey. At Glastonbury, for example, some books are kept under lock and key, volumes thought too dangerous or too seditious to be viewed by any but the most senior, and therefore most incorruptible, of the monks.'

She glanced sharply at me, as if suspecting me of irreverence towards the Holy Church and its officers, but I smiled blandly back and she was reassured.

So was Dame Joan when I repeated what I had told her niece. 'That *is* good news.' She said a benediction and we began our meal, but she still needed a little reassurance. 'You're certain there's nothing there that could implicate Peter in any form of magic?'

'Quite certain. You may rest easy on that score.'

'Then whatever can have happened to him?' she asked. No one made answer and she looked again at me. 'What do you plan to do now, Roger?'

I wiped my mouth on the back of one hand. 'I should like to ride to the Pennards' farm and have a word with young Abel Fairchild. Would I meet with any opposition from your friends, do you think?'

I had to wait several moments while Mark emptied his mouth of food, but eventually he replied with a shrug of his shoulders, 'They're not really friends, just people with whom we have commercial dealings. But they're all of them pleasant enough, and would probably raise no objections to you speaking with Abel, provided you don't keep him too long from his work. They must be as anxious as we are to resolve this business. After all, Peter's disappearance happened on their land, and it may harm their reputation as well as ours if no solution's found soon.'

'I'll ride with you,' Cicely offered, hurrying to finish her dinner. 'You'll need someone to show you the way.'

'I already know the way,' I retorted firmly. 'If you recall, we passed over Pennard land yesterday, and you pointed out the farmstead.'

'You'll stay here,' Mark informed her roughly. 'You can help Mother in the house.' He turned back to me. 'Will you ride the Duke's horse?'

'He was lent to me for my use,' I answered. 'Can you think of a good reason why I shouldn't take him?'

My host was only too anxious to endorse my claim, not wishing to put Dorabella to any further exertion for a while.

Consequently, as soon as dinner was over, I set off in the direction of Northload Street and the stables. As I passed the north gatehouse of the abbey I heard my name called in such quavering accents that they were almost drowned out by the rattle of a passing wagon. Turning my head I saw the fragile, stooping form of Brother Hilarion, who had been Novice Master during my novitiate, and who doubtless still enjoyed that thankless office. It was he, more than any other, who had patiently listened to all my fears and misgivings concerning my fitness for the religious life, and who had tried to answer my questions as honestly as he knew how without straying into the realms of heresy. Moreover, it was he who had persuaded Abbot Selwood that, in spite of my promises to my dead mother, I must not take my final vows, as much for the sake of the abbey as for my own.

He was standing outside the porter's lodge, and I crossed at once to greet him.

'Brother Hilarion! Peace be with you!'

'And with you, my child. What brings you back to Glastonbury?'

'Chance,' I said. Then, with those faded blue eyes fixed trustingly upon me, I amended, 'God's chance. I am staying with Dame Gildersleeve and her family. I was given the commission of escorting Mistress Cicely home from Farleigh Hungerford when . . . when her cousin Peter failed to arrive to claim her.'

The gentle old face crumpled in distress. 'Ah! Yes! We have heard. The whole enclave, indeed the whole town, is buzzing with rumours regarding the strange circumstances of his disappearance. How are Dame Joan and her niece bearing the uncertainty? I hear that Mark and the two apprentices were out searching all day yesterday, but found no trace of Peter. Yet Tom Porter tells me that he saw John Longbones down by the mill stream this morning, lifting skins from the vats, and that the shop is open.'

I laughed. 'Glastonbury hasn't changed, I see – gossip is still its staple diet. So, what else are the good citizens saying about how Master Gildersleeve vanished?'

Brother Hilarion looked even more troubled. 'People are always suspicious of one of their own kind who can read, and especially of one who spends money on books and keeps a chestful of them in his workshop,' he replied evasively.

'You mean they're saying that he was in league with the Devil?'

The old monk was a shade too swift with his denial. 'No, no! It's much too soon for that sort of talk. Peter may yet turn up with a perfectly reasonable explanation of what has befallen him.'

'But if he doesn't . . .?'

Brother Hilarion shivered. 'We won't think of that, my child.' Almost involuntarily, he crossed himself. 'Let us pray that these signs of normality in the Gildersleeve household mean that they have some knowledge of his whereabouts.'

'They don't, Brother,' I told him bluntly, 'but I ask you to keep that information to yourself. Mark and Dame Joan have entrusted the task of finding Peter to me.'

'To you?' Brother Hilarion was naturally astonished. 'But you are a stranger to them, by your own account thrown in their way by chance.'

'It would take far too long to make all plain to you now. I have work to do. But I promise to visit you as soon as possible and tell you everything that has happened to me since I left your care. Can you be patient?'

He smiled ruefully. 'Patience is no inconsiderable part of our calling – as you should know, for you were never much good at practising that virtue.'

I laughed, bade him farewell and continued on my way down the busy thoroughfare, across the bustling market place and so to Northload Street and the stables, where I could almost have sworn that Barnabas was pleased to see me.

I was equally warmly welcomed by the Pennards when, just under an hour later, I rode into the courtyard of the long, low, single-storey farmhouse, with its slate-tiled roof and ample-sized undercroft, to make known my errand and to beg a word with Abel Fairchild.

'A bad business. A bad business,' Anthony Pennard said, rubbing his forehead in perplexity with a workmanlike hand.

He was a smallish man with such gnarled and weather-beaten features that it was difficult to guess his age. But his hair, although liberally streaked with grey, retained much of its original brown colour, and his dark eyes had a direct, unclouded gaze, both of which suggested that it was the elements rather than time that had not dealt kindly with him. Moreover, Mistress Pennard was a sprightly woman with cornflower-blue eyes and dimpled cheeks, who I should not have reckoned to be much more than forty. Therefore, unless she was considerably younger than her husband, Anthony Pennard was still some way short of his fiftieth birthday.

'What's happened to poor Master Gildersleeve is a mystery, and that's a fact,' Mistress Pennard chimed in, her mouth puckered with anxiety. 'And it occurred on our land, too! I was in Wells market earlier this morning and I fancied several people tried to avoid me. I saw one or two whispering behind their hands. But what am I thinking of? Won't you sit down and have a stoup of ale, Master . . .?'

'Stonecarver,' I said, reverting to my original name before it seemed to have been changed for ever by my calling. I had agreed with Mark, before leaving, that there was no need to be too frank about my connection with the Gildersleeves, and to introduce myself as a friend (albeit a recent one) of the family. 'My father pursued that trade,' I added. 'He was killed by a fall whilst working on the roof of the cathedral nave, here in Wells.'

'You're a local man, then?' Mistress Pennard said,

66

wrinkling her brow. 'Wait . . . I seem to remember a Widow Stonecarver. Blanche, her name was. She had a son called . . . called—'

'Roger,' I smiled. 'Yes, I'm he.'

After that she could not do enough for me, almost forcing me to sit at the table and drink with her and her husband before setting out to find Abel. She rejected the sallop she had been about to offer me, and sent Anthony to broach a new cask of ale. While he was gone, I learned that the house and pastures were episcopal property and that the original lease had been her father's. When William Jephcott died, however, it had been granted to Anthony Pennard, a Priddy man whom Anne Jephcott had married when she was made pregnant by him at the age of sixteen.

'Not the marriage that my parents would have chosen for me,' she whispered confidentially, 'but he's proved a good man none the less, and very few people the wiser that Gilbert, my eldest, wasn't conceived between clean sheets, as they say.'

I doubted this. Anyone who could confide such intimacies to a stranger, and all within ten minutes of making his acquaintance, was not the woman to keep a still tongue in her head about anything. I saw Anthony Pennard give her a swift, sideways glance as he returned with the cups of ale, and guessed that he was wondering what fresh indiscretions his wife had committed.

'Been giving you the family history, has she?' he asked in a resigned tone as he resumed his seat at the table.

'I'm just being friendly, that's all,' Anne Pennard rebuked him.

I smiled and swallowed my ale almost in one gulp. I had had a hot ride from Glastonbury and was thirsty.

'Do you have any thoughts yourselves on what might

have happened to Master Gildersleeve?' I asked them. 'This boy, Abel Fairchild – is he given to odd fancies or making up stories?'

They shook their heads in unison.

'He's been helping Gilbert and Thomas tend our flocks these two years past,' Anthony said, 'and never a complaint about him that I've heard. You can question my lads though, if you like. You don't have to take my word for it.'

'A thoroughly sensible young boy,' Anne Pennard confirmed. 'Neither Gil nor Tom hesitate to leave all in his charge when they're away to Priddy with their father.'

'So you wouldn't doubt that things happened just as he described them?'

'Peter's missing, isn't he?' Anthony Pennard demanded. 'And his horse was left tethered in that stand of trees. Why should we think that the boy's lying about what he saw?'

His logic was irrefutable. Even if Abel Fairchild was known to be the biggest liar unhung, it wouldn't alter the fact that Peter Gildersleeve was missing, and had been since the previous Friday. Today was Wednesday. Nothing had been seen or heard of him for almost five days.

I repeated my earlier question. 'What then do you think has become of your friend?'

Anthony Pennard was as quick as Mark had been to deny any friendship between the two families.

'We do business together, that's all. Peter and his brother have been good customers over the years, like their father before them. We go rarely to Glastonbury. Will you take some more ale?'

I refused, regretfully, and, pushing back my stool, rose to my feet. 'Where shall I find Abel Fairchild at this time of day?'

Anthony Pennard also stood up. 'He'll most likely be on

the lower slopes as it's close on noon, looking for some shade amongst the trees and scrub. It's too hot higher up in this weather. I'll come with you at least a part of the way.' He addressed his wife, 'I need to have a word with Gilbert.'

Mistress Pennard made no demur, and the two of us set out across the steeply rising pastures to locate our quarries. Clumps of gorse and clusters of trees dotted these lower slopes of Mendip, and the undulations of the ground made heavy going, especially as I had to limit my stride to the shorter steps taken by my guide. Clinging veils of heat shrouded the hilltops and made us both sweat in the midday glare. Then, suddenly, as we crested a rise and entered the grateful shade of a circle of stunted oaks, Anthony Pennard gripped my arm and pointed downwards into the dip below us.

'This is the place,' he whispered. 'There's the shepherd's hut. This is where Peter Gildersleeve disappeared.'

Chapter Six

I descended the slope at a run, much as Peter Gildersleeve must have done the preceding Friday, and on reaching level ground paused to look around me. Then I glanced up to find myself staring at a boy whom I judged to be some twelve or thirteen summers, dressed in hose and smock of brown homespun, carrying a shepherd's crook. His narrow face, beneath its thatch of straggling, straw-coloured hair, was pinched and ashen, his mouth agape, eyes wide with fear. The whole of his thin body seemed to tremble as he stood on top of the ridge above me.

From behind me, as he scrambled awkwardly down the incline, came the reassuring voice of Anthony Pennard.

'It's all right, Abel, lad! This is Roger Stonecarver, a friend of Mark Gildersleeve. He's come to talk to you and to have a look at the place where Master Peter vanished.'

The boy drew a long, shuddering breath and a little colour seeped back into his cheeks. He swallowed hard and his eyes lost their look of terror. After a few moments, when he had regained control of his legs, he came down to greet us, tugging at his forelock.

'I'm s-sorry,' he stuttered. 'Just for a second I thought . . .'

Anthony clapped him on the shoulder. 'We know what you thought, lad, and we understand. No need to apologize.'

'It was just seeing a man standing in the same spot where ... where—'

'Well, now you're satisfied that it's not Master Gildersleeve, I'll leave you to talk with Roger here.' And Anthony gave his shepherd-boy another hearty clout on the upper arm. 'You have my permission. Where's Gilbert? Have you seen him lately?'

'He's over to the west pasture with the ewes. Master Tom's higher up. Last time I set eyes on him, he was rescuing an old tup that keeps wandering away from the flock and was caught in some brambles.'

'Ay, I know the one. A stubborn, wilful old bugger. But Tom'll be a match for him. No, it's Gil I want.' Anthony Pennard turned to me. 'We'll talk later when you come back for your horse. You can tell me then if this lad's been of any use to you.'

He clambered up the slope again with more haste than dignity, skirted the copse and disappeared from view as the land shelved away to the foot of the Mendips and the marshy plain which stretched towards Glastonbury and the glimmering horizon beyond. I smiled at Abel and suggested that we sit in the lee of the hut, but he insisted on climbing out of the dell to the higher ground, so that he could keep a better eye on his sheep. These were scattered over a little distance, placidly nibbling the grass. We found some shade, cast by an outcropping of rocks, and seated ourselves with our backs pressed against the sun-warmed stone.

'Now,' I said, once we were comfortably settled, 'would you be good enough to tell me exactly what happened the other day, the last time you saw Peter Gildersleeve? To be honest, I have already heard the story from the lips of Dame Joan, but details may have got lost or added in the telling. I should prefer to hear it from you.'

He regarded me curiously, his shrewd little eyes puckered against the light. 'Why do you want to know?'

'I'm lodging with the family and hope, if I can, to aid them in discovering Peter's whereabouts. By removing that burden from Mark's shoulders, it leaves him free to attend to his business, otherwise he loses both time and money.'

The boy, satisfied with this explanation, looked slowly around to make sure that none of his charges had wandered out of sight, then recounted his version of events. But in fact this varied very little from the one I had had from my hostess.

'I was standing on that upper ridge there, just above that fold in the ground—'

'I know,' I interrupted. 'I rode the same way only yesterday. You can see directly down into the next dip where the shelter stands. You can also see the copse and the Pennards' house.'

'That's right.' He nodded eagerly. 'But then they disappear from view. Well, as I say, I was on that upper ridge and I saw Master Gildersleeve walking down the lower slope from the trees. When he reached the bottom, by the hut, he glanced up and waved.'

'Did he seem pleased to see you?' I asked, interrupting for a second time.

Abel looked faintly surprised, as if he had not previously considered this point, and answered thoughtfully, 'He didn't smile, now you come to mention it. And . . . yes, I remember he was slow in raising his hand. Grudging, like, in his greeting. You may be right, Master Stonecarver. Perhaps he wasn't pleased to see me. Does it matter?'

'Call me Roger,' I insisted, ignoring his question. 'You make me feel old with such a formal mode of address. Go on – what happened next?'

'I ran down into the dip, rounded up a couple of sheep who showed signs of straying, and up the other side.'

This, I reflected, must have taken more time than the few seconds attributed to Abel's fleetness of foot by Dame Joan.

'How long, would you say, was Peter Gildersleeve out of your sight?'

He pursed his mouth and stuck out his underlip, flicking at it with a grubby forefinger. 'A minute, perhaps. No more.'

In my own mind, I doubled this up to two. But even so, not long enough for a man to hide unless it was inside the hut itself. Anywhere else and surely Abel must have caught a glimpse of Peter as he bolted for cover, for that particular fold of ground was innocent of any of the trees and scrub that dotted the rest of the surrounding landscape.

'So! When the hut came into view again, Master Gildersleeve had vanished. What did you do?'

The boy regarded me as though I were a simpleton. 'I searched for him, of course.'

'Why?'

'Because I meant to find out what he was doing, roaming around the gaffer's land on his own. If he wanted to speak to Master Pennard, or Master Gilbert or Master Tom, he should've called at the house, or the sheds where we store the fleeces. And I knew Mistress wouldn't have sent him off on a wild goose chase after them, for they were all three over to Priddy that day.'

'So you looked in the hut, but there was no one there. Are you quite certain of that?'

Abel spoke in a tone of withering scorn. 'Have you been inside it?' He did not wait for my reply, but went on, 'You can't have, because if so, you'd know there's

74

nothing in there but a heap of old sacks.'

'The hut has only a small window,' I pointed out. 'Its interior must be dark. Could Master Gildersleeve have been hiding behind the door as you opened it?'

Abel smiled triumphantly. 'I thought of that. And he wasn't.'

'You looked?'

'I looked.'

'And did you go right inside?'

'No need. When the door's open, there's enough light to see everything that there is to be seen.'

I sighed. 'Very well! You've convinced me that your quarry was not in the hut. What did you do next?'

'I walked all round the outside.' Abel shivered suddenly. 'Master Gildersleeve wasn't there, either. He wasn't anywhere in sight.'

'And did you search further afield?'

'I went back and forth round the hut a few times more and looked inside for a second time, but by then I was truly scared.' His voice sank to a whisper. 'I reckoned Peter Gildersleeve had been snatched by demons – they say he was a man who never had his nose out of a book and had forbidden learning – so I ran to the house as fast as I could. Mistress was angry at first because I'd left my flock, but in the end she sent one of the maids with me to see what she could discover. Susanna was as terrified as I was, but we did find Master Gildersleeve's horse tied up among the trees. We went back and told Mistress, and she said I was to round up my sheep and bring 'em down to the home pasture without delay. Suppertime, Master and young Masters returned from Priddy and I was sent for to tell my tale again.

'Old Master didn't make much of it at first, but later,

when he and Master Tom and Master Gil had walked to the copse and found the mare still tethered there, he began to think differently. He said Master Gildersleeve would never have abandoned the creature willingly, and that Gilbert must ride to Glastonbury straightaway, before it got dark, to see if Dame Joan or some other could throw light on the subject. He said the family would be getting worried on account of all the robberies there've been lately in the district. Though what that had to do with anything, I can't for the life of me see. The robberies have all been at night. Houses and farmsteads broken into, goods and money taken. We've been sleeping with all the shutters closed in spite of the hot weather.'

This explained Mark's reluctance to leave his chamber windows open. I asked what the Sheriff's officers were doing about the robberies, but my informant didn't appear to know the answer. In any case, I felt we were drifting into uncharted waters and made a bid to put us back on course. I got to my feet and reached down a hand to assist him to his.

'I'd like to look inside the hut for myself,' I said. 'Will you come with me?'

Abel was right. Despite its paucity of light, the hut was so small that with the door wide open it was possible to see into every corner. Heaped in one of them was a pile of old sacking, but the remainder of the beaten-earth floor was bare and swept clean. There were a few scuff marks just inside the entrance – presumably made by Abel when he had peered around the door to ensure that Peter Gildersleeve was not behind it – but otherwise all lay undisturbed. No one had taken refuge there for quite some time.

I stepped back a few paces, the better to view the outside

of the hut. Made of stone, with a roof of latticed branches overlaid with moss and twigs, it would be used in inclement weather as a shelter by both men and beasts. The apex of the roof was a foot or two higher than the top of the incline behind it, and although from the front it appeared to be built directly up against the bank, upon closer inspection I discovered that it was possible to walk all round it on level ground.

The dell, as I had recollected earlier, was devoid of either bush or tree. The nearest hiding place, apart from the interior of the hut, was the stand of trees where Peter Gildersleeve had left Dorabella, and it was extremely doubtful if he could have reached its cover without being glimpsed by Abel. Yet if the latter were to be believed, Peter had vanished without trace from this very spot. Still loath to abandon the idea of a rational explanation, I climbed once more to higher ground, Abel following at my heels, and surveyed my surroundings.

From where I now stood, I could see to my left the well-worn track, leading from the upper heights of Mendip, which Cicely and I had ridden on Barnabas yesterday afternoon. It was a rough and bumpy ride, but one which lopped quarter of an hour or more from the journey to the Glastonbury road. It went in a direct line, making no concession to the unevenness of the terrain – a reminder that, centuries ago, the Romans had been mining for lead in these parts.

I spun slowly on my heel in a full circle, and had begun to do so again when my eye was caught by a second track which I had not previously noticed. It curled around the bluff of rising ground to the right of me, leading deep into a ravine between the hills. I wended my way along its length, but at the end there was nothing more than a fall of matted foliage cascading down the cliff-face from a crevice high above to the valley floor beneath. I moved aside some of the greenery, but it concealed only a narrow fissure in the rocks, so I retraced my steps and returned to Abel and his sheep.

He cocked his head knowingly to one side.

'There's nothing to see, is there?' he grinned cheekily. 'I could have told you that if you'd taken the trouble to ask. Sometimes I have to go round there to rescue sheep.'

'It must be a lonely life up here in the winter,' I remarked, glancing about me.

'I don't mind.' Abel shrugged and laughed. 'These hills are full of surprises.'

'What sort of surprises?' I enquired.

One hand made a sweeping gesture. 'Oh, just things,' he answered vaguely. 'I found a coin once with a man's head on it. Gaffer said it was Roman. Another time I found some bits of an old pot. He said they were Roman too.' His brow creased into a disapproving frown. 'Whoever these Romans were, Master Stonecarver, they were very careless.'

I was about to repeat my request that he call me Roger when a man's voice exclaimed, 'Here you are, Abel! I've been . . . Hello! Who's this?'

The young man who had so silently approached while we had been busy talking, was also serviceably dressed in homespun and carried a shepherd's crook. He was about my own age, perhaps a little younger – it was difficult to tell, but there was no doubt whatsoever that he was Mistress Pennard's son. He had the same cornflower-blue eyes and dimpled cheeks, the same plump and stocky body. In one respect only did he resemble his father, and that was in the way the elements had weathered and tanned his skin to a rich and leathery brown. It needed few powers of deduction to guess that this must be Thomas, who had been minding his flock higher up and as yet knew nothing of my presence on Pennard land.

Abel, somewhat confused, made us known to one another, and I explained again my reason for taking upon myself the investigation into the whereabouts of Peter Gildersleeve.

'A strange business! A strange business!' Thomas muttered, scratching his right ear. With a quick, deft movement, his other arm shot out to hook back a straying sheep from the brink of the little dell where the hut stood. 'What conclusion have you come to, Master Stonecarver?'

'None so far,' I admitted ruefully. 'For the present I'm as nonplussed as everyone else seems to be. However, I haven't yet given up all hope of discovering some simple reason for Master Gildersleeve's disappearance. And now I must return to your stable to fetch my horse before riding back to Glastonbury.'

'I'll come with you,' Thomas said. 'I want a word with my father. Abel, lad, keep an eye on my flock for me while I'm gone, particularly that old tup. He's as crafty as Satan.'

'Master Pennard may not be at the house,' I remarked as we moved off in that direction. 'He was going to the west pasture to look for your brother after he left me with Abel.'

But whatever business Anthony Pennard had had with Gilbert, it had been of short duration, for he was seated at the table in the kitchen as we entered, laboriously trying to add a column of figures written on the piece of parchment in front of him.

He looked up in relief. 'By Our Lady, I'm pleased to see you, Thomas, my boy! You've a clearer eye and a quicker brain than your old father. See if you can find the answer to this sum. It's plaguing me silly! Figures and letters – damn stupid, jiggling things! They never make sense when I look at them, but just go dancing around all over the paper. Well, Master Stonecarver, and was Abel of any use to you?' I shook my head regretfully and he continued, 'I can't say I'm much surprised, for there doesn't seem to be any rhyme or reason in the way Master Peter vanished. There's no shaking the boy's story, and as I said to you a while since, I can't see why he should lie about Peter Gildersleeve's disappearance. And he *has* disappeared, that much is for certain.'

I accepted a cup of ale from Mistress Pennard, who, instructing the two maids to continue with the baking, sat down beside her husband. I took a stool on the opposite side of the table. Thomas, meantime, had removed himself to some other part of the house in order to grapple with the addition which was giving his father so much trouble.

'The track which crosses your land,' I said, 'does it date from Roman times?'

Anthony Pennard shrugged. 'Who can say? It's certain that it's very old and has been a common right of way as long as anyone round here can remember. But the Mendips are covered with such tracks. Some lead somewhere, some don't. Some lead to the great gorge. Have you ever seen it?'

I shook my head. 'No. Oddly enough, I've never been that way, but they say the old Saxon kings used to have one of their dwellings on the heights above it.'

'That's as maybe. I never heard so, at any rate. So, Abel wasn't of much use to you, eh? You're none the wiser as to what's happened to Peter Gildersleeve?'

'Not one whit,' I acknowledged. I drained my cup and stood up, refusing the goodwife's offers of further refreshment. 'I must be getting along now. My thanks to you both for bearing with me.'

Master Pennard rose and clapped me on the back. 'I'm sorry there's not more we can do to help. If only we'd had the foresight to keep Abel's testimony quiet, then it might have been thought that Peter had ridden off on his own somewhere. We could have returned Dorabella to the Gildersleeves later, when they'd had time to think up a story.' He sighed. 'But there you are! We all took fright, Mark Gildersleeve included, and now the damage is done as they say. The gossip is spreading, and I daresay we'll have the Bishop's men poking and prying about the place once they get wind of the tale.'

'You're probably right,' I agreed, 'unless I can discover something first. But at the moment, I'm floundering around in the dark with nothing to go on. Only one thing is certain, and that's that a man has disappeared in the twinkling of an eye in most mysterious circumstances.'

'Aye, that's for sure, Chapman,' Master Pennard nodded. 'Sure as Christ came to Priddy!'

As Barnabas and I plodded sedately back along the raised causeway between Wells and Glastonbury, I pondered on that strange expression: 'Sure as Christ came to Priddy'. It was one with which I had been familiar all my life, and I knew its origins.

The story, handed down from father to son to grandson for hundreds of generations past, said that during the Roman occupation, when they were mining for lead in the Mendips, merchants had arrived from Palestine to do business, chief amongst whom was Joseph of Arimathea. On one visit Joseph had brought with him a young boy, who was our Lord and Saviour, Jesus Christ. The two had lodged at Priddy, and during his stay the Christ Child used to roam the countryside, coming eventually upon the Tor. He was so struck by the sanctity of the place, that He decided to build a church at its foot in His Mother's honour: thus it was Christ Himself who miraculously raised the earliest church at Glastonbury.

After the Crucifixion, Joseph had returned to Somerset to carry on the work of the Christian faith. Did we not have the Holy Thorn to prove it? Blossoming every year at the time of Our Lord's nativity, it had first sprouted from Joseph's staff where he had planted it in the ground. The stories had not always held the prominent position in the religious life of the abbey that they did today, but John Selwood was among those abbots under whose spiritual guidance the cult of Joseph had grown.

For my own part, credulity struggled with disbelief for dominance in my mind. On the one hand I desperately wanted the stories to be true, to believe that the Christ Child really had walked among the Mendip Hills and the pleasant green Somerset valleys; on the other, I knew that such tales, along with those of King Arthur, brought untold wealth and prestige to the abbey in the shape of a constant stream of pilgrims and the claim to be the oldest Christian foundation in the country, if not the world. Abbots of Glastonbury, following the example set them many centuries earlier by Saint Dunstan – until, that is, the saint became Primate of All England himself – tended to go their own way regardless of Canterbury.

With such thoughts jostling around in my head, the five miles between Wells and Glastonbury passed like one. I barely noticed the mid-afternoon heat or the crowded causeway, and was surprised to find myself descending through Bove Town almost before I knew it. As I passed the church of Saint John, Cicely came running up the street to meet me and catch at the horse's reins.

'Oh Roger, I'm so glad you're back,' she said in a high-pitched, breathless voice. 'Come into the house at once!'

'Let me settle Barnabas first,' I protested, and proceeded towards the market place. Besides stabling the horse, I needed to retrieve my cudgel which I still had not collected from the livery stable.

I handed over the cob and the necessary payment to one of the grooms and followed Barnabas into his stall, where my stick was still propped against the manger. Emerging again into the courtyard, I was astonished to find Cicely waiting for me just inside the big double gates.

'You've had a wasted journey, I'm afraid,' I told her gently. 'I know no more about what has happened to your cousin than before I went to the Pennards'.'

I saw the tears well up in her eyes and start to trickle down her cheeks. I put an arm around her shoulders. 'Don't cry. I don't despair yet of finding Peter.'

'It's not just that,' she said, and I felt her tremble. 'Oh Roger! Now Mark has disappeared as well!'

Chapter Seven

My grip on her shoulders tightened. 'What do you mean, "disappeared"?' I demanded. A foolish question, perhaps, for what could the word mean but one thing? Nevertheless, I was not ready to accept as yet that Mark Gildersleeve might have suffered the fate of his brother. 'No, no,' I added, 'don't tell me here. Say nothing further until we reach your aunt's house.' I held up an admonitory finger. 'Leave it for the moment.'

Within five minutes we were once again entering the shop in High Street to be met by Dame Joan, who, I was relieved to notice, although plainly worried, was far less agitated than her niece. A glimpse into the workroom from the passage was also reassuring, showing me Rob Undershaft and John Longbones, the latter now returned from the vats, proceeding unconcernedly with their craft. I mounted with the two women to the solar above, feeling Cicely was making much out of little.

'Very well,' I said as we sat down, 'tell me what has happened. When did you last see Mark, and where was he going?'

Aunt and niece immediately broke forth in concert, so that nothing made sense and I was forced to beg for quiet. 'Stop!' I protested. 'Stop!' I turned to the older woman, who seemed the calmer of the pair. 'Dame Joan, let me hear you first, if you please.'

She looked a trifle bemused. 'There's not a lot to tell, I suppose,' she eventually admitted. 'After dinner, after you'd gone, Mark said that he was going to go to Beckery Island, to see the priest there.' She gestured towards Cicely. 'We both asked him why, but all my son would say was that he wanted a word with Father Boniface. I asked was it to do with Peter's . . . well, his disappearance, but Mark didn't answer. He just instructed me to keep an eye on the apprentices while he was gone, and said he would be back some time after noon.'

'And it's now past three o'clock,' Cicely interrupted, 'and there's still no sign of him!'

'My dear child,' I objected, 'half a dozen things might have delayed your cousin, but the most likely, surely, is that he has met a friend and gone with him to an ale-house for a cup of wine or beer. Or he has got into conversation with one of the pilgrims – if memory serves me aright, there are always pilgrims lodging at the priest's house in Beckery at this time of year. Or perhaps some business has demanded his attention. You are letting your imagination run away with you. Mark will be home soon, safe and sound. You'll see.'

I had succeeded in reassuring Dame Joan, who smiled and nodded before hurrying downstairs again to the kitchen to oversee Lydia's preparations for supper. Cicely, however, was clearly still worried.

'Why did my cousin suddenly take it into his head to visit Beckery?' she demanded, chewing her bottom lip.

'To deliver some merchandise?' I suggested. 'The priest there must have need of parchment in the course of his work.'

She brightened slightly, but asked, 'Then why didn't he

say so? What need could there be for secrecy?'

I sighed. 'People don't always act in a predictable fashion. How dull life would be if they did! Maybe Mark was irritated by his mother's questioning. He's a grown man; he doesn't have to account to her for his every movement.'

Cicely thought this over before agreeing, albeit grudgingly, that I could be right.

'All the same,' she coaxed, 'I'd like to go to Beckery Island and make sure he really went there. It would put my mind at ease. It won't take long. We'll be back before supper.'

'We?' I groaned resignedly.

She got resolutely to her feet. 'Come along,' she insisted, 'and you can tell me what happened at the Pennards' as we go. I haven't asked you about your visit there yet.'

'I've already told you that there's nothing much to say. I've no solution to offer. I'm as mystified as the rest of you in regard to your cousin's whereabouts.' I heaved a second, more heartfelt sigh. 'Oh, very well! I'll come with you. But I've no doubt that we shall either meet Mark returning, or, in any event, that he'll be home before us.'

I was proved wrong on the first count. We did not encounter Mark on our way to Beckery Island.

It is not really an island, of course. It may have been once, centuries ago, when all the low-lying land in these parts was under water and only the hills stood clear. The great Tor itself, rising above the abbey, and which can now be reached dryshod, is still known as the Isle of Avalon – Ynys Afalon in the old Celtic tongue, the 'Island of Apples'. Beckery, which lies about a mile south-west of the town, was originally called Becc-Eriu, meaning 'Little Ireland'. Saint Bridget is said to have visited it over a thousand years before to work and pray, while Saint Dunstan was instructed there by Irish teachers.

The other story connected with Beckery is that King Arthur, while resting at Glastonbury, was told by an angel in a dream to go to the hermitage on the island, and when he did so, he was favoured with a remarkable vision of the Virgin and Child.

In that late summer of 1476, however – already nearly half a century in the past as I recount this story; how the years spin by us as old age takes its toll! – Beckery was what it had been for many years: a halt for pilgrims approaching Glastonbury from the west, either by land or along the waterway of the river Brue. A small, compact chapel, a simple oblong in shape, catered for their spiritual needs, while the priest's house itself, together with another long, low, single-storey building, provided them with accommodation for rest and refreshment. Ditches and a substantial fence protected the whole compound and separated the chapel from the secular buildings. A lavatorium had been added to the north-east corner of the house, a more than welcome sight, no doubt, to dusty and footsore travellers.

Upon enquiry, Cicely and I were told by one of the pilgrims that the priest was within the chapel, getting all ready for Vespers, which was only a half-hour distant. Our journey had taken us longer than we'd expected, the heat having slowed our progress and made several rests necessary for comfort and well-being. We were directed to the building's only entrance, a door which opened into the nave, where the tiled floor added to the general coolness induced by thick stone walls and a roof of Cornish slates.

The priest, a slender young man wearing the black Benedictine habit, was in the chancel, lighting the altar candles and making certain that all was swept and garnished for the evening service. Cicely and I paused for a moment, silently regarding him while we recovered our breath, before advancing. Our shoes made very little noise, but something – a sudden draught of air, perhaps, or the faint creaking of a door hinge – alerted him immediately to our presence. He turned and came towards us with a friendly smile, wiping his hands on the skirt of a linen apron.

'Have you come far, my children? Do you require accommodation? We have a space or two. All our overnight visitors have moved on to the abbey, and we have had less than a dozen replacements.'

Cicely forestalled me. 'No, no, Father! We're not pilgrims. We've come to ask after my cousin, Mark Gildersleeve, who set out to pay you a visit this morning and has not yet returned home. Did he arrive here? And if so, did he stay long?'

The priest frowned for a moment, then his brow cleared and his narrow features lifted into a smile.

'Yes, yes! Mark was with me today, round about noon. He came to bring me a present of a new sheet of vellum.'

'A present?' I repeated. 'It was not something you had ordered from him then?'

'Oh no! It is extremely fine vellum. A very generous gift indeed by Master Gildersleeve, but far too good for my mundane needs. I shall, however, pass it on to the abbey scriptorium, where it will doubtless be used to the best advantage.'

Puzzled, I said, 'But Master Gildersleeve must have known that the vellum was too valuable for your household accounts and suchlike. Why did he bring it?'

Father Boniface's smile grew rueful. 'I think it was in

the nature of a small *douceur*. He hoped I could give him some information.'

'What information?' Cicely and I demanded in the same breath.

The priest looked somewhat taken aback by our eagerness. 'He asked me about a paper which I had given to his brother some two or three months ago, knowing of Peter's interest in all things antiquarian. Mark wanted me to explain its contents to him. Alas, I was unable to do so.'

'Why was that? Had you not read it?'

'Yes. Well, I'd seen it.' The priest shivered suddenly. 'It's cold in here,' he said, laying a hand on my arm. 'Let's go outside and sit for a while in the sun.'

Cicely and I, who were both still feeling the effect of our long, hot walk, reluctantly followed him out of doors and sat beside him on the top of the knoll. Daisies and buttercups starred the grass, and here and there I could see the bright sapphire-blue of a speedwell. Beyond the inner fence hens pecked in the dust for grit and the scattered remains of their morning's feed, while a fat black cat lay curled contentedly in the doorway of the house, sleepily oblivious to the pilgrims forced to step over it as they left or re-entered the building. A cow lowed plaintively from a neighbouring field.

After a long-drawn silence I prompted, 'Why then, Father, were you unable to explain this paper?'

The priest turned his mild blue eyes upon me with a look of vague astonishment, as though he had, for a moment, forgotten my presence. 'Ah, yes. The paper. I couldn't explain its contents, my son, for the simple reason that I couldn't understand them.'

'They were written in a foreign language?'

'You might say that. The message, if it was one, consisted

of a number of horizontal and vertical lines. The latter, some upright, some sloping, were arranged in groups, varying in number between one and five, either above, below or aslant the former. And that, as I also told Master Gildersleeve this morning, is the reason I gave it to his brother. I hoped Master Peter might discover how to decipher it.'

'How did you come by this paper, Father?'

'It was given into my hands for safekeeping over a year ago by an Irishman, who had travelled to Beckery in the steps of Saint Bridget. From Glastonbury he was going to the shrine of Saint Thomas at Canterbury, and he asked me to look after it until his return, in case it was either lost or stolen from him on the journey.'

Cicely shifted restlessly beside me. All she wanted now was to go home to discover if Mark had reached there before us. Her arms were clasped about her raised knees, her hair, unconfined by net or ribbon, tumbling about her shoulders in an untidy profusion of pale golden-brown curls. Those huge violet eyes were veiled by blue-veined lids, and her sullen expression only served to emphasize the thin lips and heavy lower jaw, making her look almost plain. A ladybird was crawling slowly down her arm, like a drop of blood oozing from a wound.

I ignored her obvious impatience and turned once more to the priest. 'But did this Irishman tell you nothing about the paper? Didn't he explain the meaning of these symbols you describe?'

'The paper was folded and sealed with wax. Naturally, at that time, I did not suggest opening it.' Father Boniface sounded offended. 'What it contained was not then my business. I merely put it away to give him again when he came back.'

'But he has not come back?'

'No.' The priest removed his apron as he began at last to feel the heat. He raised the skirts of his habit above his ankles, stretching out his scrawny white shins and sandalled feet to the caressing rays of the sun. 'He did however tell me his name, Gerald Clonmel, and that he came from the parts about Waterford which, he said, is in the very south of Ireland. But I have no means of knowing whether this is true or not, having no knowledge of the world beyond this island.'

I nodded. 'Indeed it is. The people of that region have long trafficked with the merchants of southern Wales and with Bristol.'

'Ah!' The priest smiled in satisfaction. 'Then that would add weight to his story. It is the tradition in his family, he told me, that this paper was taken to Ireland by one of his remote forebears who came from hereabouts.'

'And did *he* understand its message?'

Father Boniface spoke slowly, as one dealing with a simpleton or a child. 'I have already explained that when it was given into my keeping I had no notion what the paper contained. When Gerald returned from Canterbury he could share the secret of its contents with me or not, just as he pleased. But as you have surmised he did not return, and a little over three months ago I learned that he had died shortly after he had fulfilled his lifelong vow to worship at the Holy Martyr's tomb. A fellow pilgrim who had been with him at the end, and who was on his way home to Wales, told me that Gerald had been buried in Canterbury.'

'So you opened the paper?' I was not condemning Father Boniface, which he seemed to understand; I should have done the same in his place, as, I think, would anyone.

'I did, and have told you what I found. Of course I could make no sense of its message, and so, a little while afterwards, when Peter Gildersleeve brought me a fresh supply of parchments, I gave it to him to see if he could puzzle out its meaning.'

'And you have no idea whether he did so or not?'

'When I last saw him, four or five weeks since, he said he thought he might have some news for me very soon.' The priest's face grew deeply troubled. 'And now I understand that the poor young man has disappeared in mysterious circumstances.' He shivered again, more violently than before, and his hand, when he laid it on mine, was icy cold in spite of the heat. 'I fear I might unwittingly have enmeshed him in some terrible evil. I did not know until this morning, when Mark Gildersleeve came to visit me, what had happened. We are isolated here. News takes a day or two to reach us.'

I scratched my chin, where tomorrow's growth of beard was already making its presence felt. When, I wondered, had Mark discovered this paper? He had not known of it last night, or he would not have asked me to carry out my search this morning. So, sometime between then and now he must have chanced upon it.

'Do you suppose,' I enquired of Father Boniface, 'that Mark also associated this strange message, whatever it may be, with his brother's disappearance?'

'It is possible, my son.'

'Did he have the paper with him?'

'I asked him that. I thought that perhaps we might have studied it together in the vain hope of finding some clue to its meaning, but Mark said no, he had left it at home.'

'Did he know its history?'

'No, for his brother had never spoken to him about it. I

gathered from his discourse that he does not share Master Peter's interest in antiquities.'

'That's true enough.' I frowned as a thought occurred to me. 'But if, as you say, his brother neither showed him this paper nor discussed it with him, how did Mark know that it had been given to Peter by you?'

The priest nodded sagely. 'That question also occurred to me. It would seem that my name had been written on the reverse side of the parchment by his brother.'

Of course! I had seen similar annotations on the books and folios I had looked at that morning; names written either at the beginning or at the end of the script which, then, had had no meaning for me. Now I understood. They were the names of the people from whom Peter had acquired them.

I turned to Cicely, only to find that she was not attending to the conversation. She had been busy picking the daisies which surrounded her and fashioning them into garlands. She had a chain about each wrist and a third, longer one, perched on her curls like a flowery coronet, but slipping towards her left ear, which gave her a slightly rakish appearance. I realized that, in spite of her airs and graces, she had not really grown up yet, which gave her the childlike ability to detach herself from time to time from the worries and concerns of everyday life and enter, however briefly, a secret world of her own.

Suddenly conscious of my eyes upon her, she returned my look defiantly. 'We should be getting home,' she said, scrambling to her feet. 'It will soon be suppertime. Mark and Aunt Joan will be waiting for us.'

The thrust of her chin dared me to contradict this statement. It had been proved that, after all, her cousin had indeed visited Beckery Island as he had said he was going to do, and she was now ashamed of her former state of panic. She obviously felt that she had been foolish, and tried to make up for this by descending the knoll with her most queenly gait. Unfortunately she had forgotten the daisy chains, until the one on her head slipped forward over her eyes and she snatched it off and stamped on it with a most unladylike display of rage. I only made matters worse by being unable to control my laughter, and she swung round, pummelling me hard on the chest.

'I hate you! I hate you!' she shouted, and would have continued hitting me had she not caught sight of the young priest's scandalized face. She then tossed her curls, divested herself of the daisy bracelets and proceeded on her way without a backward glance.

I paused at the foot of the slope to thank Father Boniface for his time and trouble and, above all, his frankness in answering my questions.

He made the sign of the Cross and gave me his blessing. 'And if you hear anything at all of Peter Gildersleeve, my son, please send me word. I shall not sleep soundly until I know that the paper I gave him has nothing to do with his disappearance.'

'Even if it has, Father,' I consoled him, 'it was a gift made in all innocence. No one, not God Himself, can blame you for such an act.'

'Do not presume to speak for God, my son,' he answered severely. 'It is difficult enough trying to fathom the hearts and minds of our fellow men, without aspiring to interpret the thoughts of the Almighty.'

Suitably chastened, I closed the gate of the inner fence in order to keep the hens out of the chapel precinct, called a greeting to two of the pilgrims who had just emerged from the house in anticipation of the Vespers bell, and followed Cicely through the door in the outer stockade and on to the track which led to Glastonbury.

We trudged in silence for a while, the green mass of Weary-all Hill keeping us company, until at last I was forced to express contrition.

'I'm sorry,' I said, 'I shouldn't have laughed at you like that.'

Cicely sniffed, but her back grew a little less rigid. 'It was unkind,' she chided.

'I know. I've said I'm sorry.'

She seemed to accept this, waiting for me to catch her up and slipping her right hand beneath my left elbow. 'What was Father Boniface saying to you about Mark?' she asked.

'You should have listened.'

She withdrew her hand abruptly. 'Don't be horrid! You sound like my father.'

So I repeated all that the priest had told me – a good test to discover how much I could remember, which was very nearly everything. (My memory has always been excellent, and even now, in my seventy-first year, I can oftentimes recall whole conversations almost word for word.)

When I had finished, Cicely took my arm again, her face troubled. 'Do you think this paper important?'

'Mark does; so important that he visited Father Boniface as soon as he could after finding it, to discover if the priest could shed any light on its meaning.'

'Do you think Mark has told Aunt Joan about it?'

'No. If he had, she would have told me, for she would see no need for secrecy.'

'He might have sworn her to silence.'

I shook my head. 'She is an open-hearted woman and would not keep either of us in the dark.'

Cicely sighed. 'You're right. But why would Mark keep

his find a secret? Why did he not mention it while we were having dinner?'

I shook my head. I had no more idea than she did. 'What is equally to the point,' I said, 'is where did he find it? And where has he hidden it now?'

'You must demand a sight of it as soon as we get home,' Cicely urged. 'Mark's surely bound to have returned by now.'

She stumbled over a loose stone in the road and I put an arm about her waist to steady her. Some travelling players, who were passing in their gaily painted and beribboned cart, gave a cheer, and one shouted a well-intentioned (but highly reprehensible) remark. I glared at the offender, but Cicely did not even blush, and I realized that she was too innocent to have understood its meaning. She had been sheltered all her short life and, as yet, knew very little of existence, in spite of her desire to present herself as a woman of the world. I hoped that she would not have too rude an awakening.

We arrived at the Gildersleeves' house, footsore and tired and late for supper, to be met on the doorstep by Dame Joan in a greater state of agitation than when we had left her, and I realized that the second of my predictions had also been wrong.

'Mark still hasn't come back,' she told us, 'and Rob has discovered that Dorabella is missing from the stable.'

Chapter Eight

'We should have guessed that Mark would have ridden, not walked, to Beckery,' I said.

Cicely, Dame Joan and I were seated at the kitchen table, together with the two apprentices, while Lydia scuttled around behind us, ladling a savoury-smelling stew on to our plates. As well as the rich scent of the meat, with its juices and gravy, the whiff of rosemary and garlic and sweet wild thyme teased my nostrils and made my mouth water. A basket of hot oatcakes graced the centre of the board alongside a jug of ale, filled to the brim and running over. In spite of the heat, my walk had made me ravenous, and it was all I could do to wait for my hostess to say a benediction over the food before falling to. Cicely, although hot and tired, had clearly also developed an appetite, and it was not until we had blunted the edge of our hunger that Mark's continued absence was discussed.

'I don't see why he couldn't have walked to Beckery,' Dame Joan complained. 'Dorabella has been ridden hard these past few days and could do with a rest. It's only a mile and wouldn't have taken him much more than half an hour on foot.'

'And another half-hour back again,' I pointed out, adding with a certain amount of feeling, 'An hour too much, perhaps, in this broiling sun.' I spooned stew into my mouth and went on thickly, 'But maybe he meant to ride on somewhere else when he had concluded his business with Father Boniface.' I swallowed and turned to Rob Undershaft. 'Did Master Gildersleeve give any hint to you, or John Longbones here, concerning his intentions?'

Both apprentices shook their heads vigorously, continuing to wolf down their belated supper. At last John, the first one of them to clear his plate, said, 'Master told us he was going to Beckery, that was all. Told us the priest there was in need of a sheet of vellum, which he'd promised to let him have today.'

Rob nodded in confirmation.

'An untruth,' I declared flatly. 'Father Boniface was neither expecting, nor in need of, a sheet of vellum.'

Dame Joan cut in. 'But why should Mark lie? Tell me again, if you please, exactly what passed between you and the good Father.'

So, with more hindrance than help from Cicely, I repeated my conversation with the priest as accurately as I could, but left my hostess almost as bewildered as before.

'Peter said no word to me of any gift received from the Father.' She considered this for a moment, then continued fair-mindedly, 'Although I have to admit that he did not often show me his books or parchments, for what would have been the use, knowing I cannot read? No, I suppose there was no reason why he should have mentioned this particular paper to me, if it had no pictures. For it's the pictures I like to look at. I can understand those.'

'There were no pictures in this manuscript,' I assured her gently. 'Nor, apparently, any words that were recognizable as such, if the priest is to be believed.' And I repeated Father Boniface's description of the strange arrangement of lines.

With a furtive gesture, so that the apprentices should not notice, Dame Joan made the sign to ward off evil before addressing me again.

'And you think Mark must have come across this paper sometime today?'

I nodded and she turned a scared face towards me. 'Do you think these strange symbols have anything to do with Peter's disappearance? And have they now worked their evil spell on Mark?'

I noticed that she had started to tremble, and took the liberty of reaching out a hand and squeezing one of hers. But what comfort could I offer when I was not sure myself of the answer?

'Dame Joan,' I urged, 'we don't yet know that anything *has* happened to your younger son. The fact that he rode to Beckery instead of walking hints that he intended to travel further afield if he got no satisfactory answer from the priest. We cannot know where, or for what purpose, but there is every likelihood that he will return home before dark.'

She smiled tremulously. 'Yes. Yes, of course.' Her look became less strained and anxious. 'But did you learn nothing from Abel Fairchild or the Pennards that could explain what might have happened to Peter?'

'Nothing more than what you have already told me. I'm sorry.'

'And Abel remains constant in his story that Peter vanished within moments?' Once again I nodded. 'But are *you* satisfied that there was no other means of concealment anywhere at hand?'

'Apart from the hut? No, I'm afraid not, and Master Gildersleeve was not inside it. Abel had wit enough, seemingly, to look behind the door, but there was no one there. The interior of the hut is small, with nothing but a pile of sacking in one corner. There is nowhere else anyone could hide in such a short time.'

'So what is to be done now?' my hostess demanded tearfully. 'Tongues are already wagging, and will do so in earnest if Peter's fate is not discovered soon. And if it should prove that Mark, too, has vanished . . .' She did not finish, but let the conclusion go as something too awful to contemplate.

Even Cicely seemed struck by the seriousness of the situation. She rose from her place and went to comfort her aunt, kneeling beside the older woman's chair, putting her arms around her and kissing the suddenly careworn cheek. Then she raised her head and glared fiercely at me.

'Can't you do something, Roger? According to you, you're so clever at solving mysteries! Why is it that you can't solve this one?'

'I only arrived here yesterday evening!' I protested warmly. 'You're unreasonable, Mistress!'

Dame Joan agreed, at the same time smoothing her niece's hair, anxious to antagonize no one. 'Roger has done a great deal already, my love. And he has done it out of the goodness of his heart, for he is under no obligation to assist us.'

Cicely gave her aunt a final hug and returned to her place, grimacing at me across the kitchen table. 'I know. I'm sorry,' she said, and blew me a kiss.

Dame Joan gave a strangled cry of protest.

Later, walking with Cicely in the little garden, the scent of blown roses all about us, thick as incense, I took her to task, reminding her of her betrothal to her elder cousin.

'It was a marriage arranged by our parents. I'm not in

love with Peter,' she whispered, and I was aware of the gleam of tears in those huge violet eyes upraised to mine.

'And you're not in love with me either, my girl,' I answered briskly, 'any more than I am with you.'

The tears miraculously vanished. 'You're horrid and rude, and I hate you!' she retorted with venom.

I laughed. 'So you've told me once already this afternoon. Just try to remember how much you dislike me and we shall rub along véry well together. Your aunt is in great distress. Her burden should not be increased by anxiety about your conduct.'

The violet eyes gleamed again, but this time with pure temper. 'I'm going indoors,' Cicely announced. 'Don't dare to follow me!'

'I am yours to command!'

I thought for a moment that she would strike me yet again, but after half raising her hand, she must have decided that a dignified departure would be more impressive; so, gathering up her skirts, she swung on her heel and disappeared inside the house.

I smiled to myself and sat down on the stone bench that ran along the wall beneath the workroom window. From the kitchen I could hear the clatter of pots and dishes as Lydia went about the evening's work, assisted by her good-natured mistress, and the low rumble of the apprentices' voices as they discussed, no doubt, this latest development in their hitherto uneventful lives. Their future prospects must look bleak to them at present, I thought, with first Peter, and now possibly Mark Gildersleeve missing.

The westering sun speared through the branches of both the medlar tree and an apple tree that grew in one corner of the garden. The round, reddening globes of fruit nestled against the velvety darkness of the leaves, and the slender trunk rippled like water under the running light. Birds sang in the branches, for it was still far too early for them to go to roost, and just for a moment I let my body slacken and cleared my mind of thoughts, refusing to contemplate the Gordian knot which I had yet to unravel . . . and in no time at all I was sound asleep.

I awoke with a start to the sudden conviction that something I had said recently, some remark uttered to Dame Joan during supper, had been of great significance. The feeling was so strong that I desperately tried to recall our conversation word for word, but however often I went over it in my mind I was unable to pinpoint anything which seemed to be of any importance. I was still racking my brain, without success, when Dame Joan herself emerged from the kitchen, Lydia hard on her heels. They crossed to the stone bench and sat down, one on either side of me, each emitting those little grunts and gasps which, I have frequently noticed, women give when their chores are temporarily finished and they can take the weight from their feet.

'Where's Cicely?' her aunt inquired in a tone tinged with alarm. It was plain that she found her niece and prospective daughter-in-law both headstrong and wilful.

'She's gone indoors. I think she's very tired,' I answered, abandoning for the present all attempts to solve my riddle.

'She's a good girl really,' Dame Joan excused her, 'but at that age, when she's longing to spread her wings . . . Poor child!' And the older woman heaved a sympathetic sigh.

I thought then, as I think now, that it must be hard for women, going as they do straight from the authority of parents to that of a husband. They know so little freedom in their lives – that freedom which allows a man to take charge of, and order, his own existence.

From the other side of me, the quiet shadow that was Lydia gave a half-suppressed cough and muttered, 'Mistress . . .'

'Ah, yes!' Dame Joan seemed to recollect herself. 'Lydia has something to tell you,' she said.

I turned to the little kitchen-maid who, with her hood awry and a smudge on her nose, was impatiently swinging her legs to and fro, her tiny feet some inches from the ground.

'What is it you wish to say?'

She giggled self-consciously. 'It concerns this paper you were talking of at supper. I knew about it already.'

'*You knew about it!* But surely . . . surely Master Peter didn't mention it to *you*?'

'Lord, no!' Lydia gave another giggle. 'It was Maud.'

'Who's Maud, in the name of heaven?'

'Maud Jarrold,' Dame Joan explained. 'Our other maid, who left us two days ago and went back to her parents' cottage in Bove Town.'

'But why would your son confide in her?' I demanded, puzzled.

Lydia was scathing. 'Master Peter didn't *tell* her anything, stupid! She saw it. She wasn't meant to, and Master Peter was very angry about it.'

'So how did it happen? How did she come to see it?'

'Sometimes, at the end of the day, when the shop's shut, Master Peter will take some of his books and go in there to read and study them . . .'

'That's true enough,' Dame Joan confirmed from my other side. 'He says it's quieter than the solar.' She grimaced. 'And I daresay he's right, for I have to admit I am a bit of a chatterer.'

'But what about Mark? Doesn't he go in and out of the shop?'

'Not once it's closed for the day. He's always off to some tavern or ale-house. Mark likes company. He has a lot of friends.'

It crossed my mind that Dame Joan's life must have been very lonely before Cicely's arrival, with one son's nose permanently stuck in a book and the other out drinking as soon as work was finished. I turned back to Lydia. 'Go on,' I said.

She wriggled into a more comfortable position on the hard stone.

'Well, it was one evening some three or four weeks ago – I can't remember exactly when. It was just beginning to get dark. Maud was coming out of the workroom where she'd been talking to John and Rob.' Lydia sniggered. 'She was a bit sweet on Rob Undershaft. She'd never confess it, but she was.'

'I didn't know that.' Dame Joan was intrigued.

'Oh yes, and—'

'*What happened?*' I interrupted them both ruthlessly.

Lydia collected her rambling thoughts and continued: 'Well, Maud told me that Master Peter must have heard her come out of the workroom and called to her to fetch him a candle. When she returned he wasn't there – he'd had to leave the room for a few minutes – so she put the candle on the bench and started looking at the books and papers that were spread out all over it. There was this one sheet of parchment, she said, which was nothing but a lot of lines. Just a lot of little strokes arranged in bunches. That was her word: "bunches". I mean, Maud can't read any more than I can, but we know what proper writing looks like.'

'And then?' I prompted.

'Master Peter came back, and when he realized what it was she was looking at he flew into a rage. Maud said she'd never seen him so angry, because normally he's a polite, mild-tempered man.' Dame Joan nodded in agreement. 'But he bundled her out of the shop as fast as she could go, shouting all sorts of silly things at her. She was really frightened.'

'What sort of silly things was he shouting?'

'Lord, I don't know. She may have told me, but I've forgotten.' Lydia screwed up her face in an effort to remember. 'Something about the paper being very valuable, and it wasn't to be touched.'

'Valuable?'

'I think that's what Maud said. Anyway, Master Peter was quite himself again the following morning and apologized to her for being so hasty. Pretended he'd been feeling unwell – but Maud didn't believe him.'

After a short silence while I mulled over this information, I asked, 'Are you certain you can't recall anything else Maud might have told you?'

Lydia shook her head, suddenly losing interest in the proceedings. She stretched her arms and gave a cavernous yawn before announcing that she was off to prepare the dough for tomorrow's bread. She slid wearily off the bench and went into the kitchen.

After a few moments I said, 'Dame Joan, with your permission I'd like to see this Maud Jarrold for myself. If you'll tell me where she lives, I'll go at once. I want to know in more detail what passed between her and your son.'

'Do you consider it so important? You've had a tiring day. Can't it wait until tomorrow?'

'I'd rather go this evening. The sooner we know all there is to be known, the better.'

'Perhaps you're right. Very well, then. Go as far as the

pilgrims' chapel of Saint James, and beside it you'll see a lane, running northward. There are half a dozen cottages there which house some of the lay workers of the abbey. John Jarrold's is the last, the farthest from the road. Maud's father helps the brothers with the heavier digging and planting in the orchard and the kitchen gardens. He's a rough-tongued man and won't take kindly to your wanting to question his daughter. But at this hour of the evening you may be lucky and find him from home. He'll be in one of the ale-houses.'

I thanked her and rose to my feet.

She smiled up at me, her eyes deeply troubled. 'Take care, my dear boy,' she said, and I promised her that I'd try.

I left her sitting on the stone bench, alone with her uneasy reflections.

There was still a great deal of activity in the lower part of the town, for the fine summer evenings meant that men could work longer, or sit with their womenfolk out of doors gossiping with their neighbours. Children not yet in bed were playing games up and down the street: bowling hoops, trying to kick a blown swine's bladder between two sticks planted upright in the ground, throwing discarded horse-shoes at a given mark, and – the most favoured pastime, as I remembered from my youth – taking sling-shots at birds, or indeed at anything that moved.

Higher up, however, beyond the turning to Lambcook Street where the climb becomes steeper, there was far less noise. Here, in those days at least, the dwellings were sparser. Not so many people lived in Bove Town, and those who did seemed to be of a less friendly disposition; so I trod more warily, keeping my eyes on the road ahead and offering no greetings. I knew the chapel of Saint James well enough; indeed, most of my recollections of Glastonbury were as fresh in my memory as though it were only five weeks, and not five years, since I had last been there. The chapel stood some furrow's length below the causeway to Wells, on the left-hand side as one walked eastward, and at right angles to it, as Dame Joan had said, ran a narrow lane.

The six cottages were close together, with a patch of ground at the back of each where a pig or cow could be kept during the day and a few vegetables grown in season. The goodwife who lived in the first cottage was already driving her animal indoors for the night – a little premature, I thought, as it would not be dark for a while yet.

I knocked on the door of the last cottage, where the lane dwindled to a rough and narrow track, and waited in some trepidation for it to be opened. To my relief, my summons was answered by a young girl, while a woman's voice from within shouted, 'Who is it, Maud?'

'I don't know, Mother. A stranger.' And Maud Jarrold turned a look of enquiry on me, waiting for an explanation of my presence.

I asked, 'Can I come in?'

Immediately the goodwife was behind her daughter, barring the entrance with a pair of brawny arms. 'My man's from home at present, but he'll be back very shortly. What is it you want?'

I explained as well as I could, and the woman's face darkened with suspicion.

'Maud can't tell you anything. Her father took her from that house as soon as he learned what had happened to Peter Gildersleeve. There were strange goings-on there. Too many books, for one thing; it isn't safe for a man to read as many books as he did. And then there was that piece of paper my girl saw which had nothing but lines on it! Witchcraft, that's what my John says!' Recollecting herself, the goodwife took a step forward to peer nervously down the lane, afraid that one of her neighbours might have heard her.

I said eagerly, 'It's that paper I wish to know about.' I addressed myself directly to her daughter. 'Lydia told me what happened – the night that you saw it, spread out on the bench in the shop. What did Peter Gildersleeve say to you when he returned?'

Maud, swelling with self-importance, spoke up before her mother could stop her. 'He was furiously angry. I've never known him behave like that before.' She went on to repeat more or less what Lydia had said: 'He's usually so calm and gentle. He thought I'd touched it, but I hadn't. I wouldn't.' She shivered. 'Not a thing like that. Black magic, I reckon it was. The work of the Devil.'

'But what did he *say*?' I repeated.

Maud thought for a moment or two, her rather plain features hardening into lines of furrowed concentration. At last she said, 'I was very frightened, you understand, because he was in such a temper, but I do remember him saying that it was . . . now, let me see . . . yes, that if he'd int . . . interpreted it aright – ' she stumbled a little over the unfamiliar word – 'it was "valuable beyond price". That was it! "Valuable beyond price".'

'If he'd interpreted it aright,' I repeated slowly. 'Did he say anything else that you can recall?'

'She's answering no more of your questions,' the goodwife told me angrily. 'What's more, she's never going back to work for the Gildersleeves. And you can tell Dame Joan so, if she asks! You'd better be off before my man gets home, or he'll grind you into mincemeat.' She paused, taking stock of me. 'Well,' she amended honestly, 'he'd try; my man's not scared of anyone.'

I decided it was time to be gone. I should get no more out of Maud, and I had no wish to be confronted by her irate father. And I had gleaned something for my trouble.

So I said my farewells and hastened down the lane towards Saint James's chapel. As I rounded the corner into the main thoroughfare a big, burly man with a belligerent expression on his unattractive face passed me, going in the opposite direction. Impossible, I felt, that he should be anyone but John Jarrold, and I was glad that our paths had crossed so briefly.

The heat of the day was giving way to a soft warmth, which made for pleasant walking. At the side of the track, willow herb and ragwort stood sentinel, rose-purple and dusty gold, their petals beginning to furl against the coming dusk. I thought again of the paper Father Boniface had given to Peter Gildersleeve, and which Peter had told Maud was 'valuable beyond price if he had interpreted it aright'. What had he discovered about it between receiving it from the priest and the time that he had vanished? And did it really have anything to do with his disappearance?

I passed the turning to Lambcook Street and re-entered the lower part of the town. The children were being rounded up now and shepherded indoors, goodnights were called, gossip was abandoned until tomorrow. I turned into the Gildersleeves' house and was met by Dame Joan, coming along the passageway from the garden.

I raised my eyebrows in silent enquiry, and she, just as silently, shook her head.

Mark had not yet come home.

Chapter Nine

Nor had he returned by nightfall, when the rest of us (with the exception of Dame Joan) went soberly to bed: the two apprentices to their pallets in the workroom, Lydia to her kitchen corner, Cicely to her chamber and I to Mark's.

'Won't you come too, Aunt?' Cicely pleaded. 'You can do no good by depriving yourself of rest. If my cousin arrives home during the night or early morning he'll knock loudly enough to rouse one of us. You'll achieve nothing except to give yourself that sort of headache which comes from dozing and waking in a chair.'

But Dame Joan was adamant. 'I must know the moment he returns,' she said. 'Roger, lad, fetch me down an armchair from the solar, if you'd be so kind, and place it in the shop. I'll leave the door into the passageway open, then I'm certain to hear him. Lydia, child, run and fetch me a spare blanket from the cedarwood chest. It'll be sufficient covering on a warm night like this.'

The maid (whose attempt to say something was angrily hushed) and I did as we were bidden. Cicely tucked the rough grey blanket around her aunt's legs.

Dame Joan thanked her and patted her cheek. 'You're a good girl,' she told her.

Cicely and I each took a candle and mounted the stairs, saying a muted goodnight to one another before entering our respective rooms. The door to Dame Joan's chamber stood wide open, showing a glimpse of a four-poster bed, with its tapestried canopy and snowy white cover. I thought of the hard armchair and the draught from the passageway, and hoped, like Cicely, that my hostess would not have cause to regret her decision tomorrow morning, when she would almost surely suffer from fatigue and aching bones.

I lit the wicks of the two horn-paned lanterns and snuffed out my candle before sitting down to pull off my boots. My day had been long and hard. I had been to the Pennards' and back again, a total distance of some eleven miles, walked to and from Beckery Island in all the glare of the afternoon's heat, and, finally, paid a visit to the Jarrolds' cottage in Bove Town. I should have been dog-tired. Indeed, I was – and a few moments earlier my one ambition had been to climb between the sheets, sink into the goose-feather mattress and lose myself in sleep; my racing thoughts, however, prevented me from doing so. I sat there on the blue damask coverlet, one boot off, the other still grasped in my hand, staring before me at the open window but hearing and seeing nothing. Where had Mark gone? He had ridden to Beckery, that much I could be sure of, but I had no idea what had happened next. Absentmindedly I finished removing my second boot, then, elbows propped on knees, chin resting on my hands, I considered such information as I possessed.

Mark had told both Dame Joan and his cousin that he was going to see Father Boniface, but had offered them no explanation – and he had lied to the apprentices about the reason for his visit. The truth was, however, that he had hoped the priest could interpret the contents of the paper left behind by the Irishman, Gerald Clonmel, and had been disappointed. So what had he done then?

The question of exactly *when* Mark had discovered this mysterious document returned to tease me. He had patently not known of it last night, when he had asked me to go through his brother's books and folios this morning. It must therefore have been sometime today, before dinner – for I had set off for the Pennards' immediately afterwards, and he had departed for Beckery before I returned – and consequently prior to ten o'clock, when the meal had been served. We had been much together during those early hours – washing, dressing, breakfasting, shaving – but naturally I had not had him in view every second. There were many moments when our eyes had been averted from one another, and a full ten minutes when I had been in the privy next to the stable.

It was most probable, I decided, that he had chanced upon it then, and somewhere in this room. His brother had originally stored the paper with his other books in the workshop, but as Peter had come to appreciate its value, or what he thought was its value, he had grown more secretive, keeping the chest locked and flying into a rage when Mark had questioned this unaccustomed action. And, eventually, he had removed it from the chest (which he had not bothered to relock) and hidden it elsewhere.

One of my legs was growing numb from the weight of my elbow pressing against my knee, so I straightened my back and looked around me. If Mark had indeed discovered the paper in this room it might still be here, probably in the same place in which he had found it. For unless he had lied again, this time to Father Boniface – and I could see no good reason why he should have done – he had not taken it with him to Beckery. My gaze ranged over the clothes-chest and the oak cupboard in the corner, but I dismissed them out of hand: they were neither of them places in which to hide something that needed to be kept secret; Dame Joan and the maids would have had constant access to them both. Instead my glance rested upon the remarkable bed-head, with its posts of carved acanthus leaves, and, in between, its score or so of tiny drawers and cupboards.

Suddenly I recalled the scene in the workshop, when Mark had produced the key to the book-chest. I remembered his words: 'It was in one of the drawers of the bed-head. It occurred to me last night that that was where it might be.' And he had found the paper at the same time. He must have done! There was no other explanation.

I knelt up on the bed and, with hands that shook a little, opened every drawer and cupboard in turn, peering excitedly into each one, certain that in the next I should find what I was seeking. But there was nothing. Disbelieving, I started over again, but this second search was just as fruitless. Almost weeping with disappointment I then looked in the clothes chest – even rifling through the pockets of the garments it contained – and the corner cupboard, but without success. I stripped the bed of sheets, blankets and mattress, all in vain, and had to remake it before I could sleep.

By this time, however, I was so tired that I could barely stand, and so I reluctantly abandoned any further search until the morning. I thought that in spite of my weariness I shouldn't know a moment's rest all night, but I was asleep as soon as my head touched the pillow.

I awoke with the crowing of the cocks and the early morning sunlight shining through the open window. With Mark absent, I had not closed the shutters but left them wide to the cool night air. Nor had they been closed during the intervening hours of darkness, a fact which alerted me, almost before I had come fully to my senses, that my bedfellow had not returned. Immediately I was wide awake, dragging myself up by my elbows and looking anxiously towards the other side of the bed.

My fears were well founded. It was still as empty as when I had fallen asleep last night. The pillow was smooth, the sheets cold to the touch. No one had occupied that space, not even briefly.

I judged that it was yet some time before the bells would ring for Prime, but I could already hear the rumble of cart wheels up and down the High Street. Today was a feast day, and a great many people would be crowding in from the surrounding countryside to attend the abbey's celebrations. There would be small chance of a private word with Brother Hilarion; he would be too occupied with supervising the novices and making sure they did all that was required of them. Though I stood in urgent need of his quiet wisdom and sound common sense, I should be forced to practise the patience which I had preached to him yesterday.

Sleep, once banished, would not return, so I got out of bed and pulled on my breeches. Before going downstairs however, I decided to look yet again for the missing paper. That Mark had found it here, somewhere in this room, I was as certain as I possibly could be, but still its whereabouts remained a mystery. He had come across it by accident while searching for the key, and I was therefore unable to escape the conclusion that he must have been lying when he told Father Boniface that he did not have it with him yesterday. There was, after all, no reason why he should have scrupled to carry it with him – having no idea that his brother had deemed the paper 'valuable beyond price' – not unless Maud had informed him of the fact. But that, of course, she plainly had not done, or Mark would have known of the paper's existence earlier. He would have questioned Peter on the subject and, having wrung the truth from him, would most likely have demanded his share of the value that his brother placed upon it.

Lydia was the only person Maud had told, during that time of shared confidences, after dark, when the rest of the household was sleeping and the pair of them were snuggled down on their pallets in the kitchen. They would have discussed and wondered at Peter's unusual spurt of ill temper, commiserated with one another on the unpredictability of employers, perhaps whispered with thrilling voices about cabalistic signs. In the morning, however, the incident would have been forgotten as they resumed their normal, humdrum lives. It was only when Peter had suddenly vanished in such mysterious circumstances that Maud Jarrold had thought again about the paper she had seen. But even so, she had mentioned it to no one but her father, and then not until after he had removed her from the Gildersleeves' house. Lydia, far from connecting it with Peter's disappearance, had only recollected Maud's story when she overheard our conversation at supper the previous evening.

I was convinced in my own mind that my assumptions were correct, but I resolved to make sure by asking Lydia for confirmation.

It was still very early; not even Rob and John were up yet. I washed and dressed and went downstairs to the garden, only to find the kitchen door wide open and the little maid bustling around, already making preparations for breakfast – not just for myself and the two apprentices, but also for Dame Joan and Cicely who, like the rest of the world and his wife, would be abroad betimes, getting ready to go to Mass. After a little small talk, I asked Lydia if she had mentioned the paper to Mark.

'No, I said nothing to him. I never took much notice of Maud's tales, and that's a fact. She could be a bit of a liar at times.'

'But not on this occasion.'

'Seems not.'

'Did Dame Joan stay downstairs all night?' I asked, looking up from my shaving, which operation I had begun carefully performing at the kitchen table.

'She did, more fool her.' Lydia began beating eggs in a basin. 'She's gone up to her room now to lie down for half an hour. She'll be worn out by the time this day's over.'

'Mark didn't come home then.'

It was not a question; I already knew the answer. But Lydia treated it as such.

'No, not so far.' She finished beating the eggs and put the bowl down on the table. I sensed that there was something more she wished to say, and smiled at her encouragingly. After a moment's hesitation, she went on, 'This isn't the first time that it's happened.'

'That what's happened?'

'That Mark's stayed out all night . . . He'd be furious if he knew I'd told you, for he swore me to secrecy. Said he'd have me dismissed if I so much as breathed a word to his mother.'

'Go on,' I said. 'I shan't betray you.'

She stooped to put a batch of risen dough into the oven next to the fire, then sat down opposite me, wiping her hands on her apron.

'It was some months back, not long after Easter – perhaps nearer to Ascensiontide, now I think of it. One night, I couldn't sleep. I wasn't feeling well. I'd eaten something which disagreed with me. Normally, I never stir until morning.' That, I thought was understandable, considering how hard she worked and how long her day. 'I needed to go to the privy.' She shrugged. 'You know where that is.'

I did indeed. Sleeping in the kitchen, she would have been forced to make her way across the garden, through the house and let herself out of the front door. The privy stood alongside the stable, and, together with the pump, was shared by the Gildersleeves' neighbours. I nodded.

Lydia continued, 'It was very nearly dawn. I remember that, because when I opened the front door, there were streaks of light in the sky over Bove Town. I was running towards the privy when I saw Mark locking the stable. It was obvious he'd only just come home. He looked frightened to death when he first saw me, then he grabbed my arm and asked what the devil I was doing up and about at that hour? I told him, and he let me go.' She grinned. 'He had to. But when I got back into the house, he was waiting for me in the passageway. Said he'd spent the previous evening drinking with a friend who lives out on the Meare road. He'd drunk so much, he'd passed out and been forced to spend the night there. That's when he said if I told Dame Joan I'd be in trouble, and he'd see to it that I was sent packing. I promised I wouldn't say a word. I was still feeling so bad I'd have promised to kill my grandmother, so he'd let me get back to bed. It wasn't my business, anyway.'

She rose from her seat and went to take a batch of oatcakes out of the second oven on the other side of the fireplace. 'So you see, I think the Mistress and Mistress Cicely are making a fuss about nothing. Only I daren't tell them, because when Mark does come back – and I'm sure he will be back sometime – he'll be livid if he knows I've let on. And I don't suppose it was the first time it'd happened, either.'

'Did his brother know, do you think, that he occasionally stayed out all night? After all, they shared a bed.'

Lydia wiped the sweat from her forehead with the back of one small hand. 'He might've done, if he'd woken up. But he never said anything. He wouldn't. There's not a lot of love lost between Peter and Mark, not since the old Master died, but neither would tell tales on the other.'

'Why? Are they frightened of Dame Joan?' I asked, puzzled. 'She seems a very sweet and gentle lady.'

'Oh, they aren't *frightened* of her!' Lydia laughed at the very notion. 'But if either Mark or Peter does something she doesn't approve of she can make their lives a real misery with her tears and her reproaches. She can go on for days and days until she has their solemn word that they won't ever do it again. So most of the time they don't tell her what they're up to.'

It crossed my mind that this revelation of Lydia's might cast a new light on Peter's disappearance, but then I dismissed the idea as absurd. The conspiracy of silence between the brothers would surely never extend to abandoning a horse and vanishing without a word for almost a week – for it would be a week tomorrow since Peter Gildersleeve was last seen alive.

I had finished shaving. I pushed away the bowl of tepid water and returned my razor to my pouch. I looked at Lydia who was now stirring the porridge, bubbling in the pot suspended from the cross-bar in the chimney.

'You said just now that there isn't much love lost between the two brothers since their father died. Why's that?'

Lydia turned her flushed face towards me. 'Because the old Master left the shop and workshop to Peter, I reckon. And his second-best bed. Dame Joan has the best one, of course.'

'It's natural for the elder son to inherit,' I pointed out. 'Why should Mark resent it?' Yet I had guessed myself that he did.

Before she could answer, the door opened and Rob Undershaft and John Longbones came yawning and stretching into the kitchen, sniffing appreciatively the smells of new bread and oatcakes and porridge. They were still young enough for the needs of their stomachs to be the most important thing in their lives. And today, whether Mark returned or no, there would be no work done. They would be at the abbey with the rest of us.

Cicely came in shortly after the apprentices, dressed in her Sunday best gown, her hair brushed and neatly braided. She looked apprehensive. 'Mark's not returned?'

Lydia shook her head. 'He'll come back, though, don't you fret, Mistress.'

A thought struck me. 'If he'd arrived in the middle of the night, or . . . or early this morning before anyone was stirring, is there any way in which he could have entered the house without rousing someone to let him in?'

'I don't know,' said Cicely. 'I haven't been here long enough. But I do know that the street door is always bolted after curfew, my aunt told me so herself. That's why she sat up.'

I caught Lydia's eye and twitched my eyebrows in enquiry. She gave the faintest shrug of her shoulders. I realized that the one time she had encountered Mark returning at dawn, she would have left the street door open; so she, like me, was none the wiser. Yet on that occasion, Mark could not possibly have foreseen that she would be up and about, so he must, therefore, have known of some way to enter the house without knocking.

Before I could pursue the thought further, Dame Joan

entered the kitchen. She, too, was dressed in what was plainly her best gown, a violet silk which must once have been as bright as her eyes, but which now, like them, was a little faded. Her snow-white cap and veil were freshly laundered, while a girdle of purple leather, tagged with silver and studded with small amethysts, emphasized that, although middle-aged, she still retained her trim figure. But her face showed increasing signs of strain, and the two dark circles beneath her eyes seemed more apparent than they had been the previous day.

She took her seat at the kitchen table and Lydia put a bowl of porridge in front of her.

'You eat that all up, Mistress,' the maid said with a brusqueness which concealed her true concern, 'every last bit of it.'

Dame Joan smiled faintly and picked up her spoon. 'Mark didn't come home,' she remarked to no one in particular.

'We were just debating,' I said swiftly, seizing my opportunity, 'if there is any way to enter this house without knocking for admission.'

My hostess shook her head. 'It's an awkwardly built house, as you can see, with this kitchen at an angle to the rest of it. It was added on later by my husband's grandfather, when the original kitchen was turned into the workroom. In *his* father's day, the parchment making was carried on in the shop. I've heard my husband say that it was the old man's intention to make a second door in that wall over there, the one that backs on to the stable. But he never did, and like most inconveniences it continues to be tolerated, in spite of constant talk about putting it right. There's only one entrance to this house, and that's the front one.'

'So there's no other choice for anyone returning home

late than to rouse a member of the household to let him in?'

Dame Joan shook her head. 'No, none at all.'

I glanced thoughtfully across at the two apprentices, who were busy scraping the last mouthful of porridge from their bowls. Both young faces were bland with indifference, neither, apparently, taking anything but the most cursory interest in our conversation. Rob Undershaft, his fair hair falling as ever into his eyes, pushed his bowl away from him and glanced around the table. He reached out one skinny arm towards the dish of oatcakes, took one and began to munch it stolidly, staring into space. John Longbones, his red curls still unkempt from sleep, followed his companion's example, his nimbler fingers managing to secrete a second oatcake in the palm of his hand, his short-sighted gaze fixed on nothing in particular. It was well-nigh impossible to determine if either of them had anything to hide.

Yet when the others had all dispersed to finish getting ready for church, I lingered in the kitchen with Lydia. I took a cloth and began to dry the dishes as she washed them. 'That evening,' I said, 'when you were ill and met Mark returning in the early hours of the morning . . .'

'Yes?' she asked cautiously. 'What about it? I've told you all that I can remember.'

'Think very carefully,' I urged her. 'You had to run through the house to reach the privy, but do you recall having to unbolt the street door, or was it already unlocked?'

Lydia paused in her task of scouring out the iron pot in which she had cooked the porridge, her bunch of hazel twigs poised in mid-air, her eyes suddenly enormous in her tired little face. 'I . . . I can't remember,' she answered slowly. 'Wait . . . Wait!' She resumed her scouring, but in a half-hearted manner. 'I ran along the passageway and . . . and I just opened the door,' she finished on a note of surprise. 'I remember now! Fancy me not thinking that strange at the time! But I was in such a hurry, had such awful pains in my belly, that I never gave it a thought. You're right!' She turned her wondering face towards me. 'Normally, to reach the top bolt in the morning, I have to fetch the little footstool from the shop, and I have to stand on it to get the key down from its nail. Oh, why has that never struck me until now? I am so stupid!'

'No,' I smiled, giving her shoulders a friendly squeeze. 'As you say, you had other things on your mind. But someone had unlocked the door for Mark that night, and probably on other nights, too, when he stayed out drinking.'

'Who?'

I shrugged. 'There are are only two likely suspects: either Rob or John. But which one of the two, I wouldn't like to guess at present. Perhaps both of them are culprits.'

'Do you think it's important?'

'That Mark has stayed out all night on previous occasions? It might be, insofar as it means that we don't need to give up all hope of seeing him again.'

Chapter Ten

The muttering of the congregation faltered and died. The great west door was flung wide, and the candle-buds blossomed in a thousand draughts. Abbot Selwood led the procession of monks and novices from the Lady Chapel, up the steps of the Galilee into the crowded nave and all the glitter and colour of the abbey church. The sun, filtering through the stained-glass windows, traced jewel-like patterns on the rush-strewn floor and washed in ripples of rainbow hue over the intent and straining faces of the congregation. And because of my height, I could just see over the heads of the people in front of me the black marble tomb in the middle of the choir, which housed the remains said to be those of Arthur and Guinevere.

Dame Joan and Cicely stood either side of me, having arranged themselves thus as we had entered through the north door, as though I were the man of the household. To begin with it had made me a little uncomfortable; but when I noticed the way in which some of their fellow townsmen and women shrank from them as they passed, the whispering behind raised hands, I was glad if my presence afforded them some measure of comfort. The two apprentices and Lydia had followed behind, and Mark's absence could not fail to be noticed. I had seen people nudge one another, staring hard, first at us and then at the open doorway, waiting for him to appear. And when it became apparent that he was not coming, expectation gave place to dismay and then to fear, as suspicion festered into speculation that he had met the same strange fate as his elder brother.

It was not surprising, therefore, that none of us paid as much attention to the Mass as we should have done; we were too busy brooding on other things. Cicely and her aunt stood with downcast eyes, but I could see by their faces that their thoughts were elsewhere. At last however, after the paeans of praise had been raised to God, the Three in One, and to all the hierarchy of Heaven, and after Abbot Selwood's sermon and the Mass itself, the service was nearly over.

It felt strange to be standing once more in the abbey, not among the novices, but as a member of the laity. I wondered if discipline among the monks had improved at all since my departure. John Selwood, Abbot here for almost twenty years, had not, in my day, been noted for the strictness of his rule; and in spite of several official inquiries into this lack of authority over his flock I doubted if improvements had been made or steps taken to remove him from office. He was too well liked by both his peers and subordinates for any serious complaint to be lodged against him.

And, of course, it was he who had taken in the body of the Earl of Devon six years earlier, when, on the orders of the Earls of Warwick and Clarence, Humphrey Stafford had been executed after the battle of Banbury. (If I glanced over my shoulder, I could see the tomb on the south side of the nave.) King Edward would always vigorously defend anyone who had been loyal to his cause during those difficult days when his own brother and cousin had tried to reinstate King Henry on the throne and take Edward prisoner. I had been still a member of the abbey fraternity then, and I can recall even now the arrival of the bloody and mutilated corpse, the way we novices crowded around the cart, repelled but at the same time fascinated. Abbot Selwood had not hesitated to accept it for burial.

As we streamed out of the abbey into the mid-morning heat, I was again aware of that edging away of our fellow worshippers, the twitching aside of the women's skirts, until Dame Joan, Cicely and I were walking in isolation, a path opening up for us as we made our way towards the north gatehouse. Rob Undershaft and John Longbones had prudently slipped away into the crowd, and only the faithful Lydia still followed in our wake. I wondered how long it would be before the two apprentices quit the Gildersleeve household for good, and I prayed that when we reached the shop we should discover Mark waiting for us with an explanation of his overnight absence.

My hostess made several attempts to speak to friends and neighbours, but there was a general reluctance to return her greetings, and the reason was not hard to find. The burly figure of John Jarrold, accompanied by his wife and daughter, was moving purposefully among the dispersing congregation, whispering in the ear of this one, exchanging a few muttered words with that. Heads turned briefly in our direction, eyes met ours only to turn hurriedly away, and worried frowns replaced the first natural inclination to smile. The story of the paper with its mysterious signs was spreading rapidly, and causing consternation wherever it was heard. If the townspeople of Glastonbury had at first dismissed the rumour of Peter Gildersleeve's disappearance as being attributable to the Devil's work, subsequent events, and now this tale of Maud's, were making them change their minds.

Fortunately, the Gildersleeves' house was close to the gatehouse, on the opposite side of the street, and on leaving the abbey precincts, a very few steps brought the four of us safely to the door. Dame Joan, having unlocked it and carefully replaced the key on its customary nail in the passageway, hastened from room to room, upstairs and down, hopefully calling 'Mark! Mark!' But there was no answering cry. Mark Gildersleeve, like his brother, had still not come home.

The two apprentices reappeared at four o'clock, just in time for supper, and crept into the kitchen, where the rest of us were seated round the table looking both shamefaced and defiant.

'Where have you been?' Cicely demanded angrily before her aunt could question them.

John Longbones, after some hesitation, admitted having paid a visit to his mother, an absence which he well knew would not have been tolerated in normal circumstances. Rob Undershaft, on the other hand, countered truculently with, 'Where's Master Mark, then? Not back yet?' And when Dame Joan shook her head, he added, 'My father says if he's not returned by tomorrow, I'm to go home. He'll not have me stay here any longer.'

'You can't break your articles of indenture!' Dame Joan exclaimed, finally roused from the apathy which had cloaked her like a shroud for the past few hours.

'We're indentured to Master Peter, and he ain't here,' Rob pointed out triumphantly – and not, I felt, without some justification. 'We can't go on working, Mistress, without someone telling us what to do. It wouldn't be right. Besides . . .'

'Besides what?' Cicely asked, raising her chin belligerently.

Rob and John exchanged a quick sidelong glance before their eyes fell once again to their still empty plates.

'Besides . . . ?' I prompted, adding my mite, and they both wriggled uncomfortably.

Rob Undershaft took a deep breath. 'My father says he'll not have me stay in a house where there's devil's work afoot. He . . . He's been talking to Goodman Jarrold,' he added by way of excuse.

'And you, John?' Dame Joan's gentle voice held a note of pleading. 'What does Widow Longbones have to say?'

The carroty head hung even lower. 'The same,' he mumbled.

Dame Joan bit her lip in desperation. Unless the riddle of Peter's and Mark's disappearance could be resolved soon, she faced the prospect of being ostracised by her God-fearing neighbours, if nothing worse. To calm her over-wrought nerves she sipped an infusion of basil and rosemary which Cicely had thoughtfully prepared for her.

Lydia got up and went to the pot over the fire, ladling generous portions of frumenty on to the apprentices' plates, which she banged down on the table. 'It's more than you deserve,' she hissed at Rob and John. 'I'd let you starve.'

Her mistress reproached her with quiet dignity. 'That will do, Lyddie. While they remain under my roof, I shall honour Peter's side of the bargain to provide them with three good meals a day.' She turned to me. 'Chapman, what are we to do?'

'Yes, what *are* we to do?' Cicely added waspishly. 'If you can't help my aunt, I suggest the sooner you're on your way, the better. She can't afford to keep feeding you and your great appetite with no money being made in the shop.'

Dame Joan turned a scandalized face towards her niece and bade her hold her tongue. 'You really must learn to show more civility, my dear,' she scolded, almost angrily for her, 'to anyone to whom you have offered hospitality.'

I smiled understandingly at Cicely. I had met many young girls like her, just blossoming into womanhood, blowing first hot then cold, fancying themselves in and out of love with any and every reasonably good-looking man who crossed their path, confused by previously unknown emotions and trying hard to cope. In reply she stuck her tongue out at me when her aunt wasn't looking, and stirred the half-eaten mixture of vegetables and oats around her plate.

I addressed Dame Joan. 'Mistress, give me a day or two longer to try to solve this puzzle. But if I haven't done so by then, your niece is right, and I should be on my way.' All three women, including Cicely, gave a little cry of protest, but I held up my hand to hush them. 'What else can I do? My family are expecting me in Bristol. My duty is first to my mother-in-law and child. If it proves that I can truly be of no assistance to you, then I can no longer delay my return home.'

'And desert us in our hour of need!' Cicely spat at me across the table.

Her aunt sent her a bewildered glance before shrugging her shoulders, evidently abandoning all attempts to understand these violent swings of opinion.

'You must do as you see fit, Chapman,' she told me quietly. 'Whatever you decide, it will be with my thanks and blessing. Meanwhile, do you have any idea at all as to what can have happened to my sons?'

I glanced across the table at the maid, who had just sat down again to resume her own interrupted meal.

'Lydia,' I said, 'it's time to tell your mistress what you told me this morning.'

Before Lydia could protest, Dame Joan's head jerked round. 'My child,' she asked reproachfully, 'what have you been keeping from me?'

'How *could* you?' Lydia demanded tearfully of me. 'You promised you'd keep it secret! You *promised*! You know I told you Mark would have me dismissed if I betrayed him to the Mistress!'

Dame Joan said firmly, 'Whatever this is about, you are *my* maid, Lyddie, not Mark's. How could you believe that I should let myself be influenced by him in such a matter? You know I promised your mother I'd look after you. Do you really think I would go back on my word?'

Lydia looked uncertain. 'I ... I don't know,' she muttered.

'Then it grieves me very much to hear you say so. Now, what is it that you have to tell me?'

The story was haltingly repeated, and when Lydia had finished, I jogged her memory about the open door.

'So you see,' I concluded for her, 'someone aided and abetted Mark that night. Mark knew he was going to be late, in spite of telling Lydia that he'd unintentionally drunk too much and had had to spend the night at the house of a friend.'

Dame Joan regarded me straitly. 'This is the reason you were asking all those questions at breakfast this morning, wanting to know if there was any other way into the house without having to rouse a member of the household.' I nodded. 'So!' She drew a deep breath. 'You obviously don't believe, Roger, that this was the first occasion Mark had stayed out all night.'

'To be honest, Mistress, no. I think it had probably happened before, and maybe since. No man anticipates getting so drunk that he cannot ride home, unless he does it regularly.'

133

Dame Joan nodded her agreement and turned to look at the two apprentices. 'Which one of you unlocked the door at nights for Mark?'

Neither boy seemed inclined to speak first, but it was obvious that both had lost their appetites. The speed with which they were shovelling the frumenty into their mouths began to slacken, then stopped altogether. After a protracted silence, Rob laid down his spoon and raised his head.

'We were doing nothing wrong, Mistress. We were only following orders. If Master Mark chose to stay out all night and not let on to you, then that was his business. And if he told us to hold our tongues – well, it was natural that we obeyed him. He's a grown man, after all, and no harm was done to you or anyone.'

This was unanswerable, and I could see that Dame Joan was nonplussed. She felt she had been betrayed by their silence, but knew also that she had no good reason to feel so. It was true that Mark was a grown man, and that she had no jurisdiction over him, but like most mothers she found it hard to accept that her sons were no longer children. Women will let their daughters go, treat them as equals and companions, but in a mother's eyes her son is for ever in leading strings, the little boy she dandled on her knee.

'And where did he go when he stayed out all night?' she asked. 'Did he tell you?'

Once again, the two apprentices exchanged sidelong glances. John Longbones raised his sandy brows, and Rob Undershaft gave an infinitesimal shrug of his shoulders. Both were obviously calculating what their chances of escaping a beating would be if Mark were suddenly to reappear in our midst, and realizing that they were slender. But after a few moments' deliberation, Rob, who seemed to me to be the stronger character of the pair, decided to speak out and brave the possible consequences.

'He went drinking and gambling. You know, the way men do.'

Dame Joan wrinkled her little nose fastidiously. The washed-out violet eyes held a spark of contempt.

'Drinking and gambling don't normally keep a man out all night,' she said. 'What else was Mark up to?'

For a third time the two boys silently consulted one another, then Rob unwillingly admitted, 'He used to visit places.'

'What places?' Dame Joan was as close to real anger as I had ever seen her.

Rob fiddled with the spoon on his plate. 'You know, Mistress, places . . . women,' he muttered indistinctly.

The silence stretched like a thin, bright thread, which snapped suddenly when the outraged Dame asked furiously, '*Whore-houses?* Are you telling me, Rob Undershaft, that my son frequented whore-houses?'

'That's what he said, didn't he, Jack?'

John Longbones nodded unhappily.

Dame Joan's cheeks were scarlet with mortification and embarrassment. It was a second or two before she could catch her breath. 'No wonder he didn't want me to know anything about it,' she said at last. 'And Master Peter . . . did *he* know what was going on?'

'Couldn't say, Mistress. Master Mark never said one way or the other.'

My hostess considered the probability, avoiding both Cicely's eyes and mine. 'How often did Mark stay out all night?' she asked.

'Once a month maybe. Sometimes twice, sometimes not at all.' It was John Longbones who answered this time.

'And how long has this . . . this depravity been going on?'

John wrinkled his forehead. 'A while now, I reckon, wouldn't you say, Rob?'

'A fair while, yes. I'd say so.'

Dame Joan now looked as pale as she had previously looked red. 'Then unless Peter slept as soundly as the Seven Sleepers of Ephesus, I don't see how he could possibly have remained ignorant of these nocturnal excursions. In short, he encouraged his brother by his silence.' There was a pause before she added tearfully, 'I am deeply disappointed in both my sons.'

I caught Lydia's eye and she grimaced, as much as to say 'I told you so'.

'Dame Joan,' I said, carefully picking my words, 'your sons are men, and men do these things. Otherwise there would be no need for such places. And it's only natural that one brother should keep the confidences and secrets of the other, especially if Peter understood how much the truth would upset you.'

But Dame Joan refused to be comforted, and continued to sniff and mop at her eyes until Cicely, who had tried to appear unmoved by the revelations, lost patience with her.

'Oh, Aunt,' she begged, 'please stop snivelling. If you'd seen as much of the world as I have in the service of the Duchess, you'd realize that it's fashionable to visit whore-houses. The brothels of Southwark are all owned by the Bishop of Winchester.'

I hastily covered my mouth with one hand so that Cicely should not suspect that my lips were twitching. The part she was playing at the moment was that of the woman experienced in the ways of the world, and I had to admit that she did it very well. But underneath, I suspected, she was as shocked as Dame Joan. These were her cousins, the chief culprit her future brother-in-law; and, like everyone else, she did not expect members of her own family to be tainted with the same vices as the rest of mankind.

At her niece's unfeeling words, Dame Joan burst into a flood of tears and announced her intention of taking to her bed. 'I shall be in my chamber if anything should happen,' she sniffed, 'if Mark should come home. Not that I ever want to clap eyes on that reprobate again! And you can tell him so, before you send him up to see me! Lyddie, be a good girl and make me another infusion of rosemary and basil. My head feels as if it's going to split in two.'

With her departure, calm descended on the kitchen. The apprentices finished their supper and slunk away to the workshop, presumably to beguile the hours until bedtime with a few games of hazard. Lydia began washing up the supper things and Cicely offered to dry the dishes. So, left to my own devices, I went into the garden and sat on the stone bench under the workshop window. The casement, was open, and I could hear Rob and John whispering and, occasionally, giggling together, but their voices were subdued. For them, as for the rest of us, it had not been a pleasant day.

Where, I wondered, was I to go from here? How was I going to make good my boast to solve this puzzle? I went back over the apprentices' revelations concerning Mark Gildersleeve, but could see no way in which they shed any light on his or his brother's disappearance. It was a common enough story of a young man keeping his youthful sins from his mother in order to be spared her reproaches, and of a brother who kept his own counsel so as not to get drawn in. Mark's dismay and anger on the morning he encountered Lydia were now easily understood, as was his hurriedly concocted tale of having got drunk and spent the night with a friend.

I sighed, and suddenly realized how tired I felt. The inactivity of the afternoon – those dragging hours when the women had begged me not to leave them because they feared that the hostility of their neighbours might result in some form of physical attack – had fatigued me far more than being up and doing would have done. But up and doing what? I seemed to be in the centre of a maze where all the exits led only to dead ends. There was no way out. Every path was closed. I thought perhaps sleep would help clear my brain, but it was far too early to go to bed. The sun continued to shine and the heat was still intense; Mark's bedchamber would be even hotter. But I knew that at any moment Cicely and Lydia would finish their chores and most likely join me on the bench. Solitude was suddenly inviting.

I was along the passageway and mounting the stairs almost before I was aware of my actions. Dame Joan's door was closed, but I could hear her muffled sobs. Lydia had guessed correctly why Mark and Peter kept secrets from their mother: her reproaches would, in the end, wear down even the most heartless of sons.

I entered Mark and Peter's room and shut the door behind me. Somewhere in here, Mark had chanced upon the mysterious paper belonging to his brother. I had almost come to believe that he had lied when he told Father Boniface that he had not taken it with him to Beckery – but suppose, after all, he had been telling the truth . . . Where then had he hidden it?

Common sense argued that he would have left it where he had found it, if the original hiding place had been a good one. I stared once more around the room but could see nowhere more likely than the little drawers and cupboards of that fantastic bed-head. Yet I had thoroughly searched every one of them the previous evening. Nothing could be lost, however, by trying once again. If I still did not find it, I should know that any further search would be a waste of time. I pulled off my boots, knelt up on the bed and began, slowly and methodically, to open the tiny cupboards and drawers.

I explored each cavity in turn, some of them no wider than half the span of my hand, and eventually arrived at the centre drawer at the top of the bed-head. I had noticed before that it appeared larger than its fellows, yet when I examined it more closely, it seemed shallower than it should be. My heart began to beat a little faster and I groped around feverishly, feeling for . . . feeling for what?

But when I found it, I knew at once that this was what I sought. There was a small metal catch at the back of the drawer, on the right-hand side, and how I had come to miss it last night I could not imagine. My fingers were trembling as I pressed it . . .

Immediately the floor of the drawer slid back to reveal a secret compartment in the base and, more importantly, what it contained. Carefully, as though it were a rare and precious jewel, I lifted out a piece of folded parchment.

Chapter Eleven

I understood at once why Peter Gildersleeve had not wanted the parchment touched by less careful hands than his own, and also why Mark would have been wary about carrying it upon his person. It was very old and extremely fragile, its mottled, yellowing surface overlaid with the patina of age, one corner already beginning to crumble into dust. I could see where Father Boniface had cut the seal, but the hard medallion of wax bore no imprint to indicate where this ancient document might originally have come from, or to whom it had belonged.

Gently and with the utmost care I began to unfold it. When it was finally laid flat upon the bed it proved to be far larger than I had expected: probably some eighteen inches square and chequered with creases, many of which had cracked, leaving rents in the parchment. But its contents were surprisingly clear. The ink, however it was made – with blackthorn bark and gum or with oak galls – had retained its colour despite the passage of time. The writing with which the paper was covered was still readable; if, that is, you knew how to interpret what it said . . .

And there was the rub. I knew no more than Father Boniface how that could be done. The priest's description had been a good one, and accurate as far as it went. The parchment was ruled from top to bottom with horizontal lines, and either above, below or aslant them, groups of vertical pen-strokes were arranged, ranging in numbers from one to five. Some of the strokes were longer, some thicker than others, and there were also (which Father Boniface had failed to mention) a saltire cross, a double saltire cross, a small circle, a symbol which resembled a figure six and another like two little dots, placed side by side.

I stared long and hard at the parchment in growing frustration, and at the end of an hour or more, had reached only one conclusion. It was probable, I thought, that each group of lines or symbols represented a single letter, separated from its neighbours by a gap of less than quarter of an inch, and that the longer gaps of double that length indicated the spaces between words. For a moment or two after hitting upon this idea I experienced a wild sense of elation. If, I told myself, I could work out short, regularly repeated words that might very well prove to be 'the' and 'and', then I should at least be able to recognize specific letters, and from this small beginning it would be possible, eventually, to decipher others. My mood of self-congratulation was however short-lived when cold reality raised its ugly head. This was a very ancient document, and therefore almost certainly not written in English; and even if, by some remote chance, it were, it would be in the old, pre-Conquest form of our language, before the coming of the Normans changed it for ever.

Yet – and my heart leapt at the thought – Peter Gildersleeve had managed to discover its meaning, and if he could do so, why could not I? To whom had he turned? Who had he visited in those months before he vanished? And did this parchment indeed hold the clue to his disappearance, or was it simply a distraction which I did not need?

I folded it again and replaced it in the secret

compartment of the bed-head's middle drawer, before un-
dressing and climbing between the sheets. In the morning I
would show my discovery to Dame Joan and Cicely, but
not, I decided, to the two apprentices (such confirmation of
the tale spread by Maud Jarrold and her father could only
precipitate more trouble for the Gildersleeve family – or
what remained of it). Afterwards, I would visit the abbey
and seek out Brother Hilarion to ask his advice.

I knew that I was dreaming, but could do nothing to shake
myself awake.

I was standing outside the shepherd's hut with my hostess, while Cicely sat on the bank above us, picking daisies
and fashioning them into chains. I was conscious that she
was laughing at me for my failure to find her cousins,
although she addressed no word to me and kept her eyes on
the task in hand. Once she turned to speak to Father
Boniface, who had materialised beside her in the mysterious
way that people do in dreams.

For my own part, I was saying earnestly to Dame Joan,
'Peter is not inside the hut, you can take my word for it. He
is not inside the hut.'

'But where is he then?' she demanded. 'And where is
Mark . . .?'

I was suddenly wide awake, the morning sun pouring in
through the unshuttered casement, warm on my face, and
the plaintive query still ringing in my ears.

Later, over breakfast, I could see the same unspoken
question in both women's eyes. I waited until Rob and John
had finished eating and had retired to the workshop – with
firm instructions from Dame Joan to finish whatever work
there was in hand – before asking them to accompany me
upstairs to the solar. Lydia gave me a resentful glance at

being thus excluded, no doubt guessing from my manner that I had something of interest to impart, but I thought it better that, for the time being at least, she should know nothing. She probably remained friends with Maud Jarrold, and might encounter her in the market place or at the shops. If we swore her to secrecy the importance of her knowledge would doubtless be visible in her small, expressive face and the added consequence of her manner, and Maud was sharp enough to draw her own conclusions.

When Cicely and her aunt were seated I fetched the parchment from its hiding place and, with infinite care, spread it out on the table. Both women shrank back in their chairs as though I had placed a poisonous serpent in front of them.

'Wh-where did you find it?' stammered Dame Joan. When I had explained, she frowned. 'I didn't know there was a secret compartment in that middle drawer. My husband never said a word to me about it. He must, however, have told Peter at some time or another, perhaps when he made up his mind to leave him the bed in his will. My sons have always slept in it, you understand, from their youth, but now it is Peter's rightful property.'

'It looks very ancient,' Cicely remarked of the parchment, one hand creeping towards it, only to be hurriedly snatched back again without quite making contact. 'What . . . what do you think it is?'

'Could it, perhaps, be a spell or an incantation?' Dame Joan whispered, regarding it with fear.

'I've no idea,' I answered truthfully. 'That is something I must try to find out.'

'And how will you do that?' Cicely inquired, a note of mockery creeping into her voice.

'I think we should burn it!' her aunt exclaimed. 'Before it does harm to anyone else!'

I refolded the parchment with a haste which enlarged at least two of the rents, and laid both hands over it, fearing for its safety.

'Mistress,' I said earnestly, 'we have no proof yet that this document is connected with the disappearance of either of your sons. I'm going to the abbey to seek out Brother Hilarion and ask his advice. He's the Novice Master and taught me all I know. I would trust him with my life. You can be sure that he will spread no stories or rumours, nor even discuss my visit with anyone at all – not even Father Abbot – if I ask him not to. He has a wisdom which comes with age, and a faith which makes him unafraid of anyone or anything.' And I glanced down significantly at my cupped hands, under which lay the paper.

Dame Joan nodded. 'Very well, you must do as you think fit.' She added resignedly, 'What else is there to be done? It's a week ago today since Peter vanished, and it's now nearly two whole days since we last saw Mark. Only for heaven's sake, Chapman, promise that you won't let that parchment out of your sight, or allow it to be seen by anyone except Brother Hilarion.'

'I can't promise that, but I will be guided by his advice. And don't forget,' I warned, 'that if Peter solved the riddle of this strange writing, it's improbable – although, I have to admit, not impossible – that he did so on his own. There may already be at least one other person in this town who is aware of the paper's existence, as well as Father Boniface.'

I rose to my feet. 'Now, if I'm to carry it around with me, it will need stronger protection than my pouch can offer. Dragging it in and out of that would only cause yet more damage, and it's fragile enough already. If I might borrow one of Master Gildersleeve's books I can place the parchment between the leaves, and the cover-boards will keep it from further harm.'

'Take whatever you need.' Dame Joan fidgeted with her leather girdle, knotting the ends around her fingers. The washed-out violet eyes roved unseeingly about the room. Never a big woman, she seemed to be growing even smaller, as though fear and care and worry were like physical burdens, crushing her with their weight. She was withdrawing into herself, suddenly frightened of the world beyond her doors – a world which had, in the past week, become such a menacing and terrifying place. 'I think,' she added, 'that I shall go back to bed. Cicely, my dear, tell Lyddie I shall require only a little broth at dinnertime.'

'Aunt, you must eat . . .' Cicely was beginning, when she was interrupted by the clatter of feet on the stairs. A moment later the solar door burst open and Lydia almost fell into the room.

'Mistress,' she panted, holding her side, 'you'd best come down. There's someone asking to see you.'

Dame Joan scraped back her chair, her eyes alight with sudden hope. 'Is it Mark?' she demanded.

The little kitchen-maid shook her head. 'No, no, Mistress! But . . .'

'But what? Speak out, you stupid girl!' Dame Joan was trembling.

'It's Edgar Shapwick from the stables in Northload Street. He says he wants to speak to you. Urgent.'

Disappointment seemed to have rooted Dame Joan to the spot, but Cicely and Lydia each seized one of her arms and urged her out through the door and down the stairs. For the time being, I concealed the parchment inside my pouch and followed them.

I recognized Edgar Shapwick at once as the man who

looked after Barnabas and to whom I paid my daily fee for the cob's board and lodging. He had a couple of boys to assist him, but he was the owner. I had already judged him to be a pleasant fellow, and it was apparent from the manner of Dame Joan's greeting that she regarded him as a friend.

'Edgar, what brings you here? I didn't hear you knock.'

He was standing just inside the street door, and at Dame Joan's approach he tugged the forelock of yellow hair which fell almost to his eyes. 'Lyddie was coming out to sweep the step just as I arrived.' He indicated the long-handled broom propped against one wall where Lydia had abandoned it, and shifted uncomfortably from one foot to the other. 'I thought I'd better . . .' He paused uncertainly, then blurted out, 'Are they true, Mistress, the rumours that Master Mark has disappeared along with his brother?'

Dame Joan groped for and clutched her niece's hand, holding it in a fierce grip. 'My younger son is from home at present, on business,' she lied. 'He will be back soon, although we aren't sure exactly when. You may say so on my authority to anyone who asks you, Edgar.'

The brown eyes avoided hers, and again the man shuffled his feet. 'I'll do that, Mistress, if that's what you want. But it ain't true, is it?'

'How dare you!' Dame Joan drew herself up to the full extent of her unimpressive height. 'Do you doubt my word?'

Edgar Shapwick sighed and forced his glance to meet hers. 'I haven't any choice but to doubt it, Mistress. A man – a stranger, fortunately – in the town on business, just brought your Dorabella into the stables. Found her wandering out on the moors, midway between here and Godney.'

There was a moment's silence charged with disbelief, but that soon gave way to panic.

'Are . . . are you certain it's Dorabella?' Dame Joan asked in trembling accents, as soon as she could speak.

'Not a doubt of it, Mistress. Don't I know the mare as well as any horse that's in my stables? Better, in fact, than most, who spend only a night or two before their owners ride them away again. It's Dorabella all right. Come and see for yourself.'

But Dame Joan was in no state at that moment to go anywhere. With a queer little sigh, her knees buckled under her and she fainted. I caught her in my arms as she fell and, on the vociferous instructions of Cicely and Lydia, carried her into the shop where the armchair, used during her vigil the night before last, still stood beside the counter. While Cicely hovered agitatedly around her aunt, the more practical Lydia ran to the kitchen, returning several minutes later with a cup of water and a handful of feathers. These latter she piled in a heap on the floor, and proceeded to light them by means of the tinder-box kept on a shelf in the room. The acrid smell was soon making all our eyes water and searing our throats.

As I wiped away the tears with the back of my hand, I became aware that Rob Undershaft and John Longbones were standing in the open doorway, the voices and commotion having naturally aroused their curiosity and brought them creeping out of the workshop to discover what was going on. There was no chance of keeping Dorabella's return, riderless, a secret from them – indeed, Edgar Shapwick was already regaling them with the story – and therefore no hope of preventing the tale from spreading. Even if Dame Joan could have persuaded Edgar to hold his tongue, neither of the apprentices would do so. Their parents had already aroused their fears, and Rob's father had ordered him home if Mark failed to return today. There

148

was small likelihood now that he would do so, unless, for some reason, he had been thrown . . .

Dame Joan was recovering, her eyelids fluttering against her pallid cheeks. She began to cough and splutter as the pungent aroma of burnt feathers assaulted her nostrils, and she brushed indignantly at the drops of water which had been splashed in her face. She stared around her vacantly for a moment or two, trying to recollect where she was and what had happened. Then the pale eyes widened in shock and fear as memory came flooding back.

She tried to rise from her chair. 'I must go to the stables at once,' she protested feebly as Cicely and Lydia forced her down again. 'I must see the horse for myself and make sure that it really is Dorabella.'

'Mistress,' Edgar Shapwick assured her earnestly, 'I swear to you that it is. There's no need for you to come to the stables. You're not fit; you should be laid down upon your bed, and that's a fact. Don't worry your head about the mare. I'll look after her for as long as is necessary. You can settle with me when the time is right, but there's no need for any haste. Meantime, if it will set your mind at rest, one of these lads can accompany me back to Northload Street and inspect the horse for you. Either one of 'em's bound to recognize her.'

Dame Joan glanced at the apprentices. 'I suppose it's useless to ask you two to keep still tongues in your heads,' she said bitterly. 'You'll be off home now to your families with this latest tit-bit of gossip.'

But to our astonishment, Rob Undershaft and John Longbones, after another of their wordless consultations, proved themselves staunch and loyal allies after all.

'We'll stop, Mistress,' Rob said, 'for as long as we can be of any use. You never know,' he added ominously, 'you might yet be glad of two extra men about the house.'

Cicely, Lydia and Dame Joan were torn between thankfulness and further anxiety by these words, but in the end gratitude prevailed. The Dame tearfully embraced them both and called them good boys before allowing her niece to escort her up to her room.

I turned to Edgar. 'Do you happen to know the name of this stranger who brought in the mare?'

'He did say, but I didn't rightly catch it. Gilbert, was it?' Edgar scratched his head. 'Ay, Gilbert something – but Gilbert what? That's the question. Perhaps you'd better come down to the stables too. One of my lads might remember what he was called.'

So he and Rob and I set out for Northload Street, and while the apprentice went to look at the mare, I had a word with the stable-boys.

'Oh ay, I remember his name all right,' said the smaller, freckled one of the two. 'Gilbert Honeyman his name is. A beekeeper from near Bristol. Leastways, that's what he told us, and no cause that I can see to think he's lying.'

The second stable-boy nodded vigorously in corroboration, and I thanked them.

'Do you also know whereabouts in the town he was headed?' I asked.

At this point we were joined by Rob Undershaft and Edgar Shapwick.

'It's Dorabella all right,' confirmed the former, nibbling at a piece of loose skin on one thumbnail. 'And by the appearance of her, she's been out on the moor for some time, wouldn't you say so, Master Shapwick?'

Edgar looked glum. 'She's tired, hungry and thirsty, and hasn't been groomed for a day or two. Ay, lad,' he said heavily, laying a hand on my shoulder, 'she was abandoned a while ago, I reckon. Moreover, she's saddleless and bridleless, so Mark wasn't thrown. It seems like the rumours going round about him, how he's met the same fate as his brother, might be true after all. Whatever that fate may be,' he added hastily.

'Do you know where I can find this Gilbert Honeyman?' I asked.

'Oh, ay! Honeyman, that was his name. A beekeeper, I mind it now. He had panniers attached to his saddle and said he was in Glastonbury on business.'

The two stable-boys murmured confirmation. 'We already told him that,' said the freckled one.

Edgar ignored him. 'So, where would he be going? Not selling from door to door; the abbey hives supply most of the town with honey, though the brothers keep the best wax for their own candles. If this man's as well-heeled as he looks, I reckon he's a Bee Master and must have a fair-sized apiary, so the probability is that he's come with a load of the stuff for the chandler. Anyway, if I were you, I'd try there first. Martin Toogood on Fisher's Hill.'

I smiled at him. 'Master Shapwick, I think I should enlist your aid to help me solve this riddle. You've a thinking brain.'

He coloured, disclaimed, but looked pleased none the less and sent the stable-boys off about their work with renewed authority.

I turned to Rob Undershaft. 'I'll speak to this Gilbert Honeyman if I can find him. Go home,' I instructed, 'and tell Dame Joan what's happened and where I've gone. I'll follow you before I visit Brother Hilarion at the abbey. Ask Mistress Cicely to look out one of Master Peter's books for me from the chest in the workshop. One with a good, stout cover.'

Rob stared in perplexity for a moment, then shrugged, sensibly coming to the conclusion that the less he knew the better. I added, 'There's no need to spread the news about Dorabella yet a while.' I glanced at the stable-boys, whispering together as they mucked out one of the stalls, and sighed. 'It'll get around fast enough, heaven knows!'

'You can rely on John and me,' Rob answered gruffly, and I suddenly felt sure that I could.

I watched him leave and said my farewells to Edgar Shapwick.

'Tell the Dame not to worry about the mare,' he said. 'I'll take good care of her. By the way, your cob's getting restive. He needs exercise.'

'Get one of the lads to ride him,' I suggested, as I took the hint and handed over the day's payment for Barnabas. 'I may have need of him later.'

He nodded and swung on his heel, jingling the coins in his pocket. I crossed the stableyard to leave, but as I was about to step outside I heard the patter of feet behind me, and someone tugged at my sleeve. Turning, I saw the freckle-faced stable-boy holding something clenched tightly in his fist.

'What is it?' I asked.

Carefully he unfurled his grubby fingers to display a coil of brown thread. 'This was snarled up in the mare's mane,' he said. 'I don't suppose it's important, but I thought you might like to see it. Do you want it, or shall I throw it away?'

I took the thread and stretched it to its length, revealing it as a piece of rough homespun yarn. It had certainly not been torn from anything that Mark Gildersleeve was wearing.

I placed it in my pouch along with the folded parchment.

'I'll keep it,' I told the boy. 'You never know, it might have some significance. Thank you. You're a clever lad.'

He grinned cockily. 'So my mother says! I'll tell you something else,' he went on, 'which I don't think the gaffer mentioned – leastways, not that I overheard. There are bits of straw in the mare's coat, like she's been shut up in a stable or a barn, and flecks of . . . well, something sticky.'

'Sticky?' I queried, puzzled.

The boy nodded, beginning to move away. 'I'd better get back to work. I thought you'd like to know, that's all.'

I thanked him yet again and turned slowly into Northload Street on my way to Fisher's Hill, unsure as yet just what value this information had.

Chapter Twelve

I had no need to go as far as the chandler's shop. I met Gilbert Honeyman at the bottom of Fisher's Hill, riding a brown bay and travelling northwards along Magdalene Street in the direction of Market Place. I guessed it must be him by the two large panniers, one on either side of his mount, swinging loose and bumping against the animal's flanks, and obviously empty. A big man, middle-aged, with a thick grey beard and very dark blue eyes, he had that indefinable air of prosperity about him which had made Edgar Shapwick describe him as 'well-heeled'.

He drew rein when I hailed him by name, and regarded me curiously.

'Do I know you, lad?' he asked. 'If you're wanting to buy wax you're unlucky. I've just sold my whole stock to the chandler, and I shan't be back this way now for a month or two. It'll most likely be October before I'm in Glastonbury again, but you could always ask at the abbey if a small quantity is all you're needing.'

'No, no,' I assured him, 'I don't wish to buy wax. I want to talk to you about the horse you found wandering on the moors. If you can spare me a moment or two of your time, that is.'

Gilbert Honeyman swung himself out of the saddle. 'There's nothing much to tell,' he said, 'but such as there is

155

might as well be told over a drink, instead of full in the sun's glare in this hot, dusty street.' He indicated the row of houses opposite the western wall of the abbey precinct – and one in particular, which sported a bunch of leaves on a pole outside its door. 'Shall we try there? It's clean and wholesome, if I remember rightly. The beakers are properly scoured and the rushes changed regularly. But that's probably something you know already.'

I didn't bother to contradict him, and waited while he tethered the bay to the rail which fronted the house before following him inside.

It was too early in the day for the tavern to be over-full, although there was still a surprising number of people occupying the tables and benches. We found seats in a secluded corner and Master Honeyman called for the pot-boy and ordered two mazers of their finest mead.

'One of your metheglins,' he warned, 'properly flavoured with herbs and spices. None of that rubbish which is usually palmed off on unwary drinkers: just honeycomb washings with a little pepper added. I shan't have it, and neither will my friend! And I shan't pay for it either, you can tell your master so. Disgusting swill of that sort isn't even fit for pigs!'

Having delivered himself of this diatribe on what was plainly one of his favourite topics, the Bee Master then settled himself to his satisfaction and turned to me. 'Right, my lad. You know my name. What's yours?'

I told him, and because he was a man who inspired confidence and trust I allowed my tongue to run away with me. By the time the metheglin was set before us – certainly one of the finest meads I had ever tasted – Master Honeyman was in possession of most of the facts concerning Mark and Peter Gildersleeve, and my involvement with them. When, at last, I finished my story, he pulled thoughtfully at his beard.

'A strange business,' he commented. 'A very strange business indeed! Well, all I can tell you about the mare is that I found her this morning, early, wandering on the moors. I left home yesterday and spent the night at Priddy. I was on my way again just after daybreak, and came down over Mendip by the Holly Brook and started off along the causeway which joins the Wells road. I'd gone about a furlong when I noticed this horse, roaming loose and riderless, and stopping every now and then to crop the grass. I was too far away at that point to be able to see much of the animal, and thought it one of the moorland strays. But later, as I approached Glastonbury along the main track, near the turning which leads to Godney, I saw it again – this time close to – and I could tell at once that it was a thoroughbred, even though the coat was rough and staring. There was no bridle or saddle, but she's a docile, well-mannered creature and came to me when I called. Luckily I had a stout piece of twine in my saddle-bag and I was able to use it as a leading rein. I'd noted the stables in Northload Street on one of my previous visits to the town, so I took her there. To my relief, the owner recognized her right away, and I was able to get on about my own affairs with a clear conscience, knowing that she was in safe hands. But I'd no idea that she was a part of such an intriguing tale.'

'How long do you think she'd been riderless?'

Gilbert Honeyman swallowed a deep, satisfying draught of his mead before replying. 'Judging by the state of her, I'd reckon a day, maybe even longer.'

'That's Master Shapwick's opinion too. And he rules out Mark having been thrown, because of the lack of saddle and bridle.'

The Bee Master cavilled at that. 'There are plenty of unscrupulous folk about, unfortunately. A loose horse and no one near . . . well, it could tempt an honest man to his limits in these difficult times. A good saddle would fetch a fair price, and no questions asked.' Once more he stroked the luxuriant beard. 'No, I wouldn't rule out the possibility that the mare's rider had been unseated, and might, even now, be lying out there somewhere with a broken leg, or maybe worse.' He glanced at my face and added, 'Now, what have I said to make you look like that?'

I smiled ruefully. 'You've put me in a dilemma. I feel now that I've no option but to abandon all my plans and ride out across the moors to look for Mark, although I'm convinced it will prove a fruitless errand.'

Gilbert Honeyman frowned. 'In that case, why not notify the Sheriff's Officer and get him to raise a posse from amongst the townsfolk?'

'No, no! That wouldn't do at all. The longer we can conceal Mark's disappearance from people the better it will be for Dame Joan and her niece. There are too many whispers about Peter Gildersleeve and his dabbling in the black arts already. If the inhabitants were to know for certain that his brother has vanished as well, it would only make matters worse for them. I shall have to go myself.'

'It will be worth it, however, if you find this Mark Gildersleeve . . .' Master Honeyman was beginning, but I shook my head.

'I've told you, I don't believe I shall. I'll just be wasting my time.'

The Bee Master finished his mead, wiped his mouth on the back of his hand and continued to stare into the empty mazer for several seconds. Then, coming to a decision, he pushed it away and turned his head to look at me.

'Let me search for this friend of yours,' he offered. 'I've completed my business more quickly than I expected. I thought to be here for at least another twenty-four hours, and I shan't be looked for at home until early next week, today being Friday and Sunday being a day of rest.'

I stared at him in sudden hope – but felt, nevertheless, that I ought to protest. 'I can't possibly let you do it. Why should you become embroiled?'

He spread strong, blunt-fingered hands. 'Why should *you*? As far as I can gather from your story, these Gildersleeves have been thrust upon you quite by chance. Your part was played when you delivered the girl safely to her aunt. But you stayed on and are doing your best to solve this mystery. We're all put on this earth to help one another, lad. And if I'm honest I have to admit that this tale interests me more than somewhat. So, what do you say?'

Misinterpreting my hesitation, he continued; 'If you feel you know too little about me, I can soon remedy that. I'm a bee-keeper – as my father was before me, his father before him, and many of my forebears – well-known and well respected in the village of Keynsham, where I live. I'm fifty-nine years old, a widower with one daughter about your own age, which I judge to be three or maybe four-and-twenty. Am I right? Ay, I thought as much.' He sighed. 'Rowena's a headstrong, masterful lass, as unlike her dear mother as can be. The saints alone know where she gets it from.' He slapped his hands on the table and rose to his feet. 'Now, let's proceed! Tell me which is Dame Gildersleeve's house, and I'll report there as soon as I return from my mission, probably close on suppertime. Meanwhile, lad, you can go about your business, whatever it is you have in mind to do.'

I thanked him fervently, but had another proposal to

make. 'I'm returning to the house now, before I visit my old friend and mentor Brother Hilarion at the abbey. If you'd like to accompany me there, we can acquaint Dame Joan and her niece of our plans and seek their approval before you set out.'

Dame Joan, aroused from an uneasy doze by Cicely, descended from her bedchamber to give us her blessing. Both women seemed unflatteringly grateful to have such a solidly respectable citizen on their side, a man whose advanced years bestowed upon him the wisdom which they were afraid I lacked. Master Honeyman was persuaded to stay to dinner before pursuing his quest, and during the meal – which was served, to save Lydia's legs, in the kitchen – I was amused to note that our hostess's appetite had been miraculously restored to her. Instead of the broth which she had earlier requested from Lydia, Dame Joan did full justice to a baked carp in Galentyne sauce, with a side dish of buttered vegetables, followed by strawberries stewed in red wine. It was, by pure chance, one of Lydia's better meals, and the Bee Master was plainly impressed.

He listened intently while the two women regaled him with the circumstances of Peter's disappearance, politely suppressing any hint that I had already told him the story.

'Young man,' he said, addressing me across the table as their recital ended, 'when you have solved this mystery, you must call upon me on your way home and let me know the answer to this riddle.'

'If he manages to solve it,' Cicely snorted, unable to resist the jibe.

'He'll do his best, you can be certain of that,' my new friend assured her heartily – but without, I felt, expressing too much confidence in my powers of deduction. 'My guess is that he's cleverer than he looks.'

With this dubious accolade still ringing in my ears, I went after dinner to collect the book which Cicely had, at Rob's request, searched out for me. She had chosen well, demonstrating unexpected common sense in her selection of a quarto not too rich in appearance, which would draw little attention to what I was carrying. It was bound in a strong, plain cloth made of hemp or jute, with only a few copper studs for decoration, and it had ties of the same material at both top and bottom and in the middle, with which the covers could be safely held together. I eased the parchment from the pouch at my waist, laid it carefully between two of the pages and fastened the strings.

I took my leave of Dame Joan and her niece, with a word of sincere thanks to the latter, and said farewell to Master Honeyman, expressing the hope of seeing him again at supper.

'You will, lad! You will! And if Mark Gildersleeve's out there to be found, I'll find him.'

I squeezed his arm in unspoken gratitude, but was certain in my own mind that he would have nothing to report when he returned for the afternoon meal. Then I crossed the road and entered the abbey by the north gate, the porter deciding after a long, hard stare that there was little in my appearance to which he could take exception. I knew that, at that time of the morning, the Chapter meeting would be over and the monks all busy about their various employments. Brother Hilarion would be at his task of instructing the oblates and novices; and from my own past experience, I remembered that when the weather was fine he often conducted his classes in the cloister garth, deeming it sensible for his pupils to be in the open air as much as possible.

As ever, the abbey precincts were teeming with people,

both lay and clerical, for Glastonbury has always been one of the most important religious foundations in the country, and is almost certainly the wealthiest. (How does the old saw go? 'If the Abbot of Glastonbury were to marry the Abbess of Shaftesbury, they'd be richer than both King and Pope together.') Messengers came and went, to and from the Abbot's parlour; a cart laden with building stone nearly ran me down, accompanied by curses from the driver; and pilgrims jostled for position as they made their way inside the Abbey. It was this constant stream of humanity, ensuring daily contact with the outside world, which had been yet another factor in my desire to quit the monastic life. I had never experienced the peace and quiet of a lesser church, and so had had no real chance to settle.

Brother Hilarion was indeed in the cloister garth, his pupils ranged about him in a semi-circle on the grass. His subject for the morning's lesson – I could hear him holding forth as I approached – was Joseph of Arimathea and his connections with the abbey, how he had come across the sea to Britain after the Crucifixion to establish the first Christian church at Glastonbury. I recalled that this was a subject dear to Abbot Selwood's heart, as indeed it had been to the hearts of many of his predecessors, for the claim established not only Glastonbury's superiority over Canterbury, but also over the entire ecclesiastical world. And it encouraged, too, a greater flow of pilgrims, legend linking Joseph to the Arthurian stories as the ancestor of Lancelot and Galahad.

As I trod soft-footed across the grass to stand behind him, Brother Hilarion had just reached the hotly-debated argument concerning the actual date of Joseph's arrival in Britain: 31 AD or some years later.

'At the Council of Pisa, and again at the Council of

Constance, the French bishops demanded precedence over the English because, they said, Saint Denis had brought the faith to Paris not long after his conversion by Saint Paul. But our bishops, in their turn, demanded precedence over the French on account of Joseph of Arimathea, who had come to this country immediately after the Passion of Our Lord. And at the Council of Siena the great Richard Fleming, Bishop of Lincoln, upheld England's claim against the combined opposition of French, Castilians and Scots. Less than fifty years ago, at the Council of Basle, we took on the mighty Alphonso Garcia de Sancta Maria, doctor of law and Dean of the Churches of Compostella and Segovia . . .'

He broke off, suddenly aware of someone watching him, and turned his head to see who it was. When he saw me, his gentle old face creased into a smile, and he welcomed me with a hand raised in blessing.

'You've come then.'

'I said I should.' I looked towards the novices. 'Are you too busy to spare me a few moments of your time?'

'No, no. Brother Oswald here is in training to take my place when I grow too old to cope any longer with the vagaries and high spirits of youth.' He smiled and indicated a young monk who had been standing a few paces in the rear, his head respectfully bent, listening intently. 'Brother Oswald, pray continue with the life of Joseph while I have a word with my friend. I think, at this point, that you might deal with the miracle of the Holy Thorn and the founding of the early Celtic Church.'

He took my arm and drew me apart into the shelter of the cloister and lowered his voice. 'Now, is there any news yet of Peter Gildersleeve? And there are also rumours that Mark is missing, including further gossip this morning that

163

the mare, Dorabella, has been brought in riderless. Is this true?'

'Alas, yes,' I said. And as briefly as I could – for I was beginning to tire of repeating the story – I told him as much as I knew and of my part in it. He listened without interruption until I had finished and then sighed, pulling down the corners of his mouth.

'It sounds worse than I feared. The testimony of the shepherd lad will prove to be the most damning, of course. Had Peter Gildersleeve not vanished into thin air before his eyes, it might have been possible to still people's clacking tongues with some plausible explanation. As it is . . .!'

'Brother Hilarion,' I reproached him, 'you don't believe that a man can vanish into thin air, as you put it. That would be to say that you believe in magic.'

He made the sign of the cross and glanced furtively about him. 'My child,' he whispered, 'this whole realm of Avalon is full of magic. In their time, great wizards have lived here: Merlin and Gwyn ap Nud, the Lord of the Wild Hunt, to name but two. And Satan is about his work both night and day. We cannot deny that his evil presence is constantly amongst us, even though we acknowledge that Christ will triumph in the end.'

'And you seriously believe that Peter Gildersleeve had truck with the Devil?'

Brother Hilarion shook his head sadly. 'My child, I pray hourly that it is not so, for the sake of his immortal soul and of his family.' He hesitated a moment, before adding, 'There is one thing . . .'

'What?' I queried sharply.

He looked uncomfortable. 'It may mean nothing at all. I probably shouldn't mention it.'

'Tell me anyway,' I implored him.

My old teacher continued to look unhappy, and fidgeted with the rope girdle that encircled his waist.

'Tell me!' I repeated, desperate for any crumb of information in this increasingly baffling affair.

Brother Hilarion glanced sideways at one of the novices, a tow-haired lad, paying scant attention to Brother Oswald's lecture, and nodded in his direction.

'A month or so back – maybe a little longer, maybe less – Humphrey there was assisting Father Elwyn in Saint Michael's Chapel, on the Tor, working in the bakehouse – for he knows something about bread-making, his father being a baker by trade—'

'Yes, yes!' I interrupted impatiently.

Brother Hilarion went on, slightly ruffled, 'Well, it would seem that during this time – the time, that is, that Humphrey spent assisting at Saint Michael's – Peter Gildersleeve visited Father Elwyn to consult with him on some private matter.'

'So?'

'So, I overheard Humphrey telling one of his fellow novices about it yesterday, during a discussion between them concerning Master Peter's disappearance. Of course, I reprimanded them severely for discussing the subject at all, when there are so many more important things to occupy their minds—'

Once again I cut in ruthlessly. 'What significance did young Humphrey attach to this visit? Did he say?'

'No, nor did I ask him.' Brother Hilarion was offended. 'To do so would have been to encourage the gossip. I feel that I have been very wrong in repeating it to you now, for the visit was doubtless entirely innocent. Indeed, what reason is there to place any other construction upon it?'

'None at all,' I agreed. But Brother Hilarion had thought

it worthy of repetition. And he told me that something in the young novice's tone of voice and general demeanour had implied that he thought there might be a connection between Peter's call on Father Elwyn and his later disappearance. I did not pursue the matter, however, merely asking, 'Do you truly believe that Joseph of Arimathea founded the original church at Glastonbury? Do you indeed have faith that he came here at all?'

After a momentary confusion caused by this abrupt change of subject, and after an even briefer attempt to look scandalized at such heresy, Brother Hilarion gave my question the same grave consideration which he had always given my past doubts and queries. He was not a man easily shocked.

'My child,' he said at length, 'I cannot answer you with the certainty of Father Abbot or even of some of my brothers. All I can say is that where a tale or a person is strongly connected with a particular place, as Joseph is with Glastonbury, and where that belief persists down through the centuries, handed on from father to son for endless generations, I think there is good reason to believe that the story could be true – in spite of the Dean of Compostella and Segovia's contention that Joseph was still imprisoned in Jerusalem as late as 70 AD. But this is between ourselves, Roger. I can trust you not to make my doubts known.'

'You seem to have very few doubts,' I reassured him. 'Yet why should Joseph come to Britain? Had he indeed been here before, in order to purchase lead from the Romans?'

'Ah!' Brother Hilarion smiled. 'The story of the Christ Child lodging at Priddy! A charming conceit, but not one to which I give much credence.' I did not embarrass him by asking why not, seeing it was as old a story in these parts as the other, but let him continue. 'No, no! I think Joseph was directed here by God, as Mary Magdalene was directed to France – at least, so the southerners of that country claim.'

'And what of the story that he is the ancestor of Lancelot and Galahad?'

Brother Hilarion shrugged noncommitally, indicating neither belief nor disbelief in this part of the tale. 'There's no proof that Joseph ever had children,' was his answer.

He glanced anxiously over his shoulder at his charges, but apart from the errant Humphrey – and there is always a Humphrey, in every group of people I have ever known – they were perfectly well behaved. Nevertheless, he sighed and indicated that he must return to them.

I thanked him, and once more he raised his hand in blessing.

'What will you do now?' he asked.

'I must visit Saint Michael's on the Tor to find out, if I can, what Peter Gildersleeve wanted with Father Elwyn.'

Brother Hilarion nodded. 'Then let us pray that the good Father will be able to shed some light on this sorry matter.'

Chapter Thirteen

I was young and fit in those days, but even so I found myself breathing heavily as I climbed the last few feet to the summit of the Tor. Below me I could see the town and abbey precincts laid out like a chequered board, and all the people, houses and animals had turned into the playthings of some giant's child. The old Roman road, Dod Lane, leading from Lambcook Street, was nothing more now than a faint thread among the thickets and bushes crowding about the base of this strange, steep hill that rose out of the surrounding moors and marshes. Once, long ago, when water had lapped about its foot, Arthur had been brought here to die . . .

Here, too, or so the stories would have us believe, Saint Collen had come to live the hermit's life and wrestle with the evil spirits of the place. Gwyn ap Nud, Lord of the Wild Hunt, who reigned over a fairy world beneath the Tor, had tempted him with visions of a great and luxurious palace where musicians played and dancers cavorted, where tables groaned under the weight of succulent food and fountains spouted every imaginable variety of wine. But Saint Collen would have none of it, preferring his anchorite's cell and a diet of wild berries from the hedgerows. He had sprinkled holy water in the faces of his tormentors and immediately they had vanished, leaving him in peace thereafter. I could

169

not help wondering if I would have had the strength of character to resist such temptation, and the answer was no. But then I was not (and still am not) a saint, and God, however eternally hopeful of mankind, would never have expected it of me.

A strong breeze was blowing, whipping my hair across my cheeks, and I recalled that the top of the Tor was renowned for always being windy, even on the most still and sultry of days. But this was something more. For the first time in weeks the sky was growing overcast and there was a smell of rain in the air. I suspected that one of those brief but torrential summer storms was brewing, and I hoped that I should be under shelter when it finally broke.

The chapel of Saint Michael and its attendant outhouses – kitchen, bakehouse, barn – were built on the small, flat, slightly sloping area at the Tor's summit. Over two hundred years before, the original chapel had been destroyed during an earthquake which shook that part of Somerset, and today's church was rebuilt half a century later under the auspices of Abbot Adam of Sodbury. Made of sandstone and limestone from the Mendip Hills, it had leaded windows, a tiled floor (some of the tiles exquisitely patterned), and a portable altar of Purbeck marble – luxurious furnishings by the standard of many other small chapels.

I entered through the gate in the boundary wall and mounted the steps that brought me at last to the top of the slope. In high summer the enclave was usually crowded with pilgrims – particularly those dedicated to the cult of the Archangel Michael – but today, for some reason, it was almost deserted. One of the abbey novices, whose turn it was to assist Father Elwyn, had just emerged from the bakehouse, the sleeves of his habit rolled above his elbows and his hands covered in flour; a solitary pilgrim, a rich merchant by his appearance, was on his knees before the altar when I glanced inside the chapel – but of further life there seemed, at present, to be no sign.

I sought out the novice, who had by now returned to the kitchen, and asked for Father Elwyn's whereabouts. I was directed to the barn.

The interior was dim, the more so since clouds had begun to gather, and sunlight no longer filtered through the narrow windows or flooded the open doorway. A lantern had been suspended from a nail in one wall, and by its pale radiance I was just able to make out Father Elwyn's figure in the deepest recesses of the building, checking his stores against the approach of colder weather.

I called his name, and he swung round with a start.

'Who's that? Who's there? What do you want?' He came forward – a little, dark man with the lilting speech that betrayed his Welsh origins – and stared long and hard into my face for several seconds. 'I remember you,' he said at last. 'Weren't you once a novice at the abbey?'

'I was,' I admitted. 'My name was Stonecarver then, but nowadays I'm known as Roger Chapman.'

He nodded, as though perfectly recollecting all the circumstances connected with my departure, and enquired, 'So what do you want with me, Master Stonecarver, also known as Roger Chapman?'

I decided not to beat about the bush. 'I understand from Brother Hilarion that a month or so before he disappeared, Peter Gildersleeve paid you a visit ... You have heard, I suppose, that Master Gildersleeve has since mysteriously vanished?'

Again Father Elwyn nodded, but wasted no words on the subject, simply asking, 'Well?'

I drew a bow at a venture. 'The visit, I believe, had

nothing to do with his spiritual welfare.'

'You understand! You believe!' Father Elwyn exclaimed testily. 'I trust Brother Hilarion is not becoming a gossip in his old age! How does he know all this?'

'He overheard one of the novices – a certain Humphrey, who once helped you in the bakehouse here – telling a fellow novice.'

Father Elwyn gave a short laugh. 'A trouble-maker, that boy! I had him marked down as such from our very first encounter.'

'Nevertheless,' I pursued, 'you don't deny that Peter Gildersleeve did visit you!'

'No, I don't deny it.'

'And was it on a secular matter?'

The priest was growing manifestly more annoyed with every passing second. 'That has nothing to do with you, nor with anyone save Master Gildersleeve and myself. Now, I have work to do. I'll bid you good-day.'

He would have turned away from me, but I caught his arm.

'Father, listen! I think I might know the reason why he came to see you. Had it anything to do with this?' While I spoke, I had drawn the quarto from beneath my left arm and proceeded to loosen its ties; then, with infinite care, I extracted the folded parchment.

At the sight of it, Father Elwyn stepped back hurriedly, making the sign of the Cross high in the air between himself and the offending paper. 'How did you come by that?' he demanded.

I plunged yet again into my tale. The priest listened quietly, passing no comment until I had finished, when he urged me to let the matter well alone.

'Ever since the report of Master Gildersleeve's

mysterious disappearance reached me, I have been certain that the document you are holding had something to do with it. God forgive me! I should have told him to burn it there and then, for it had the smell of evil about it.'

'You understand what these strange symbols mean?' I queried hopefully.

Father Elwyn shook his head. 'No, but I gave Peter Gildersleeve directions to one who I thought might possibly be able to explain them to him.'

My heart missed a beat with excitement. 'Who was that?' I demanded.

'Do you really expect me to tell you, so that you too can run to put your head in the noose? Don't be a fool, my son!'

'Father,' I said urgently, replacing the precious parchment between the quarto's leaves, 'you *must* tell me. How can I possibly discover what has happened to Peter Gildersleeve unless I know the whole story?'

The priest crossed himself again. 'You won't find him,' he said in a low, scared voice. 'He has been carried off by demons. How else could he vanish into thin air?'

'Father, have you not considered that there might be some perfectly ordinary explanation for his disappearance?'

'How can there be an ordinary explanation,' the priest asked truculently, 'when a shepherd-boy sees him with his own eyes one minute, and the next he's completely vanished?'

Thus challenged, I had to think quickly. 'The ... the shepherd-boy might be lying,' I stammered. 'Have you thought of that?'

But he could tell by my expression that I had no faith in my own suggestion, and dismissed it scornfully. 'No child would make up such lies about a man he barely knew and who meant nothing to him. For what purpose? Besides, in that case, where is Peter Gildersleeve? And why did he abandon his horse?'

I sighed. The questions were unanswerable, the affair far better understood than I had bargained for. The story may not have reached as far as Beckery, but within the town and the abbey enclave, and apparently here on the Tor, it was known in some detail. So I had to fall back on my powers of persuasion.

'Nevertheless I'm still not convinced, Father, that Peter Gildersleeve has been bewitched or fallen into the clutches of Old Scratch. But even should I be proved wrong, I must put my trust in God and look to Him to deliver me from harm. I've promised Dame Joan to find out what happened to her son—' I bit off the 's' of the last word just in time, for as far as I could tell rumours of Mark having shared the same fate as his brother had not yet travelled this distance. 'And I intend to keep that promise. Therefore, I must beg you again to tell me where, and to whom, you sent Master Gildersleeve.'

Father Elwyn hesitated. Fleeting changes of expression, shadows of his internal conflict, chased one another across his face. At last, however, he said, 'So be it. But you must hold me exonerated in this world and the next should anything untoward befall you.'

I gave him my most solemn assurance that this would be the case, and found myself in the odd position of offering him absolution rather than the other way around.

'Very well then,' he agreed, albeit with palpable reluctance. A sudden flash of lightning momentarily illuminated the windows of the barn, followed by a faint rumble of thunder as yet some few miles distant, but menacing none the less. It was enough to make the priest jump and show the whites of his eyes, like a startled horse, and for a moment I thought he was going to change his mind and withhold the promised information; such signs and portents were unnerving. But after a further inward struggle, he steeled himself to tell me what I wished to know.

'It came to me, when I first looked at that paper, that it was written using the ancient Ogham alphabet – or the Bethluisnion as we Welsh call it – of the Celts. It was often used for carving inscriptions on stones, and many of them can still be seen today in Wales.'

'Would the alphabet have been known in Ireland?' I interrupted, and was rewarded by a withering glance.

'Naturally! They too are Celts! But as you can see for yourself it was an unwieldy, time-consuming method of writing much more than a word or two, and its general use died out many centuries ago. Nevertheless, I considered it just possible that it might still be known and employed in the wilder, remoter regions of my country, where you Saxons and your Norman overlords have failed to penetrate.'

'And so?' I prompted eagerly as he again paused, racked by yet more doubts.

Father Elwyn sighed. 'And so I sent Master Gildersleeve to Saint Mary's, the alms hospital in Magdalene Street, and told him to ask for Blethyn Goode.'

'Blethyn Goode,' I repeated, carefully committing the name to memory.

'That's right. Blethyn,' the priest continued, 'is a country-man of mine, but nobody knows how old he is – some reckon a hundred, and others much older than that. He claims he was already over eighty when he first arrived in Glastonbury, but no one can remember when that was. He was born, he says, somewhere in the Black Mountains, but cannot recall exactly where. He thinks he must have run away from home when he was a boy, but is vague, perhaps on purpose, about the intervening years before he finally settled here. One thing is certain, however, and that is that he is a remarkable man. He can both read and write, has a profound knowledge on many subjects, and seems almost immune to the debilitating effects of old age. Oh, he suffers in his joints and gets chest trouble in the winter, but he sees and hears as well as a person half his years. He uses spectacles, it's true, and is somewhat deaf in one ear, but otherwise is as fit as I am.'

'And did Peter Gildersleeve go to see him?'

'Now, that I am unable to say with any authority. He certainly expressed the intention of doing so, so I can only assume that he did. I haven't seen Blethyn Goode for many months. His parish priest is the priest of Saint John's, and I only visit the Infirmary if Father Jerome is sick.'

'And do you think that Master Goode may have been able to translate the parchment's message?'

'I very much fear that he must have done.' Father Elwyn shivered. 'That was only a month or so ago, and last Friday Master Gildersleeve disappeared.'

There was long pause before he added, 'Do you intend to visit Blethyn?'

'I do. Do you wish me to let you know what he says?'

The priest shook his head vehemently. 'I want to be embroiled in this affair no more than I have to. Now, leave me to my work. I've told you all I can.'

I was halfway down the Tor when it began to rain, after another flash of lightning and a clap of thunder which was almost directly overhead.

While I had been inside the barn the clouds had

continued to march up out of the west with, at their heart, a dirty, sulphurous streak. Away to my left the sun could still be glimpsed every now and then, like fire beneath a pall of smoke, and the light was a murky saffron yellow. The first few drops were as large as hailstones, increasing rapidly in quantity without diminishing in size, and the grass was soon flattened beneath their weight. I battled my way through grey ribbons of water which irrigated the parched ground with a network of tiny streams, loosened earth and stones tumbling in my wake. The world was blotted out in a torrential downpour.

My clothes hung on me like sodden rags and my feet squelched inside my boots. Yet before I had reached the end of Dod Lane, the storm was already passing, the clouds beginning to lift on faint streaks of coral; and by the time I gained Market Place, the sun was riding high again in the heavens, my soaked garments steaming gently in the heat. A couple of apprentice boys, on errands for their masters, jeered at my bedraggled appearance, and I was forced to cuff the most impudent of the two around the ears.

I had managed to keep the quarto and its precious contents dry by pushing it inside my jerkin, and now I gingerly withdrew it to make sure that all was safe. But no drop of rain, however heavy, could penetrate the leather and its scarlet lining, and the strong, coarse cloth of the book's boarded covers was unspotted.

Two thirds of the way along Magdalene Street, almost opposite the abbey mill, I found the Hospital of Saint Mary Magdalene, a refuge in their old age for eleven poor men and a Master, built some two hundred and fifty years before. It consisted then (as presumably it still does) of a long infirmary hall with twelve cubicles, six on either side, one for each man and one for the Master, and a chapel dedicated to its patron saint.

Three of the old men were inspecting one of the stone benches set against an outside wall, obviously debating whether or not it had dried sufficiently for them to risk sitting down. A thin, arthritic finger, as brittle and bent as a twig, was cautiously drawn across the roughened surface, then the owner of it sadly shook his head.

'Not yet, boys,' he said in a husky voice, 'but maybe in half an hour.'

Frustration was registered on the other two ancient faces, for at least here, through the archway, they could glimpse some of the activity of the bustling street and feel themselves once more part of the outside world. One of them caught sight of me and his leathery features creased into a toothless grin.

'Here's a visitor,' he informed his companions, and they fell on me like ravening wolves upon their prey, hands clawing at my arms and shoulders as they demanded who it was I had come to see.

'I'm looking for Blethyn Goode,' I told them, only to watch their faces crumple again into lines of disappointment.

'You're the second person who's visited him in the past three months,' the toothless one grumbled, gnashing his empty gums.

'Why should he be so favoured?'

His friends nodded in agreement, plainly irritated by their fellow's popularity and the paucity of their own.

'You can come and talk to me for a while,' said he of the arthritic fingers, his bright, avian glance busily taking in all the details of my person. 'What's that you're holding?'

'It's a book,' announced the third man gloomily. 'No use

to us; we can't read. Couldn't you have brought some food? There's never enough to eat in this place.'

The other two nodded in agreement, their resentment growing as they began to feel themselves ill-used.

'I'm sorry,' I answered, 'I didn't think. I'll . . . I'll bring you food next time I call. I promise. Meantime, I must speak to Blethyn Goode. Can you tell me where to find him?'

They were slightly mollified by my apology, and the toothless wonder indicated the door behind him. 'Inside,' he spluttered. 'He's most likely in his cubicle. Turn left and it's the one at the far end, on the opposite side of the hall.'

I thanked the three of them with exaggerated courtesy, and left them inspecting the bench once more, in the vain hope that it might now be sufficiently dry for them to sit on.

I recalled having visited the hospital twice as a novice in the company of Brother Infirmarian, when he had come to dose the sick, and realized that Blethyn Goode, and also the old men I had just encountered, had probably been here then. But it was a long time ago, and I had been no more interested in the patients than they had been in me. I must have been a sad trial to all the brothers, and there could hardly have been one who wasn't relieved to see me go without taking my final vows.

The long hall and the narrow stone cubicles on either side were much as I remembered them, and I crossed to the one in the far left-hand corner, peering inside. It was sparsely furnished with a wooden-framed bed, a single grey woollen blanket folded neatly at its foot, a stool, a shelf above the bed on which reposed a candle in its holder and a tinder-box, and a small wooden chest, presumably containing personal possessions.

The old man who sat reading on the side of the bed glanced up, regarded me indifferently for a moment or two over his spectacles, then looked away again.

'Blethyn Goode?' I inquired tentatively, entering the cubicle.

'Who wants to know? And who invited you to come in?' was the chilling reply, all without the eyes being raised from the book.

'My name's Roger Chapman. Father Elwyn sent me to see you.'

This information did evoke some response. Blethyn Goode lifted his head and glared fiercely at me. 'He's always sending people to see me! I wish he wouldn't.'

'I-I'm sorry,' I stammered, 'but . . .' My voice tailed away as I realized he was no longer listening. Vacillation, however, would get me nowhere, so I sat down beside him and untied the strings of the quarto, easing the parchment yet again from between its leaves.

Now that I was close to Blethyn, I could see that he was indeed extremely old, the skin stretched thinly across the bones and blotched with the brown pigment of the aged. Because of the day's warmth he had removed the linen hood which he normally wore indoors, to reveal a narrow skull to whose dome there clung a few determined tufts of hair, white and as fine as feather fronds. The brown eyes were faded and rheumy, but his glance, like his mind, was as sharp as a razor.

'Go away,' he instructed without turning his head; but when I ignored him and continued to sit there, he slapped the leaves of his book together with an irritable sigh and looked towards me. Immediately, his eyes fell on the parchment I was holding. 'What are you doing with that?' he demanded. 'That's the property of Master Gildersleeve.

There can't possibly be two of them.'

'He did come to see you, then? Peter Gildersleeve?'

'Of course he did. You can surely work that out for yourself! I shouldn't know anything about that piece of paper otherwise, now should I? Father Elwyn sent him to see me.'

'You know that he's disappeared? Master Gildersleeve, I mean.'

'A whisper has penetrated our seclusion, yes. Probably gone off with some woman, a young, good-looking fellow like that.'

'I don't think so. He vanished very suddenly and mysteriously, almost in the twinkling of an eye.' I tapped the parchment. 'Father Elwyn thinks this to be the cause. He believes it to be some spell or incantation which has conjured up the Devil.'

Blethyn Goode stared at me for several seconds before breaking into a snort of laughter. 'The man's a fool,' he hooted. 'I'm sorry to say such a thing about one of my fellow countrymen, but he's an idiot. You can tell him I said so if you like. I've translated that parchment. I know what's in it.'

'I'd much rather you told me what it says,' I answered. 'Can you remember after all these months?'

Again he snorted. 'I don't have to remember. I wrote it all down for Master Gildersleeve, but I also made a copy for myself. It's over there, in that chest.'

Chapter Fourteen

From around his neck Blethyn removed a leather thong on which hung a key, and nodded once again towards the chest.

'Open it,' he instructed.

I did so, and inside found a woollen cloak, neatly folded, a pair of winter boots, a spare shirt and a dozen or so books, mostly quartos and octavos, thrown in higgledy-piggledy, one on top of the other. There were also several sheets of blank parchment, an inkhorn and pen, and a second pair of bone-framed spectacles, presumably a safeguard in case the first pair were lost. But of anything else I could see no sign, and said so.

'Use your eyes, boy! Use your eyes!' said the irascible voice behind me. 'It's there somewhere! Just keep looking.'

I did as I was told and, eventually, between the folds of the cloak, I discovered a sheet of paper covered in spidery writing. I held it up for confirmation.

'That's it,' agreed Blethyn. 'I told you it was there. Lock the chest again and give me back the key. Some of my fellow inmates have more curiosity than is good for them. In this place, you daren't leave anything open or lying about that you want kept secret.'

When I had done as he bid, I sat down once more beside him on the bed and unfolded the paper.

He glanced sharply at me. 'Can you read?'

'I was once a novice at the abbey. The brothers taught me my letters.'

'In that case,' he declared, 'you might as well take the thing away with you and leave me in peace to get on with my book. You can keep it if you like. I know what's in it. I shan't be wanting it again.'

'I'd rather read it for the first time in your presence,' I said apologetically. 'There might be something I need to ask you, some point on which I should value your opinion.'

Blethyn grunted and pretended to be annoyed, but secretly, as I could tell, he was flattered.

'Oh, as you please!' he snapped, hunching one shoulder.

I settled myself more comfortably, heaving my bulk further on to the bed so that my back was resting against the wall, my long legs stuck straight out in front of me, whereupon, my unwilling host removed himself to the stool in high dudgeon, remarking that it was as though a second earthquake had struck that part of Somerset. I only laughed and held the paper up in front of my eyes, angling it until it caught the light from the cubicle's open doorway.

It must, I judged, be mid-afternoon by now, but the rain clouds had passed and the sun had reappeared so that it was not too difficult to see, even without a candle. My clothes had dried sufficiently to be comfortable again, and I felt that, at last, one part of my mystery was about to be unravelled.

I began to read.

'In this, the five hundredth year since Christ's Nativity, I, Brother Begninus of the monastery at Ynys Afalon, or Ynys Witrin as it is sometimes called, have been entrusted by my superiors with the safe keeping of the most precious possession this abbey holds, before the Germanic tribes from across the northern sea finally overrun us for ever.

'Five days ago, news reached us here that the Axe-Ones are advancing on us from both the east and the south, and many people are already fleeing northwards, across the great river and into the mountains beyond. Some of our own Brothers have also left, or are going soon. Tomorrow, Brother Percival and Brother Geraldus will start on the long and hazardous journey to their native Ireland. They will take this paper with them in case they should ever return to Ynys Afalon and I not be alive to greet them. For who can tell what the fate of those of us who remain will be at the hands of the pagan conquerors?

'Therefore, dear Brothers in God, I say to you, as I have said to Father Abbot, that the Great Relic, brought here by the one who came from over the water, is hidden in the same place in which it was concealed two years since, when we thought the Axe-Ones to be almost upon us: amongst the hills, in the hollow places of the earth, on the altar by Charon's stream.

'God go with you both, dear Brothers, and may He keep you and watch over you until we meet again, either in this world or the next.'

I raised my head and looked across at Blethyn Goode. 'Is this the whole of the translation?' I asked. 'There seems to be so little of it.'

He regarded me with indignation. 'Why should I deceive you, pray? You're as suspicious as Master Gildersleeve, so I'll tell you what I told him. The Bethluisnion is a laborious way of writing and wasteful of space. What you read there is all that is written on the sheet of parchment which you have between the leaves of that book.'

Recollecting that Father Elwyn had said much the same

thing, I had, perforce, to be satisfied with this explanation. After a moment or two I asked, 'What do you think it means?'

Blethyn had resumed his reading again, but at my question, he closed the quarto with a furious slap of its covers and glared angrily at me over the rims of his spectacles.

'Isn't it obvious, even to your impoverished intelligence, what it's saying? Surely you can work that out for yourself!'

I sucked my teeth thoughtfully. 'In the year 500 AD, one of the brothers of the early Celtic church here was empowered by his abbot to hide their chief relic before they were overrun by the Saxons. This he did, somewhere, apparently, where it had been hidden once before. He told his abbot what he'd done and, for good measure, wrote down the information for two brothers who were returning to Ireland the following day, not knowing what might befall the rest of the community at the hands of the invaders.'

'Very wise of him,' Blethyn interrupted nastily. 'I don't suppose you could trust the worshippers of Thor and Woden then any more than you can trust them today.'

I ignored this childish interruption and continued, 'Which is how the original document came to be brought back here by Gerald Clonmel, the Irishman who was on his way to Canterbury, and who told Father Boniface of the family tradition that it was taken to Ireland by one of his ancestors. Which means that he was a descendant of either Brother Geraldus or –' I consulted the translation – 'or of Brother Percival. Some sects of the Celtic priesthood, I believe, were allowed to marry.'

'And plenty of them, then as now, had children out of wedlock,' Blethyn snarled. 'Don't you believe it, boy, when they tell you that holy men and women never have bastards.

Conditions in our monasteries and nunneries have always
been a disgrace! If the inmates don't mend their ways,
something terrible is going to happen. The earth will open
and the Devil and all his cohorts will swallow them up!'

'Oh, come!' I protested mildly. 'You can't damn the
whole Church because some of its foundations are inclined
to be lax.'

Blethyn curled his lip. 'The Church is too fat, too greedy,
too lazy, too prosperous! One day – oh, maybe not in your
lifetime, and certainly not in mine – someone is going to
cast a covetous eye on all that wealth and want his share of
it.'

I laughed and rightly dismissed the notion, returning to
the matter in hand.

'What do you think this precious relic was?'

'How should I know?' was the testy response. 'There are
so many in this world that it would be impossible to guess.
Bones of the saints, girdles of the Virgin, pieces of the True
Cross, bits of the Crown of Thorns! Every church of any
size throughout the whole of Europe boasts of its relics.'

'But the monks thought this one important enough to
take special precautions with it, so that it didn't fall into
the hands of the advancing Saxons.'

Blethyn waved one gnarled hand in an airy gesture.
'God's toenails, boy! The church here wasn't anything like
as rich then as the abbey is today. Whatever it was, it was
probably their only relic and had to be kept safe, especially
if they were about to be overrun by heathens.'

I was not totally convinced by his argument, but common
sense told me that it was most likely the correct one. For
the moment, however, I let it go and moved on to my next
query.

'So where was this relic hidden?' I tapped the translation

and quoted, ' "Amongst the hills, in the hollow places of the earth, on the altar by Charon's stream." Where can that be?'

Blethyn shrugged and started to tighten the iron rivet of his spectacles with one fingernail. 'How in Heaven's name do I know? It could be anywhere.'

'No, not anywhere,' I corrected him. 'It must surely be somewhere within reach of the abbey.'

'Do you think me a fool?' he snapped. 'Of course it's within reach of the abbey! But on foot or on horseback? Either, but particularly the latter, would cover an enormous acreage of ground. North, south, east, west . . .' He broke off, shrugging his shoulders.

I could see his point. 'Do you know of any canal or brook or waterway in these parts known as Charon's stream?'

'God's toenails, boy!' he exclaimed yet again. 'Of what possible interest can it be to us now? We're talking about nearly a thousand years ago! Whatever was hidden won't still be there, not after all this time! And that's supposing the relic was left where it was hidden by this Brother Begninus. The chances are that it was recovered shortly afterwards and taken back to its rightful place in the abbey. The year of Our Lord five hundred was the year in which Arthur defeated the Saxons at the battle of Mount Badon, and so halted their advance from the east. Oh, it was only a temporary setback for them, I admit, but no one knew that at the time.'

'There were Saxons advancing from the south as well,' I reminded Blethyn, much to his annoyance.

'All right! All right!' he answered pettishly. 'Perhaps it *was* left where it was hidden. We shall never know now. But what difference does it make? As I said before, it isn't still there, waiting to be found! Apart from anything else, the landscape will have changed in a thousand years. And then there's reference to an altar! That suggests to me a church of some kind, maybe a chapel or a wayside shrine. You won't find that still standing, either. Your forebears weren't the only invaders this island has seen. Since them we've had the Normans as well as the occasional marauding Dane. Not many of *them* though, hereabouts. Thanks to King Alfred,' he added grudgingly, loath to speak kindly of one of my race.

'But . . .' I began, then changed my mind. There was no point in further argument with Blethyn, and in any case, he had pointedly opened his book again and resumed his reading. He was tired of the subject and was making it clear that it was time I was gone.

I slid off the bed and stood upright, the crown of my head brushing the cubicle's low ceiling. I held up the translation. 'You said that I could keep this. Did you mean it?'

'I never say anything I don't mean. Yes, keep it if you must, and show it to that fool Father Elwyn at Saint Michael's on the Tor. Prove to him that it has nothing to do with spells and incantations, and that it couldn't of itself have caused Peter Gildersleeve to vanish. But what good it'll do you I've no idea! As I said, you won't find any hidden relic now, even if you knew where to look for it.'

I was inclined to agree with him. Nevertheless there was no doubt in my mind that Peter Gildersleeve had believed he had stumbled upon some secret which the parchment held. Why, otherwise, would he have told Maud Jarrold that 'if he'd interpreted it aright' it was 'valuable beyond price'? Well, that was something I should have to work out, if I could, for myself. Meantime, the best thing for me to do was to return to the house and reassure Dame Joan and Cicely that the black arts had had nothing to do with Peter's disappearance. That might afford them some peace of mind at least.

It did not, however, solve the problem of either brother's whereabouts. When Mark had visited Beckery the day before yesterday he had not long discovered the parchment in the secret drawer, and had hoped that Father Boniface could enlighten him as to its meaning. When that had proved not to be the case, he had gone off on on some quest of his own. But where? And for what purpose? The only clue was that Dorabella had been found wandering on the other side of the moor . . .

I suddenly remembered Gilbert Honeyman and wondered if, by any chance, he had discovered Mark, lying out there with an injured leg or ankle, or even a broken skull. It became still more imperative that I get back to the house, and I said a somewhat perfunctory goodbye to Blethyn Goode. He merely grunted in reply, shifting from the stool to his former seat on the bed without glancing up. Nor did the three old men, now cosily ensconced on the bench, show any further interest in me. They did not bother to answer my valediction, but continued to cackle with laughter over some piece of gossip they were sharing. I went out under the arch and turned northwards along Magdalene Street.

Gilbert Honeyman had drawn a blank, as I had prophesied he would.

The Bee Master had retraced his ride of the morning, across the raised causeway leading to Wells, and then taken the path to the Holly Brook where he had begun his search.

'From there, I went as far as I could in all directions but, alas, to no avail. There was no sign of anyone lying injured on the ground. But I do assure you, Dame Joan, that only my own and my horse's weariness stopped me from starting all over again.'

'You have done more than anyone could expect of you,' that worthy assured him, her voice tremulous with gratitude, and she laid a hand on his arm. Master Honeyman patted it sustainingly.

We were eating supper, again in the kitchen, and I had promised to tell my news as soon as we had finished. Consequently, once the meal was over, although the dirty dishes were cleared from the table, no effort was made to wash them. Everyone, including Lydia, resumed his or her seat and waited eagerly to hear what I had to say.

When I had recounted the day's events, there was a moment's silence. Then Dame Joan let out a sigh.

'Does this mean that Peter wasn't dabbling in sorcery after all?' she asked.

Both Cicely and I, with assistance from Gilbert Honeyman, did our utmost to reassure her on that score. But her next two questions – 'Where is he then?' and 'What's happened to him and Mark?' – were as unanswerable as ever.

'You must give me more time,' I pleaded, 'to try to work things out in the light of this new knowledge.'

'Do you have any ideas at all?' the Bee Master demanded bluntly.

'There's a thought stirring at the back of my mind,' I admitted, 'but I'd rather keep it to myself for now.' I didn't add that the idea was so absurd I could barely give it credence, and was certainly not prepared to hold myself up to ridicule by sharing it.

'That's not fair!' Cicely exclaimed hotly. 'This is as much

our mystery as it is yours, and I don't see why you have to be so horridly secretive!'

Dame Joan immediately reprimanded her for her impertinence, but it was obvious that she was inclined to share her niece's sentiments. Master Honeyman, on the other hand, looked as though he recognized only too well the headstrong, impulsively outspoken female of the species, and sent me a sympathetic glance.

'I'm not being horridly secretive,' I answered gently, 'it's just that I can't yet see where my idea is leading me, even supposing that there's something in it, which may not be the case. I need to speak to Brother Hilarion again. I'll pay him a visit this evening and see if I can talk to him sometime between Vespers and Compline. But don't expect me to tell you anything on my return. I shall need to be on my own, to think.'

This in no way placated Cicely, who continued to sulk. Master Honeyman decided on a strategic withdrawal and announced that he must be on his way. 'I shall be at the abbey hostelry at the bottom of the street, should you need me,' he said, gallantly bowing over Dame Joan's hand. 'I've already paid my shot and stabled my horse there. If I may, I shall visit you again tomorrow, to find out how matters stand then.'

'Don't waste your time, sir,' Cicely advised him with a toss of her head, 'for I'm sure we shan't be any the wiser than we are now – except Master Chapman, of course.'

Gilbert clapped me on the shoulder and pulled down the corners of his mouth. 'You're making an enemy there, my lad,' he hissed in my ear.

I winked in reply and rose to my feet. 'I'll come with you,' I said, 'as far as the abbey's north gate.'

Once we had left the house, it was only a step or two

before we parted company, but time enough for him to say, 'What a termagant! She reminds me of my own Rowena.' He laughed. 'God preserve us from the female race!'

I smiled and waved him on his way; then I roused the gate-porter and begged admittance for the second time that day.

'Oh, it's you again,' he grumbled. 'The brothers are in the refectory, at supper.'

'I can wait,' I said. 'But I must speak with Brother Hilarion when he's finished eating.'

He made no further objection and let me pass. The precincts were just as busy as they had been earlier, and I reflected that it was an abbey which never seemed to sleep. The only truly quiet time was in the small hours of the morning, when the monks roused themselves in the cold, dark dorter and went in procession down the night stairs to sing Vigils in the church, a great pool of darkness starred with a few, faint, flickering lights. (I regret to say that when I was a novice there, I often fell into a doze while chanting my psalms, and had to be nudged awake by my neighbours.)

To pass the time I skirted the Lady Chapel, threaded a path through the old cemetery and past the cloisters towards the dorters, situated between the refectory and the latrines. Away to my right, wonderful, mouth-watering smells were issuing forth from the abbot's kitchen, and I wondered which local dignitary was being entertained this evening in the adjacent hall. No such appetizing aromas came from the monks' kitchen as I passed it; a bowlful of thin gruel or broth would have constituted their evening meal, and I recalled with almost physical agony the pangs of hunger from which I used to suffer during my novitiate.

Out of curiosity, I mounted the stairs to the deserted dormitory over the undercroft. Nothing had changed. The same two rows of blankets, straw-filled pillows and rush-mats – only the old and the sick had mattresses – lined each wall, and the same bleak crucifix hung at one end. The door leading to the night-corridor and stairs was shut, but icy draughts still seeped beneath it. As for myself, I was seized with the same urgent longing for escape that had so frequently afflicted me in the past, and I descended into the fresh air again with almost indecent haste.

I returned to the cloisters and found Brother Hilarion's carrel, hoping that he would come there for meditation, or to read the Scriptures quietly until it was the hour for Compline (always a little later in the summer months). I was not disappointed, and when supper was over and grace said, the brothers entered from the refectory and went each to his own place, some taking up pen or brush again to resume their labours on psalter or Bible or other holy book.

Brother Hilarion did not immediately perceive me, for I was sitting in shadow at the carrel's further end. When I moved, he started back with a cry.

'It's all right, Brother,' I whispered. 'It's only me again.'

'R-Roger? How you startled me! What do you want?'

'Can we talk here?'

He nodded. 'Yes, but we must be very quiet.' He slid on to the seat beside me. 'Have you discovered anything since this morning, concerning Peter Gildersleeve?'

Keeping my voice as low as possible, I told him all that had happened, producing for his perusal both the original parchment belonging to Gerald of Clonmel and also the translation made by Blethyn Goode.

His frown deepened as he looked at them. 'This is certainly no evil spell or incantation. So what can it have to do with Master Gildersleeve's disappearance?'

I countered with a question of my own. 'Have you ever

heard of any great relic which was housed here in the olden days?'

He shook his head. 'This is before the coming of our Saxon forefathers. After their conversion by Saint Augustine we might have seen the bones of Saint Patrick and Saint Aidan, relics which we still retain. And three of our Saxon kings were buried here: Edmund, Edgar the Peacable, and Ethelraed Unraed's son, Edmund Ironside. But what was here in ancient times, I have no idea. Maybe you should speak to Brother Librarian. He might have some thoughts on the subject.'

I pointed to a phrase in the translation.

'It says here that the relic was brought to the Abbey by "the one who came from over the water".' I hesitated, then continued, 'This morning, you were teaching the novices about Joseph of Arimathea, who is, we are told, the Founding Father of this place.' Again I paused, uncertain whether to proceed in case Brother Hilarion should think me suddenly bereft of my senses. But I plucked up my courage and said, 'What about the cup that Joseph is said to have brought with him from Palestine? The Passover cup, used by Our Lord at the Last Supper?'

'Ah!' The faded blue eyes opened wide in wonder and astonishment as they met mine. 'You are . . . You are talking of the Holy Grail.'

Chapter Fifteen

There was a profound silence, broken only by the whispered voices of two other Brothers speaking together in the next carrel. Then Brother Hilarion repeated on a low, wondering sigh, 'The Holy Grail.'

'Could it have been?' I asked, trembling with excitement, and grateful that my suggestion had not been immediately dismissed as the ravings of an unsound mind. 'What would it have looked like?'

My old friend and mentor raised a trembling hand, pressing it to his lips while he considered his answer. At last he said, 'If the story is true, if . . . if indeed the Grail was ever brought to this country, if . . .' He broke off in confusion, afraid to confirm or deny the existence of so legendary an object, and worried that any denial would call in question the very sources from which the abbey drew its wealth.

'Yes?' I urged him.

'Well . . . It would probably have been a plain olive-wood bowl, Our Lord and the Blessed Disciples being poor men.' He must have seen my doubtful expression, for he went on hastily, 'But naturally, a reliquary of gold and precious stones would have been made for it, which would explain why, in the stories of King Arthur, it is depicted as a chalice of beauty and worth.'

197

'Yes, of course,' I breathed. 'Of course! That would be the answer.'

'My child!' Brother Hilarion admonished me gently. 'Don't let your imagination run away with you. There must have been other relics which the monks of those days would have prized. Furthermore – and you tell me that Blethyn Goode has already pointed this out to you – anything from almost a thousand years ago is very unlikely to have survived. Even if there was in fact a shrine or chapel beside a brook known as Charon's stream, it would surely have been looted by the Saxons during their final advance.'

There was so much excellent sense in what he said that my heart plummeted, and I once more began to feel foolish. But after a few moments my natural optimism reasserted itself as I reflected that Peter Gildersleeve had thought the parchment 'valuable beyond price'. Why? Was it possible that he had come to the same conclusion as I had done? And if so, what did his disappearance have to do with it?

My thoughts were interrupted by my companion. 'Let's pay a visit to Brother Librarian and ask his opinion of the matter. He knows more about the history of this abbey than any of us. There's time, I think, before Compline.'

I was again reluctant both to expose my theory to ridicule and to be forced to repeat my story; nevertheless, I eventually gave in and meekly followed Brother Hilarion to the library, where my fears were proved unfounded. Brother Librarian, a small, rotund, pink-faced man, whom I vaguely recollected from my novice days, not only grasped the essentials of my tale with amazing speed, but also listened gravely to the conclusion that I had drawn. When I had finished, however, he shook his head.

'I should very much doubt it being a reference to the Holy Grail. I'm not saying it couldn't be, you understand –

but I think it far more likely that the relic in question was an ossuary containing the bones of Saint Patrick.'

'Saint Patrick? But surely he died and is buried in Ireland!'

The button mouth pursed itself into a tiny, fleshy, pink rosebud. 'So the Irish would have us believe. Yet there is a strong tradition of links between the saint and the church at Ynys Witrin. It is not improbable – not improbable at all! – that Patrick was born in Somerset, and that when, as a boy, he was carried off by Irish raiders, it was from around these parts; for in those days, the coast was constantly harried by the pirates and sea-scavengers of many different countries. And if that were indeed the case, would it not be natural that an old man should wish to return to his birthplace towards the end of his life? William of Malmesbury, in his *De Antiquitate Glastoniensis Ecclesiae*, tells us definitely that after coming back to Somerset, Patrick "chanced upon the Isle of Ynys Witrin, wherein he found a place holy and ancient, sanctified in honour of Mary, the Pure Virgin". And also that he climbed the Tor, where he discovered a ruined oratory and an ancient tome recording the acts of Saint Faganus and Saint Deruvianus, who had founded the chapel in honour of Saint Michael. Our Lord Himself appeared to Saint Patrick in a dream to confirm that the summit of the Tor was holy ground which must always be dedicated to the worship of the Archangel.'

'Then you believe,' I said slowly, 'that an ossuary containing the bones of Saint Patrick must be the relic referred to in Brother Begninus's letter?'

Once more, Brother Librarian's mouth formed a small, round O, but this time one of uncertainty rather than conviction. He was wary of committing himself unreservedly to the idea that the saint had been buried here, realizing

how contentious the notion would be not only amongst our
Irish neighbours, but also to many of the Church's chief
dignitaries, who were constantly alert to the danger of
Glastonbury setting itself up in rivalry to Canterbury.

'I'm not stating it as *fact*,' he recanted hurriedly, 'but
only as a far more probable interpretation of events. The
Grail story has always been a little ... um ... a little
suspect, shall I say? In spite of its figuring so strongly in
the stories of King Arthur.'

'Who, as we all know,' I cut in blandly, 'lies buried with
Queen Guinevere in the nave of the abbey, and who must,
therefore, have existed in truth as well as legend.'

I felt Brother Hilarion stir uneasily behind me, while the
round, rosy features of Brother Librarian stiffened into lines
of disapproval.

'Of course! That goes without saying. But that doesn't
mean,' he continued coldly, 'that there were no inaccuracies
made in the accounts of Arthur's life. The Grail stories,
after all, do vary. One tells us that what Joseph of Arimathea
brought with him from Palestine was a pair of cruets, one
containing the sweat, and the other the blood, of Our
Saviour. Then again, Wolfram von Eschenbach, in his epic,
Parzival, declares that the Grail is a stone or jewel, called
the Lapis Exilis. So you see, there are doubts about what
form the Grail actually took.'

'Brother,' I said, 'with all due respect, I cannot see that
your argument proves my theory wrong. Passover cup,
cruets or precious stone, the Grail could still have been the
relic hidden by Brother Begninus. Nowhere does he state
exactly what it was.'

'But can't you see,' Brother Librarian demanded in
growing exasperation, 'that the differing descriptions throw
doubt on its very existence? No, no, boy! Take it from me

that this parchment of yours refers to something else. And in my view, that something else is Saint Patrick's ossuary.'

'But that theory is as suspect as mine,' I retorted. 'In fact any Irishman would know it for a downright lie!'

Brother Hilarion touched me on the shoulder. 'I think we should be going,' he whispered anxiously, noting the swelling veins on Brother Librarian's neck and his blood-congested cheeks.

I at once felt ashamed of myself. Why do we always want people to agree with us, and resent our preconceptions being challenged? So I humbly begged the little monk's pardon, thanked him for his help, and added for good measure that beyond doubt his wisdom and superior knowledge would prevail with me, when once I had had a chance to mull things over.

I don't think he really believed me, for his face was still very red when Brother Hilarion and I emerged into the open air.

'You haven't improved, Roger,' the Novice Master reproved me sternly in the disappointed tones I remembered only too well. 'You must learn respect for your elders.'

I tried to look suitably abashed, but failed dismally if Brother Hilarion's reproachful expression was anything to judge by. But that had always been a part of my trouble: I could never accept that because a person was older than myself, he was also necessarily wiser. (And even now that I am one of the old ones I cannot feel certain that I know more than my children do. Perhaps it is just as well, for they all have very definite and forthright opinions on almost every subject.)

'Brother Librarian was most enlightening,' I said. 'I shall have much to think about when I return to Dame Joan's.'

The bell began to toll for Compline and I quickened my

step. 'Thank you, Brother, for your time and patience.'

He raised his hand in blessing. 'Won't you come to the service?' he asked.

But he knew as well as I did that I should derive small benefit from it, that my mind would be on other things. It was surely better to wait until I could concentrate my thoughts as I should. So he let me go without any further attempt at persuasion.

I sat on the edge of the bed in Peter and Mark Gildersleeve's bedchamber and tried to marshal my thoughts into some sort of order.

I had returned to the house to be told by Lydia that I was expected in the solar as soon as I set foot indoors. There I had been met by the tired, drawn face of Dame Joan and the sullen, anxious features of Cicely. The strain was making both women ill, especially now that the bracing presence of Gilbert Honeyman had been withdrawn, and the need for courtesy to the stranger within their gates was no longer necessary.

Dame Joan had lived with the disappearance of her elder son for a week now, and with Mark's since the day before yesterday. All the same, I was still not prepared to take them further into my confidence until I had treated myself to a period of quiet reflection, in order to clarify my ideas. I therefore had begged them both to excuse me, and to allow me to retire for the night.

'I told you so!' Cicely had flung at her aunt. 'I told you that we should learn nothing from Master Chapman! And why? Because, as I said before, it's my belief that all that boasting about how he's solved mysteries in the past is so much nonsense! I was never more deceived in anyone in my life.'

I had fully expected the Dame to call her niece to order as she had done previously, but the older woman seemed oblivious to the insult, labouring with some decision of her own.

'I've made up my mind,' she had remarked with sudden purpose, emphasized by tapping her fingers on the table. She looked at Cicely. 'I'm sending for your father. Where did he say the Duke was bound for when he left Farleigh Castle?'

The younger woman had wrinkled her brow. 'London, I think. Yes, London, but only for a couple of days. Father said he would leave word of their next destination, however, for anyone enquiring after him. And I do remember now,' she added guiltily, 'that he particularly asked to be kept informed of what was happening. He wanted to know that Peter was all right.'

Dame Joan had nodded. 'That settles it. I have been very remiss in not requesting his presence here earlier. First thing tomorrow I shall instruct Rob Undershaft to search out anyone in the town who is despatching goods to London within the next few days, and if there is someone his carter shall take a message from me to William. I'll visit the scrivener in the morning and get him to pen a letter, simply stating that my brother is needed here as soon as possible.'

It would have been the easiest thing in the world for me to have proposed that I write the letter for her, and in more detail than she would trust to the scrivener's discretion, but I had the feeling that the offer would not have been welcomed. I was being deliberately cold-shouldered by the aunt as well as the niece, as though I had been put on trial and found sadly wanting. So I had retired to my bedchamber in a huff, where I had spent the first half-hour making plans to wash my hands of the entire sorry business and set out for home at the crack of dawn.

I should have known better, alas, than to waste my time in this fashion, for once my curiosity is aroused I cannot rest until it is assuaged. And this mystery in particular held me in thrall, just as if it were indeed a spell cast by Merlin. But the longer I thought, the more confused I became, reason and fantasy struggling together for possession of my mind like the magical beasts of the enchanted forest, thrown up by the Wizard about his domains . . .

My head jerked forward, and I realized that I had almost fallen asleep where I sat. The Holy Grail! The Holy Grail! The words spun round and round in my reeling brain. Had it ever actually existed? And if it had, did Joseph of Arimathea truly bring it to Glastonbury after Our Lord's death upon the Cross? And if so, what form had it taken? Had Joseph himself really come here, crossing from Little Britain, which we now call Brittany, to Great Britain across the Narrow Sea? Or was that just another myth, as some of our neighbours, jealous of the standing it gave this country in the Christian hierarchy, would have us believe?

My head felt as though it was being squeezed by a band of red-hot iron, and my legs were as heavy as lead. Without even bothering to remove my boots, I swung them on to the bed and was sound asleep before my head touched the pillows.

When I awoke it was dark, the unshuttered window making an oblong of grey in the blackness of one wall. The house was silent, and I assumed that everyone else had retired for the night. I had no idea how long I had been asleep, but it was obviously for some hours. I must have been more tired than I knew.

But my rest had refreshed me. My mind, which had been so befuddled earlier, was now crystal clear. I realized, as though hit by a blinding truth like Saint Paul on the road to Damascus, that whether or not the Holy Grail had ever existed, whether or not it had taken the form of a cup, a cruet or a gemstone was of no importance. Nor did it really matter what the relic secreted by the long-dead Brother Begninus had actually been. What was of moment was the interpretation put upon the story by Peter Gildersleeve. I had to look at the riddle through *his* eyes, not through my own.

I got up and closed the shutters, for the downpour of the afternoon had been followed by a chillier night than those we had grown accustomed to during that long, hot summer. The faintest hint of autumn was in the air, the first intimation of a colder wind blowing from the east. I suddenly found myself thinking with almost nostalgic longing of my mother-in-law's little house in Bristol, of the fire on the hearth with the cooking-pot suspended over it, of my daughter perched on my knee while the winter gales roared along the Backs, whipping the river to a frenzy and howling amongst the roof-tops, leaving us cosy and warm inside.

I groped around until I discovered the tinder-box, lit the two lanterns and then retired again to the bed. This time I removed my boots, although otherwise remaining fully clothed, then banked up the pillows high enough to support my back and resumed my seat, my legs stretched out in front of me.

I had to try to imagine myself inside the mind of Peter Gildersleeve. When Blethyn Goode had translated the parchment's contents for him, what did he imagine was the relic hidden by Brother Begninus? What secret did he think it held? Had he too hit upon the possibility of the Holy

Grail? Or had he, unlike me, indulged in less outrageous flights of fancy? But whatever had been his conclusions, he had considered himself the possessor of information which was 'valuable beyond price'.

On Mark's telling, Peter had grown secretive about his books for those last few months before he disappeared, locking the chest where they were stored, a thing he had never done previously. And when his brother had idly questioned him as to the reason for his action he had flown out at Mark, cautioning him to mind his own business. And when he had found Maud Jarrold studying the parchment, which he had left spread out on the shop bench, Peter had bundled her out of the room, shouting at her and frightening her half to death. Later on, once his fear had subsided, he had realized how stupid he had been, for Maud could not even read, let alone translate the arcane alphabet of a thousand years ago, written in the old Celtic language. He had realized too that his uncharacteristic behaviour might arouse suspicion, and had therefore apologized to her and pleaded illness as the cause of his ill temper. But he had been badly, if senselessly, scared, and shortly afterwards had removed the parchment to the greater safety of the secret drawer in the bed-head.

So! After Peter had been to see Blethyn Goode, he must have decided, as I had done, that he had guessed the identity of the relic. How long it had taken him to reach his conclusion I could not say with any certainty, but it was obvious from his encounter with Maud Jarrold that he had made up his mind sometime before he had vanished. Had he been looking for whatever he thought it was during those weeks? Or was he simply mulling things over, trying to work out where his search must begin? And was it that search which had taken him on to Pennard land?

206

I was now faced with another question to which I did not know the answer: did Peter Gildersleeve's strange disappearance have anything at all to do with his acquiring the parchment and his knowledge of its contents, or were the two things unconnected? Had he visited the farm purely on a matter of business (he and Mark were accustomed to buying some of their sheepskins and cowhides from Anthony and his sons)? Yet he had not gone straight to the house or to the sheds where the fleeces were stored. Instead he had shown up at the shepherd's hut on the eastern perimeters of the holding, and there, minutes later, he had completely and mysteriously vanished, apparently into thin air . . .

I had just reached this point in my deliberations when something happened that was perhaps the most frightening experience of my life. As I have so frequently said in these tales of my youth, I inherited from my mother the capacity to dream strange dreams. I have never claimed to have the Sight, and my 'visions' usually do no more than point me in a direction which I have carelessly overlooked, or which has not been obvious to me before. The people and places in them are normally people and places I have encountered in daily life, but distorted by the unreality which comes with sleep. I have often suspected that they are no more than my own perceptions floating up from the dark and hidden corners of my mind.

But that night it was different. To begin with, one moment I was wide awake – refreshed, as I have already said, by my earlier doze – the next, I was deeply asleep . . . or was I? I have never been able to determine in all the years between then and now, and I still cannot decide today. There was none of that drifting through a twilight world, half real, half imaginary, that normally precedes unconsciousness, only an abrupt transition from wakefulness to the heart of my dream.

I was standing in a landscape both terrifyingly strange and yet oddly familiar, inside a circle of palings which housed a large, round, central building of daub and wattle with a thatched, conical roof. This was ringed by twelve smaller but almost identical huts, with paths radiating inwards from each one to the edifice in the middle. The stockade was too high for me to see over it, yet I knew without being told how the surrounding countryside looked. Bleak marshland was interspersed with swathes of primaeval forest, and the howling of wolves was borne to my ears on the ice-cold air. Thus far all was unrecognizable, but when I raised my eyes to the great mound which towered above the enclave, and to the adjoining promontory of land, I knew them at once for the Tor and Weary-All Hill.

While I watched there emerged from the twelve huts, as if by a prearranged signal, twelve men, each clad in a rough, grey shift, knotted about the waist with rope, with their hair shaved back from the brow almost to the centre of the head. The recollection came to me that the monks of the old Celtic Christian Church had worn their tonsures in this fashion, instead of on the crown; and, without being told, I knew that the central building must be the very first church here, at Glastonbury, and that this was how it had looked in King Arthur's time.

The monks advanced towards the church, every man along his own track of beaten earth and holding in his right hand a wooden cross. I knew that they were chanting, for I could see their lips moving, but I could hear no sound. All about me now was utter silence. Even the baying of the wolves had ceased. It was like being a spectator at a shadow-play, or as if I had suddenly been deprived of my ears.

When they reached the middle of the compound, which they seemed to do at exactly the same moment, the monks began walking in single file around the church. To start with they went slowly and sedately, but they gradually increased their pace until they were running as hard as they could. Then the company began to diminish, disappearing from my view and re-emerging each time one less in number until, finally, no one reappeared at all. I moved towards the church, floating weightlessly across the marshy ground, and as I did so the building grew transparent, allowing me to see through it to the other side where the monks stood in a long, straight line . . .

I was awake again without any sensation of arousal; no start, no snort, only a smooth re-entry into my own world and time. And yet surely there had been some slight noise which had penetrated my consciousness. I turned my head on the pillow and glanced towards the door. Someone had lifted the latch and was slowly, cautiously pushing it open.

Chapter Sixteen

I knew what I should do. I should slip quietly off the bed and stand behind the door, ready to pounce on the intruder. But I was still in a semi-trance-like state and my limbs refused to obey me. Moreover I felt no apprehension, no sense of danger, only an urgent desire to sleep until cock crow and maybe even longer. I was bone-weary, as though my vision had sapped all my strength.

In these circumstances, perhaps it was just as well that my nocturnal visitor was only Cicely.

But as the slim figure in the long linen shift closed the door softly behind her I was jolted into wakefulness, both mind and body suddenly alert and wary. I sat up abruptly, swinging my legs off the bed and planting my feet firmly on the floor. History was repeating itself. In just such a surreptitious manner Lillis had crept into my bed in the middle of the night, which was how I had become a reluctant husband (and so I might still have been had she not died in childbirth). When I married for a second time I was determined that it should be my own choice and not because, yet again, my hand had been forced.

'What are you doing here?' I hissed at her. 'Go back to your room at once!'

Cicely ignored this and perched beside me on the edge of the bed. 'I've told you before,' she said, 'but I don't mind

211

telling you again: I wasn't in love with Peter.'

I noticed that on this occasion she had used the past tense, seeming to have no doubt now that her cousin was dead.

'And I've told *you* before,' I retorted, 'that you're not in love with me either, any more than I am with you. And for both our sakes, keep your voice down! Do you want to be discovered by your aunt?'

'Yes,' she answered brazenly, snuggling into my side. 'Then she'd make you marry me.'

I wriggled several feet nearer the head of the bed. 'If you were my wife I'd beat you every day!'

She moved up close to me again. 'No you wouldn't. You're not that kind of man.'

'Yes I am!'

'No you're not!'

The argument was becoming childish, and I sprang to my feet, almost knocking her sideways.

'Cicely!' I exclaimed in a desperate whisper. 'I don't want to marry you, and that's the truth!'

To my horror, instead of spitting fury at me she began to cry, tears welling up and trickling silently down her cheeks. My first instinct was to turn tail and run, but, with a sigh, I resumed my seat and put one arm around her.

'Don't you even like me a little bit?' she asked pathetically, resting her head on my shoulder.

'Of course I do,' I said. 'I like you very much.'

'But not enough to marry me?'

I stroked her hair. 'My dear, you're not the girl for me, nor am I the man for you. You're better born than I am, for a start. What do you think your father and aunt would say if you announced that you were to wed a Chapman?'

'But you're not an ordinary Chapman,' she insisted. 'The

Duke of Gloucester would find you a place in his household if you asked him. You said he would.' She raised swimming violet eyes. 'Was that a lie?'

'No. It was the truth. But I don't want that sort of life. I hate being confined between four walls. I want to be my own master. And even if you could cozen your father into letting you marry a pedlar, you wouldn't be happy. I'd be off at the very first hint of fine weather, leaving you behind at home. My wife won't have to care about that. I know it's selfish, but I'm not going to change, not while I have my health and strength. Also, I have a little girl. Would you be willing to bring up another woman's child?'

There was a protracted silence while she reviewed the picture I had painted. I could feel the warmth of her body, the swell of her young breasts beneath the thin linen shift, and I was sorely tempted to take her at her word and leave the future to look after itself. But common sense prevailed, for which I thank God every night on my knees, for we should have been an ill-assorted couple. And in order to be worthy of her, I should, in the end, have been coerced into respectability and servitude. Cicely, like Lillis, was not a woman who would have been content to be on her own for long.

After a while she sniffed loudly and lifted her head, wiping her nose with her fingers.

'Perhaps you're right,' she conceded to my great relief, adding tartly, 'I daresay I'll meet a man one day who I *really* want to marry.'

I smiled to myself. She had recovered her spirit and her tears had ceased.

'I'm sure you will,' I told her. 'But you'll need one who can put up with that cursed sharp tongue of yours.'

She laughed tremulously and wiped her nose again, this

time in the sheet. Then she sobered, biting her lip.

'I'm talking as though Peter's dead,' she said. Once more the violet eyes lifted to mine. 'Do you think he is?'

I nodded. 'I think it likely. But until we find him we can't be sure.'

Cicely squared her shoulders. 'Even if he isn't, I shan't wed him now. I don't think Father would make me if he knew I had truly set my heart against the marriage. At least you've done that for me. You've made me see what it is I want – or rather don't want! Aunt Joan will be upset, but I can't help that.'

'I'm glad to have been of some assistance,' I answered gravely, pressing her hand. 'Now, it really is time you returned to your room.'

'Oh, no!' she said, sitting bolt upright. 'I'll not be fobbed off again. I want you to tell me everything you know.' She saw denial written in my face. 'If you don't,' she continued softly, 'I'll scream so loudly that I shall wake the entire household. Then you'll have no choice but to marry me.'

'You're a scheming, unprincipled hussy!' I exclaimed bitterly, and she grinned.

'I know. Most women are. It's the only way we can survive.' She folded her hands in her lap. 'I'm waiting.'

I realized that the strange lethargy which had possessed me had now passed. I was still tired, but it was a natural weariness, engendered by the fatigues of a long, hard day. And even that was beginning to vanish as I decided I had no option but to take Cicely into my confidence.

Her eyes were as round as saucers, her voice hushed in wonder. 'The Holy Grail,' she whispered. 'But . . . but I didn't think it really existed.'

'I'm not sure I do even now,' I admitted, 'but that isn't

the point. The point is that I feel almost certain your cousin thought he might be on its trail.'

'Why?'

'Because he told Maud Jarrold that the parchment was "valuable beyond price". Also, the Grail was reputedly brought to Britain by Joseph of Arimathea and then, if we believe the stories of King Arthur, lost. The Knights of the Round Table spent a lot of time searching for it.'

'What about this oss . . . ossie . . . oh, whatever it was – containing the bones of Saint Patrick?'

'I don't think such a notion would have crossed Peter's mind for an instant. Brother Librarian has a bee buzzing around in his head on the subject of Patrick. He believes he died in Somerset and was buried in or near Glastonbury. It probably reflects an idea of Abbot Selwood's. Abbots get these odd notions. Glastonbury spent years arguing with Canterbury that it had the bones of its former abbot Saint Dunstan, while Canterbury just as vigorously denied that the Archbishop's remains had ever been removed from the cathedral precincts.' I added cynically, 'It's all to do with prestige, pilgrims and money.'

I saw the blank look on my companion's face and returned to the subject in hand. 'No, I'm positive that only one relic would have occurred to Peter as being of importance to the Church here in the year 500 AD. And that's the Grail.'

'Why?' she asked again with the persistence of an obstinate child.

'Because among his folios and quartos and octavos are books by Geoffrey of Monmouth and William of Malmesbury. Peter read a lot. He knew about the Grail. And it was what first occurred to me: that here, in this ancient parchment –' I drew it out from under my pillow where I had placed it for safekeeping – 'is the true story of how it was originally lost.'

Cicely's mouth was set in a mulish line. 'I can't believe it,' she said.

Of course she couldn't. She was a woman, and women deal in practicalities. They have to; who else do we men look to for succour and assistance when things go wrong? It's only my sex who are free to pursue impossible dreams, form secret societies, read and write books. Women are too busy mending, cooking and sweeping. And there are always the children.

'I'm not asking you to believe it,' I sighed. 'As I told you, what's important is what your cousin believed.'

She furrowed her brow. 'You think then that he was looking for the Grail when he disappeared?' I inclined my head and the frown deepened. 'But what about Mark? You haven't mentioned him. He's vanished too, but he didn't know what the parchment contained. No one had translated it for him, unless he also went to see this Blethyn Goode.'

'I feel sure he didn't. Blethyn would have told me. Besides, Mark wouldn't have visited him without being directed there by Father Elwyn.'

'Perhaps he was.'

'No. I only went to the Tor because of information I had gleaned from Brother Hilarion. The path is far too tortuous for Mark to have followed in the few hours between his discovery of this parchment and his going to Beckery. And nobody seems to have seen him after that. His disappearance puts me in an even greater quandary than his brother's. Where did he go, and why, after leaving the island?'

'You don't think Father Boniface was lying, and he did know what the parchment said?'

'Again, no. If he had done he would have told Peter, who would then have had no cause to visit either Father Elwyn or Blethyn Goode. And it would mean that he not only has a knowledge of the ancient Ogham alphabet, but also of the old Welsh tongue. And I think that unlikely, don't you?'

Cicely shrugged despondently. 'In that case, I don't understand it. Nothing makes sense. Peter wasn't dabbling in the Black Arts, so why should he have been snatched the way he was? Abel Fairchild said he vanished into thin air. What could cause that except the hand of the Devil?'

'I'm not sure.' It was my turn to frown. 'A night or two ago we were all talking in the kitchen – you, your aunt, Lydia, me, Rob and John. I think it was after you and I had returned from seeing Father Boniface. Later, during the night, I woke up with the conviction that I had said something of importance during that conversation, but I had no idea what it was. I still haven't. Can you recollect anything which struck you as significant?'

But she could remember nothing, and I suspected that for her, as for me, the days since our arrival in Glastonbury were beginning to run together in one continuous blur, aggravated by the fact that all our talks had a sameness about them, a single topic inevitably dominating our thoughts and utterances. How could I possibly expect her to recall something which I was unable to pinpoint myself?

'It doesn't matter,' I lied. 'It will come back to me.'

Cicely was suddenly yawning and her eyes looked heavy with sleep. She was young and healthy, and neither blighted love nor the strange disappearance of her two cousins could keep her awake for long. I smiled and gave her shoulders another squeeze. 'Go to bed. We'll talk again in the morning. Perhaps by that time inspiration will have struck.'

I had anticipated an argument, but to my surprise she slid obediently to her feet and began to move towards the door. Halfway there, however, she stopped and turned.

'Just one kiss, Roger,' she pleaded, 'and after that, I promise to be good.'

I stood up and gently took her face between my hands. 'Just one then,' I agreed, and pressed my lips full on her soft, warm mouth.

I had been half afraid that it was a trick, but she only pouted.

'That's not much of a kiss,' she protested, adding in her usual outrageous fashion, 'I'm sure even Rob Undershaft or John Longbones could do better than that. I must ask them.'

I unlatched the bedchamber door and propelled her through it. 'What you could do with, my girl,' I whispered in my best elder brother tones, 'is some discipline. It will be a very good thing if you are returned to the care of your father and Duchess Isabel for a little while longer.'

She made a face at me, then crossed the narrow landing to her own room, closing the door softly behind her. I heaved a heartfelt sigh of relief and went back to bed, pausing long enough to undress before clambering between the sheets. And this time, I really did sleep until cock crow.

I awoke not at all refreshed and with a headache nagging at the back of my eyes. For a moment I was unsure of my surroundings, then memory flooded back. I got up and opened the shutters, expecting to see brilliant sunshine, but the sky was overcast. Clouds had gathered during the night. The eastern horizon, above the Tor and a town just stirring into life, showed a long, ominous streak of crimson, heralding the arrival of unsettled weather. 'Red sky at night, shepherd's delight; red in the morning, shepherd's warning,' went the old rhyme, and was, in my experience, usually proved to be right. The storm of yesterday had not been a single summer downpour but the harbinger of more to come. Autumn and winter were indeed on their way, and I longed more than ever to solve this mystery and go home.

I descended the stairs, let myself out of the front door and went round to the pump at the side of the house. Here I stripped and began to wash, shielded from the gaze of people already passing up and down the High Street by the wall of Dorabella's empty stable. The air struck chill and I finished my ablutions as quickly as possible, the contrast reminding me sharply of that morning three days earlier when Mark Gildersleeve and I had bathed here together. That, in its turn, jogged my memory regarding the events of the preceding night, when, leaning from the bedchamber window, I had thought I saw someone moving in the shadows. I recalled how Mark had forbidden me to accompany him when he went to investigate, and also how, the next morning, he had scuffed over the ground in order to erase what he declared to be nothing more than his own footprints. He had explained that he wanted to save the women any anxiety which such marks might have aroused, had they got up and gone to the pump before him. At the time I had considered it a sufficiently unconvincing explanation to be, as is so often the case, true, and in consequence had relegated the incident to the back of my mind.

Now, however, I wondered about it. All at once I felt that I had been reprehensibly foolish in not pursuing the matter. I should have ignored my host's instructions and crept down after him. Had I done so, should I have discovered him talking to someone? And if so, to whom, and what about?

It could, of course, have been a friend, wanting to know why Mark had not been seen of late at one of his usual haunts in the town, one of the brothels which, as I recalled from my novice days – although not, I hasten to add, from any first-hand knowledge – were grouped about Cock Lane . . .

I stood staring before me, lost in thought. Then, having scoured my teeth with my willow bark, I went back through this inconvenient house and crossed the garden to the kitchen, where the tireless Lydia was already boiling water for my daily shave.

'Lyddie,' I said, taking my razor out of my pouch and laying it on the table, 'the night you were ill, the night you went out to the privy and met Mark returning from one of his excursions . . .'

She poured hot water into a wooden bowl. 'What about it?' she asked without looking up.

'You told me – at least I think you told me – that when you first saw Mark he was locking the stable.'

She nodded, pushing the bowl towards me. 'That's right. Why?'

'You're sure of that?'

'Yes. Does it matter?'

'I don't know. I think it might. Rob and John said that Mark visited the local whore-houses, so that must be what he told them – they wouldn't make it up.'

'No, I suppose not.'

'So why would Mark need Dorabella to go only as far as Cock Lane? A man on horseback attracts more attention than one on foot.'

She sat down on the stool opposite mine and propped her elbows on the table. 'That's true,' she admitted. 'I hadn't really thought about it. And practically everybody in the town knows Dorabella. Tying her up outside one of those places would have told everyone who saw her that he was inside.'

'Him . . . or his brother.'

Lydia shook her head decisively. 'No. No one would have thought of Master Peter. He was a pious gentleman. Mark was always the more unruly of the two, especially when they were younger. According to Dame Joan he was jealous of his brother because he said his parents favoured Peter over himself. And the Mistress also says that after the Master died and left the business and his second-best bed to Peter, Mark grew even more disgruntled. He didn't show it, I must admit, but she's his mother and she should know.'

Carefully I began to remove the fine, blond fuzz of hair from my chin and upper lip. 'All the same,' I grunted, 'I find it difficult to believe that even Mark cares so little for his reputation as a respected burgess of this town that he is foolhardy enough to ride Dorabella, and so advertize his presence in the local brothels, when it would make more sense for him to walk.'

'It does seem strange now you mention it.' Lydia screwed up her nose in puzzlement. 'Why are you asking all these questions?'

I dipped my razor in the water again and began scraping the other side of my face. 'I was just wondering . . .'

'What?'

'Oh, nothing. It may not be important.'

Unlike Cicely, Lydia never demanded to be admitted to confidences which might be none of her concern. She kept secrets herself and accepted others' right to do so. Now, she simply got up and began to attend to the breakfast.

This proved to be a meal of long pauses and few words. The two apprentices were content to eat their food in silence, while Cicely, after one swift glance at me from beneath lowered lashes, addressed herself solely to Dame Joan and Lydia. The older woman, however, was pre-occupied with her forthcoming visit to the scrivener, and judging by the soundless opening and closing of her lips, was busy composing her letter to her brother. She roused herself eventually to instruct Rob and John to be off about the business of discovering a carter bound for London, and to inform her the moment that they found one.

No one inquired as to my intended movements until, just as Lydia was in the process of clearing the table, Gilbert Honeyman arrived from his hostelry further down the street. His genial presence was like a breath of fresh air in a musty room and cheered us all considerably. He refused all offers of food and drink, having breakfasted, he said, extremely well off soused herring, broiled venison and medallions of mutton. This being far superior fare to the bacon collops and oat cakes served up by Lydia, I felt very envious of him and immediately my stomach began rumbling with dissatisfaction.

Dame Joan acquainted the Bee Master with her intention of sending for her brother, a plan at once applauded by him as the wisest action she could take, praise which brought the faintest flush of colour to her drawn cheeks. She asked Master Honeyman to go with her to the scrivener's, but was denied his company by Cicely's belligerent claim that she was the most proper person to help compose a missive to William Armstrong.

'He's my father, after all. I know better than Master Honeyman what you should write to him.'

Dame Joan sighed, recognizing that Cicely was in one of her intractable moods and, if not allowed her own way, would be quite capable of making trouble. She was obviously too tired and too depressed to argue, and therefore apologized to Gilbert with a half-smile and a vague flutter of her hands. Master Honeyman acknowledged her dilemma with an understanding nod, directing a disapproving glance at Cicely's departing back, then seized my elbow and piloted me into the garden, leaving Lydia to collect and wash the dirty dishes.

'If that girl were mine,' he began menacingly, 'I'd . . .' But then he laughed and shook his head. 'Who am I to talk? I can't even manage my own Rowena. Now!' He squeezed my arm. 'What have you been up to since I saw you yesterday?'

I regarded him thoughtfully for a moment before asking, 'I wonder if you'd care to accompany *me* instead of Dame Joan?'

'I might,' he answered cautiously. 'Where are you going?'

I grinned. 'I'm paying a visit to all the whore-houses in the town. So what do you say? Will you come with me?'

Chapter Seventeen

There was a moment's pause before Gilbert Honeyman gave a somewhat uncertain laugh.

'I daresay you have a reason, lad, for visiting these places – apart, that is, from the usual one.'

'I do.'

'And will that reason help to find these two young men who are missing? Will it assist Dame Gildersleeve?'

'I'm not sure,' I replied honestly, 'but it might move us one step further on in this inquiry.'

He sucked his teeth for another two or three seconds, then clapped me on the back, a prurient curiosity seeming to have overcome his natural reluctance. 'Very well! I'll come with you, provided that I don't have to enter any of those dens of vice.' He puffed out his chest. 'I'm a respected citizen and I wouldn't want anyone to get the wrong idea about me.'

'I promise that you needn't do more than wait for me outside. Now, if you're willing, we'll be off.'

Cock Lane was a narrow twisting street well away from the main thoroughfares of the town, dark because the overhanging eaves of the houses met almost in the middle. The central drain was piled high with refuse, including the rotting carcass of a sheep, and rats ran openly in and out of doorways. The muckrakers, who had been busy in the High

Street when we quit the shop, had not yet reached this far, and by the look of things were not too punctilious at any time in their duties hereabouts.

Gilbert Honeyman held his nose and picked his way fastidiously through the litter. For my own part I was less cautious, but my boots were stout and had survived worse conditions than those at present prevailing underfoot. I noted that there was only one house where a rail outside provided for the tethering of horses, and I made directly for it. Two girls, wearing striped hoods to indicate their calling, were leaning from the upstairs window, both amply proportioned and in a state of undress. One was quite pretty, but the other had a pronounced squint which marred looks already rendered plainer than necessary by several layers of white lead paste.

'Can I come in?' I called up to them. 'Is the house open yet?'

The girls exchanged glances then burst into raucous laughter. 'You're a bit early, my dear, aren't you?' Squint-eyes giggled. 'Your goodwife have a headache last night, did she?'

I waited for the hilarity subsequent upon this sally to subside before telling them, 'I'd like a word or two with your Madam.'

There was further merriment. 'She doesn't do anything, my old acker,' the prettier one said, using a local term of endearment, 'except take the money.'

Her companion nodded, her smile vanishing. 'Ay, she's good at that, but not so generous when it comes to sharing it out.' She focused her good eye on me, while the other seemed to stare off into space. 'But come in, all the same. Nice-looking fellow like you won't have any difficulty fixing himself up with a partner, early though it might be, and half of us not yet awake.'

I didn't argue with them but went inside, leaving an uncomfortable Gilbert Honeyman hovering in the shadows, trying to render himself as inconspicuous as possible.

He breathed a huge sigh of relief when I reappeared after only a couple of minutes. 'Can we go now?'

'Not yet, but I promise to be as swift as I can.'

By the time I had called at every house in the alley, however, Gilbert had withdrawn from the vicinity of Cock Lane and awaited me in a neighbouring street. Here he had located another tavern which he deemed worthy of his attention, after a conversation with the landlord concerning the method of brewing and the contents of the latter's various ales.

'Come in! Come in!' In the dark interior, he guided me to a table where two pots of ale were already set out – 'and paid for,' Gilbert assured me – indicating the settle along-side it. 'Sit down, lad, and drink up.'

He raised his beaker and gave me the old Saxon form of cheer, still often heard in western parts: '*Was heil!*'

'*Drink heil!*' I responded, but absently, my mind on other things.

'Tell me then!' he ordered once he had quenched his initial thirst. 'Did you find out what you were hoping to, or have you been wasting your time and mine?'

'No,' I answered, setting my beaker down on the table and wiping my mouth with the back of my hand. 'I made a discovery.'

'Go on!' he urged, as I hesitated. 'Explain to me why were you so anxious to visit the town brothels.'

I had told him most of the facts relating to Mark and Peter Gildersleeve the previous day, but, because I had then thought it unnecessary, I had mentioned nothing of Lydia's encounter with Mark on the night she was taken ill, nor of Rob and John's explanation of these nocturnal expeditions. I was therefore obliged to do so now.

Gilbert Honeyman was much shocked. 'That poor creature!' he exclaimed, referring to Dame Joan. He shook his head despondently. 'But it only goes to show that even the best of women can breed a wayward son.'

'Undoubtedly,' I agreed. 'But whatever Mark Gildersleeve has been up to, it isn't whoring. Not one of the madams in Cock Lane could recollect ever seeing him, nor entertaining him, in her establishment. And he's a familiar enough face in the town to be recognized by all of them.'

Gilbert frowned. 'So what does that mean?'

'It means I was right when I thought it unlikely that Mark would ride his horse, especially one so well known as Dorabella, on such an errand. First of all, it would let every passer-by know of his presence, and secondly, the animal could be stolen under cover of darkness; both of which reasons add up to taking an unnecessary risk when there was a safer alternative.'

Gilbert looked relieved. 'Then you'll be able to inform Dame Joan that her fears regarding her younger son's conduct are unfounded. That at least must be of some comfort to her.'

'Must it?' I regarded him straitly. 'Why, if it wasn't true, did Mark tell the two apprentices that he had been whoring when he hadn't? And where in fact *was* he during those nights when he was absent from home?'

'Ah!' Gilbert Honeyman grimaced. 'I'm growing old. My wits aren't as sharp as they used to be.' He cocked an eyebrow. 'So? What's your explanation?'

'I haven't one yet,' I answered. 'I wish I did. It might throw some light on his and his brother's disappearance.'

Gilbert finished his ale and bade me drink up. 'We'll have one more before we go. I find there's nothing better than good ale for clearing the mind.'

I was extremely dubious about this pronouncement, my experience being that the better the ale the more muddied my thoughts were likely to become. And one thing I could be sure of, potent liquor always loosened my tongue. Now, after only two or three sips from my second cup, I found myself telling Gilbert where I had gone and what I had done yesterday evening, after he and I had parted company at the abbey gate. When I had finished, I turned to see him regarding me with much the same expression in his eyes that I had noted in Cicely's.

'Look here, lad,' he said at last, patting my arm in an avuncular fashion, 'I know we're in Avalon and that King Arthur and Queen Guinevere lie buried in the abbey, but to tell you the truth I've never more than half believed those stories myself. And as for this business of Joseph of Arimathea and the Holy Grail, well . . . !' He broke off with an expressive shrug of his shoulders.

I answered defensively. 'But there's no proof that Joseph *didn't* come to Britain after the Crucifixion, any more than there's proof that he *did*. Perhaps we ought to respect ingrained, age-old beliefs that are part of the very air and soil of a region, legends and stories that go back into the mists of time. They had their origins somewhere, in some event or other . . .' I drank the dregs of my ale. 'Nevertheless, in this case I'm not saying that I necessarily believe the story of the Grail, or that it's the relic referred to in the account of its concealment by Brother Begninus. But I feel sure it's what Peter Gildersleeve thought.'

'Why?' Gilbert Honeyman was sceptical.

I repeated the reasons I had given to Cicely the previous

night. They sounded feeble enough now as then, but I was still convinced that I was right.

Gilbert pursed his lips. 'I'm not much of a one for reading,' he said, 'and I can't make head nor tail of stories and yarns and suchlike. I know enough to keep my accounts in good order and to be sure that customers aren't cheating me, but that's about it. But I had my girl, my Rowena, taught her letters by the nuns at Shaftesbury. There are some who say educating girls is a waste of time, but I don't hold with that. She's my only chick and she'll need all her wits about her when I die. However, that's beside the point – which is that she knows all these tales of King Arthur and his knights, and now and again, of a winter's evening, she's related bits of them to me. And those knights weren't searching around Glastonbury for the Holy Grail – leastways, not as I remember it. They went here, there and everywhere, up and down the country, but mostly overseas. And what adventures they had! Enchanted halls and castles! Angels, magicians, fairies! Wonderful things were involved. People who appeared and disappeared . . .' His voice faded to an embarrassed silence as he realized what he had just said, then he coughed and went on hurriedly, 'Yes, well . . . there you are. You see what I mean.'

'Of course I do! But don't *you* see that those are the legends?' I urged excitedly. 'As I said just now, most such tales are probably rooted in a grain of truth. With the passage of centuries they become distorted as layer upon layer of romantic invention is added bit by bit. But long ago, in the dim and distant past, something actually happened that gave birth to the original story. Have you never, as a boy, rolled a snowball down a hill and watched it getting bigger and bigger before it reached the bottom? Legends must grow like that.'

The Bee Master peered into his beaker, and finding it empty called the pot-boy. I hastily declined his offer of a third cup of ale, and was treated to a diatribe on the inability of modern youth to hold its drink. This however was mercifully brief, Gilbert being anxious to get back to the subject under discussion.

'So, what you're saying,' he continued, as soon as his beaker had been replenished, 'is that the legend of Arthur's knights looking for the Holy Grail is based on the fact that this Brother Begninus hid some relic or other because the pagan Saxons were approaching, and afterwards people had to try to find it again?'

I reflected that there was nothing wrong with Gilbert's understanding, and that he was quicker on the uptake than many a younger person of my acquaintance.

'Exactly!' I said. 'Perhaps Brother Percival and Brother Geraldus, the two monks mentioned by Begninus as departing the following day for Ireland, never returned. Perhaps Brother Begninus himself, and the Abbot and the other inmates of the church at Ynys Witrin, were all killed by a Saxon raiding party, or died naturally, one by one, of old age and disease. If the latter, maybe the Abbot decided that it would be wiser to leave the "great relic" where it was, rather than bring it back to the church. Even though 500 AD was the year of the battle at Mount Badon, when Arthur is said to have inflicted a heavy defeat on the Saxons somewhere away to the east, there were still other bands of invaders coming ashore along the south coast and gradually making their way inland.'

'So when the monks died, the secret of the relic's hiding place died with them?'

'Yes. But the relic was famous enough for other people to have heard of it, and to make them anxious to find it again. Both before and after the completion of the Saxon conquest it was searched for, probably over a period of many years. And gradually the hunt became a part of the stories about King Arthur and his Knights of the Round Table. The quest for the Holy Grail.'

Gilbert swallowed another draught of ale. 'That's all very well,' he demurred, 'but surely no one in their right mind could imagine that it is still possible to find it today, after almost a thousand years!'

It was the same argument advanced by Blethyn Goode and Brother Hilarion, and still as unanswerable as when they had posed the question.

I could only give the same response. 'Peter Gildersleeve, by my reasoning, thought it possible, and we must therefore try to think as he did.'

The Bee Master grunted doubtfully. 'What was the wording of this precious parchment of yours? Where did this Brother Begninus say that he'd hidden the relic?'

I quoted, for I knew the words now by heart: ' "Amongst the hills, in the hollow places of the earth, on the altar by Charon's stream." '

'Well, there you are then! A chapel, or a shrine maybe ... But no building of that age could possibly be standing today. The idea defies all reason. And so Master Gildersleeve must have known. He doesn't sound a fool by anything I've heard tell of him. No, I think you've been sitting on a mare's nest, lad, and you've hatched out a three-legged donkey.' He sighed. 'But it doesn't alter the fact that both that poor woman's sons have disappeared and no one is any the wiser as to where they've gone or why. But what anyone can do about it, I don't know. You've done your best, Roger, and you can't do more. You'll have to forget it. Even if, by some wild stretch of the imagination, you're

right about the way Peter Gildersleeve's mind was working
– but I think it's unlikely – you can only follow his logic so
far. And how did he vanish so completely within the span
of just a few moments?'

The ale-house was filling up, the clamour of voices
growing greater by the minute. I felt defeated, useless, and
leant back against the settle, closing my eyes. Immediately
I was caught up once more in my strange half-dream, half-
vision, watching the monks process, each man along his
track of beaten earth, until they reached the thatched,
circular building in the middle of the enclosure. Again, I
could see their lips moving, but heard no sound: utter
silence engulfed me. As on the previous night, they began
walking in single file around the church, slowly at first,
then increasing their pace until they were running. Now
they were diminishing in numbers, one less appearing after
each encirclement. Finally, no one re-emerged at all. I
floated weightlessly towards the central building with its
conical roof and, as before, it became transparent. Through
its walls, I could see the monks standing in a row on the
other side . . .

'Are you all right, lad?' Gibert Honeyman's voice was
taut with alarm. 'You're looking very pale. You're not ill,
are you?'

I passed a hand across my forehead. I was sweating and
filled with that same, strange lassitude that had afflicted
me last night. The noise all round me seemed deafening,
and I noticed that people were beginning to stare at me.
With a prodigious effort, I pulled myself together.

'No. No, I'm just a little drunk, that's all,' I lied. 'This
ale must be more powerful than I thought.'

'Ay, it's potent stuff all right. Nevertheless, I think you'd
better let me accompany you back to Dame Gildersleeve's

and ask her to dose you with one of those concoctions women always seem to have in the medicine press. And then I'd think seriously if I were you about my advice to go home and leave others to solve this mystery. If there *is* a solution, that is. You're suffering from a touch of the sun if you want my opinion. It's been a hot enough summer, goodness knows, to affect the strongest constitution. And then all this thinking and teasing of your brain – it's no good for anyone.'

I realized that it was pointless to argue with him. I should never convince Gibert that I was perfectly hale and hearty and in my right mind. To tell the truth, I knew a moment's doubt on the subject myself. I had never before had a dream without being asleep, and it worried me, until my companion put me a little more at ease on that score.

'You're tired,' he went on. 'Just now you nodded off for a second. You need to get some rest.'

'Perhaps you're right,' I answered.

All the same, I knew that I should get no rest until I had worked out what it was that my dream was trying to tell me.

Gilbert Honeyman accompanied me as far as the shop, but declined to enter. 'Give my respects to Dame Gildersleeve, lad, and say that I shall call to make my farewells before I leave for home on Monday.' He lowered his voice to a confidential whisper. 'Why don't you ride with me, as we're going in the same direction? Get out, before this sorry business really turns your brain.'

I hesitated. His offer seemed suddenly very tempting. But then I knew with absolute certainty that I must not accept it. God had sent me here, as He had sent me elsewhere in the past, to uncover evil. If I failed to do so, I failed Him as well as myself – and I had already done that once in my life. I could not do it again.

I embraced Gilbert. 'You're a good man,' I said, 'but I must see this through to the end.' I braced my shoulders. 'And who knows? With God's guidance I may have solved this mystery by Monday. I might, after all, be free to ride with you.'

I could see that he thought it unlikely, but he clapped me on the back and answered with a false heartiness, 'Ay, so you might at that, lad! I'll pray that it's so. Now, I must go and take a look at that horse of mine and make sure he's being properly treated.'

Gilbert administered me a second boisterous clout before disappearing into the crowds which thronged the High Street on this Saturday morning. It was warm and airless, with little sign of the sun breaking through the clouds which continued to pile up in the east, turning Saint Michael's chapel and its enclave on top of the Tor into nothing more than a two-dimensional black shape against a grey background. The streak of red which I had noticed earlier in the sky had correctly presaged a stormy day.

As I turned to enter the Gildersleeves' shop I felt a sudden desire to speak to Brother Hilarion again, so I crossed the street and presented myself once more at the porter's lodge. It was a different lay Brother this time, and he informed me that my old friend had not long ago conducted a party of pilgrims into the abbey church, where I should doubtless still find him. I thanked the man and joined the tail end of yet another band of pilgrims who had entered just ahead of me, processing beneath the north porch and into the nave.

Some of the pilgrims turned to their right, down the Galilee steps to the Lady Chapel, but I followed those who moved to the left, in the direction of the choir. A few stopped in the north transept to pray in the chapel dedicated to Saint Thomas à Becket, but most continued towards the tomb which reputedly housed the remains of King Arthur and Queen Guinevere. It was, after all, this which they had travelled many hard and weary miles to see. It was not a holy relic, and no one bowed the knee in worship, but they stared in awe and wonderment at the great shrine of black marble, a cross guarded by two carved lions at its head, and an image of the king, flanked by two more carved lions, at its foot.

I perused the inscriptions slowly and with difficulty, translating my rusty Latin into English: *Here lies Arthur, the flower of Kings, the kingdom's glory. His morals and virtues commend him with everlasting praise.* And also: *Arthur's fortunate wife lies buried here, loved by Heaven for her virtues.* For those pilgrims unable to do it for themselves, Brother Hilarion was reading aloud, while a few of them stooped to gain a better view of the carvings.

One, a goodwife, straightened up with a piercing shriek.

'A mouse! There! *There!* At the base of the tomb.'

Most of the women scuttled clear while Brother Hilarion tiptoed cautiously around the shrine, looking for the offending animal.

'I think you're mistaken, my child,' he said at last. 'I can't see anything.'

A man who was standing near gave me a nudge and pointed in the direction of the choir, where a field mouse was just whisking out of sight behind a pillar. I nodded and grinned. My neighbour had seen, as I had done, exactly what had happened. Neither of us said anything, however, and the pilgrims proceeded on their way to offer up prayers before the high altar. But I stayed where I was, staring unseeingly at the shrine and thinking about the little creature . . .

And suddenly my dream became clear to me. I knew what it was trying to tell me, and what it was that I had been too dense to understand all along. I made for the north door without more ado, and within five minutes was entering the Gildersleeves' shop.

Cicely and Dame Joan had returned by this time from the scrivener's house, and the former met me in the passageway.

'Where have you been?' she demanded.

'I've been visiting whore-houses in Cock Lane with Master Honeyman,' I answered. Ignoring her gasp of astonishment and outrage, I gripped her wrist. 'Where's your aunt?' I demanded.

'In the shop. Rob's found a carter going all the way to London, and she's arranging for him to carry her letter to my father. What do you mean, you and Master Honeyman have been visiting—'

'Never mind that for now,' I cut in impatiently. 'I'll explain later.' I shook her arm. 'I think I've discovered how your cousin Peter disappeared!'

Chapter Eighteen

Cicely's mouth fell open and she stared at me for several seconds in uncomprehending silence, then she gasped. 'You know what's happened to Peter?'

'I think,' I corrected her, 'that I know why Abel Fairchild was deceived into thinking your cousin had vanished. What I don't know is where Peter went after Abel ran away.'

'You mean Peter wasn't seized by Old Scratch?'

'I've always thought that unlikely, haven't you? People abducted by the Devil are always people no one has ever met. Such reports are always hearsay, recounted by the friend of a friend of their cousin's brother-in-law's mother's niece.' I added soberly, 'But I'm not holding out any hope that Peter is still alive.'

Cicely giggled nervously, then shivered, her thoughts turning to Dame Joan. 'We must tell my aunt at once what you've just told me.' She turned, and would have made her way into the shop had I not caught her by the arm.

'Not yet. I must test my theory first. Come outside with me to the stable.'

She looked puzzled, but did as I asked. The stable, as I have already described, stood between the Gildersleeves' shop and the neighbouring house, and it was possible to walk freely all round it. It was still empty, Dorabella

239

remaining for the present in Northload Street, cared for by Edgar Shapwick.

'Well?' Cicely was puzzled.

'I want you to pretend,' I said, 'that the stable is the shepherd's hut and that you are Abel Fairchild. I shall play the part of your cousin.' As I spoke, I moved towards the building. 'Abel was coming down from the upper slopes of Mendip with his flock when he spied Peter and waved to him. Almost immediately after that, because of the lie of the land, Peter disappeared from his view. So I want you to shut your eyes for the same length of time, and promise that you won't cheat by peeping.'

'All right,' Cicely agreed reluctantly. 'I give you my word. But what do I do then?'

'You behave exactly as Abel Fairchild did.'

'And how was that? I've forgotten.'

'Then listen carefully.' I was pleased to note that I had her attention. 'First of all, you look in the "hut" to see if I'm there. When you're satisfied that I'm not, walk right round the outside of the building, and then walk back again. Repeat this two or three times, remembering that Abel was growing ever more frightened and cautious with each second that passed, and in all probability walking slower and slower. Now, do you think you can do that? Can put yourself into Abel Fairchild's shoes?'

'Of course I can!' was the lofty response. 'I shall pretend I'm just a silly child who's convinced himself that something dreadful has happened to Peter.'

'Isn't that what we all thought?' I asked, and she had the grace to blush. 'Very well,' I continued, 'let's begin. Wave to me and then close your eyes. No looking, mind! You've promised!'

Cicely did as I bade her, and after a minute or two, I

heard the stable door creak open as she went inside. There were rustling noises from within as she made a pretence of searching among the straw, then a second creak told me that she had come out again. She walked slowly, clockwise, around the stable, before turning and going withershins; but by the time she had repeated this manoeuvre several times more she had no need to simulate Abel's increasing alarm. She was herself growing frightened.

'Roger! Roger, where are you?' When I did not answer, she ran out from behind the stable and stood facing the door. 'Roger! Stop it! This has gone far enough!' Her voice was trembling.

Deliberately, I waited a few more seconds before strolling into view.

'Here I am, as you can see, alive and well.'

The violet eyes widened. 'Where have you been?'

'Only two or three steps either behind or in front of you all the while.' I smiled at her confusion. 'There's really precious little mystery about it. We have to assume that your cousin was on Pennard land not on business, but for some purpose of his own, hoping against hope that he wouldn't be seen by any member of the Pennard household. He may even have known, by some means or another, that Anthony and his sons had gone to Priddy that afternoon. But unluckily for him, he was spotted by Abel Fairchild. He returned the boy's wave, but as soon as Abel was out of sight, in the hollow, Peter hid behind the hut, trusting that when the boy found him gone, he would simply proceed on his way. After all, why should he bother to search for your cousin when he had his sheep and their welfare to attend to?

'But your cousin reckoned without Abel's natural curiosity and his sense of duty. Abel wanted to discover what Peter was doing, roaming around so far from the farmhouse on his own, so he started to look for him. First he searched inside the hut, even peering round the door, in order to make certain that his quarry wasn't hiding behind it, then he began walking around the outside. After a while, Abel must have begun to grow uneasy because he couldn't understand how Peter could possibly have vanished in so short a time, and he was probably moving cautiously enough for your cousin to keep several steps either ahead of or behind him. As Abel turned one corner of the hut, Peter disappeared around the next, as I was doing just now.'

'But I turned and went in the opposite direction as well,' Cicely objected. 'You told me to. So why didn't we meet? Why didn't Peter and Abel Fairchild bump into one another?'

'Because it's possible to peep very quickly around each corner to see what the other person is doing. If your quarry moves with sufficient speed to begin with, he is behind the hunter, watching his back. But when the hunter shows signs of retracing his steps, the quarry does the same, quickening his pace until he is again following the person who is looking for him. Do you understand what I'm saying?' Cicely nodded solemnly. 'In my case, of course, there was no danger of our meeting because I knew in advance what you were going to do, that as soon as you had circled the stable once you would turn and go withershins, as I had instructed. Had your cousin and Abel come face to face, however, Peter could easily have claimed to be playing a joke on the lad. He would then have offered some excuse for his presence so far from the house, mounted Dorabella and ridden away, postponing whatever it was he had gone there to do until another day.'

Cicely's eyes narrowed as she thought about what I had

said. 'You mean Peter didn't disappear at all?' she asked at last. 'At least, not just then. And if anyone had been watching from a distance, he would merely have seen two people stalking each other round and round the hut?'

I nodded and she started to laugh, a little wildly. 'But why didn't one of us think of that before? It's such a simple explanation.'

I grimaced. 'When it's been pointed out to you, yes. But the answer didn't fully occur to me until half an hour ago, in the abbey, when one of the pilgrims swore she'd seen a mouse by King Arthur's tomb. The Brother who was with her went all round the shrine but could find no sign of it, and swore that the woman had been mistaken. But my neighbour and I had seen the animal scuttling around just ahead of his pursuer, until he finally broke away and vanished behind a pillar.' I made no mention of my half-dream, half-vision, but went on, 'I think that at the back of my mind I must have worked out the answer already. I knew that something I'd said a night or so ago, at supper, should have alerted me to the truth, but I couldn't remember exactly what that something was.'

'So you mentioned before. And have you remembered it now?'

'As far as I can recall, your aunt asked me if there was any other means of concealment near at hand, in the hollow. And I answered no, not apart from the hut, and that Master Peter was not inside it.'

'So?'

'So, I should have realized that if he was not *inside*, he had to be *outside*. And if there was no time for him to make good his escape without being seen by Abel, then he still had to be where the lad had first spotted him.'

'Unless he had been snatched by the Devil.'

I smiled down at her. 'I thought we'd agreed that that was most unlikely.'

She eyed me askance, uncertain whether or not I was speaking heresy. A denial of the Devil might logically mean a denial of God, although Cicely perhaps would not think of it quite like that.

I hastened to reassure her. 'It's just common sense,' I said, adding, 'Our Saviour had a lot of common sense.'

'Did He?' she queried doubtfully, and again regarded me uneasily, still not certain that it was permissible to speak of the Lord in such terms.

I smiled and held out my hand. 'Let's go to dinner,' I said. 'It must be well past ten o'clock, and Lydia will grumble if we're late.'

At this moment Dame Joan came out of the shop with Rob Undershaft and a swarthy-looking man with a weather-beaten face who was clutching a letter in one hand and several coins in the other, obviously the carter bound for London. The Dame was still issuing a number of confused instructions, but the man cut short her meanderings.

'I shan't have any difficulty in discovering where the Duke of Clarence is lodging, Mistress, don't you trouble your head about that. And if he and his household have already left the city, I'll make certain someone gets your letter and knows that it's to be passed on urgently to your brother, Sergeant Armstrong.'

He nodded perfunctorily at Cicely and me before wishing Dame Joan farewell and disappearing into the hurly-burly of the High Street.

My hostess twisted her hands together. 'He didn't want to take it, you know,' she whispered. 'He didn't want anything to do with me, in case he might be jeopardizing his immortal soul. It wasn't until Rob here –' she summoned up a watery smile for the apprentice – 'reminded him that we had put plenty of work his way in the past that he agreed, but then only with the greatest reluctance.' She wrung her hands again. 'We are becoming outcasts in this town.'

Cicely linked one of her arms through her aunt's. 'Come and have dinner. Lyddie had it ready ages ago. Roger and I have something to tell you.'

'You mean . . . you mean there isn't anything strange about what happened to Peter?'

In spite of her immense relief, Dame Joan sounded almost as if she had been cheated, an emotion reflected on the faces of Lydia and the two apprentices. They were all finding it difficult to accept my explanation.

'It's the fault of that stupid boy,' Lydia exclaimed wrathfully, 'frightening us with his talk of the Devil!'

'I don't think that's being fair to Abel Fairchild,' I reproved her gently. 'After all, Peter *has* disappeared. This solution resolves only a part of the mystery: how he escaped Abel's vigilance before going off about his own concerns.'

'Ay, that's true enough,' John Longbones said thickly through a mouthful of goat's milk cheese. 'What was Master doing over at Pennard's, anyway? He said nothing to us about needing more skins, and by my reckoning we had plenty in store.'

Dame Joan nodded her agreement. 'And if it was on business,' she added, repeating what had been said before, 'why didn't he go to the house or the sheds?'

I caught Cicely's eye across the table and almost imperceptibly shook my head. I was not yet sure myself that Peter's foray on to the Pennards' land necessarily had anything to do with his quest (although I found it hard to believe otherwise; I suppose I was tired of the incredulity with which my theory was constantly greeted), nor did I want Rob Undershaft and John Longbones spreading the story all over town. To my relief – and, I have to admit, somewhat to my surprise – Cicely remained silent.

Lydia said, 'There's Master Mark as well. He's vanished too. You seem to have forgotten him.'

'How can you suggest such a thing, Lyddie?' Dame Joan reproached her. She began to cry again. 'When my brother comes, he'll know what to do.'

I felt my hostess was being over-sanguine. Furthermore, it could be many weeks before William Armstrong reached her, depending upon whether or not my lord of Clarence had moved on before the carter arrived in the capital. Moreover, Dame Joan was right: an uneasy atmosphere had permeated the town for several days now whenever she or her niece had appeared in public, and I was sure that the continued calm was only a result of the influence exerted by such friends as Edgar Shapwick. This fear proved to be well-founded when, shortly after dinner, a dead cat, with a halter tied about its neck, was found lying outside the front door. Lydia's scream brought us all running to see what had caused it, and one look at the gruesome discovery was enough to send Dame Joan into strong hysterics.

'I knew it! I knew it!' was all she could utter coherently between sobs which racked her from head to foot.

The practical Lydia, although badly shaken, was more concerned for her employer than for herself, and insisted that Dame Joan drank an infusion of herbs in order to calm her overstretched nerves, followed by a draught of lettuce juice in order to make her sleep. Consequently it was more than an hour later, when the household was at last quiet and its mistress laid down upon her bed, that I was able to take myself off to the garden and sit on the bench beneath the medlar tree, where I could think undisturbed.

But I had barely managed to get even the most trivial of my thoughts in order when I looked up to see Cicely treading purposefully towards me across the grass. I sighed audibly as she sat down beside me.

She ignored this mark of disapproval. 'You haven't told me yet,' she said, in the determined tone of voice I was beginning to dread, 'what you and Master Honeyman were up to, visiting the whore-houses in Cock Lane earlier this morning.'

My hope that she had forgotten this unguarded remark was dashed. But there was no good reason why she should be kept in ignorance concerning Mark's nocturnal activities, so I felt obliged to tell her what I had discovered.

She was, of course, as mystified as I was. 'But if he didn't go whoring, what *did* he do?' she demanded.

'I don't know.'

'You don't know much, do you?' she snapped.

We were growing extremely edgy with one another; the discovery of the dead cat had shaken us all more than we cared to admit.

'No!' I snapped back. 'And I don't know what significance this has, either.' I opened my pouch and drew out the coil of brown homespun thread which Edgar Shapwick's stable-boy had given me.

Cicely took it from me gingerly. 'Where did it come from?' she asked.

'It was snarled up in Dorabella's mane when she was found wandering yesterday morning. She also had bits of straw in her coat, as well as flecks of something sticky.'

Cicely had unwound the coarse woollen thread and was pulling it through her fingers in an effort to straighten it further. She frowned. 'There's something sticky on this as

247

well.' She examined the strip more closely. 'Yes, look!' she said. 'There! In the middle. You can probably feel it better than you can see it.'

She was right. When she handed the thread back to me I was just able to make out, halfway along its length, a speck of some black foreign matter which undoubtedly felt glutinous to the touch. I raised it to my nose and sniffed, but it was too small an amount to have retained any smell.

'Well?' Cicely asked impatiently. 'What do you think it is?'

When I shook my head, she jumped up from her seat, holding out an imperious hand for me to accompany her. 'We'll ask the others,' she said, 'and see if they have any ideas.'

I followed her meekly, first to the kitchen, where Lydia was boiling some bones in a pot over the fire, the preliminary step to making a nourishing broth for her mistress's supper.

But she could offer no solution. 'Take that nasty bit of stuff away,' she ordered crossly, 'before you drop it in the water.'

We then repaired to the workshop, where the two apprentices were scraping skins in a desultory manner, more to keep themselves occupied than from a belief that the work was of any importance. They were glad of a diversion, and both scrutinized the thread curiously as they listened to my story.

'Found in Dorabella's mane, eh?' said Rob thoughtfully. 'I'd say it's a piece of homespun, unravelled from somebody's clothing.'

'Well, of course it is!' Cicely raised her eyes to the ceiling in a mute appeal for patience. 'But what's that sticky blob in the middle of it?'

Rob shrugged his shoulders. 'How should I know? I can barely see it.'

'Wait a minute.' John Longbones took the thread from his friend, carrying it over to the window and holding it up to the light. This was poor, the heaviness of the day still not having lifted, even though the hour was approaching noon. Then he rubbed the yarn between fingers and thumb, testing the consistency of that little black speck. After a moment or two, he said, 'I think it's tar.'

'Tar?' Cicely repeated vaguely, while Rob and I looked equally mystified. We were many miles from the sea and the nearest port.

John nodded. 'Stockholm tar.'

'But that's used in the building and repairing of ships.' I had lived in Bristol long enough by now to have some knowledge of seafaring matters.

'It's also used on sheep,' John Longbones insisted. 'One of my mother's brothers keeps a flock near Wedmore. He always carries a little box of it around with him to treat fly-blow and maggots and cuts and grazes.'

'I thought they used broom water for that sort of thing,' I argued, childhood memories of watching local shepherds beginning to stir.

John gave me a look which showed plainly that he regarded me, however mistakenly, as a townsman who knew nothing of country ways. 'Only the poorest herdsmen use broom water nowadays,' he informed me pityingly. 'It's not nearly so effective. Haven't you heard the saying, "It's a pity to lose a good sheep for a ha'p'orth of Stockholm tar"?'

I had to admit that I hadn't, but I was far too excited to worry about John Longbones's poor opinion of me. Peter Gildersleeve had been on Pennard land when he disappeared, and the Pennards owned sheep. Now it seemed that

Mark too might recently have been on Pennard land, and he had also vanished. Yet why would he have chosen to visit Anthony and his sons when he knew that I had done the selfsame thing that very morning? Why did he not return home from Beckery to hear first what I had to say? But if he had indeed gone, what could have befallen him? For what possible reason would the Pennards wish to harm either him or his brother?

I turned to see Cicely's eyes blazing with an excitement equal to my own, which she was unsuccessfully trying to conceal in front of Rob and John. Fortunately, neither apprentice was very perceptive and, with a casual remark about us still being none the wiser regarding her cousins' fate, she was able to drag me outside once more without arousing their suspicions.

'Well?' she breathed as soon as we were out of earshot. 'What do you think? Has this mystery something to do with the Pennards?'

We sat down again on the bench surrounding the medlar tree while, for the hundredth time, I tried to put my thoughts in order. 'Anthony Pennard and his sons certainly wear brown homespun,' I conceded. 'And a man might well wipe his hands clean on his tunic or hose after rubbing tar on a sheep. A thread pulled loose from a rent in the cloth or from an unravelling hem could carry with it a speck of that tar. But we mustn't forget that there are other shepherds and other flocks in this region from whom your cousins may have bought fleeces.'

My companion was rightly scornful of this argument. 'Peter was visiting the Pennards when last seen. And if Mark wanted to find out more about his disappearance, he wouldn't have gone riding off to see anyone else, now would he?'

'No,' I agreed, suitably chastened.

'Then it's obvious that the Pennards' land is where we must begin the search for them both.'

'Not "we",' I corrected sternly. 'I must certainly confront the family again in the light of what we now know – or think we know – but you will stay here with Dame Joan. It's where you're most needed, and you would only be a handicap to me if there should prove to be danger. I don't know why the Pennards should wish any harm to your cousins, and can think of no good reason, but I can't, and won't, take the risk of letting you go with me. You understand that?'

'Yes,' she answered submissively, which surprised me a little, until I realized that she had not previously considered the possibility of danger.

'Good,' I said, and then went on, 'At least now I think I know why Peter was there, what he was looking for, and how he evaded Abel Fairchild's curiosity. But I still have no idea where he went after Abel returned to the house to raise the alarm. Why was he in that particular spot? It's so bare and desolate.'

Cicely nodded, and then repeated something she had said to me once before. 'I suppose that's why it's called the Sticks.'

Chapter Nineteen

I turned my head and stared at her unblinkingly for several seconds.

'What is it?' Cicely asked nervously. 'What have I said? You look so strange.'

I quoted once again: ' "Amongst the hills, in the hollow places of the earth, on the altar by Charon's stream." Perhaps,' I added, 'that stretch of ground is not called the Sticks, but the Styx.'

It was my companion's turn to stare. 'Whatever are you talking about?' she demanded peevishly. 'You're not making sense.'

'How did that particular parcel of land get its name?' I asked. 'Do you know?'

She thought for a moment, then shook her head. 'My father called it that,' she said at last. 'Whenever we visited my aunt and uncle in the past, we always travelled the last stage of our journey along the old Roman road, which as you know cuts across the Pennards' holding. The Pennards don't like it but the land belongs to the Church, and all the Bishops of Bath and Wells, including Bishop Stillington, have insisted that the route remains open to pilgrims and other wayfarers. Not many people use it, though, because it's so lonely; they prefer the busier highway which leads through the city, even though it takes them longer if they're going further afield.' She paused, frowning, confused by this digression. 'Where was I? Oh, yes! My father! He'd say the same thing every time we reached the lower slopes of Mendip: "Now we're crossing the Sticks."'

'You never thought to ask him how it got its name?'

Cicely grimaced. 'No, why should I? It's always been called so as long as anyone can remember. In any case, I don't think he knows or he'd have told me.'

'No, I don't suppose he does,' I sighed.

Probably no one knew. It was just a name which had been passed on from generation to generation down the centuries, until its original meaning had been lost. But had it once, in the dim and distant past, been called the Styx, after that river of ancient mythology? The Greeks had believed that their souls must traverse the Styx before they could reach the Underworld, and they would be rowed across by the boatman, Charon.

'What does it all mean?' Cicely wanted to know. 'And why are you asking me all these questions?'

She listened patiently, and with a brow furrowed in concentration, while I explained things to her. 'But there's no river there,' she objected when I had finished. 'It's nothing but pasture.'

'But there might have been water there once,' I insisted. 'A thousand years and more ago, there could have been a river known for some reason as the Styx.'

Charon's stream! But where had it come from? And where was its source? I thought suddenly of the great gorge away to the north-west, near Cheddar. I had never seen it, as I had told Anthony Pennard, but I had heard it described by many pilgrims who visited the abbey in the days when I was a novice. And I recalled one old man, more learned than many of his fellows, and more patient with the

questions of a green youth hungry for any scraps of knowledge which came his way, who had told me that this ravine
between the towering heights on either side had probably,
long, long ago, been the bed of a river which, century after
century, had carved a course for itself through the Mendip
Hills.

Hard upon the heels of this thought came a recollection
of the lie of the land close to the shepherd's hut, the narrow
valley which sloped gently downhill from the sheer cliff-
face. I remembered too that there was a well-worn track
which curled around the bluff, and which ended in a fall of
matted foliage, trailing ivies and ferns that grew in a fissure
of the rock higher up. Had that little valley also been a
river-bed a thousand years ago? But if so, where had the
stream come from? Had it trickled down from the slopes
above? Unlikely, because in that case it would surely have
worn away the rocks in its path, just as the constant flow of
water had done in the great gorge. And yet the only other
place it could have come from was out of the cliff-face
itself, trickling down through the porous limestone from
the sink-holes on top of the Mendip Hills.

A cave! Of course! Why hadn't I thought of that sooner?
I recalled one of the brothers at the abbey once telling me
that caves are nothing more than the beds of dried-up
underground rivers, after the water has been diverted into
another channel.

Underground river . . . Charon's stream . . .

I turned again to Cicely, who was regarding me
anxiously, unable to follow my racing thoughts. 'Let's go
and see Rob and John again,' I said, getting to my feet.

The two apprentices had given up all pretence of working
by now and were crouched on the floor of the workshop
playing at fivestones.

'Have you ever heard of there being caves,' I asked them, 'on that part of the Pennards' land known as the Sticks?'

'Or the Styx,' Cicely smirked, thereby thoroughly confusing her listeners and distracting their attention from the question.

At last, however, I was able to learn from Rob Undershaft that there were indeed any number of caves in the Mendip Hills, far more perhaps than anyone knew about; and he cited the terrifying experience of one of his cousins who had crawled into what appeared to be nothing more than a hole in the ground, only to find himself in an underground cavern, from which he had eventually been rescued with the greatest effort and difficulty.

'But I've never heard of any on the Pennards' land,' he went on, 'though that isn't to say there isn't one. The best person to ask, surely, is Anthony Pennard himself. Why do you want to know?'

'No particular reason,' I lied, daring Cicely with a look to contradict me.

I reflected with rising excitement that the Sticks was the area of hills within easiest reach of Glastonbury, close to its sister town of Wells, and which would probably have been most familiar to the monks of Ynys Witrin. Brother Begninus might well have known of a cave through which ran an underground river, a river which found its outlet through an enlarged fissure in the rock and flowed on down the hillside into the great marshy plain below. Perhaps there had been a dry area within the cave, and a rock formation which resembled an altar ... Perhaps Begninus had hidden the church's holy relic there once before when danger had threatened, and used the place again during that year when news of a fresh Saxon advance had reached him and the other brothers, when he had once

256

more been charged with its concealment.

'Amongst the hills, in the hollow places of the earth, on the altar by Charon's stream.' The words kept spinning round and round in my head. Had Peter Gildersleeve followed this same line of reasoning? There was no way of knowing, but somehow I felt it more than possible that he had. And had he also concluded that the entrance to the cave must lie at the head of that little valley?

Once more, I could not know the answer. But just supposing I was right – why had he not come back? Whether he had found what he was looking for or no – whether he was about to become one of the most honoured men in Christendom, feted by kings and cardinals alike, or was a very deeply disappointed man – he should have returned. Where, too, was Mark? And why had Dorabella been found with traces of tar and bits of straw in her coat? The riddle was not yet solved, nor would it be until I put my theory to the test and went to see for myself if it were sound or no.

When we quit the workshop, leaving the apprentices to resume their game, Cicely would have returned to the garden for further discussion, but I shook my head.

'The time for talking is past,' I said. 'I'm going to fetch Barnabas from the stables and ride as far as the shepherd's hut where Peter disappeared.'

'And what good will that do? she demanded, eyeing me with suspicion. 'I've been watching you closely while you were talking to Rob and John, and something's going on in that brain of yours. And why were you asking about a cave? You still haven't told me everything, have you?'

I smiled and kissed her lightly on the forehead. 'Better you don't know. Give my respects to Dame Joan when she wakes, and say that I hope to be with you by suppertime.'

'Why do you say "hope"? You said earlier there might

be danger. Were you serious?' she challenged.

'Maybe. But God will protect me,' I answered, wishing that I felt as confident as I sounded.

'But . . .' Cicely began.

'No "buts",' I answered. 'Listen carefully! You are to remain here and say nothing of where I've gone to anyone.'

'But if there's danger,' she persisted, 'why don't you ask Master Honeyman to go with you? Two would be better than one.'

'No,' I answered firmly. 'I won't imperil him for something that's not his business.'

She gave a reluctant nod. I went swiftly upstairs to collect my cudgel and the tinder-box and flints from the bedchamber, dropping the latter into my pouch before running down again to the kitchen. There I begged from Lydia a few of the linen strips dipped in melted fat which she used for wrapping and preserving joints of meat. Then, ignoring Cicely's plea of 'Wait!', I was out of the front door and along the crowded High Street almost before I knew it, making my way towards Edgar Shapwick's stables.

I flattered myself that Barnabas recognized me, for he threw up his head and whinnied as one of the stable-boys led him into the courtyard for saddling. He looked well-groomed and cared for, but he seemed restive for so placid an animal.

'He needs a good gallop,' said Edgar Shapwick, coming up behind me. 'We haven't had much time to exercise him. Are you leaving us at last, Chapman?'

I did not answer, but mounted the cob, positioning my cudgel awkwardly across the saddlebow, then paid the rest of what I owed for his stabling. I glanced up at the darkening sky.

'Ay, there's going to be a storm, Chapman,' the stablemaster confirmed, 'as sure as Christ came to Priddy!'

I had given Barnabas the office to start, but Edgar's words made me tug violently on the reins. I turned to stare at him, and he returned my look with interest.

'Something bothering you?' he enquired.

After a moment's hesitation I said, 'Supposing I wanted to get from Beckery to the foot of Mendip, are there other paths I could take beside the road to Wells?'

'Lord love you, yes!' Edgar laughed. 'Plenty of tracks for those that know them. But I wouldn't recommend them to strangers.'

I nodded. Then for the next few minutes I spoke long and earnestly to Master Shapwick, watching his face lengthen first with astonishment and then with consternation. To his credit, however, he made no attempt to interrupt me with questions, and spared me any exclamations of disbelief. And when at last I had finished, he simply reached up and clasped my hand.

'You may rely on me,' was all he said.

As I rode back through the town and along the causeway which leads towards Wells, I felt happier for having taken the stablemaster into my confidence. (I have always thought it wrong to lay all the burden for my well-being upon God's shoulders when there are precautions I can take myself.) It was now past midday and the heat was growing oppressive, although there was only an occasional glimpse of sun between the lowering clouds.

With Wells visible on the horizon, I turned off the main causeway on to a rougher, narrower path which took me across the moor directly to the foot of the Mendip Hills. Here it forked, one track leading on to the Pennards' house and its outbuildings, the other joining what remained of the old Roman road. I urged Barnabas along the latter until

I came to the stand of trees where Peter Gildersleeve had tethered Dorabella eight days earlier. Here I dismounted and did the same with the cob, stroking his nose.

'I'll be back,' I assured him.

He showed me the whites of his eyes, as though sensing danger, before lowering his head to crop the grass. I paused to look around, but there was no point in wasting time, so I took my cudgel from the saddle-bow and swathed one end in the strips of the fat-soaked linen, which I extracted from my pouch. As I stepped clear of the trees I glanced up at the heights above me, searching for any sign of human life, any indication that I was being watched. But I could see no movement except for the sheep, placidly grazing. I wondered uneasily where Abel Fairchild was, and also Anthony Pennard's two sons. At the same time, I was thankful for their absence.

I descended into the hollow, glancing briefly at the shepherd's hut, but it no longer held any interest for me. I hoped I had solved that riddle, and also that I knew where Peter had gone once Abel had made off in terror. As I mounted to the higher ridge of ground which separated the hollow from the little valley, the first drops of rain began to fall. Somewhere away to my right, above the crest of Mendip, thunder rolled, preceded by a jagged flash of lightning. I quickened my pace, proceeding as best I could with the wrapped end of my cudgel protected beneath my jerkin. It was awkward but I managed it somehow, making my way around the bluff until I reached the matted curtain of foliage.

My heart was beating so fast that I could scarcely breathe. Now was the moment when I should discover if my powers of deduction had steered me aright, or if this strange case, with its echoes of events almost a thousand years old, was beyond my ability to solve. I pushed aside the hanging trails of ivy and ferns and the long, attenuated branches of some tree to reveal a narrow fissure in the rock-face. And cautiously I eased myself through the gap, stepping into the darkness beyond.

It took a moment or two for my eyes to adjust to their surroundings, so little daylight filtered through the foliage which hung down across the almost invisible entrance. From the outside, looking into the blackness, I had been able to see nothing except what appeared to be solid rock; but once past that curtain of fronded green I found myself standing in a cave. I felt exultant, and it was several seconds before I mastered my elation sufficiently to get on with the business in hand and light my home-made torch.

I withdrew the tinder-box from my pouch and struck a spark from the flint. As soon as I had kindled a flame I set light to the fat-soaked linen strips which bound the end of my cudgel, and immediately I could see that I was in a kind of passageway whose floor was liberally studded with rocks and with what appeared to be frozen icicles hanging from the ceiling. I moved forward cautiously, my makeshift torch illuminating my path through the muffled darkness, and as I did so colours rushed at me along the walls – green and brown, pink and red – only to be engulfed in the following gloom as the light swept onwards. Fear and excitement made my hand shake, and hovering somewhere at the edges of my mind was the image of a bejewelled reliquary housing the fabulous Grail of the stories and legends – those legends in which I did not believe, but which I was half convinced might, after all, prove to be a reality.

My footfalls echoed dully in that rock-bound tunnel until suddenly the quality of sound altered; and even before the flaring light from my torch told me the reason I was aware of a withdrawing of the rocks, a sense of height and breadth and space. I was standing in the cave proper; a vaulted chamber where the varying density of shadow marked boulder and stone, and whose ceiling was ragged with the same frozen icicles I had noted in the passageway: some a pure, ethereal white, others leaden grey or a faint, translucent pink. Yet more tumbled down the walls, as though Merlin had transformed them with his magic wand and turned the cascading waters into stone.

All this I noticed in the first few, fleeting moments before other things began to encroach upon my consciousness, the chief of which was the realization that there was a far greater brightness all around me than my single light could possibly provide. The reason for this was not hard to discover. Three or four iron stands supported torches of which my own was but a poor, truncated imitation. The smell of pitch and burning rags assailed my nostrils as the flames licked sideways in a brief and sudden draught which blew through some fissure in the rocks.

At the same time I also became aware of three large wooden chests standing in the middle of the floor. One was open, its lid flung back to reveal, as I approached it, the glint of precious metal and the sparkle of jewels. Not the Holy Chalice, but gold and silver artefacts: candlesticks, goblets and gem-encrusted boxes, plates and knives and spoons. There were also belts and necklaces, bracelets and rings, all set with glittering stones . . .

How long I stood there staring I have no idea – a few seconds, perhaps, before I became aware that I was not alone. I raised my head and saw Anthony Pennard, his two sons ranged behind him, watching me from the furthest recess of the cave. They had just emerged from what I now realized was another opening which led even deeper into the heart of the Mendip Hills.

'You don't seem surprised to see us, Master Chapman,' Anthony said, strolling forward.

At his words I felt a prickle of fear which raised the hairs along my skin. I held my burning cudgel like a lance before me and slowly began to back against the nearest wall.

'What have you done with Peter Gildersleeve?' I asked. 'And where is his brother?'

'Both dead,' Thomas Pennard cut in before his father could answer. 'Once that interfering idiot Peter had clapped eyes on those – ' he indicated the chests of stolen goods – 'there was no way we could let him live.'

'No, I suppose not. Not once he realized that you and your father and brother were the gang of thieves who had been robbing the people of this district for so long. What have you done with his body?'

The eldest Pennard grinned and waved his hand towards the opening in the corner.

'Beyond this cavern is a whole warren of other caves and passageways. It would take a lifetime to master the ins and outs of all of them, and perhaps even then there would be places that a stranger would never find.'

'And what about Mark? Is his body with his brother's?'

When there was no answer, I went on, 'You've killed him too, haven't you, even though he was one of you? A disgruntled young man, jealous of the brother to whom their father had left everything including his second-best bed. Oh, Peter would have looked after Mark and seen to it that he wanted for nothing, but it wasn't quite the same as being an equal partner. He wanted money of his own so that he would be independent of his brother. When he grumbled to you and your sons, you saw him as an easy recruit; someone who heard a good deal of gossip and careless chatter in the course of his work. Mark very often delivered the finished parchments himself, both in the town and the surrounding countryside. He knew the insides of his neighbours' houses, the weaknesses of their defences, and when the occupiers would be from home. He must have been very useful to you. So why did you kill him?'

I was drawing a bow at a venture: I was not absolutely sure that Mark Gildersleeve was dead, but it seemed highly probable.

My hunch was proved correct by Gilbert Pennard. 'Because Mark got cold feet and told his brother what he was up to,' he said, thrusting forward to stand beside his father, lips drawn back from his teeth in an ugly snarl. 'How else could Peter have known about the cave? Why else would he have come snooping around, except to confirm Mark's story? Oh, of course Mark denied it! Told us a ridiculous tale of his brother finding some ancient document. Said its discovery was probably the reason why Peter was here. You never heard such a rigmarole of nonsense.'

So my guess was right. Mark had ridden here after leaving Beckery, and no one had seen him because he had travelled by unfrequented paths across the lower moor. Why had he come? To clear his name, of course, with his fellow thieves. The accusation must have been made the previous night by one of the Pennards, who had been prowling around the Gildersleeves' home, perhaps in the hope of rousing Mark and luring him away to do the deed then. But his plans had been thwarted by my unexpected presence; if Mark had not returned to bed I should have raised the alarm. The next day, however, Mark, who had probably believed that the Pennards could never seriously doubt him, had walked straight into their waiting, murderous arms.

The picture was becoming clearer to me now. Mark had arrived here while I was still with Abel, which explained why Anthony had not gone on to speak to Gilbert Pennard, as he had intended, but remained close to the house. Mark had concealed himself and Dorabella until I had gone, but he had had time to tell Anthony enough about me for the latter to address me as Chapman when he saw me off, in spite of the fact that I had informed both him and his wife that my name was Stonecarver. To my everlasting shame, I had not noticed his slip at the time.

'How did you discover Peter's presence here?' I asked. 'I thought you had all three gone to Priddy that afternoon.'

Anthony laughed shortly. 'We were on our way back, unluckily for him. We were descending towards the Sticks when we saw him dismount and walk down the slope to the hut. Didn't think anything of it to begin with, except it was a bit strange he should be so far from the house. But then we witnessed his little charade with Abel – which I'll give a clever fellow like you the credit of having worked out for yourself – so we grew suspicious and lay low to wait and watch. After Abel ran away, Peter went back to where he'd tethered his horse, and when we saw him again he had a lantern in his hand, which he must have brought with him in his saddle-bag. He came straight here.'

'So you followed, and killed him.'

Thomas Pennard drew a wicked-looking knife from his belt. 'That's right,' he agreed. 'Just as we're going to kill you.'

'No!' yelled Cicely, breathless with running as she erupted into the cave. 'If you do, you'll have to kill me and Master Honeyman here as well.'

Chapter Twenty

Our heads turned simultaneously towards her and her companion, but although this momentary distraction on the part of the Pennards should have given me a chance to fell Thomas, who was nearest, astonishment rooted me to the spot.

'So,' the Bee Master grunted, advancing further into the cave, 'you haven't dealt with him yet. What in the Devil's name are you waiting for?'

Cicely and I both stared at him in horror. I wondered briefly if some magic power had robbed me of my senses.

'What on earth do you mean?' Cicely quavered in a voice which she could barely master. 'You've come to help Roger.'

Gilbert Honeyman glanced at her with a certain amount of compassion in his eyes, and when he spoke a faint note of regret informed his tone. 'I'm afraid not, my dear. But I'm very grateful all the same that you came to me for assistance, otherwise I might have had a very unpleasant shock.' He turned to me. 'I must apologize to you too, Roger. It must be distressing for you to discover that I'm not quite what I seemed.'

I could not answer him, I was filled with such self-disgust at having been so easily been taken in. The Bee Master had seemed to me a pleasant, honest man, only too anxious to assist his fellows. Nothing he had said or done had made me suspicious of him. And yet suddenly I could see where he fitted into the Pennards' schemes. The one thing that had been perplexing me since I stumbled across the stolen goods was now made plain.

Gilbert nodded understandingly. 'It must be galling for a clever young lad like you to be deceived by an old codger such as me. All the same, I was right in warning these three not to underestimate you.'

'We didn't,' Anthony grunted. 'One of us has been keeping watch in the inner cave since you came to see us yesterday. And by great good fortune it so happened that we were all present when he arrived.'

Cicely found her voice again. 'But . . . but I don't understand,' she said hoarsely, appealing to me. 'Why should Master Honeyman be in league with Master Pennard and his sons? And what is it that they've been doing?'

I directed her attention towards the three chests ranged side-by-side in the middle of the cave. 'They are the thieves who have been plaguing this district for so long.' I added more gently, 'And I'm sorry to have to tell you that Mark was one of them. He supplied the information as to which houses were standing empty while their owners were from home, or which were the easiest ones to rob. Master Honeyman, I think, was recruited to shift some of the booty in those great baskets of his, and to sell it in Bristol and elsewhere.'

The Bee Master grinned. 'You've got it almost right, my lad, except that I'm not in the pay of Master Pennard and his sons. They are employed by me, and they're not the only ones. I have several dozen people working for me in various parts of the countryside – wherever, in fact, I take my honey and wax for sale. It's a sweet set-up, as you might say.' And he laughed immoderately at his own joke, although no one else saw fit to join in.

In spite of the gravity of our situation, or maybe on account of it, and because my nerves were on edge, I couldn't forbear from upbraiding Cicely. 'I told you to speak to nobody! Why did you ignore my instructions?'

'But Master Honeyman is – was – our friend,' she wailed. 'I thought he'd advise me what to do. You said that you might be in danger.'

'But you didn't know where to find this cave! I didn't give you instructions because I wasn't sure if my hunch was right or no. So didn't it make you suspicious when Master Honeyman knew exactly where I'd be?'

'I . . . I never thought about it.'

Of course she hadn't; she had been concerned only for my safety. And it was natural that in her confusion she should have turned to the one grown man who was sufficiently privy to the story to be of any use, and who had no need of time-consuming, tortuous explanations. She had run to find Gilbert Honeyman at his hostelry and poured out her tale. He would have needed no second bidding to spring into action, nor any persuasion to take Cicely up before him on the bay. Indeed, he could not well have left her behind even had she desired to stay, for she knew too much. His security was threatened; she had to be silenced along with me.

I wondered if Edgar Shapwick trusted me sufficiently to have carried out the instructions I had given him when collecting Barnabas, but the thought was fleeting. The four men were closing in on me, their faces set and purposeful. The last few shreds of cloth on the end of my home-made torch had almost burned themselves out, but a flame or two continued to lick at the rags.

With a suddenness that took him by surprise I lunged at

Thomas Pennard, catching him a blow between the eyes. His hair was singed, and a brand appeared on his forehead which made him scream and drop his knife, clapping both hands to his wound. The other three, unnerved by the incident, hesitated for a second or two before Anthony Pennard leapt forward to retrieve the fallen blade, but I had been too quick for him, placing my right foot on top of it.

'Run, Cicely!' I yelled. 'For Heaven's sake, run!'

But she had already made her move – not towards the entrance of the cave but to fling herself at Gilbert Honeyman, her arms coiled about his neck in a strangle-hold. He had been fumbling for the dagger at his belt but was forced to abandon any attempt to draw it in order to shake off his assailant.

Meantime, Anthony Pennard had made a bid to unsheath his own weapon, but was foiled by a glancing blow from my scorched and smoking stick. At the same moment, out of the corner of one eye, I saw Gilbert Pennard reach into the chest behind him and grab a heavy silver candlestick, which he brandished like a club.

And here I made a terrible mistake. In order to parry the blow which he aimed at me, I slid my right hand further along my cudgel to bring it into a defensive, horizontal position; but the blackened end was still smouldering and the charred wood burned my flesh. I let it go with a resounding curse, but through my pain I kept sufficient wits about me to retain my grasp of the the other end.

Gilbert Honeyman had at last managed to loosen Cicely's grasp, and with a final heave sent her sprawling on the ground. In a sweat of fear and fury, he raised a ham-like fist and would have dealt her a murderous blow had she not rolled clear and scrambled quickly to her feet. I was only vaguely aware of all this, however, my attention being focused on Gilbert Pennard and his candlestick. He was aiming for my head, and, ignoring the agony of blistered palm and fingers, I again took hold of my cudgel with both hands, just in time to save my skull from being crushed.

But in doing so I had shifted my stance, exposing the knife which Thomas Pennard, still in something of a daze, was nonetheless able to stoop and retrieve. His father had also managed to draw his dagger, as had Gilbert Honeyman, and once again all four men were advancing towards me, their evil intentions writ large on every face.

Using my stick to hold them at bay, and completely unconscious now of my painful right hand, I stepped back the two or three paces which in the past few moments I had allowed to open up between me and the wall of the cave. Four pairs of eyes were fixed unwaveringly on my person, and I realized with awful clarity that even if I could lay one man low, I could not escape the vengeance of the others. Only a miracle could save me . . .

Even as the thought entered my head, Thomas Pennard tripped over one of the many stones and small boulders which littered the ground. He recovered his balance almost immediately, but the accident had caused him to fall a step or so behind the rest. In consequence, he could see that Cicely, whose existence had been temporarily forgotten in the general desire to dispose of me, had copied his own example and armed herself with another of the weighty silver candlesticks. She was already creeping up on Master Honeyman when Thomas shouted a warning.

'Gilbert! Watch out! Mind your back!'

The effect of this was to deflect the attention of both the Bee Master and his namesake Gilbert Pennard, who each whirled about, knives at the ready. Taking advantage of their momentary distraction I swung my cudgel with all my strength to the side of Anthony Pennard's head, felling him to the ground, and I knew that he was unlikely to rise again for some little time.

One down, but there were still three to go.

I heard Cicely scream. She retained her hold on the candlestick, but was now using it as best she could as a means of defence against Gilbert Honeyman's lunging dagger. I forced myself away from the wall, expecting opposition from the Pennard brothers, but to my astonishment Thomas had dropped to his knees beside his father, while Gilbert stooped over the pair of them, arms hanging limply at his sides.

I staggered across the cave's uneven floor towards the Bee Master, who turned to meet me, calling upon the Pennard brothers to assist him. Although I was able for the moment to keep him at cudgel's length, I knew that I must lay him low before either Thomas or Gilbert Pennard recovered his senses. At any moment now, their anxiety for their injured father must surely give way to concern for their own safety, for as far as they knew Cicely and I were the only two people who could deliver them into the arms of the law.

Still holding Gilbert Honeyman at bay and judging my moment to strike, I saw one of the brothers slowly raise his head and shake it, like a man gradually awakening from a dream. I could delay no longer, or I should throw away my unlooked-for advantage. I raised my cudgel but my adversary, moving with extraordinary speed, ducked in under my guard and rushed forward with his knife aimed straight at my heart. I twisted out of his path with less than an inch to spare, at the same time catching him a glancing blow to the side of his head. It was not a serious knock, but together with his own momentum it brought him crashing to the floor where he lay gasping for breath.

But it was a losing battle. The two Pennard sons were now coming for me, each armed with a knife, and even if I managed to hold them off, Gilbert Honeyman would not be winded for long.

I yelled again, 'Run, Cicely! Run!' And this time she obeyed. She must have realized that there was nothing else she could do to save me, and that if she at least got away, whatever my fate, the villains would be brought to justice. She scrambled towards the entrance to the inner cave and vanished into the darkness of the passageway beyond.

And then I heard her scream, a high-pitched, desperate cry that was broken off abruptly. The Pennards stood rooted to the spot, like men who had looked upon the head of the Medusa. Gilbert Honeyman, who had risen halfway to his knees, also stiffened into immobility, as frozen as the stone waterfall behind him. But the silence which had succeeded that Banshee wail was suddenly broken by the reassuring murmur of men's voices and a gasp of relief from Cicely. A moment later she reappeared in the cave.

'Roger! Roger! It's all right! Edgar Shapwick is here with the Sheriff's men!'

There is a certain satisfaction in bringing the guilty to justice, and I feel sure it is God's Will that evil men and women should be punished for their crimes. Yet in all the years that I have acted as an instrument of that Divine Intent I have found very little pleasure in doing it; except, perhaps, on one or two occasions when those concerned have been wicked beyond all possibility of forgiveness. But for the most part, it has been my experience that nearly everyone has some good in him or her which, had things chanced differently, might have kept that person on the straight and narrow path to redemption.

You can tell that I am getting on in years, my children, for only the elderly pontificate in this self-righteous fashion. Nevertheless I have written no less than the truth, for always the innocent suffer with the guilty, snared in a web of other people's making – innocents like Dame Gildersleeve, who had not only lost both her sons but had to endure hearing one of them posthumously branded as a thief. She might also have been deprived of her livelihood with Mark and Peter dead, had not Cicely decided to remain with her aunt and take on the running of the business.

That girl knew nothing about parchment-making, but I had no doubt that she would learn. Someone in many ways little older than a child had run into that cave, but a woman had come out – a woman who had proved to herself her own courage and worth, and who was ready to tackle the world. I felt almost sorry for Sergeant Armstrong when he eventually arrived in Glastonbury, expecting to find the same easily biddable daughter from whom he had parted.

Another innocent to suffer was Rowena Honeyman. Before he was dragged off to prison, and knowing that he was gallow's meat, Gilbert had begged a word alone with me.

'Promise me that before you go home you'll seek out my daughter. Take her to my late wife's sister at Frome. It'll be some miles out of your way, but I beg you to give me your assurance that you'll do it. Once I'm dead my holding will pass to my half-brother, and we never could abide each other. Apart from the shame and disgrace which will be attached to my name he'll make my child's life a misery, and she'll not fare well either at the hands of the neighbours. A felon's daughter – who'll want to know her? Who'll want to marry her? She'll be powerless now. But her aunt will give her a home and look after her as best she can. Will you do this for me?'

How could I refuse? To all intents and purposes he was a dead man. He promised me that he had known nothing of the murder of Mark and Peter Gildersleeve until he had called upon the Pennards on his way to Glastonbury two days previously. Dorabella, who had been shut up in one of the outhouses of the farm, had somehow managed to break loose, and it had been pure chance that he of all people had come across her roaming the moor.

But as he was bound and led away by the Sheriff's officers, I could not help but reflect that although Gilbert Honeyman may have been innocent of the brothers' killing, he had been nothing loath to help murder Cicely and me. Once we had proved ourselves enemies to his safety, he had not scrupled to advocate our deaths. Yet his villainy could not be laid at his daughter's door, and so I agreed to do what little I could for her.

Mistress Pennard was a different matter, and there was nothing that anyone could do to ease her lot. She vigorously denied all knowledge of what her husband and sons had been up to, and as the three of them upheld her claim she was, after rigorous examination, allowed to go free. But she had lost her home, her livelihood and her friends. What would become of her in the end, I could not hazard. She would probably end her days in the shelter of some religious house, alone and friendless. As I said, the innocent suffer as much as the guilty.

Dame Joan begged me to stay with them for a little while longer. 'Just until my brother arrives,' she pleaded, her expression lost and frightened.

But who could say what length of time it would take for her letter to reach him? And now that my task was done I wanted to be home. Yet even that would be further delayed by the return of Barnabas to Farleigh Castle and the fulfilment of my promise to Master Honeyman, who now languished in prison. So I hardened my heart and said that I would spend the Sabbath beneath her roof, but that I must be on my way no later than the following day.

Cicely, I noticed, did not entreat me to remain, as she might have done a day or two earlier. Rather, she seemed impatient for me to be gone, sparing me but little thought as she held conference with Rob and John on the intricacies of the task before her.

'We shall miss you, of course,' she said on Monday morning, absentmindedly reaching up to peck my cheek before hurrying into the workshop.

I smiled to myself, then went to take my leave of Brother Hilarion at the abbey. He was plainly both relieved and distressed by the outcome of my investigations.

'A bad business. A bad business,' he kept repeating over and over.

I asked him to keep an eye on Dame Gildersleeve and to invoke Father Abbot's protection for her against the malice of her neighbours. 'At least the stigma of a son who dabbled in the Black Arts has been removed, but she will still be branded the mother of a thief.'

Brother Hilarion sighed his acknowledgement and gave me his blessing. As I turned away he called urgently after me, 'Roger! My child, wait a moment! There's something I must ask you.'

But just at that moment I was hailed by one of the brothers who had been a novice with me in those days when he had been plain Nicholas Fletcher. And by the time we had traded memories of our time together, and recalled his brother Martin, whom I had met the preceding year in far from happy circumstances, Brother Hilarion's attention had been claimed by two of his pupils. I wondered idly what he had wanted, but I was too eager now to be off, and bade Brother Nicholas make my farewells for me.

I did not loiter but went straight to Northload Street and the stables to take my leave of Edgar Shapwick.

'But for you, I should be dead,' I said, embracing him.

'I only carried out your instructions to contact the Sheriff's men,' he protested. 'You were wise not to trust the Pennards, it seems. Did you know what you were going to find?'

I shook my head. 'Although perhaps I should have guessed. But I only knew that the disappearance of Mark and Peter Gildersleeve must be linked to them, once those traces of tar had been found in Dorabella's mane. It has been a muddled, unsatisfactory business in many ways.'

'What led you to suspect there was a cave in that part of the hills?' Edgar inquired, holding Barnabas's head while I mounted.

'It's a long story,' I answered, then clapped a hand to my mouth as I realized just what it was that Brother Hilarion had been about to ask me.

'Is something wrong?' my companion enquired, noting my consternation.

'N-no,' I answered slowly. 'No, nothing!' I leaned from the saddle. 'Once again, thank you for your good offices, Master Shapwick.'

'It's we, the folk of Glastonbury and the villages around, who should thank you,' he protested. 'You've done what the Sheriff's men were unable to do and cleared up the mystery of these robberies. There will be many a home's occupants grateful to see the return of their valuables.' He handed up my scorched and blackened cudgel and slapped the cob's rump. 'God go with you, lad, and guard you safely home to Bristol.'

I accepted his good wishes and also enlisted his support for Dame Joan and Cicely. 'They'll need stalwart friends.'

'They will that. You can rely on me.' He clasped my hand and watched me ride out of the stable before turning back to resume the morning's business.

I rode up the High Street, past the abbey and the church of Saint John, and on into Bove Town, where the pilgrims' chapel of Saint James indicated the track leading to the Jarrolds' cottage. To my right the strange, brooding hump of the Tor rose against the skyline, crowned by Saint Michael's chapel, the home of Merlin, of Gwyn ap Nud, of the early Celtic gods who had been worshipped in these parts long before the coming of the first Christians.

I remembered with a smile my longing, a week ago, to be plunged into some romantic adventure, to become a part of the the mystic, mythical world of my wildest dreams. And for a few, brief hours I had thought myself to be standing on the threshhold of one of the greatest discoveries in the history of mankind, just as Peter Gildersleeve had done before me. But now, as I turned off along the raised causeway to Wells and the Mendip Hills, I wondered heavily whatever had possessed me to believe it possible, and felt that I had been touched by a sort of madness. I had completely forgotten about the Grail in the aftermath of what had happened in the cave, and had only recollected the object of my search just now, prompted by Edgar Shapwick's question. I felt stupid and dull, as if I had just awakened from a long, deep sleep. Well, it was too late now. I should never be able to prove what Brother Begninus had concealed from the Saxons a thousand years ago, or where he had hidden it . . .

And then, suddenly, as a shaft of sunlight pierced the clouds which had hung like a pall over the countryside for the past two days, my spirits rose, and I was glad that I had not found the Holy Grail. Down through the centuries it had grown to symbolize so much more than just a great Christian relic. It had come to stand for Man's quest for everything worthwhile, for his better nature, for hope in an unfriendly world. If it could be reduced to nothing more than an object of gold and precious jewels it would lose its significance, and the world would be a poorer place because it had lost an ideal.

And as I urged Barnabas to a trot, I began to smile.